KANE

ALSO BY GRAHAM HURLEY

The Spoils of War Collection

Finisterre
Aurore
Estocada
Raid 42
Last Flight to Stalingrad
Kyiv
Katastrophe
The Blood of Others
Dead Ground
Kane

DI Joe Faraday Investigations

Turnstone
The Take
Angels Passing
Deadlight
Cut to Black
Blood and Honey
One Under
The Price of Darkness
No Lovelier Death
Beyond Reach
Borrowed Light
Happy Days

DS Jimmy Suttle Investigations

Western Approaches
Touching Distance
Sins of the Father
The Order of Things

Enora Andressen

Curtain Call
Sight Unseen
Off Script
Limelight
Intermission
Lights Down

Other Fiction

Rules of Engagement
Reaper
The Devil's Breath
Thunder in the Blood
Sabbathman
The Perfect Soldier
Heaven's Light
Nocturne
Permissible Limits
The Chop
The Ghosts of 2012
Strictly No Flowers
Acts of Separation

Non-fiction

Lucky Break
Airshow
Estuary
Backstory

KANE

GRAHAM HURLEY

An Aries Book

First published in the UK in 2025 by Head of Zeus,
part of Bloomsbury Publishing Plc

975312468

A catalogue record for this book is available from the British Library.

ISBN (HB): 9781035908271
ISBN (E): 9781035908264

Cover design: Matt Bray | Head of Zeus

Typeset by Siliconchips Services Ltd UK

Printed and bound in Great Britain by
CPI Group (UK) Ltd, Croydon, CR0 4YY

MIX
Paper | Supporting
responsible forestry
FSC
www.fsc.org
FSC® C013604

Bloomsbury Publishing Plc
50 Bedford Square, London, WC1B 3DP, UK
Bloomsbury Publishing Ireland Limited,
29 Earlsfort Terrace, Dublin 2, D02 AY28, Ireland

HEAD OF ZEUS LTD
5–8 Hardwick Street
London, EC1R 4RG

To find out more about our authors and books
visit www.headofzeus.com
For product safety related questions contact productsafety@bloomsbury.com

'Los Angeles? Any further, *hombre*,
and you fall off the edge.'

– Gustave Leaman

To
John Mills
1937–2024

Book One

1

Just another Sunday. Quincy Kane awakes in darkness, aware of the soft pad of the dog patrolling the icy spaces of his modest DC apartment. The dog, renamed Dexter, once belonged to his elder brother. Danny called him Vasco for reasons Kane has never properly fathomed. Neither Washington nor 'Dexter' have been much to the dog's taste, and lately the skinny mutt has surrendered to insomnia. He misses Boston like he misses Danny, and the greyhound's plaintive whine has become the soundtrack of this never-ending winter.

Kane takes an upper-body wash, dresses and checks his weapon before pausing beside the door. The automatic is still in his hand, a round chambered, the magazine full. Lack of sleep has wrecked Dexter's appetite. Last week Kane returned from the butcher with yet another bag of soggy offcuts, but again the dog left the bowl untouched. Maybe, just maybe, they might still become friends, but the sweetest temptation is to bring Dexter's troubled tenancy of the apartment to an abrupt end. They study each other for a long moment, then Kane shakes his head and opens the door. No one in this neighbourhood shoots a dog on a Sunday morning.

*

'Mr Kane? Cold enough for you?'

The uniformed guard at one of the side entrances of Secret Service District Sixteen skips the body search and barely glances at Kane's proffered ID. A grey dawn has appeared over the nearby Potomac River and Kane can taste snow in the air.

Secret Service District Sixteen is the White House. A handful of agents work a regular shift system and eight o'clock in the morning is handover time. Mike Reilly, an Irishman, has been the overnight volunteer stand-in to release a fellow agent for his son's bar mitzvah, and can't wait to get home.

'Any word on the fire drill?' Kane has opened his monthly paycheque, retrieved from his personal mailbox in the usher's office off the north portico that now serves as the agents' retreat.

'Tuesday,' Reilly is frowning. 'The guy from downtown won't leave me alone. Our big mistake was letting him in here in the first place.'

Kane nods. The eager young inspector from Fire Department HQ has a big career planned for himself. He's figured the nation's best address as a catastrophe in the making and recently spent an entire working week walking the corridors, surveying room after room to tally the more obvious fire risks. The US Treasury is expecting his report any day now and are doing their best to head him off. Hence the imminent drill.

Kane pockets his payslip. The figure at the bottom, he's long concluded, is plenty enough for a single man with a taste for his own company.

Reilly is winding his favourite green scarf around his neck before reaching for his gloves. After a nap, he has plans to take his wife for Sunday lunch at a place they like out in Maryland but the guy from the Fire Department is beginning to obsess him.

'Too much time on his hands,' Kane grunts. 'Maybe he needs a dog. Let me know, yeah?'

Reilly gone, Kane heads for the White House private quarters. Responsibility number one is protecting the President and the sensible place to start is making sure he's still alive. FDR's bedroom is on the second floor, up the modest sweep of the central staircase. He takes his usual route, passing the presidential valet on the long second-floor corridor. Alonso Fields is a big man, tall, black.

'Everything OK?' Kane asks.

'Washed and shaved, Quince. All yours, buddy.'

Buddy.

Kane pauses for a moment outside FDR's bedroom. One of the things he's grown to appreciate about this place is the feeling of home. People like each other here, by and large, and that's a tribute to the man in charge.

Kane raps twice, hears FDR clearing his throat, steps lightly inside. The first time he set eyes on this room, he'd fought his gut reaction. The word was disappointment. He was disappointed by how bare and spartan it was. By the narrow white iron bedstead, slightly angled towards the window. By the old-fashioned rocking chair with its scatter of cast-off clothing. This was the world's most important leader, the planet's most powerful guy, and here he was spending half his life in a bedroom that might have belonged in a rooming house.

That first week Kane had challenged himself to number the items on FDR's bedside table. After tallying the bottle of aspirin, the nose drops, the stubs of pencils, the scraps of paper, the worn old prayer book, the watch with scratches on the back, the open packet of Camel cigarettes, he'd given up. And since then, nothing had changed. Same prayer book. Same watch. Probably the same pencils.

Kane had first met Roosevelt in Boston five years ago. Kane was a cop in his home city. The President was standing for re-election. The motorcade had been snarled in traffic on a busy downtown intersection. FDR, as everyone called him, had beckoned the rangy uniform on the sidewalk closer to the presidential limo. That moment, Kane has since reflected, changed his life. Forever.

'We can get this thing moving?' That ready smile.

'No problem, sir.'

'Good man.'

Good man. The phrase had pursued Kane through the intervening years, and now was no different.

'Good man,' FDR is sitting up in bed, an old sweater draped around the broadness of his shoulders, fondling his mutt, a bad-tempered Scottie called Fala. Kane has collected a copy of the *Chicago Tribune* en route to the second floor, and now lays it carefully among the spread of East Coast newspapers on the rumpled counterpane.

FDR takes a glance at the Chicago headlines and then wants to know about the fire drill. Kane is looking at the iron brace his president has to wear simply to stand erect. Pounds and pounds of ironwork, testament to the pinked, slightly raised welts on his skinny legs, paralysed and useless after an attack of polio.

'The guy from downtown is saying the day after tomorrow, sir. It may never happen.'

'You think it should?'

'Yes.'

'I agree. And me?'

'We carry you down. As usual.'

'And if the stairs are on fire?'

'There'll be another way.'

'That's why God invented fire drills. Am I right, Agent Kane?'

'You are, sir.'

'Good man.'

Kane lurks by the still-open door. His time here is done and both men know it. It was Reilly a while back who broke FDR's big secret. The man fears absolutely nothing, he'd told Kane, except fire. 'Which is why we need to make him safe here,' Reilly had tapped his own temple, 'in his head. A good night's sleep will keep the country safe. That's the least we owe him.'

True. After an affable exchange of banter about the Redskins' prospects in this afternoon's game out at Griffith Stadium, Kane retreats from the bedroom. This morning, like every Sunday morning, is minor key stuff. Downstairs, there's a pile of correspondence overdue for Kane's attention, thanks to a busy week. These are hundreds of letters sieved by the White House secretaries. Over a mug of thin coffee, Kane skim-reads them, looking for the trademark insults levelled at the guy in the second-floor bedroom.

Shit-for-brains. Commie-lover. Mr Hand-Out. No-good Russkie-loving bastard. Stuff like this would upset most folks. The more rabid threats upset even Kane. Who'd want to be garrotted with a length of barbed wire? Or drilled by a volley of dumdum bullets? Simply because he was still trying to make life just a little sweeter for tens of millions of fellow Americans beached by joblessness and hunger and plain bad luck?

Each of these trash letters has to be traced to an address, wherever that may be. The details will go, in the first place, to the FBI's General Intelligence Division but, at Kane's insistence, local cops will pay a visit, make notes, suggest some other outlet for this rage, and if the campaigning FDR ever happens within shooting distance of the scribbled name at the bottom of the letter, then the guy – and it's always a guy – will be locked up for the duration of all the presidential hoopla.

Kane knows FDR is aware of all this, not in detail, not in terms of what might be coming his way, but as part of the complicated deal he's made with the American public. Listen to me, trust me. In return, on your part and mine, I will fear nothing. Except fire.

Good man.

A couple of minutes after half past one Kane is scanning a scrawled note from a cowhand in Montana who claims once to have been in uniform. His beef with the President is the much-loved fireside chat slot on national radio. Folks, he writes in big capital letters, have no need of nanny-crap like this. Out here in sight of the Rocky Mountains life teaches you a thing or two about getting by. At the bottom of the letter is a poorly rendered cartoon face inside a pair of crosshairs. The message, thinks Kane, couldn't be plainer. Keep your fucking distance.

Another file for J. Edgar Hoover's attention? A Category Two threat or Category Three? Kane is reaching for a pen when the door to the Secret Service office bursts open. Shirley operates the White House switch on alternate Sundays and has long taken a shine to Kane.

'You're not gonna believe this.'

'I'm not?'

'The Japs have just bombed Pearl Harbor.'

'You mean Hawaii?'

'I mean Pearl Harbor. Battleships, Quince. Hundreds dead. Maybe more.'

'When?' Kane is on his feet, putting on his jacket.

'Half an hour ago, and it ain't over yet. No bullshit. I've been trying to get Colonel Starling but he's out of town. Next best has to be Mr Wilson.' She's nodding at the phone. 'Better the news comes from you.'

Frank J. Wilson is Chief of the US Secret Service. Kane has talked to him just twice in his life.

'He knows about Pearl?'

'I doubt it,' she's heading for the door. 'I'll put you through.'

Kane takes the call, trying to figure out how much to trust of what little he's heard. In the event, it doesn't much matter because Wilson has sources of his own.

'I'm talking to Agent Kane?'

'Sir.'

'Then listen up, son. The Japs are making war on us. God knows where this ends. We need to quadruple the standing guard around the White House. I'm waiting on a call from Fort Myers. We're talking machine-gun crews on the roof. Ack-ack batteries in the grounds. Tomorrow your man will be heading for the Capitol. We'll need armed soldiers every damn yard of the way and I want you, Agent Kane, to make sure he gets there in one piece. Wraparound protection from start to finish. You got that?'

While Wilson pauses to take a breath, Kane can feel the weight of his automatic nestling in his shoulder holster. Are the Japs massing down Pennsylvania Avenue? Will the White House roof carry the weight of machine-gun crews? Is DC ready for a mass parachute drop as tomorrow's sun comes up? Should Kane be thinking about an extra magazine for his automatic?

'Something else, son.' Wilson is back on the line.

'Sir?'

'We reinstate armed protection around Roosevelt, including indoors. Twenty-four hours. We keep the bedroom door locked. Two guards in the corridor. More on the lower levels. You hear me, Agent Kane?'

Kane was gazing out of the window. Already he can see a scatter of hunched figures stamping the cold from their feet and staring into the White House grounds through the iron railings. Back when he first moved into the White House, one of FDR's first acts, according to Reilly, was to keep his bedroom door unlocked and ban armed agents to the far corners of the mansion. 1600 Pennsylvania Avenue, to him, had always been a family home, not some damn fortress.

'The President may have views on that, sir…'

'And so may we, son. We're charged with protecting the guy. Constitutionally, Secretary Morgenthau is calling the shots.'

Morgenthau is Treasury Secretary and therefore Wilson's boss. Kane says he'll pass the message on.

'Order, son. Not message.' The line goes dead.

★

Shirley has returned to the White House switchboard. She has a checklist of every Secret Service agent assigned to District Sixteen and Kane asks her to call them all in. Using a spare line, he talks to the duty liaison at the Army's base at Fort Myers. It turns out that Wilson has gotten there first and that three machine-gun crews have already been despatched, with three more standing by in reserve. Shirley has summoned extra help at the switch, and Kane is looking at three pairs of hands patching incoming calls through to every corner of the building.

A brief moment of calm brings Kane to Shirley's side.

'FDR?'

'In the Oval Study.'

'Alone?'

'Harry's with him. Sandwich lunch.' Harry Hopkins is Roosevelt's trusted aide.

'And Rover?'

'She's hosting a lunch of her own. Thirty guests last time anyone counted.' Rover is Secret Service code for Eleanor Roosevelt, FDR's wife. These days they lead largely separate lives.

'She knows about Pearl?'

'Dunno,' she shoots Kane a look. 'Is that relevant just now, Quince?'

Kane takes the hint, tells himself to slow down, to focus. The guy he really needs is Mike Reilly. Just now he might be eating lunch with his wife in some fancy out-of-town Maryland restaurant. If so, news of the Jap raid will take him to a phone.

Reilly's on the line shortly after two o'clock. Kane updates him. The machine-gun crews have arrived and the lieutenant in charge is up on the roof plotting overlapping fields of fire. Extra armed guards have been posted in the grounds, each detail accompanied by Secret Service agents with orders to detain or turn away anyone without ID and demonstrable cause for gaining entry. The latter group, including key secretaries plus presidential aides and assistants, have already appeared in the ground-floor corridors. Little groups gather around someone who may have fresh news. Disbelief, says Kane, has given way to something closer to bewilderment, often laced with anger.

'Sounds like the ball game you thought you had in the bag,' Reilly has the softest chuckle, good to hear. He'll drive straight back. Shame about dessert.

By the time he arrives, Kane has managed to snatch a moment or two of Roosevelt's time. FDR is sitting in his wheelchair in the Oval Study alongside his bedroom. Between phone calls, Kane does his best to brace the President for tighter personal protection but can tell he's barely listening. Within seconds he's back on the next call, leaving Kane with Harry Hopkins.

Hopkins probably sees more of FDR than anyone else alive just now. He has a bedroom of his own on the second floor and unlimited access to the Chief. He's a tall, thin, untidy looking guy with great eyes and some mysterious medical problem that no one seems to understand. His prowess with women has long been the talk of District Sixteen's secret agents and he drinks far too much, but for years he's been brushing down many of FDR's wilder ideas and standing them on their own two feet. Kane has never met anyone so conversationally direct. He has a talent for getting along with anyone, no matter how mighty or how inconsequential, and he has a tongue – in Mike Reilly's phrase – that can scorch paint. Kane loves him. Always has.

'Wilson means it.' Kane has explained about the phone call earlier.

'You're telling me that's news? Wilson always means it.'

'But for real.'

'Sure,' Hopkins gestures across the office at FDR. 'You know who he talked to just now? Chiang Kai-shek. It's God knows what time in Peking. They had to get the guy out of bed. Chiang hates the Japs. Wants them all dead and buried. The moment the Chief told him about Pearl, and the Japs declaring war on us, he put a record on and danced round his goddam bedroom. The Chief put the phone on loud. Crap music, the worst. Our enemy's enemy is our very good friend. Never fails, even in China.'

Kane passes the story on to Mike Reilly, along with the news that FDR has summoned a Cabinet meeting for this evening. Reilly has been doing some thinking in the car. Two guys outside the Oval Study on the second floor where the Cabinet meeting will take place, the door an inch or two open for ready access. More agents on the first landing and the ground floor. Reilly, like Kane himself, can't figure how the Navy got caught with their pants down like that. Didn't anyone spot a bunch of aircraft carriers heading their way? Do brains turn to mush in all that Hawaii sunshine?

'Maybe it's down to bad habits,' Kane has been listening to Shirley, who'd eavesdropped on calls at the switch. 'Word is they don't pay much attention to the radar at weekends. Plus they line up all the aircraft wing to wing on that big old airfield to cut down on security. A handful of sentries? Neat little targets just begging to be bombed? Even the Japs couldn't miss.'

'You're kidding me?'

'If only. The first most folks knew was a very big bang when the *Arizona* went to the bottom. Direct hit on the forward magazine. Maybe a bomb, maybe a torpedo. Some guys aboard never had a chance to wake up. This is a Sunday, remember. No one starts a war on a Sunday.'

The Cabinet convenes for twenty after eight in the evening. Departmental Secretaries from various corners of DC shuffle into the Oval Study, some sparing Kane a grim nod of greeting. Even in the depths of winter, they look greyer and more strained than usual. One pauses, his gnarled old hand on Kane's arm.

'They'll pay for this, son. And that's a promise.'

At this point the door is wide open and Kane catches a glimpse of FDR in his usual chair at the centre of the table. His head is bowed, his face drawn. Cabinet members have gathered round, a gesture of raw physical support, and after Roosevelt has waved them into their allotted seats he says he has an announcement to make. He's suffering from a cold and a headache, and his voice is low, barely a whisper. With the door open an inch or two Kane strains to hear properly.

This, according to FDR, will be the most consequential Cabinet meeting since 1861. Then, with civil war in the offing, the very future of the nation was at stake, and now is no different. Maybe four battleships have gone down, plus most of the rest of the fleet. Hundreds of planes have been shot to pieces on the tarmac at Hickham Field. Thousands of men are dead or dying. The Japs, meanwhile, are also turning their attention to the Philippines, Guam, Wake Island and possibly Midway. As Roosevelt tallies the dead and dying, Kane catches a low collective murmur from around the table. Sympathy? Anger? He has no way of knowing.

The Cabinet meeting wraps up forty minutes later. Kane finds himself alone in an alcove on the second floor with Mike Reilly. The Irishman is a presidential favourite, a reliable source for the ripest stories, but even he has been unable to persuade FDR that a declaration of war might be grounds to keep his bedroom door locked.

'Won't hear of it, just said no,' Reilly shrugs. 'And you know something else? We're riding to Congress tomorrow and he wants to use the '38 Caddy. Can you believe that?'

Kane does his best to mask a smile. The V-16 Cadillac is FDR's favourite, an open limo he favours at election times. Barely even semi-armoured, it invites the attentions of any passing crazy but Roosevelt has never paid the slightest attention to sensible precautions or the workings of fate.

'So what do we do?' Kane asks.

'We double the on-board protection, wrap ourselves around him, keep the man warm, keep the man alive.'

The Man. Kane's last glimpse of him as this long day comes to an end occurs after midnight. Two presidential confidants, NBC's Ed Murrow and a buccaneer outlaw called Wild Bill Donovan, have been summoned to the White House for beer and sandwiches and it falls to Kane to take them upstairs to the Oval Study. Murrow has just returned from an assignment in London and wants to know about Harry Hopkins.

'He just got out of the hospital,' Kane says. 'A month of blood transfusions.'

'So what the heck's wrong with the guy? He looks like someone dropped him and broke the important bits.'

Kane says he doesn't know, raps on the door of the Oval Study, stands to one side as the two men file past. Roosevelt catches sight of him at the door.

'20–14, Agent Kane. Can you believe that?'

'Sir?'

'Out at Griffith, this afternoon. Philly Eagles brought down to earth.'

Kane nods, robbed for once of anything sensible to say. The Pacific Fleet in ruins. Thousands dead. Certain war in the offing. And yet this president has time to celebrate the score in the DC game. Truly remarkable.

That night, Kane remains on duty in the White House, fielding telephone calls, patrolling the corridors, ascending to the second floor to check out the presidential bedroom door. After years of keeping its distance from foreign wars, America is fast adapting to the prospect of a very different future. Rumours are sweeping DC that some of the Jap planes over Pearl Harbor carried swastikas on their wings and tailplanes. Might American boys once again be despatched across the Atlantic?

Next morning, just before noon, Kane joins other agents outside the southern entrance to the mansion. Here, in warm sunshine, a motorcade has assembled for the three-mile dash to Capitol Hill. Mike Reilly is in charge of the on-board protection detail and assigns Kane the mortuary slot to FDR's immediate right. Should anyone open fire on the President from the sidewalk the bullets will have to go through Kane first.

On a hand signal from Reilly, the motorcade begins to move. Overnight, the news from Hawaii has only become grimmer. More than two thousand servicemen and civilians confirmed dead. Hospitals brimming with casualties. The Pacific Fleet counted out in the first round.

At the bottom of Fourteenth, the Caddy slows for the turn into Independence Avenue. Kane is watching the faces behind the armed soldiers lining the route and detects none of the usual enthusiasm for FDR. Instead, folks are silent, watchful, maybe apprehensive. A disaster like this was on no one's Christmas list, and even the nation's president, normally so glad to be free of the White House and his bank of telephones, is grim-faced, his eyes fixed on some distant point way beyond the windshield. Kane can feel the heat of his body through his own suit. As they finally slow to a halt beside the Capitol, he pats Kane's thigh.

'Let's get this thing done,' he murmurs.

Transferring FDR in and out of limos is silky-smooth, a marvel of co-ordination: the wheelchair readied at the kerbside, two men on either side, the President using his upper body strength to lever himself across the gap. Blink twice, as Reilly always says, and you've missed it.

They're on the move already, wheeling the presidential chair across the sidewalk, up the ramp and into the building with a curt nod from the trio of armed Marines at the door. Inside, Kane hears the expectant murmur of hundreds of conversations from the House of Representatives before they round the final corner and pause at the entrance to the chamber.

FDR's son James is waiting to help his father to the podium. Kane knows the exact distance to the podium because he's had to measure it. What he also knows is the immense effort FDR has to make to somehow convince a watching nation that a polio cripple can become their president. To onlookers, this walk has the makings of a conjuring trick. Only close family and secret agents know the price in effort, sweat and raw pain. Even the brief speech that follows will mean a shirt change within the hour.

At the sight of father and son, hundreds of senators and congressmen rise to their feet and give their president a standing ovation. They need leadership, they need reassurance. Stiffly, one careful step after another, FDR makes his way to the podium where his big hands grasp the wooden top while he sways a little, before gesturing for the applause to stop.

His address extends to barely twenty-five sentences and Kane counts every one of them. This, he knows, is history in the making. He can visualise packed taverns across the country, bartenders turning up the volume on the radio, hushing drinkers for a little quiet. He can imagine his own family back home in Boston, his mom and dad probably at the lunch table, his little sister in charge of the volume knob on the big old Bakelite. FDR has already rebadged 7 December as a day that will live in infamy and he's in the process of confronting the many sacrifices that lie ahead when a strange noise overhead breaks the tense silence inside the chamber.

Congressmen peer upwards. Secret agents exchange glances. The noise grows louder, and louder still, and it's Kane who recognises the tell-tale patter of footsteps. This is serious. The executive and legislative heart of America, hopelessly vulnerable, is a sitting target, Congressmen trapped in their seats are at the mercy of something totally unforeseen. Might it be a bomb? Might the ceiling shortly collapse on the beating heart of this hapless nation? First Pearl Harbor? Now the Capitol itself?

Mike Reilly has already disappeared towards the service stairs that lead to the roof. Another agent, gun in hand, follows him. But FDR, stubbornly upright behind the podium, pays not the slightest attention. He's closing his address, asking Congress to confirm that a state of war now exists between the United States and the Japanese Empire. His audience return their attention to the podium and, once again, rise to acclaim their President.

The vote goes through with a single dissenting voice, and FDR makes his way back towards the big doors through a forest of clapping hands. Kane walks behind him, scanning faces on either side of the aisle, looking – as ever – for anomalies and warning signs of yet more trouble to come. Out in the sunshine, Mike Reilly is already preparing to mastermind the transfer of FDR back to the Caddy.

'And?' Kane gestures up towards the roof of the House of Representatives.

'One of our guys,' Reilly shakes his head in mock despair, 'chasing shadows.'

That afternoon, Reilly and Kane conference with a guy from the Treasury Department. Among the Department's many trophy confiscations is a part-armoured saloon that once belonged to Al Capone, and Reilly is very welcome to have it as a sensible replacement for FDR's Caddy. Kane, amused by the thought of Roosevelt taking advantage of a gangster-ride of his very own, thinks it a fine idea but it turns out that Reilly is already in conversations with Ford in Detroit, who – in the spirit of Pearl Harbor – have offered to build a bespoke Lincoln with guaranteed all-round protection. At this, the Treasury guy gathers his papers and departs, leaving Reilly with a long list of items still needing resolution.

One of them, anticipating Jap air raids over DC, proposes painting the White House black. Another suggests changing the course of the Potomac and Anacostia rivers to deny enemy pilots an obvious path to the presidential mansion. A third, truly radical, would involve moving the nation's capital hundreds of miles inland.

Reilly and Kane agree that this crazy stuff is time wasted but when Reilly does his best to co-opt Kane onto an emergency working group to troubleshoot the construction of an air raid shelter under the White House lawn, Kane shakes his head. What he really needs just now, after thirty hours flat out, is a decent night's sleep. He's phoned a neighbour to take Dexter for a walk but the woman is Chinese and might be nervous about showing her face on the street. For his own sake, and the dog's, Kane is off home.

A pat on the back sends Kane to the door. Tomorrow's another day, my friend, but get rid of that bloody dog of yours. Kane raises a tired arm, doesn't look back. Pearl Harbor in flames? Unbelievable.

The apartment is on a quiet street near Cleveland Park, normally a fifteen-minute drive from the White House. Heading north from downtown DC, the roads are virtually empty, and Kane does it in ten. Dexter is whining behind the door and the moment Kane steps into the apartment, he knows the Chinese woman hasn't appeared.

He finds one coil of shit, then a second, and he's in the process of looking for a third when he hears a knock on the door. Cursing the intrusion, he pads back to the entrance hall. Standing regulations stipulate every agent equips himself with a spy hole but Kane has only been in residence for a couple of months and has yet to get round to it.

And so he opens the door, wondering how to handle the smell, and then pauses. The last time he set eyes on this woman was more than a month ago at the Los Angeles airport out at Inglewood. She's way shorter than Kane and has an indefinable physical presence that turns heads in any bar. Kane had spent a very happy couple of weeks in LA, once again trying to put the essence of this woman into words, and had failed completely. Saying goodbye at the departure gate put her on tiptoes, her arms once again round Kane's neck, her body pressed against his. She smells now, as she smelled then, of a French perfume called L'Origan.

'Mahoney,' Kane gestures her inside. 'My apologies for the fucking dog.'

2

More about Mahoney. Her first name is Lou, the sawn-off version of her mother's favourite American author, Louisa May Alcott. Reading *Little Women* was a rite of passage for this only child of a failed Californian marriage, and the teenage Mahoney warmed to the notion of four sisters in the book, each burdened with a flaw. For Kane's benefit, the first time they met in LA, years back, she tallied each of them on the fingers of her left hand: shyness, selfishness, vanity and getting in other people's faces.

'And you?' Kane had asked.

'Ambition. Which I guess is the OK version of the last one.'

'You get in people's faces?'

'I do. It's called journalism.'

It turned out she wasn't kidding. Working as a runner on the *Long Beach Tribune* at the age of sixteen, junior reporter on the *Los Angeles Evening Express* a couple of years later, and now – at twenty-nine – a share of a desk on the editorial floor of the *LA Times*.

'College never interested you?'

'Never. You need money for that, and time. I had neither.'

'A girl in a hurry?'

'A girl on her own. If you have no taste for solitude there are ways of making real life your friend.'

Real life. Before meeting Mahoney, Kane had dated a succession of women in Boston, two of them beauty queens. One of them was great in the sack, and the other trailed a vengeful ex-suitor in her wake, but neither held Kane's attention. There followed a series of interviews with the Secret Service over three days in DC. Two weeks later he quit the Boston PD, served out his notice period, and took the train west to California where he joined a bunch of secret agents breaking a counterfeiting ring centred on one of the big Hollywood studios. The painstaking operation swallowed a great deal of time and the final bunch of arrests brought a torrent of media enquiries, including a surprise visit from Lou Mahoney.

Much like now.

'This is your forever pal?' Mahoney is fondling the dog. She seems to like him, and the feeling is clearly mutual. Kane has rarely seen Dexter so animated.

'Here—' Kane has found a can of beer.

'A Gansett?' She's weighing it in her hand. 'You remembered?'

'How could I not?'

Mahoney abandons the can and leads Kane to the sagging sofa he acquired with the apartment. She wants to know why there are no hotel rooms in this town.

'You've checked?'

'Of course I have. It's what us reporters do. Old habits, Quince.'

'And?'

'Everywhere's full. Is Christmas in DC unmissable? Or should I be blaming the Japs?'

'Neither. This is where folks come for a favour or two. This is where the jobs are. You need somewhere to stay. That's why the hottest money goes into hotels.' He fetches a glass from the tiny kitchen and pours the beer.

'I'm drinking alone?'

Kane smiles, says nothing. The bottle of Jim Beam beside the radio set has barely been touched. He pours himself three fingers to celebrate her arrival.

'You're planning on staying the night?' He settles on the sofa again.

'I'm planning on asking you whether that might be OK.' She touches her glass to his, then kisses him softly on the lips. 'Agent Kane.'

She wakes him in the middle of the night, another kiss. Barely hours ago, he'd noticed bruising on one side of her rib cage, but had said nothing. Now, as she straddles him, he's looking again. Hints of an old swelling around her face, too.

'How come?' His fingers find the biggest bruise.

'I got in a fight.'

'How?'

'I've taken up boxing.'

'You're serious?'

'Ask the woman I was fighting. She won, by the way, but I got through to the end. Black lady. Answers to Dolores. Faster than me, and stronger.' She shrugs. 'This time round.'

'You're telling me you've agreed a rematch?'

'No kidding. She's got a great left hand, which is why I still hurt down here,' she nods down at her rib cage. 'The lady came in close, all three rounds, knew exactly what she was doing. Bam – bam – bam. At first you think it's nothing.

No way do body shots really matter. Wrong, Mr Kane. In the end you can't breathe properly and after that you're done. The trick is to learn the lesson. Next time I'll knock her out.'

Kane shakes his head. Says he's never heard of girl-on-girl boxing.

'It's probably an LA thing. Think showbiz. If someone's making a buck, it'll happen.' She's gazing down at him. 'Does that surprise you? Disgust you, maybe? Be honest.'

Kane reaches up for her. The word on his lips is why. Why do it? Why open the door to all that pain?

'Because…' she says.

'Because what?'

'Just because.' She ducks low, taking him by surprise, whispers in his ear. 'You wanna know more? The whole story?'

She slips him inside her, begins to move very slowly, her eyes never leaving his face in the chill of the underlit bedroom. She's already borrowed a sweater of his, a souvenir from the long-ago days when he was playing semi-pro football, and now she's draped it across her bare shoulders, the arms hanging down. He loves the swell of her breasts, and he loves as well the pitch of her voice when she gets into storytelling: low, intimate, a voice built for remembered details salted by a lightness he finds deeply pleasing. This is a woman who seems to have built an entire life on careful observation. Her world appears to belong to other people, and if she figures at all, it's at the very margins of visibility.

She's told him many stories during their meetings in LA, and she's told them well. Some of them were stories from her youth, often about her father. His name was Frank and he drank a great deal, often from frustration and bewilderment after yet another screenplay came winging back from this studio or that. He'd kept their tiny, busted family afloat by fixing broken plumbing around the neighbourhood but his real mission was to break out and pitch his tent downtown in Hollywood. He'd died a couple of years back, a ghost of a man emptied by disappointment and cirrhosis, but she never stopped loving him and every time she earns another byline in the *LA Times* she knows how proud he would have been. He'd kept a scrapbook of every story she'd ever had published, a secret she'd only discovered after his death. He'd pasted them into a kid's album he must have picked up from some place and leafing through a near-decade of fading newsprint had made her cry, something that Kane suspects is extremely rare.

'This is good?' She's barely moving now.

Kane nods. 'You promised me the full story,' he says. 'About the boxing.'

'You really wanna know?'

'Yes.'

'Why? Because violence turns men on?'

'Sure.'

'Especially women beating up on each other?'

'Especially you. You want the truth? I don't get it. You have everything. Looks, talent, a job that matters. Folks pay attention to that paper of yours. You have presence. So why spoil the party?'

The question seems to please her. Her eyes stray briefly towards the door. Dexter has appeared, as silent and reproachful as ever, then she's back with Kane, a gentle squeeze, and then another. The fights, she says, take place at a private venue, invitation only, men with money and a trophy starlet to impress. Mahoney had first attended on the arm of a guy she knows from one of the studios, intrigued by what she might find. She'd liked the guy enough for them to fuck a couple of times and when he'd told her she had a body that belonged in the ring, the comment had stuck.

'You trained?'

'Train. Four nights a week. Hard, really hard. This is time I can't really afford but after a while it becomes something you can't do without. You're asking your body questions it's never been asked before, never dreamed of entertaining, and you get to realise you're worth more than you thought. My trainer says that's the whole point.'

'He?'

'She. Her name's Billy-Jean. From Tennessee. She was years in the ring herself. That's all you need to know.'

Kane nods. Mahoney raises an eyebrow and quickens just a little. Kane nods again.

'Perfect,' he closes his eyes. 'Tell me about Dolores.'

'She's black, like I say. Slightly smaller than me, much stronger than me, a little knot of something most folks might call rage.'

'Why's that?'

'I never got to find out. The woman was out of reach the moment we met. You try for contact, any contact, but it never happened. God's truth, I couldn't lay a glove on her. Wouldn't talk. Wouldn't answer a single question. Wouldn't stay still so I could hit her. She beat me up good, which is what all those men had come to see, and maybe the women, too. After the fight, you go back through all the tables around the ring to the locker room. The lights are still down, which is a blessing because you're not looking your best, but there's an envelope waiting with the appearance money inside. They pay well – at least a hundred dollars for showing up – but then come all those hands from the darkness, folded notes stuffed wherever they can get to, tens and twenties mainly, plus phone numbers sometimes, and suddenly you're back in the locker room, and Dolores is counting her wad, and me, too, but even then she wouldn't risk a conversation.'

'You're telling me you do it for the money?'

'Not at all. I do it because I trained to do it. And because I was curious.'

'About what?'

'About what it felt like. Feels like. A guy once told me the ring is the loneliest place on God's earth and now I know that's true. There's nowhere to hide. Absolutely nowhere.'

'And that's worth finding out?'

'For sure.'

'You fight under your own name?'

'God, no.'

'So what do you call yourself?'

Mahoney shakes her head, won't say. Kane is frowning now. Something doesn't feel quite right.

'So why didn't you tell me any of this before? When I was out in LA?'

'Because you never asked. Don't ask, don't get.'

'And no training the last time I flew out? For two whole weeks? You didn't mind?'

'I loved you for it. You made me take a vacation and everything was much sweeter afterwards.'

'You're still fighting?'

'Sure. Dolores has agreed a rematch sometime in the New Year. Full house guaranteed so they've doubled the appearance fee. Two guys have already offered to be my agent. In a town like LA, that matters, believe me.'

Kane laughed. He wanted to know about that last round with Dolores.

'Talk me through it,' he murmured. 'Take me to the final bell.'

Mahoney knew exactly where this was leading, the kind of telepathy that never failed to turn Kane on, and she shifts her weight, leaning forwards, her arms outspread on either side of Kane's body, thrusting down, her rhythm beginning to quicken, her lips inches from Kane's face. How tired she'd felt, rising from the stool, stepping forwards onto the lit canvas of the ring, raising her gloves, trying to anticipate how Dolores planned to end the fight. She describes the way Dolores liked to crowd her into the neutral corner, the corner where the richest dudes had a perfect view, and there she did her best work, a torrent of blows to the head and the upper body, mixing the combinations, searching for that killer moment when Mahoney might lower her guard.

Twice, maybe three times, Mahoney managed to dance free, back to the safer spaces in the middle of the ring where she could kill precious time, but Dolores' eyes never left hers. They were dead, she says, the eyes of a shark, intent only on that final spasm of violence that would put Mahoney on the canvas. And so she found herself back above the rich dudes, fighting for breath, fighting to stay vertical, fighting for what felt like her very life.

At this point, with maybe thirty seconds to go, Dolores bluffed her into dropping her guard and the moment that happened, Mahoney knew that the fight was probably over. The left hook, perfectly angled, was Dolores' signature move.

It drove into Mahoney's unprotected face and she felt her head explode.

All she could hear was the roar of the crowd. All she could think about was sucking just a little air into her lungs. She clung onto Dolores the way you might say goodbye to someone you never wanted to lose, someone you loved really bad, and then – God knows how – came a moment when Dolores took a tiny step back, meaning to finish the fight, and it was then that Mahoney summed the very last ounce of what little she had left.

'Now?' She's vertical again, riding him to the finish. 'You ready for this?'

Kane nods. 'Now,' he grunts.

'Two shots,' she whispers. 'One into thin air. The other bang on her jaw. That expression on her face? I'll never forget it. No way was she going down. I doubt I even hurt her. But this was a woman robbed and that was a kind of victory. I had a mouthful of blood, and the referee was taking a good look at me, but that didn't matter because the bell had rung and it was all over. I'd survived. I'd gotten through. That was the sweetest moment of my life.' She's gazing down at him, briefly still. 'Would now be good? Just give me a clue.'

Kane nods, responds to her final thrust, groans, reaches up for her, pulls her down. For long minutes, after she'd covered them with a blanket, they lie together. Then comes a scuffling noise from somewhere nearby and Kane opens one eye to see Dexter standing beside the bed, staring up at Mahoney, transfixed.

Mahoney sees him, too, and she laughs softly, raising herself on one elbow beneath the blanket before reaching down for the bottle of Jim Beam, already half empty, parked beside the bed.

'I'm guessing you've had a busy old time this last day or two, Agent Kane,' she murmurs. 'You wanna tell me about some of that?'

3

Four days later, first thing in the morning at the White House, Kane spots the previous day's edition of the *LA Times* on the pile of papers he's due to deliver to FDR up in the second-floor bedroom. Fifteen hours earlier, Hitler had declared war on the USA and this second bombshell is splashed over every front page, including the *LA Times*. The West Coast flagship also carries a banner promotion for a six-page special supplement telling the inside story of Sunday's attack on Pearl Harbor.

Kane thinks nothing of it. Mahoney has been gone a couple of days. She's taken the dog with her – no explanation – and the note she left suggests that neither she nor Dexter will be back for a while. Missing Mahoney has become a way of life. Every time they meet she brings something new to the table and he's become uncomfortably aware that this solitary life of his brightens up the moment she arrives.

Boxing in front of a paying crowd? Putting her looks and everything else on the line? Kane is an investigator, and a good one, but never has he anticipated a development like this. Pressed for more details she'd shaken her head, telling him that patience is a virtue, promising a fuller account next time around, but the real surprise just now is the realisation that he misses the goddam dog, as well. I'm in trouble, he thinks. Missing animals as dumb as Dexter is what old folks do.

FDR, unusually, is already up and dressed and sitting in the wheelchair behind his desk in the adjacent Oval Study. In the shape of a restless, bulky, middle-aged figure in a dark suit he also has company. J. Edgar Hoover, as Kane knows only too well, is the Director of the Federal Bureau of Investigation.

From a distance, Kane has been watching this man's relentless rise to power at the head of the nation's leading crime fighters, intrigued by stories slipping out through a handful of his otherwise mute federal agents. The man runs a ship so tight you'd never believe it. The man is a fuss-budget watching every dime. The man gets seriously upset the moment you gain a pound or two and start to bust out of the FBI mould. The guy still sleeps in his childhood bedroom and kisses his mama goodnight before she retires. And here he is, a fidgety presence evidently chewing the presidential ear.

FDR looks up to find Kane at the door and pushes aside his notes, seemingly grateful for the interruption.

'We're talking internment, Agent Kane, mass arrests, lots of bodies behind the barbed wire. Mr Hoover, to his credit, has constitutional doubts. Is that fair, Edgar?'

Hoover is staring at the intruder with his armful of newsprint. Who is this guy? And how come he has the run of Roosevelt's private office?

When the silence becomes uncomfortable FDR laughs, retrieving his pad of jotted notes.

'Everything evidenced,' he reads. 'Every arrest justified. Everything shipshape in court.' He looks up. His smile is quizzical. He's pretending to be confused. 'Out there on the street, I get the feeling everyone's baying for blood. First Jap blood, now Heine blood. We're at war, gentlemen, and the gloves are off. Maybe that's where we should be starting this debate. Something the matter, Agent Kane?'

The gloves are off. Kane can't help thinking about Mahoney and those three torrid rounds with Dolores.

'Nothing, Mr President.' He's arranging the papers on the low table beside FDR's desk, aware of Hoover watching his every move.

'So give me a steer here, Agent Kane.' FDR again. 'You guys look, you listen, you're around a lot. The Free World isn't to Tokyo's liking. Hitler would love to give us a taste of Blitzkrieg if he could. So do we turn the other cheek? Refuse to take offence? Do the right and proper constitutional thing when half our fleet is history and two thousand men are dead? Or do we take a peep at the press, all of it, coast to coast?' A sweep of his big hand takes in the fan of morning papers. 'Just once in a generation these guys get to agree with each other, and that time is now.' He lifts a front page, adjusts his glasses to peer at a headline. 'Clamour for revenge. Perfect. Not a word out of place. You agree, Edgar?'

Hoover's pudgy fingers are fiddling with a button on the jacket of his suit. The FBI's fabled Director is way out of his depth, wrongfooted by FDR's cheerful disregard for the etiquette of privileged executive discussion, and it shows. A glance at his watch, a stagey clearing of his throat, and he's on his feet.

'Tell me later, Edgar. Yeah?' FDR is gazing up at him.

'Tell you what, Mr President?'

'How best you figure this next step of ours. By lunchtime would be good. A war on two fronts waits for no man.'

Kane can only agree. For the rest of his working day, he's plunged into the world of an administration getting back on its feet and brushing itself down. The longer the military and the grown-ups in the Department of Justice try and lock Roosevelt away in the White House, the more FDR is minded to get out among his people and tell them that everything is gonna be just fine.

Kane instinctively understands what drives this strange knot of contradictions at the heart of the presidency. He's long applauded America's judgement and maybe luck in electing a man as complex and opaque as Roosevelt not just once but three times, and when Mike Reilly yesterday passed word that the presidential train must be readied to depart at a moment's notice, destinations withheld in the interests of security, it's Kane who has to figure out exactly how to work this trick.

The train itself, comprising the armoured presidential carriage plus a bunch of assorted rolling stock to accommodate aides, hangers-on, pressmen and FDR's personal physician, is permanently readied in a subterranean siding beneath the Treasury building, a five-minute drive away. Railway staff who make any presidential excursion happen have already been security checked but two declarations of war in just five days demands a brand-new trawl to net any evidence of Japanese, German or Italian sympathies.

White America, by definition, is the last, best hope for millions of European immigrants, many of them with enemy blood in their veins, and as Kane's afternoon lengthens at his borrowed desk he begins to understand J. Edgar Hoover's reservations about mass arrests and incarceration.

One of the guys who drives the big engine on the presidential train is a first-generation import from Munich. Does that put him alongside the Nazis who saluted the young Adolf Hitler? And should that be enough to have him arrested? The woman assigned to the on-board catering crew who bake some of FDR's favourite pastries comes from Predappio, the small Emilia-Romagna town with intimate connections to Mussolini. Is it really Kane's job to deny FDR another plate of her matchless Baba al Rum?

Questions like these, Kane knows, are the shortest cut to insanity and he's about to put a call through to the Secret Service field office in Los Angeles when the tall figure of Steve Early appears at the door of the office where Kane has found a temporary perch. He's sharing the office with two others, both women.

'Ten minutes, ladies,' Early is holding the door open. 'And knock before you come back in.'

Early has a fearsome reputation around the White House. He serves as presidential Press Secretary, a job with a long history of career train wrecks, but he's weathered storm after storm since joining the first FDR administration back in 1933, and Kane knows exactly why. He's gruff, blunt and has a fierce belief in his own judgement. FDR uses him as a shield, warding off attacks from pressmen who will never make nice, and his job is secure as long as he wants it.

The women gone, Early produces a copy of the *LA Times* special supplement and tosses it onto Kane's desk.

'No need to read the whole thing,' he grunts. 'I've marked up what deserves a little of our goddam attention.'

Kane is staring at the front page. Beneath a stock black and white shot of the White House, photographed on the sunniest of days, is a seven-word caption: *Will the Black House Fool the Enemy?* Kane blinks, feeling an icy chill deep within him, checks a second time and then turns the page. Another photo, this time an aerial shot that captures the confluence of the Potomac and the Anacostia, DC's two rivers that meet just a mile south of the presidential mansion. Another question: *How Do You Divert the Nation's Favourite River?*

Kane glances up. Early has helped himself to a nearby phone and is tearing lumps out of some hapless journo. He shoots a look at Kane and signals for him to turn the page again.

This time an entire paragraph has been boxed with heavy red ink. It describes in some detail the discussions under way to dig a presidential air raid shelter under the South Lawn.

Early has finished his phone conversation. He replaces the receiver with a delicacy that surprises Kane, and then gazes down at him.

'You're getting the picture here?'

'Sure. I'm guessing you wanna know where all this stuff came from.'

'In one, Agent Kane. It has to be an inside job and you're the guy to ask the hard questions. It's either us or the Feds on the case and sure as hell we don't need them up our ass.'

Kane nods, remembering Hoover's heavy presence in the Oval Study. Another piece of scuttlebutt Kane has picked up along the way is the man's sheer appetite for new areas of the administration to make his own. Hoover can scent unprotected turf at a thousand yards and gorges on every passing opportunity. Not a square foot of DC is safe from his attentions.

Kane turns to the supplement's final page, looking for a list of contributors, all too conscious of exactly where some of the responsibility lies, but Early has got there first.

'No names, my friend. Not a single goddam clue. I called

the *LA Times* this afternoon, talked to the editor. I got the feeling it was a conversation he'd already rehearsed.'

'And?'

'Nothing. Sweet fuck-all. Not a single name. When I threatened him with the Feds he told me I'd never be that stupid.'

'So we keep it in-house?'

'Just you and me, buddy, and Mr Roosevelt once I get a moment of his time. This stuff has to be an inside job. Someone has blabbed, and blabbed good.'

'And me? What do you want me to do?'

'You find the guy and give me his name.'

'And then?'

'I shoot the bastard. Somewhere dark. Maybe blame it on the Japs.' A short, mirthless bark of laughter. 'Coupla days max, Agent Kane. Run this guy to earth and I'll owe you.'

'How come you think it's a guy?'

'I don't. Just testing is all.' He checks his watch, then nods down at the supplement. 'You know any woman with that kind of access?'

At the end of a very long day, Kane goes home via Washington's Union Station. All too aware that he may be walking into a trap of Early's making, he wants to leave nothing to chance.

Lou Mahoney had poured bourbon down his throat and fucked him witless in – as she saw it – the line of duty. Kane had shared far more of that unforgettable Sunday in the White House than was maybe wise but in a strange way he doesn't regret it. Neither does he blame Mahoney for taking advantage. It's what this glorious woman does. It's the way she's engineered, the way she's wired, the way she's built.

Kane has been around her for a while now and should have seen it coming. The moment he let her in through the door, the responsibility for what followed was his, and his alone. She remains the sweetest fuck, and the smartest conversation afterwards. He never wants to wake up with any other woman in his bed and more and more his instincts tell him she feels exactly the same way.

The only question that matters now is exactly how far to trust her. Not in terms of this spectacular act of larceny, journalistic theft on the grandest scale, but with the stuff that truly matters. Has she really got involved in the fight world? Or is Dolores, and the rich dudes beneath the neutral corner, just fictions she's tossed his way?

Kane makes the call from one of the phone booths at the back of the station's main concourse, knowing there's no chance of a listening ear on the line. The guy he's phoning is a good friend. His name is Gustave Leaman, 'Gus' for short. He's fluent in five languages, including Russian, and he works out of the Secret Service field office in downtown LA. Kane has a limited supply of dimes – no quarters – and keeps the conversation short.

Gus has met Mahoney twice, both times with Kane, and needs no introduction. When Kane describes the Dolores fight and takes a guess at a possible date, Gus whistles softly, a sign of approval.

'You're telling me she won in the end?'

'I'm telling you she lost. Badly. But the way she sees it, just staying on her feet is all the winning she needs. Like I've told you before, this is a woman who lives in her head.'

'She uses her own name? In the ring?'

'No. I asked for a name but she wouldn't come across.'

'Sure. Probably wise. This town is full of crazies who'd make her life a misery, but I guess you know that already.'

Kane nods, smiles. 'You can run this thing down?' he asks. 'Make an enquiry or two?'

'About?'

'Whether the fight ever happened.'

'You don't believe her?' Gus is laughing.

'I don't believe anyone. Never did. Never will.' Kane breaks off, realising he's just fed his last dime into the slot. He's trying to remember the Russian phrase they always used to end every conversation out on the coast and at last he's got it.

'*Удачной охоты*,' he grunts, mangling the vowel sounds. Good hunting.

Kane hangs up and buttons his coat against the swirl of wind across the concourse. As he does so, he spots a face that feels unaccountably familiar, half a dozen booths down the line. A second later, the guy has turned on his heel and gone.

4

Saturday already, but this war has no respect for weekends. All leave remains cancelled, like all rest days, and Kane finds himself locked in conference with Mike Reilly. Reilly has finally got the better of the Fire Department downtown, insisting that no one in the White House has time for fire drills, and he's also managed to come up with a solution in the event of a bombing raid. The Treasury Department has volunteered to construct a temporary cave in the bowels of their building that might well be perfect. All the Secret Service has to do is get FDR there in less than two minutes.

Reilly, celebrating his victory over the guy in the Fire Department, is calling it Bomb Drill. He's acquired a wheelchair and a sink belt from local cops on the Dive Squad who search the Potomac for bodies. Reilly is familiar with FDR's current weight and has figured that seventy pounds of lead should do the trick. Kane is the tallest of the District Sixteen detail and is volunteered to play FDR.

Reilly is Kane's boss. Kane knows that Reilly is a slave to the smallest print and that it might take the entire morning – maybe the entire day – to hit the golden target time. In the meantime, Kane has spent half the night trying to figure out how to counterfeit a report on the *LA Times* leak that will keep Steve Early happy. In reality, of course, it's Kane's fault that half the nation is now privy to White House secrets but confirmation of the source of the leak will put Kane on the street. Or, even worse, send him to the chair. Treason, just now, is the simplest of propositions.

Reilly has gathered three agents, including Kane, and has charted the most direct route to the Treasury. Should this morning's trials go right, a tunnel will be dug to connect the two sites but in the meantime the agents must cross a minor road and then keep to the marked paths across the cropped grass. The first bid is a disaster. Reilly has arranged for traffic to be stopped on the East Executive Avenue but a delivery van ignores the cops and narrowly avoids bringing Kane's current troubles to a messy end. Kane will be haunted for days by the image of the driver's face staring out at him as the little Ford panel van swerves to avoid them. Shit, they both think.

After that, it gets better. The two other agents are taking turns to do the running and the pushing and all Kane is left with is another bone-jarring one hundred and twenty seven-seconds or so with a stopwatch in his lap. Twice he volunteers to do some pushing of his own and twice Reilly wags his head and so, in the end, Kane does his best to ease the pressure of the weight belt and tries to figure out what it must be like to be FDR.

I'm a kid from a rich family. I go to a fancy school. I end up at Harvard with other rich kids. I spend whole summers in yet another family home way up on the Canadian border and I fall in love with the ocean, with swimming, with fooling around, and above all with sailing. I'm good at sailing. It challenges and pleases the bits of me that matter. I also get married, a tall, serious gal, a distant relative with the same name as me. She happens to be the first to say yes after a few duds. But that's another story.

We have kids, four of them. Like my Uncle Teddy I get into politics, and like my Uncle Teddy I naturally want to end up in the White House. That's looking a distinct possibility until I get sick up there on the Canadian border. A doctor attends. Then comes a second opinion. I've contracted polio. If polio doesn't kill you it can take your legs away and turn you into a cripple. At thirty-nine, I'm pretty much guaranteed the rest of my life in a wheelchair.

What next? How would you ever cope with news like that? How come the road to Washington now looks like one of God's unfunnier jokes? Kane has been pondering these questions for a while now, ever since he first joined the guys at District Sixteen, and he does so because FDR has such a special knack of getting along with folks.

Kane believes that he and the nation's president really are close – in mindset, in a shared sense of humour – but that may simply be the impression he leaves with everyone: the politician's grin, the hand that settles briefly on your shoulder. One day, the relationship may be put to the test but in the meantime Kane holds his Chief in something more than reverence. He truly believes they are friends, and just now that matters a great deal.

By five minutes short of noon, the guys doing the pushing have got the time down to two minutes and two seconds. At this point Reilly has disappeared into the White House to emerge moments later with two Hershey bars. Kane watches him toss them to the guys relaxing in the sunshine.

'And mine?' Kane says.

'You do the sitting, buddy. They do the work. That's the way it is, Quince. Me? I'm thinking of your weight.'

'Appreciate it,' Kane turns his face upwards. He can feel just a hint of warmth in the winter sunshine, and he closes his eyes and thinks once again of Mahoney. The two guys behind the chairs are demolishing their Hershey bars and telling Reilly they may need another to bust the goddam time. Then comes the crunch of footsteps on gravel, closer and closer, and Kane opens his eyes to find Steve Early gazing down at him. He's been watching the morning's entertainments from his office and he's yet to figure out how Kane has pulled the sweet spot.

'Sweet spot?' Kane pats the weights beneath his shirt. 'I'm getting to know Mr Roosevelt a little better here. Ain't no problem in the world that can't be resolved. We agree on that?'

Just a hint of a smile ghosts across Early's face. He neither nods nor shakes his head. Then he's gone.

The Hershey bars do the trick and the next run is the last one. Milton Lipson is the fittest of the two agents, and probably the bolder. The traffic has been stopped once again on the road beside the White House and Lipson takes an even tighter line through the corners on the other side, yelling at pedestrians and cops to get out of the way, and throwing Kane left and right as he desperately hangs on. By the time they get to the finish line, Lipson is forcing air deep into his lungs and has to make the four yards to a trash can before throwing up.

Kane is staring at the stopwatch as Reilly arrives, panting hard.

'Well?'

'Three seconds under,' Kane looks across at Lipson as he wipes his mouth. 'Can you believe that?'

★

Reilly is delighted. A phone call to his contact in the Treasury, and another item off his ever-growing must-do list. Kane, still thinking about Steve Early, is sitting behind one of the two desks in the agents' retreat when a call comes from Grace Tully, FDR's aide. The President would appreciate a word with Agent Quince. Now, please.

Kane mounts the staircase to the second floor. Every step upwards deepens his sense of dread and when he finally makes the Oval Study, the sight of Steve Early in one of the armchairs does nothing for his blood pressure.

'Mr President?'

FDR mutters something Kane doesn't catch. He's deep in a newspaper and he doesn't look up. His mother, Sara, has only been dead a matter of months and Kane knows that he's taken the loss hard. He's been wearing a black armband ever since her demise in September, and word around the mansion suggests he'll keep it on a full year.

Finally, he pushes the report to one side and gestures Kane into the other armchair. The First Lady, he says, is out on the coast for a week or so and he wants to pick Kane's brains.

'About?'

'Lotsa stuff, but let's start with this.' He gestures down at the newspaper. 'You were in LA for a couple of years, right?'

'Yes, sir.'

'Got on with the natives OK?'

The question is loaded and Kane senses at once that all three men know it.

'I got on with Californians,' Kane says carefully. 'There's lots to like.'

'Sure. My guess is that it has to do with the sunshine. California is where the dreamers go to pitch their tents. Where else would you ever make movies?' FDR's gaze returns to the newsprint and he frowns before looking up again.

'You know about the First Lady and the OCD?'

The OCD is the Office of Civilian Defense, one of FDR's pre-war initiatives. Eleanor Roosevelt had come on board at the invitation of NY Major, Fiorello La Guardia, plunging into the world of aircraft spotters, air raid wardens and volunteer fire brigades. Just now, she's taken herself off to California, pledging whatever help OCD can muster in the face of possible Japanese attacks.

'She's doing great work, sir, the way I'm hearing it.'

'Really? I'm not sure everyone agrees with that.' FDR is peering at the paper again. 'The First Lady is calling for tolerance, as she so often does, but just now people are getting riled up. Here's a direct quote, Agent Kane. "When Eleanor Roosevelt starts bemoaning the plight of the treacherous snakes we call Japanese, with apologies to all snakes, she has reached the point where she should be forced to retire from public life".' FDR looks first at Early, then across to Kane. 'Can you believe that, gentlemen? My wife? This nation's First Lady? Shown the door by the likes of the *LA Times*?'

Kane tries to hide his discomfort. He's been around FDR far too long not to know exactly where this conversation is headed. Sub-plots within sub-plots, everything artfully hidden, the reefs beneath the seeming innocence and hurt.

'That's harsh, Mr President,' Kane agrees.

'Harsh,' a vigorous nod from behind the desk. 'Exactly. So what do we do about it. Mr Early? Any ideas.'

'We need them to tone this stuff down, Mr President.

Maybe issue some kind of rebuttal. Maybe even get them to carry a piece coming from a different point of view.'

'Sure. And how exactly do we make that happen?'

'I can talk to the editor. No problem. But I'm guessing there might be another way.'

'Someone further down the food chain?'

'Neat idea, Mr President. You have a name in mind?'

FDR shakes his head, says nothing. Then his gaze turns to Kane.

'Anything you might do, Agent Kane? In the way of helping us all out here?'

Early evening, the White House blacked out with heavy drapes at every window, Kane makes his way to a speakeasy he knows off Pennsylvania Avenue. Before crossing the big road he pauses to check behind him but can see no trace of a tail. The speakeasy, Mario's Place, has a private booth at the back where customers can talk on the phone. Mario himself is long dead but Kane knows his son, a big Redskins fan.

'You'll take a beer, Quince?' Carlos is already reaching for the cooler.

Kane nods towards the booth, hidden behind a curtain.

'Free?'

'All yours.'

Kane settles himself in the booth. First he needs to talk to Gus. When Kane gets through, it turns out he's just got up after an all-night surveillance job in the San Fernando Valley and he's thinking of heading for the beach.

'Lucky guy. Anything on Mahoney?'

'Sure. The fight thing is kosher. She's appeared twice at a private venue off Sunset Boulevard. Calls herself Flo.'

'Just that? Flo?'

'Fightin' Flo,' Gus confirms. 'First time out, the way I'm hearing it, was a slam dunk. She was up against another white girl, much younger, thin, possibly ill.'

'And?'

'Mahoney knocked her out in the second round. Did the job good by all accounts. All those rich bastards lapped it up. That's what they come for.'

'A result?'

'Pain. Blood. Twenty bucks a ticket, you need to fill your boots. In the trade they call little girls like that carrion. If you're lucky, the appearance fee covers the hospital expenses. Stick to soccer, Quince. Give yourself a little respect.'

'And Dolores?'

'A woman of colour, my friend, just the way you described her.'

'And?'

'Payback time for your gal but she stayed on her feet, refused to bend the knee, tried to fight back before she took a big one on the jaw. That's a hundred years of history rewritten in three rounds if you happen to be black. The crowd loved her which I guess is why she's keen to go back.'

My gal, Kane thought. If only.

'Anything else?' Gus is keen to catch the last of the sunshine on the beach.

'Nope.'

Kane hangs up, gazes at the phone a moment, then ends the conversation. He produces a slip of paper and phones another LA number. He's looking at Mahoney's script, cursive, perfectly formed, unhurried. My new Santa Monica apartment, she'd told him. You'll love it.

'Yeah?'

To Kane's surprise it's a male voice on the line. When he asks to speak to Lou Mahoney the guy thinks she's gone to the grocery store.

'You wanna leave a message? My pleasure.'

'When's she back?'

'Could be minutes, my friend. Could be longer. It's a Saturday, buddy, and the sun's out. Maybe later, eh?'

Kane ends the conversation without volunteering a name and steps out of the booth. He sinks two bottles of Bud and then makes his way back to the phone booth. This time it's Mahoney who answers. She seems glad to hear him.

'You OK over there?' she asks.

'Sure.'

'Missing me any?'

'Sure.'

'Good. Right answer. The dog sends his best, by the way. Getting him on the flight was a nightmare but one of the flight crew was Irish, Galway guy, so that solved everything.'

'And?'

'Everyone loves him. They loved him on the aeroplane and they love him here. He's a dog reborn, Agent Kane, and if I ever want to bring him back east with me the plane guys see no problem. Dexter redux, Quince. You've been living with a legend.'

Redux? Kane hasn't a clue what she means but knows it doesn't matter. On two bottles of Bud, he's hot for her already.

'Listen—' he's fighting the urge to ask who the man on the

phone earlier might be '—we need to talk about that paper of yours.'

He explains briefly about the attack in the press on Eleanor Roosevelt, says her husband has taken it personally.

'This is the President? FDR?'

'The very same.'

'Holy shit, Quince. My guys will be hanging out the flags. A response from the Man himself? I never knew fame could be so easy.'

'This was a private conversation, Lou. Just like the one we had the other night.'

'Aaah…' There's a long silence, then she's back on the line. 'Is that why you phoned? To tell me I was out of order?'

'Close.'

'You read that supplement piece?'

'I did.'

'And it got you into trouble?'

'Deep shit.'

'Because?'

'Because we go back a while. Because we have a little history between us. Because these guys keep names and dates and build files. That's what they're good at, probably best at. DC can be one big fight ring on a bad day and it's best to stay outa trouble.'

'Right.' For once, she's sounding thoughtful, even repentant. Kane seizes his moment.

'So why did you do it? Care to give me a clue?'

'That's a big question, Quince. To be honest I'm not sure I can tell you. Did I knock on your door to pick your brains? Of course I did. Did I leave in a different state of mind?

That's another yes. It matters, Quince, you and me. Don't ever believe otherwise.'

'So why screw me?'

'Because...'

'Because what?'

'I dunno, and that's the truth. They sent me east because they knew you work where you work. This whole country runs on access, Quince, and you have plenty.'

'You're telling me it's their fault? Your bosses' fault?'

'I'm telling you I'm ambitious. I'm telling you I do their bidding when it seems to matter. That supplement has raised all kinds of shit nationwide. We journos call that a success. Bigtime.'

'And me? Us?'

'We're tight. We're together. We're where this story begins and ends. You think I'm bullshitting?'

'Christ, no. I want to believe you, maybe need to believe you.'

'Good. Great. So what do I do next?'

Kane blinks, takes his time, then bends to the phone. He's wanted to nurse the conversation to exactly this point.

'I'm guessing you scored a lot of points with that piece.'

'You guess right.'

'So maybe there's scope for another piece. Eleanor Roosevelt brings light into darkness. That's her phrase, not mine. Most of the Japs on the West Coast are American citizens and she thinks they deserve a break. Is that asking too much?'

'Giving them a break?'

'Sure. And you writing a piece to suggest it.'

This, Kane knows, is the crux of the conversation, the

point when all his careful planning can come off the rails and end up a pile of junk in the weeds beside the track. But to his astonishment, and maybe a little bewilderment, she starts to laugh.

'I've said something funny?'

'Not at all. Happens I agree with you completely. The Japs and the Mexicans and all kinds of so-called trash over here get the bummest of deals. The way it's been feeling this last week is real scary. To be white and rich and righteous is to carry a gun. If I was Jap I'd be heading for the hills so maybe internment camps isn't such a crazy idea, if only for their own sakes.'

'You don't mean that.'

'You're right, Quince, I don't.' Another pause. 'I have a piece in my head. I wrote a draft a couple of nights back. It isn't quite right but I could work on it.'

'And what does it say? This piece of yours?'

'It says we need to think a little harder, make a space for one or two things.'

'Like?'

'Tolerance, for starters. And maybe even more than that. Spread the love, Quince. Never did us any harm.'

Kane nods. From nowhere has come the germ of an idea.

'Eleanor Roosevelt is out west for six days,' he says. 'She's back in DC on the fifteenth. Make contact with her. Mention my name. Meet her. Interview her. Try and see this crazy war her way. She'll have lots to say, because she always does, but make sure you give her a fair hearing.'

'And then?'

'Write a piece for that paper of yours. You want some

kind of incentive? If you do it right, I won't be going to the electric chair.'

'That bad?'

'Probably worse.'

She begins to laugh again because she knows he's kidding but likes his chutzpah. This is Hollywood, Kane thinks. Everything exaggerated, everything for effect.

'Do I hear a yes?' he asks.

'You hear a maybe. Sure I'll run the lady down. Sure I'll bid for an interview. And there's nothing the honchos on the editorial desk like more than controversy. It's what they might do to my copy that matters.'

'They change stuff?'

'All the time. There are ways a gal can get round that but you don't want to know more.'

'Sure.'

'I mean it, Quince.'

'Mean what?'

'That I'll do my best. You know what, pardner? I'm not sure what you ever did with the rest of your life but you were wasted on other women.'

'Happens I agree. One last question, yeah?'

'Go ahead.'

'That guy I talked to just now. Who the fuck is he?'

Mahoney started to giggle, a sound Kane had never heard from her before.

'His name's Virgil,' she says at last. 'He writes dream film scripts and he's crazy for guys.'

'All the time?'

'Most of it, Quince, but hey, none of us are perfect...'

5

Kane hears nothing from Mahoney for the next week or so but then, in the third week in December, he's summoned to Steve Early's office to find FDR's Press Secretary studying one of the inside pages of the weekend edition of the *LA Times*.

He pushes the paper across his desk, a gesture so gruff that Kane can only fear the worst. Mahoney, or her editors, or even Eleanor Roosevelt herself have screwed Quincy Kane once again.

'Just read it,' Early grunts. 'Happy Christmas.'

Early rarely smiles. He views it as a weakness, one of the many reasons FDR cherishes his presence, but just now appears to be an exception. He's even produced a bottle of Jim Beam.

Kane is gazing at the proffered article. It carries Mahoney's byline, along with a photo the size of a postage stamp. Her smile is slightly ambiguous, Kane thinks. She might mean it, she might not.

A much bigger photo accompanies the article. Eleanor Roosevelt is snapped addressing a largely female audience in San Francisco. She stands tall at the lectern in a polka-dot dress and a wide-brimmed hat worn at a rakish angle. The shot is taken from the side of the stage and hundreds of watching faces recede towards the back of the hall.

'Read,' Early has little patience.

Kane does his bidding. The thrust of Mahoney's interview is obvious from the start. She wants the First Lady's thoughts on the threat of mass arrests of Japanese the length of the West Coast. Entire families may be taken into custody, regardless of whether they hold citizenship or not, and Eleanor Roosevelt regards that as a stain on American tolerance and what she calls the American soul.

Only these last few days, she says, the President has taken the opportunity to address the nation through one of his fireside radio chats. War production on countless factory floors needs to quadruple. Assembly lines must be tended night and day. This huge collective effort can only happen if everyone lends a hand. Hasty pledges to put a hundred thousand Japanese behind the wire is therefore a foolish act of self-harm, with the authorities obeying the instincts of the mob. These Japanese folk are as American as everyone else. The moment we forget that fact is the moment that this war of ours is lost.

'Powerful stuff.' Kane means it.

'Go to the end. Cut to the chase.'

Kane's eyes drift down through the columns of newsprint. The interview, to his surprise, occupies an entire page and in the final paragraph Mahoney records the reception for the First Lady's speech.

'The President's wife,' she writes, 'earned a standing ovation from the assembled audience. All of them had enrolled in the OCD crusade to defend the heart of America, and it was impossible to find a voice raised against what she had to say. Interviewed afterwards, women admitted they hadn't thought through the issues at stake. Eleanor was right. A war for civilisation was, in the end, about the values that we all hold dear.'

'Beautiful,' Kane is full of admiration. 'The President's read this?'

'Of course he has. It won't make much difference, the Japs will still get locked up, but that's not the point. His wife deserves her say and thanks to your friend out there, that's exactly what she's got. That makes her very happy, and if she's very happy, the President can get on with running the rest of the war.'

Brutal, Kane thinks, but probably the way it has to be.

'My friend out there?' he murmurs.

Early ignores the comment. He's decanting two hefty shots of Jim Beam. He passes one glass to Kane and raises the other.

'Here's hoping the bastards burn in hell,' he's smiling again. 'No offence, eh?'

'The bastards?'

'The Japs. All of them.'

My friend out there. Kane can only assume he's home safe. Mahoney's article appears to have diluted Early's wrath about the leaks that found their way into the *LA Times* special supplement, and there's been no more mention of an in-house manhunt for the perp. With the White House slowly coming to terms with a war on two fronts, Kane's even making cautious plans for a brief descent on Boston to celebrate Christmas with his family.

My friend out there. Kane calls her late that night from the phone in his apartment. In LA, it's barely eight o'clock.

'You're out of breath,' Kane says at once.

'The goddam gym again. An hour of ring work and other stuff and then I run home with that crazy dog. Virgil thinks I'm nuts, too, and some nights, like tonight, I think he may have a point.'

'So how do you feel?'

'Empty. I keep putting the gas in and nothing happens.'

'You're still fighting Dolores?' Kane is hoping for a no.

'Every night. Awake, asleep, it makes no difference. That woman's found a perch inside me. She won't let me alone. Bam-bam-bam. Tonight I had fifteen minutes on the punch bag. I kidded myself it was her. Bam-bam-bam. My turn.'

'And?'

'Empty, like I say. On the way home I covered her from block to block, tried to overtake, tried to trip her up, tried to nudge her into the traffic. Result? She just skips away. Was she really there? Of course she wasn't but that's not the point. Put a name and a face on certain death and you're looking at Dolores. Do I deserve this, Quince? Do I? Help me out here. Be honest. Be my friend.'

Kane is staring at the phone. Mahoney has never been needy before.

'Maybe you could use a drink,' he suggests.

'Sure. And maybe something a little stronger, too.'

'Like?'

'You, my sweet baby. You know the real story behind the stuff I gave them for that supplement?'

'Tell me.'

'Sure. This is about why crazy folks like me do what they do. Hollywood calls it motivation. In this case it comes with a dash of that mad Irish cunning. In my dreams they read the piece, figure out where it came from, take your badge away, probably your gun as well, and then leave the rest of you, the best of you, for little me. We find somewhere horizontal and not too cold and pick up the story where we left off. Might that strike you as any kind of plan? Just say yes.'

Kane says nothing. In Mahoney's world, this is foreplay, a rich overture before the curtain rises. She's done it before, a number of times, and it never fails to excite him.

'I've phoned to say thank you,' he grunts.

'What for?'

'Your piece about the First Lady. Aside from anything else, it's kept me in a job.'

'Shit,' she's laughing now. 'Then I've failed, haven't I? Totally screwed up. So much for motivation. When do we get to fool around again?'

The question haunts the days that follow. Kane books a ticket to take the train north to Boston for his brief Christmas break, a decision that delights his mother, but every time he finds himself in bed, trying to grab a little sleep, he can think of nothing but Mahoney's body hanging over him, the way she can read his every thought, satisfy urges that get steadily more pressing, laugh together over the wreckage of the bed afterwards. He wants to possess her, knowing that he never will. He wants her in his life day and night, suspecting that it wouldn't – couldn't – last but wanting it just the same. And he needs, above all, to share just a little bit of where he came from. Words on paper, he decides. Something I've never risked with anyone before.

On Christmas Eve, Kane takes an early train to Boston

via New York. He has a sheaf of paper and a couple of pens, and he buys a pack of Christmas cards with reindeer on the front, one for Mahoney, the rest for his family. The train is busy but Kane finds a table, settling back to watch the last of the DC suburbs slip past, brightened by a fresh fall of snow. Once they hit open country, he reaches for his pen and a pad of lined yellow paper he'd lifted from the White House.

'You pronounce it Kane, as in sugar,' he writes, 'though way back it was Kanet, as in "Kar-nay". My grandfather on my dad's side was Québécois. As a young guy he lived in a settlement on the banks of the St Lawrence and traded with the few Indians still living in those creepy woods downstream from Trois-Rivières, beaver pelts mainly in return for second-hand tools and a bunch of knives. One of those pelts, in the shape of a hat, was still in the family, and I remember it clear as day. It belonged first to that same grandfather, Jean-Paul Kanet. He got in deep shit with more or less everyone and was chased over the US border after fleeing arrest. Somewhere between the border and Boston this Jean-Paul dropped the "t" in the family name and told himself he'd never go back. He got a job as a labourer on the waterfront downtown, and sometime later bought a horse and cart to deliver coal ahead of those shitty New England winters. Not once did he tell us why he was wanted by the Canucks, though as a very young kid I remember him speaking his native language to the end of his life and when he was dying, and we were all standing round the bed waiting for it to happen, he made us promise to keep the language in the family. That's how I got to speak Québécois French, Lou. My mom promised it would make a man of me so I'm guessing it might have worked.'

Kane pauses, unaccountably pleased with this small

moment of revelation, trying to picture Mahoney reading it. Would she be interested enough to follow this story of his? Would she be flattered? Puzzled? Would she start thinking motivation again? Why is he letting me in so close? How come the man never told me any of this stuff before? The questions spool on with the busy clatter of the train and after a while Kane succumbs to the warmth of the sunshine through the window and falls asleep.

He wakes maybe an hour later. Baltimore has come and gone and off to the right of the tracks is the picturesque sparkle of the Susquehanna River, one of his favourite waymarks on this journey. Kane reaches for the pen again. Another confession, or maybe a moment of shared history.

'You remember the evening we first met, Lou? Me and a couple other guys had bust the counterfeit ring at Sunrise Studios. The operation had taken far too long and the real perp had fled to Mexico but we had the rest of those clever guys from the studio's design department in the slammer and even our bosses in DC were creaming themselves because Roosevelt had sent each of them some kinda personal note. So me and the other two guys are busy getting canned and there's a spare space at our booth and suddenly no one's drinking anymore because that space has gone. You, Lou. The beautiful lady with the notepad and the scarlet nails and some kinda BS about the *LA Times*. We all thought it was a set-up. One of the guys asked about group rates, maybe a discount if we did it good, took turns. None of it was funny, which is often the way when guys try too hard, but what stuck with me that night is how you dealt with us. I get it now. You'd arrived with a question or two. You'd gotten the story written already, God knows how, and now you were riding your luck and rightly figured that three federal drunks couldn't be able to hold their tongues. They didn't, and you wrote it all down, and later that night you told me what you really thought. You said they were assholes, the guys that took you for a hooker, and it happens that you were right that night, but the real point about all this is to say that you'd taken them by surprise, at a moment of weakness, which was clever on your part, but that in real life these guys were class operators, good people, smart as hell. I recall offering to buy you a drink to make up and I watched you not listening, just busy with that pen of yours, and because you were alongside me in the booth I could read what you were writing. The Mirador. Room 887. And no thank you to the drink.'

Kane is blessed with total recall, every last second of that first night, and now he starts to play with the pen on the train, twirling it between his fingers in the way that still makes Mahoney laugh. She'd soaped him down in the shower and told him he was edible, and then proved it.

They'd spent the rest of the night talking about what had taken Kane to the Secret Service, about the raw magnetism of the man in the White House, and about Kane's dreams of one day taking care of him. Not one half-sentence, not one phrase had made it onto Mahoney's notepad and for that Kane was grateful.

They'd fucked before dawn because Mahoney had to be at her desk at eight in the morning, and after that they started to meet, always her call, never his, and when Kane paused for breath and a stocktake a month or so later he'd begun to understand the cleansing spirit of adventure that had stolen the hearts of so many men as they ventured west. West was an act of rebirth. West was where you became someone else. West was where continental America ran out and a bunch of talented Jews pitched their tents beside the Pacific, looked hard at their futures, and called it Hollywood. West, to Kane's eternal delight, was Lou Mahoney.

Should he write down more of this stuff? Muddle it in with everything else? Gazing out of the train window again, he decides no. Writing too much to Lou Mahoney, he figures, might be an act of trespass. Her medium, her territory, her turf, her world. And so he gathers up the lined sheets of paper, writes in her card, and folds everything into a bigger envelope. She'd once told him that successful relationships depended on two things. The first was laughter, the second mystery. The best stories remain opaque, unfinished, incomplete, she'd whispered. Consider yourself warned, Agent Kane.

It's dark by the time the train pulls into Boston. It's much colder here, big flakes of snow dancing in the wind off the harbour, and Kane skips the long queue for the few Christmas Eve cabs. The family home is three miles away and Kane does it in less than an hour, sure-footed on the frozen sidewalk. Turning the final corner off the big main road, expecting the usual Yuletide wreath hanging from the modest front door, Kane finds the house in darkness, no wreath, not a sign of a light anywhere.

He pauses, puzzled. The wreath has always been his father's contribution to the revels, an artful, beautifully composed combination of whatever he can scavenge from the local parks. He'd fashion it from ivy, and berries, and holly, and whatever else he could find, everything interlaced with lengths of ribbon, normally red, and Kane has always marvelled at the delicacy that went into this festive chuckle.

His father is a big man, huge hands, broad across the shoulders, a drinker's nose. As a kid, delivering baloney sandwiches for lunch, Kane had sometimes watched him down on the waterfront where he worked as a senior chargehand among the roughneck stevedores, and knew that his dad never put up with any shit. Yet come December, that same Larry Kane would start playing Père Noel and the whole family found themselves suddenly living with someone very different.

Have they all gone to Midnight Mass? Has his dad planned some surprise Christmas Eve treat? But in which case where's the wreath? Kane has no idea, and when he pushes in through the gate and knocks on the door there's no sign of anyone at home. He tries again. No answer. A third time: the same dead silence.

Finally he retreats to the street. The family next door are plainly at home. Kane can hear someone playing the piano, a woman's voice murdering a Bing Crosby song, then laughter. The old guy is called Vince. His second wife is Carol. They'll know, Kane tells himself.

He goes to their front door, reaches for the knocker. Footsteps this time, and then a woman's face at the door. There are streamers down the hall, and a nest of balloons, and a sprig of wilting mistletoe hanging from the ceiling. Then Vince appears, a bunch of old bones on a stick. He joins his wife at the door.

'Quincy?' He's looking troubled. 'You're telling me you haven't heard?'

6

The Children's Hospital is downtown on Longwood Avenue across from Mission Hill. Vince organises another neighbour in the next street who has a car. The guy has been drinking and after his second skid puts the ancient Chevvy half up on the sidewalk, Kane takes over at the wheel.

'No offence, buddy,' he pats the car's owner on the arm. 'I just want that we get there.'

There's a car park at Children's and it's nearly empty. The owner doesn't want to come in so Kane settles him in the back of the car, heaps a blanket around him, but keeps the key. Inside the hospital he gives his name to the woman at the reception desk.

'Kane, you say?' The name is already scribbled on a pad at his elbow. 'You're the guy works at the White House?'

'I am, yes.'

'We've been trying to get you all day. A moment, please.'

She lifts a phone, dials a number, catches Kane's eye. Kane wants her to smile, offer reassurance, give him good news. Instead, she bends to the phone. Moments after a brief conversation, a nurse arrives and escorts Kane to a small office on the first floor. A single balloon hangs from a framed photo of the Statue of Liberty. It's red with a festive sprinkle of stardust. The rest of the office is bare except for a desk, two chairs, and a filing cabinet. A guy in his forties gets to his feet and extends a hand. Too many late nights, Kane thinks at once. And maybe time for a shave.

'My name's Evans. I'm the duty consultant just now. We're talking respiratory. How much do you know, Mr Kane?'

'A neighbour told me Sis is ill. An ambulance came in the middle of the night. That's all.'

'You call her Sis?'

'We do. Her real name is Kathryn but she's always preferred Sis.'

The consultant writes himself a note, then looks up.

'How much do you know about polio, Mr Kane?'

The word hits Kane hard. He can feel his heart miss a beat. As it happens, thanks to FDR, he knows a great deal about the disease, none of it comforting.

'I bodyguard the President,' he says numbly. 'The guy's a cripple.'

'Sure. That can happen and I don't want to kid you otherwise, but these are early days. Your little Sis has contracted the virus. We brought her in last night.' He reaches for a sheaf of patient notes and flicks quickly through. 'High temperature. Headaches. Vomiting. Stiffness in the neck. Acute limb pain.'

'This has been going on for a while?'

'Three days, according to your mother.'

Kane nods, wondering why she'd never mentioned it. A winter cold, she must have thought. Maybe the flu.

'And you're sure?' he says. 'That it's polio?'

'Ninety per cent. The tests haven't come back yet but the pathology rarely lies. Once the virus gets in, it goes crazy, gets a free ride in the bloodstream, multiplies everywhere, the throat and the gut especially, later all kinds of other places. I'm afraid your Sis is one sick little girl, Mr Kane.'

'You're telling me she's dying?' Kane can't believe it.

'I'm telling you she's very ill. We're here to take care of kids like her and that's exactly what we do, but it's best, at this stage, to be honest.'

'I get to see her?'

'Of course. The rest of your family are here and they're very welcome.'

'They're with her?'

'Kinda.'

'What does that mean?'

'Polio is highly infectious. We have a room adjacent with a big window. Your family can talk to her. She can talk back. A disease like polio, it doesn't pay to take chances, Mr Kane.'

Christ, Kane is thinking. Sis is just thirteen years old, the baby of the family, the cherished late arrival who took everyone by surprise. She's been looking forward to Christmas most of the year. Now this.

'She's in isolation?'

'She's on a respirator. This is a machine that does her breathing for her. We're not sure yet where the virus will head next but it sometimes closes the lungs down. Like I say, no risks.' He pauses, then gets to his feet. 'Your mother is very upset, and understandably so. I'm guessing she'll be glad to see you.'

Kane nods. He's staring at the photo of the Statue of Liberty on the wall. The consultant has opened the office door already and the stir of air lifts the balloon a little. Liberty, he thinks bitterly, picturing FDR's iron brace, pounds and pounds of metalwork he has to strap on every morning for the rest of his life.

'Mr Kane?' The consultant is out in the corridor, checking his watch.

Kane is led to a suite at the back of the hospital. He finds his family in the big observation room but the moment he steps inside he can look at nothing except the view through a rectangle of glass that occupies most of the wall.

A long metal box in a horrible dingy shade of green stands alone, angled slightly away. At the nearest end is a kind of collar; it might be rubber, it might be something else, but it forms a seal around the tiny neck of a face he recognises only too well.

His little sister looks pale and thin. Her eyes are closed, and her head lies on a cushioned rest that swivels out, but from time to time her mouth opens and a tiny triangle of pink tongue appears, as if to check her lips are still attached. Then a nurse appears, gowned and masked, and steps across to moisten those same lips with the corner of a flannel, but what really blurs Kane's vision is the sight of his father's Yuletide wreath, hanging over the end of the respirator where Sis can't miss it.

'She's exhausted, son. You can see it.' This from Kane's father. He's wearing a suit, unheard of except for Christmas and at the big mass on Good Friday at the St Mary of the Assumption Church here in Brookline.

Kane pumps the proffered hand, then turns at once to his mother. Her face is gaunt and in the couple of months since Kane was last up in Boston she's gotten old. Her flesh, stretched tight over wonderful bones, has the greyness and dryness of parchment, and the last twenty-four hours have etched a harrowing story on that lovely face.

'Mom…' Kane gives her a long hug, feels her ribcage beneath his fingers. She's crying now, partly from frustration at not being able to keep her grief at bay.

'She may be paralysed, Quincy. She may even die. Why her? Why us? Why anyone?'

Two of Kane's three brothers are here, too, one of them with his new wife. Patrick is the oldest child in the family. His first wife died when a truck ran into a queue at a downtown bus stop. He's been through all this before, as Kane well knows, but the fierce suck of family trauma is obviously new to Mairead, and she clings to her husband's hand as if these hours without end might sweep her away.

The other brother in the room, a year and a half younger, is Danny. Kane gives all three of them a nod of greeting. We meet so rarely now, Kane thinks. Christmas, and sometimes Thanksgiving, and moments like these that God saves up to test us all.

There's a longish silence. Everyone is looking at the nurse, still bent over little Sis, still wetting her lips.

'She talks to you at all?' Kane finally asks.

'All the time, Quincy.' This from his mother. 'She's so glad we're all here. She can't tell us enough. The shame of it is that we can't get closer. I'm not sure she understands that.'

Kane nods, trying to imagine a life with only the virus as company, then he turns to Danny, the family member he trusts most.

'And the prognosis? What are they telling you?'

'They won't really say, Quince. She says she can feel her legs OK but she can't move a thing below her waist.'

'They're stuck, Quincy.' His mother again. 'Her legs have forgotten how to work.'

'Paralysis,' his father grunts. 'She may improve, she may not, they say it's fifty-fifty.' He flutters his big hand. 'I guess it's something she may have to live with, something we may all have to live with.'

'Sure. So what else does she have to say?'

'She's been asking for you, son.' His father again. 'And before she closed her eyes just now she said something that didn't do none of us any good.'

'Like what?' Kane's gaze has returned to Sis, her mouth now closed.

'*J'ai très peur*,' his father's voice, normally so strong, is barely a whisper. 'She's telling us she's very frightened.'

Conversation limps on. Patrick bows his head and asks God to take care of little Sis in her hour of need. Moments later, the door opens and an orderly appears with an enormous pot of coffee and a plate of cookies which he swears are home-baked. At the sight of the cookies, Kane can't suppress a smile. The answer to our prayers, he thinks. Happy Christmas.

But no one has any appetite and after a while Kane volunteers to take care of what he calls the night shift. He has the keys to a neighbour's car in his pocket. There's room for at least four if the guy in the back shifts over.

'What's his problem?' Kane's father grunts.

'Too many beers is my guess, Dad. Nice of him to lend us the car, though.'

Kane's father nods. He's obviously thinking about the beers.

'Lucky guy,' he nods at the view through the glass. 'I'm not sure I can take much more of this.'

Kane's mother bristles and tells him he should be ashamed of himself. Mairead is looking uncomfortable but it's Danny – as ever – who takes charge. He'll stay with Quince. The rest of the family need a good night's sleep. Anything important, he'll be on the phone.

'So keep hold of the car,' he says. 'You may need to come back.'

An exchange of glances, an exhausted nod from Kane's mother, and the observation room begins to empty. Kane's mother pauses on the way out to kiss the cold glass, lingers for a moment or two, then she's gone.

Danny is a lecturer at a local college, the only member of the family to trouble a proper education. All his life he's been a loner by instinct, never seeing the point of marriage or even a regular girlfriend, and Kane has always enjoyed his company and the way he handles himself around other people. Danny is the guy you'd be wise to get alongside when times are tough. Like now.

Kane kicks off his shoes and rearranges the armchairs, two apiece, face to face, makeshift beds for the coming hours. He and Danny talk a little about Sis, nothing to say really except to hope she gets a whole lot better, then the conversation drifts to Kane, and the FDR White House, and the sudden knowledge that the nation faces all kinds of chaos in the big unknown Danny has always called Abroad.

'Coping OK?' he asks.

'Just. Roosevelt is built for moments like this. You never see him sweat a tough decision, ever. He plays around with the options, you can watch him do it, and then – bam! – it's done and he moves right on. I guess the way he figures it, there are a whole bunch of things worse than Pearl Harbor, or Tojo, or Hitler, or any of those other Heine clowns, and just now…' Kane nods at Sis's tiny face next door, '…he's probably right. When the rest of your life ends up in the hands of strangers, you start to figure out what really matters.'

'I meant you, Quince, not that boss of yours.'

'Me?' Kane is genuinely surprised. Very few people these days ask him a question like that, so direct, so unfathomably difficult to answer.

'Yeah, you,' Danny again. 'I'm guessing the pressure never stops, and that's just peacetime. Add Pearl to the pot, and now the Germans, and most administrations would fold. Eye of the storm? Does that sound fair? Or should I dream up some other cliché? Either way, I need to know you're getting by.'

Kane is cautious now, trying to gauge Danny's direction of travel. Should he do himself a favour? Tell this clever, subtle, often tender brother of his about Mahoney? The Californian force of nature who's bust in through Kane's otherwise sturdy door and kicked over the furniture and made a nest for herself where it matters most? Might full disclosure, Jim Beam and all, put a smile on the face of this ratshit Christmas? Or might there be another way of ending up at the same destination?

'Don't get me wrong, Danny,' Kane is looking at Sis again. 'Down in DC it's been crazy sometimes, maybe most times, but doing what I do, what I've done, you get to see a lot of stuff. Some of it comes in through the post. Some of the crazier dudes get a home visit and that can be a revelation.

You've no idea how much hate there is out there. Sometimes I wonder how the whole thing hangs together at all.'

'Whole thing?'

'Us. Society. America. Once I thought it was all home runs, and killer plays in the fourth quarter, and some serious bar time afterwards. I was wrong, Danny, though it gives me no pleasure to say so. Sometimes I think we're all fucked and fucked good.'

'Because?'

'Because we've been spoiled. Wall Street put paid to that, greed chasing money out the window and down the street, and suddenly millions of men, women, families, whatever the heck, are struggling just to put food on the table, but then FDR happens along, and a guy called Harry Hopkins who does most of the heavy lifting, and suddenly times aren't quite so desperate any more. Tough we can deal with. Plenty's a whole other problem. You're getting the drift here, Danny?'

'Sort of.'

'Yeah? That's my fault, Danny, not yours. I'm looking at our kid sister just now and pretty soon that badass fucking machine may be all that stands between her and lights out. The way I hear it, it's a clever piece of engineering on someone's part but that's not the point. We're all grateful she's still with us but some days, the worst days, I'm looking at the whole fucking nation crammed into that tight little box, fighting for air, fighting for survival. There's a name for it, isn't there?' Kane gestures next door again. 'Remind me, Danny.'

'An iron lung, Quince. It's called an iron lung. And I hate to spoil this little party of yours but just now I get the feeling we should all be grateful.'

Kane nods, still gazing at Sis, then extends a hand towards this brother of his and gives his arm a long squeeze.

'Sorry, Dan. My fault. You're right, as always.'

Danny shrugs. He has another question.

'So who is this woman?' he asks.

'Woman?'

'Yeah. The voice that phoned up this afternoon. I was at Mom and Dad's, getting the bird ready for tomorrow, and then the phone rings and I'm talking to a voice, a woman's voice, and she's telling me she's hooked up with someone at the White House and that she's really, really sorry and she wants you to know that.'

'Sorry about what?'

'Sis. Like I say, the White House people know about Sis, about what's happened. Someone's told them.'

'And she left a name? This woman?'

'Sure,' Danny is on his feet now, pouring himself a cup of lukewarm coffee. 'Said her name was Lou.'

Mahoney? Wonderful. Beyond wonderful. Kane says yes to a cookie, then tells Danny to make that two.

'Something else,' Kane says. 'That lovely woman's got your dog.'

Kane calls LA from a phone booth at the hospital's entrance. Between them, he and Danny have mustered enough small change to manage a few minutes of coast-to-coast conversation, which is all Kane is good for.

'My brother says you called the White House.'

'Your brother's right. Nice guy, by the way. Must run in the family.'

'But you knew I was heading home. Up here. Boston.'

'I was talking to the First Lady. The paper wants another interview and I had to check it out with her. We're quite the item, Quince, me and Eleanor.'

Kane is smiling now. He believes every word.

'And?' He wants more.

'She told me your father had phoned. He wanted to make sure you were coming on account of your little sister being so ill and your mother taking it so bad. The hospital was trying to find you, too. Eleanor got to hear about the calls. She's been around polio forever, Quince, saw the first reel, knows the entire plot. When we talked, she couldn't have been nicer.'

'And FDR?'

'I'm guessing he must know, too. You want to keep this thing a secret?'

'I want Sis to get better.'

'And?'

'I get the feeling that ain't gonna happen.'

'It will, Quince. Getting better is an act of belief.'

'You say.'

'I say.'

'Care to explain that a little?'

'You, me and time, Quince. *Semper fi*. Keep the faith.'

'What's that got to do with Sis?'

'Everything. Believe me. Trust me.'

Kane grunts, says nothing. Then he starts to tell her about the observation room, and his dad's precious wreath hanging from the iron lung, and Sis with her eyes closed, and his little Boston tribe falling apart in the face of so much grief.

'But that's so often the way. It happened to me a while back and I guess someday I'll tell you the whole story.'

The whole story. Kane had dropped his envelope of jottings in a mailbox at Boston South station. By now, he thinks, it might be halfway across the country.

'I wrote you,' he says, 'yesterday. Have a drink before you read it, yeah?'

'You're saying goodbye?'

'I'm explaining how come I love you. Big word, Lou. Especially here. And especially now.'

Kane hangs up, pockets the rest of his change, becomes aware of a black guy mopping the floor just yards away.

'Happy Christmas, buddy.' The guy smiles.

Kane nods, says nothing, walks away.

7

The flowers arrive next morning, a special Christmas Day delivery, fancy wrapping around an explosion of pink and red roses latticed with gypsophila and silver eucalyptus. Kane's mom is more impressed by the message on the accompanying card, and the flourish that is the presidential signature.

'It's really him? He wrote this? That's the way he does his name?'

'Sure, Mom. He's a kind man. Stuff like this moves him.'

'And you told them where we live?'

'Sort of.'

Kane glances at the message again. It's never as bad as you think it is. You'll get through this thing, believe me. Our sincere sympathies. Franklin D. Roosevelt.

Kane's father has descended from upstairs. He grunts Happy Christmas to no one in particular and then takes a look at the card while Mom readies a vase for the flowers.

'Decent man, son?' He seems impressed.

'The best. Polio should have made the rest of his life impossible, but he pays no attention. He thinks pain's an opinion. Nothing seems to lay a finger on the guy.'

'Good to hear. And Sis?'

'Still asleep, Dad, by the time we left.' This from Danny.

'Anything happening? Any improvement?'

'No.'

Heads nod around the room. This is a strange moment, Kane thinks, Christmas but not Christmas, everything normal and festive suddenly disappearing into the emptiness which is little Sis. For a busy family, waiting couldn't be worse.

'Someone has to be there,' Danny insists.

'Me,' Mom shoots a look at her husband. 'Who's going to drive me over?'

The pair of them depart with Danny, who claims to have gotten a good night's sleep in the observation room. Kane takes a long nap in the spare bedroom upstairs and awakes to the sound of the phone. It's Mike Reilly, calling from the White House. He says he's sorry about Kane's 'troubles' and wishes him a Happy Christmas. In the meantime, District Sixteen appears to be in a state of some chaos.

'How come?'

'There's a fat little guy arrived coupla days ago. You got the hell out just in time, Quince. The man drinks like a fish and treats the place like a hotel. Up all hours of the night, but naps during the day between bottles of champagne. Won't leave the Chief alone. Rover wants the guy back where he belongs. Thinks he's a very bad influence.'

'This has to be Winston Churchill, right?'

'Right. The Limey. He's stretching us every which way and I'm guessing he's gonna be around for a while. There's a night train out of Boston at eleven, Quince. I've booked you a sleeper berth. That comes as a present from the First Lady, by the way. She's guilty as hell about your Christmas dinner, and says she owes you over some article or other. Carriage 4, berth 32, Quince. Write it down.'

The phone goes dead, and Kane finds himself a pen.

Carriage 4, berth 32. Some article or other? Kane assumes this must have to do with Mahoney. Out in LA, he's watched her in company and always marvelled at the way she can cast a baited line into a bunch of strangers, and get them on the hook, and play them along. Eleanor Roosevelt will be as open to Lou's smile and her artful sincerity as anyone else, maybe more so, and just now that matters a great deal. A decent night's sleep on the journey south is a nice gesture and Kane is more than grateful. To be honest, he also finds the sheer weight of family grief hard to handle. Just like his dad.

Kane wanders into the kitchen. Danny has stuffed and trussed a turkey and there are a bunch of vegetables awaiting attention, but Mom seems to have lost interest and Kane doesn't blame her. For the rest of the morning, he scrubs and peels and dices and wonders whether anyone will have the inclination to sit around the table and put on funny hats and trade silly jokes from the box of crackers he's found in a cupboard next door. Will Patrick and Mairead be coming? Will it feel odd to have no kids, no Sis, around?

His mom and dad are back by mid-afternoon. Neither of them can face a plate of roast turkey this evening, though the news from the hospital appears to be marginally better. The consultant has done tests on Sis's respiration, switching off the machine for a brief trial period, and he thinks the virus may have stopped short of the nerves that control her breathing, but for the time being the iron lung is back in action. Sis still has no control of her legs, but when a nurse spooned a small bowl of festive jello into her mouth, she had no problem swallowing.

'So brave, Quincy,' his mom tells him. 'That little girl of

ours is so brave. Will you tell Mr Roosevelt? When you thank him for the flowers?'

The news that Kane has to travel back to Washington overnight appears to come as no surprise. Kane's father even seems to regard his son, and perhaps all of them, as part of the President's extended family, yet another tribute to FDR's mastery of life's smaller gestures.

'Tell him he's welcome any time, son. I hear he drinks whiskey sours.'

Kane takes the borrowed car back to its owner after dark, along with a plum pudding his mom had prepared weeks back. Vince gazes at the car with some surprise. He's been drinking again, and Kane wonders whether he even recognises the beaten-up old Chevvy.

Danny drives Kane to the hospital in his own car, coming to a halt outside. Danny nods at the big entrance doors. 'You want me to come in with you?'

'No.'

'You're sure?'

'I'll be fine. Sis knows about the flowers? The card from the White House?'

'She does. Mom could talk of nothing else. I'm not sure the nurses believed it but Dad put them right. You're famous in there, Quince.' He nods at the main entrance. 'Sis doesn't know you're coming, by the way. Be nice to surprise her. Take care out there, buddy.' He's giving Kane a searching look. 'And don't give up on us, eh?'

Good advice. Kane gives Danny a wave as they depart. The door to the observation room, when he finds it, is an inch or two ajar and he stands beside the window, gazing at the disembodied little face poking out of the iron lung. Someone, presumably a nurse, has wound a twist of red ribbon into Sis's ginger ringlets, and Kane spots a tiny hand mirror on a side table. The splash of scarlet is the smallest gesture in the face of catastrophe, but Kane feels a prickle behind his eyes.

A white Bakelite switch on a control panel opens the microphone. Kane stares at it for a moment or two, wondering whether to wake her up, but decides against it. He has a full hour before he has to leave for the station.

Sis wakes when a nurse brings her a drink, slipping the straw between her lips. Kane hits the switch, offers a name. The nurse stiffens, taken by surprise.

'You're the guy from the White House?'

'He is,' Sis's voice is barely audible. 'He's my brother, too.'

The nurse nods, says nothing, finishes up with the drink, leaves them to it.

Shy, thinks Kane. My sick little sister's gone shy on me.

'Hey...' he murmurs. 'Remember when?'

'When what?'

'When Danny took you to Washington. When I showed you some of those special rooms in the White House and we went Downtown afterwards. You had a hamburger with fries.'

'I had pancakes.' Gamely, she's trying to smile. 'Not a burger. And then I had pecan pie with ice cream.'

'Sure. You win. Then you and Danny stayed over.'

'And the dog,' she says. 'Danny's dog. How is he?'

'He's good.'

'Who's looking after him?'

Kane is frowning now. Kids can be so direct, so logical. Kids, he thinks, can find you out.

'Just now he's on vacation,' he says.

'Dogs don't have vacations. They have bowls. They're always hungry. They need feeding. So where is he?'

Kane is tempted deeper into the weeds of this lie. His Chinese neighbour, maybe. The kindness of strangers, or a favour repaid. Silly. Pointless.

'He's gone to LA,' he says instead. 'Dexter always wanted to get into the movies and now's his big chance.'

'How did he get there?'

'He flew.'

'Dogs can't fly. Birds fly. Dogs don't.'

'He went on an aeroplane. All the way.'

'And you went, too? To keep him company?'

'No. Someone else.'

'Who?'

'A friend.'

'She's a lady?'

'Only some of the time.'

'What does that mean?'

'It means she can be naughty.'

'You tell her off?'

'I try.'

'Do I know her?'

'No.'

'Will she come and see me?'

'She might. One day.'

'And is she nice? Will I like her?'

'She's very nice. You'll love her.'

'And me? Will she love me?'

'Hard not to, Sis.'

Sis nods, the tiniest movement of her head, rueful, resigned. That one gesture seems in one brief moment to take in the enormity of everything that's happened. Kane waits for what feels like an eternity, unsure where to take the conversation next. Then Sis musters that same smile.

'I guess she better hurry, then…' the smile dies, '…before it's too late.'

Too late? Kane wonders whether to press her a little, the way you might try and drain a wound, and he's still standing mute at the cold glass when she spares him the decision. She tells him that it's scary to be where she is. She tells him that the nights are worst because they keep the lights on. And she tells him that she's never felt so alone.

'You mean lonely?'

'Not that. Not lonely. Alone is different. No one around here ever touches me, except when they're wearing gloves. That's horrible. And scary, too. Will anyone ever touch me again? Or is this forever?'

Kane does his best to reassure her. This is the speech about the risks of infection, and doing stuff for everyone's sake, and making sure she gets better just as fast as she can, but a single glance tells Kane that she's way beyond this clumsy adult bluff. For whatever reason, on Jesus Christ's birthday of all dates, God has put her in a truly frightening place and she can't figure out why. Or what next.

'You get better,' Kane tells her.

'That's a promise?'

'That's an instruction. That's me being bossy.'

'Sure,' she turns her head away. 'At least you're not crying.'

At least you're not crying. Kane carries the thought out of the hospital and into the cab that drives him to the big pillared entrance at South Station downtown. He can hear the squawk of seagulls in the wind off the nearby ocean and when he looks up he catches the whiteness of a perfect pirouette against the darkness of the night sky.

He'd done his very best back there in the observation room, trying to inch his kid sister away from her bleaker thoughts. Throughout their conversation she'd paid him the compliment of being honest and before he'd left she'd made him promise to bring his naughty lady friend the next time he happened by. He'd been more than happy to say yes, and when she'd demanded a name he'd fogged the cold glass with his breath and then inscribed the three letters backwards so she could see it.

'Lou?' she'd murmured. 'Lou what?'

'Lou Mahoney.'

'Mahoney?' She repeated the name twice, then again, oddly content, as if Kane had given her some kind of keepsake. Then her eyes fluttered and closed, and after a while Kane was gone.

8

Mike Reilly insists on a meeting with Alonso Fields. Kane's been back in the White House no more than ten minutes. Sole occupancy of berth 32 has given him a full night's sleep on the journey south from Boston and he feels like a man reborn.

'Just as well, buddy. You gotta hear this from the horse's mouth. No one makes this stuff up, least of all Alonso.'

Alonso Fields is FDR's personal butler, possibly the man physically closest to the President. He's a commanding figure, black, with a courtly physical presence and a sharp eye for detail. Kane sees a great deal of him in his dealings around FDR and admires his stewardship of the President's best interests.

The two men shake hands, exchange belated Christmas greetings. Reilly has excused himself.

'This is about our guests, right?' Fields is on a tight schedule. 'Have you been upstairs at all? Second floor? The Brits have taken over. Not a shot fired in anger, Quincy. Total surrender.'

Fields starts to describe the whole sorry mess that began in haste and has – in his words – just gotten shittier and more shitty.

'For a start the guy was due Tuesday. Arrived on some damn battleship up there in Hampton Roads. Decent night's sleep.

Then we plan to get him down to DC, all the arrangements made, everything neat and tidy. But what happens? We get a call Monday. The guy's a fidget. Doesn't know what to do with himself. Wants a plane laid on. Wants to get here early. The First Lady sees her plans fly out the window and – hey – naturally she's upset.'

'The guy...' Kane says softly. 'We're talking Churchill?'

'Sure. That's exactly who I mean. You've met him? You know him at all?'

'Never had the pleasure.'

'Fat. Small. Rude. First time I laid eyes on the guy we're up on the President's corridor, top of the mansion, and he's going from bedroom to bedroom, testing all the mattresses. The First Lady has assigned him the Rose Room but it turns out that might not be to his liking and so we all wait until the guy makes up his mind. In the end the Rose Room's just fine but the guy hasn't finished. It's me he has to deal with this time. The First Lady does the introductions and he looks me in the eye, little as he is, and tells me the way it's gonna be. First off, no whistling. He hates people who whistle. So nice and quiet the length of that second-floor corridor. Second of all, he's very picky about that schedule of his, what happens day after day, hour by hour. He wants the papers in bed first thing, plus all the overnight stuff from London, plus breakfast, plus... wait for it... champagne. This is nine in the morning, Quincy, and no ordinary champagne. Had to be Pol Roger, some fancy brand. Had to write the damn name down. After that he needs a bath running, and time to think, and maybe down a little more of that Pol Roger. Then it's nearly lunch time, and after that he has a nap, and then another bath, and by this time the Pol is well and truly done and he has to make do with plain man's champagne the rest of his working day, which takes him nicely to dinner, where he keeps everyone up until God knows what time in the morning, story after story, all about him, brandies by now, and the President is a goner, but our fat little guy knows that America is the home of the brave, also the home of limitless brandy, and so on he goes until every other head has hit the tablecloth, and he's only got himself to keep amused. You're wondering how I know all this? Talk to the First Lady, Quincy. Being rude to guests doesn't come easy but she can't figure out what else to do.'

It's true. Fields makes his excuses and leaves Kane to track down Eleanor, to whom he owes a thank-you for a good night's sleep. He finds her behind her desk in the first-floor room she uses as a study. Kane's relationship with the First Lady has always been a little distant, which he thinks altogether appropriate, but now she greets him like an old buddy. At once, she wants to know about Sis. The way she phrases the question makes Kane wonder whether she's somehow been part of the family for years.

'She's upset,' Kane says. 'This is all strange to her. She's frightened, too. You can see it.'

Eleanor nods. This, she tells him, is to be expected. When FDR first caught the virus, it knocked the family sideways. The only one to keep his nerve, oddly enough, was her husband.

'He's been that way these past few days, too,' she adds. 'Give him really bad news and he's at his very best.'

Kane agrees. He's long believed that America's third-term President has nerves of steel. What would have crushed lesser men simply seems to make him stronger.

'You believe that?' Eleanor asks.

'I do, yes. Am I wrong?'

She shrugs, studies her hands for a moment or two, then looks up. When Kane thanks her for berth 32, she says it was the least she owed him.

'For what?'

'For that friend of yours. Lou Mahoney. The woman writes like a dream. So many interviews, you're talking to some man who's already made his mind up. It doesn't matter what you say, or how many times you say it, the piece is already written in his head. Your lovely friend's different. An open mind? Does that sound fair? Plus the decency and the wit to get the small details right? The ones that really matter? For once, talking on the record was a pleasure. She's welcome in my life any time, Agent Kane, and you can tell her that from me.'

Welcome in my life. The Roosevelt marriage is much discussed in the White House. Everyone knows that husband and wife have never been the perfect fit, and the non-stop pressures at the very top of the DC ant heap have never helped. Eleanor Roosevelt is a serious woman, under-cursed with good looks, a little gawky at first glance, but well intentioned and wholly passionate about stuff that doesn't much interest her husband.

FDR's wind-down time is six in the evening, a ritual he calls Children's Hour, when he gets to mix the drinks and slip another Camel into his silver cigarette holder and fool around a little. In the early days, his wife would show up with a certain look on her face and an armful of pressing issues, each with a file of its own, determined to catch her husband's attention, but those days have gone. Important issues have never played much of a part in Children's Hour and in any case Eleanor doesn't drink, mistrusting what it does to people, which is just one of the reasons the sudden whirlwind descent of Winston Churchill has thrown her world into turmoil.

'He's a nightmare, Quincy. He's someone I least expected to show up around here, not because he doesn't belong, of course he does, he's Prime Minister, we're fighting a war together, he has a right to be here, but he's so unreasonable. What he wants he must have. He's the child of your worst nightmares. You've talked to Alonso?'

'I have.'

'Then you'll know. Me? I worry about my husband. Take a look at the second floor, Quincy. We've given the Lincoln Suite to the Brits and they've also taken over the hall itself. Churchill calls it his current seat of government and that's exactly what it's become. He also demanded space for what he calls his Map Room. Maps of every kind, every theatre, Europe, Russia, and now the Pacific. Even I can see the logic, Quincy, because this man needs to keep a finger in all these separate pies. That's the way he explained it to my husband. There are people upstairs, his people, Brits, who do nothing but update those maps, little arrows here, pencilled crosses there, and you know what? My husband has fallen in love with the whole operation, the whole concept, with what he keeps calling Churchill's vision. He thinks the man's a genius. He pays him far too much attention, which I guess is an occupational hazard with a man like that, and right now Franklin wants a Map Room of his very own. There's a little closet down on the ground floor. A couple of days ago it was full of women's coats. Now? Care to guess?'

'Maps.'

'Exactly. I happened by only last night. It was late, way past the President's bedtime, but there they were, two little boys, poring over yet another damn map together, playing at war. You know what happens when Franklin doesn't get enough sleep? Everything goes to hell in that huge brain of his, and that's something that shouldn't be allowed to happen.'

Kane nods. Before he'd knocked on the First Lady's door he'd climbed the staircase to the second floor and every element of these stories he was hearing had checked out. Desks loaded with paperwork choked the hallway. Telephone cables snaked across the carpet. And the calm of the mansion had surrendered to the busy scurrying of lordly strangers with fancy accents. The last time the Brits had paid the White House serious attention they'd burned the place down. Now, generations later, they seemed to have made it their own.

'The man also keeps strange hours,' Kane murmured, 'according to Alonso.'

'Alonso's right. The man has gotten into bad habits and I'm guessing wherever he goes he takes them with him. The President's the smartest man I've ever met, and I mean that. He's also very brave and tends to hide his real feelings as you people know, but there's something about this visitor of ours that's gotten past those defences. He's putty in the man's hands, Quincy, which is probably the whole point of the exercise. I sit between them at dinner. The way I'm hearing it, Churchill came here to sell a certain version of the war, his own version, and so far the President seems totally taken in. I worry about him, Quincy. I worry about Franklin's lack of sleep, I worry about that foolish tolerance of his, and I worry about his liver holding up. There...' the briefest smile, '...a state secret, Agent Kane. For your ears and no one else's.'

Kane retires to confer with Mike Reilly and gather up the threads of whatever else has been happening. Already, Christmas Eve and the journey home to Boston seem to belong to a different world but he makes time to phone his brother. Sis, Danny tells him, appears to be making progress at last. The prognosis, as far as her legs are concerned, remains dire, but after a brief medical conference all three consultants on her case agree that the threat to her respiration has come and gone.

'She's out of that fucking bellows thing?' Kane asks.

'Probably tomorrow. You'll be the first to know once we've hung out the flags.'

'And Mom and Dad?'

'Better, much better. You coming up was what they really needed. That and those lovely flowers.'

'It was the card, Danny. Classy move on Roosevelt's part.'

'You've said thank you?'

'To his wife? Yes. I've yet to touch base with the man himself.'

The summons comes at the end of the afternoon. On behalf of the President, Grace Tully asks for ten minutes of Kane's time. The Oval Study, if you please, and now would be good. Kane mounts the stairs and picks his way through the busy chaos on the top hallway. He finds FDR behind his desk, attending to what looks like a letter. He looks up, pen in hand, and – unusually – nods towards the still-open door.

'You want me to close it, sir?'

'Please, Agent Kane.'

Kane does his bidding and takes a seat. When FDR enquires about Sis, he describes the view from the observation room, the ugliness of the iron lung, and touches on the many ways his family are finding it hard to cope.

'You managed any kind of Christmas?'

'Not really.'

'Don't give up. Once this party's over we should make time to get you back home again.'

Kane nods, says how grateful his family are for the flowers and especially the card, keen to let it rest there. FDR abandons his pen and eases his big frame in the chair.

'Alonso talk to you any?'

'Lots.'

'The reason we got you back, Quincy, is this. Mr Churchill, in so many ways, is a truly remarkable man. We're lucky to be fighting this war on the same side and we must never lose sight of that. Not me. Not you. Not the rest of America.'

'But?'

FDR acknowledges the obvious question with the ghost of a smile. The Brits, he says carefully, have an agenda of their own, always have done, always will.

'They're imperialists, Quincy, which is the fancy word for thieves. They put to sea and painted half the globe pink and called it the British Empire. Churchill was part of that process and he's very happy to tell you exactly how it happened. He's empire through and through, fierce in the saddle, even fiercer all these years later. India, all those Far Eastern outposts, the dominions, they're all part of the same damn trick. The Brits robbed the casino blind and Hitler, oddly enough, admires them for it. He thinks these Brit guys are ruthless and will do anything to hang onto their winnings. He's right, of course, but it takes us Yankees to draw the line. We're about to spill lots of American blood, Agent Kane, but as long as I'm behind this desk not a drop will go on defending Mr Churchill's precious empire.'

Kane nods. He hasn't a clue where any of this might be leading.

'Sir? You have something in mind here?'

'For?'

'Me?'

'I do, Agent Kane. Number one, I've fixed a meeting for you with Bill Donovan. You'll be familiar with the name. You'll have seen his face around here. He's my goddam legs when it comes to the intelligence game. He makes it his business to feed me stuff – the best stuff – from wherever it may come. Happens he's the Army's most decorated soldier, a hero among his fellow Irish, and he's smart as hell. Toss him any problem, and the solutions are on this desk of mine the same goddam day. Ideas are ten a dime in this city, but Bill's are often the best. He's working out of premises across on Navy Hill. Ask Grace for the details. He's expecting you at seven.'

'This evening?'

'This evening.'

'And Mr Churchill?'

Roosevelt nods, checks his watch.

'He'll be on his feet about now. He's in the Rose Room. Knock on the door. I've mentioned your name already, told him you're assigned a kind of watching brief. He has his own protection, of course, but as hosts we owe him a duty of care.

We know the local turf. His guy doesn't. Your job, Agent Kane, is to close that gap.'

'Happy to, sir.' One phrase of FDR's had stuck out. 'Watching brief?'

'Just that, Kane. Eyes on the street but eyes, too, on Mr Churchill. It happens that folks round here value your judgement. It also happens that I'm one of them. Do us all a favour, Agent Kane. Take a good look at the man. Then come back and tell me what makes him tick.'

The door to the Rose Room is half an inch open when Kane knocks. Faintly, he catches the gurgle of an emptying bath. Moments later he's looking at a suited figure with a long, lean face and a pair of pin-striped trousers folded carefully over his arm.

'And you are?' Flat London accent.

'Agent Kane. Secret Service.'

'Glad to meet you, Mr Kane. The name's Thompson. Walter Thompson.'

'You're the valet?'

'I'm Mr Churchill's bodyguard, though often it comes to the same thing.'

'And Mr Churchill?'

'At your service, Mr Kane. Pray enter.' The growl comes from deep inside the room. Thompson opens the door wider as Kane steps into the room. He recognises the face at once, cherubic and pink from the heat of the bath. Churchill is standing in the middle of the room, stark naked, the carpet around his hairless ankles pooling with water. Too many dinners, Kane thinks at once, and a child-like dismissal of the normal courtesies.

'You're looking uncomfortable, Mr Kane. Is it something we've said?'

'Not at all, sir. A pleasure to meet you.'

Churchill nods, says nothing, looking Kane up and down.

'Well?' he grunts at last. 'You're running an errand of some kind? Come to check we have enough to drink? Or do we owe this visit to something a little less pressing?'

Thompson has laid the trousers to one side. When he reappears from the bathroom he's carrying a towel.

'Well, Mr Kane?' Churchill again, ignoring the towel.

'The President has assigned me to offer you extra protection, sir. I'm here to explain what that might entail.'

'Riding shotgun, eh? In case Walter here forgets his little pistol? Makes a mess of things?'

'On the contrary, sir. Two guns are always better than one. I think you'll find we Yanks are generous that way.'

'Indeed, Mr Kane. Well said. Two guns better than one. Couldn't have put it better myself, eh, Mr Thompson?' Churchill doesn't wait for an answer but at last consents to wrap the towel around his ample belly. He wants Kane to know that Washington hospitality, so far, has been exemplary. Especially in the matter of keeping the lights on all night.

'Hardly, sir.' Kane nods at the heavy window drapes that serve as blackout.

'I mean outside, Mr Kane. After dark in London we live like moles in a world of rubble. The Luftwaffe, alas, are totally unbiddable. They leave their droppings everywhere. A brandy, Mr Kane? Or are there rules against celebrating an alliance as fruitful as ours?'

Without waiting for an answer, Churchill disappears

into the bathroom and shuts the door, leaving a damp patch on the carpet. It's Thompson who breaks the sudden silence.

'He means it about the brandy,' he murmurs. 'Though I imagine the answer is no.'

'You imagine right,' Kane nods at the door. 'Is there any point me staying?'

Thompson shakes his head. Churchill is singing now, an off-tune version of 'White Christmas'.

'He was due in the Map Room half an hour ago,' Thompson taps his watch. 'You'll do us all a favour by coming back some other time.'

Kane makes the appointment with Bill Donovan with minutes to spare. After camping out at a series of other locations, the new spook agency has finally pitched its tent in a three-storey, granite building at 25th and East, atop Navy Hill. The last time Kane was here was to check out a Berlin-born scientist working for the Department of Health.

The reception area looks like a war zone. Busy people toting cardboard boxes brimming with files dance around each other, headed in various mystery directions. Most of them, Kane notices, wear glasses, a fact that makes him wonder how many have ducked the draft. Enrolment as one of Wild Bill's infant army of spooks might seem a better deal than conscription in a much bigger army of grunts.

Kane offers his District Sixteen ID to a harassed-looking woman behind the trestle table that serves as a reception desk. From somewhere he can smell burning flesh.

'Elevator's still out,' she nods towards the stairs. 'Room 109. He's expecting you.'

Donovan's office commands one corner of the building, and
the contrast to the chaos downstairs is stark. Neatly stocked
bookcases, a handful of prints from the Revolutionary War,
and views in two directions from the big windows. Donovan
is sitting behind a sizeable desk within touching distance of
a huge globe. A gesture of intent? A statement of Donovan's
intended reach from the heart of this new intelligence agency?
To both questions, Kane suspects the answer is yes.

'That smell get to you yet?' Donovan gestures towards
one of the windows.

'Sure. You've fired up the barbeque already?'

Donovan's laugh is brief and mirthless. He isn't a tall man,
and his face and belly are beginning to fill out, but he has an
undeniable physical presence.

'If only,' he says. 'Upstairs on the top floor belongs to the
guys before us. They keep a whole bunch of animals up there,
monkeys, hamsters, rats, you name it. Word is they're coming
up with some fancy drug to cure syphilis. Every Friday some
damn animal dies in the line of duty and every Saturday they
cremate what's left. After a while I'm told you get used to the
smell but I've yet to see the proof.'

Kane smiles. Agents he knows and trusts like this man. He
runs a tight ship, they admit, but in no way are these guys of
his like the FBI. Donovan's people have a mind and a life
of their own. No dress code. No stern house memos about
how much you drink or who you happen to be sleeping with.
On the contrary: the only thing that matters is straying off
the reservation, dreaming up new ways of taking the war
to the enemy. On the battlefield, this guy always led from
the front, a legend among his men, and word on the street
suggests that nothing has changed.

'You talked to the President, Kane?'

'I did, sir. Yes.'

'He told you what this is about?'

'No.'

'Good.'

Donovan is suddenly on his feet. Kane notices the trace of a limp, maybe a battlefield wound, but he knows the guy is nudging sixty and to his credit it doesn't really show. His eyes are still a startling blue and it doesn't take much effort to imagine the impact he must have made on a host of doting women.

Like so many offices across DC, this one has its share of wall maps. Donovan has positioned himself beside a slice of the South of France.

'This here is Toulon...' Kane follows the forefinger with its carefully buffed nail, '...and here is where the French have parked the remains of their navy.' He turns back towards the desk. 'Mers-el-Kébir? Operation Catapult?'

Kane shakes his head. He's heard the names before but is foggy about the detail.

'This is 1940, my friend. The French Army is flat on its back and the Heinies have occupied half the damn country. Pétain, the old warrior, negotiates a peace and runs the rest of France from a dull little town called Vichy. The Army, like I say, has thrown in the towel but the Navy is still intact. It's a proper navy, good ships, new ships, big ships, lots of firepower, and Churchill doesn't want it ending up in German hands. The name Darlan mean anything? Nope? He's an admiral, runs the Navy, and in 1940 most of it is hunkered down in Mers-el-Kébir. That's French Algeria, by the way. Churchill does his best to get those boats to Britain, or maybe somewhere neutral like the West Indies, but Darlan says no, they're our boats, Vichy's boats, and they stay with us. That's no kind of damn answer from the Brit point of view and so Churchill despatches a task force from Gibraltar and gives the French at Mers an ultimatum. Sail with us or take the consequences. Darlan is back in Vichy France, out of reach, but no one talks to the French Navy this way and the guy in charge at Mers tells the Brits to get lost. The Brits give him an hour to change his mind. He still says no and so the Brits open fire. Easy targets. Heavy shells. The French lose a battleship, and all kinds of other boats, plus over a thousand men. You speak French, Kane?'

'I do, yes.'

'So think about it. The afternoon's little exchange does nothing for the *entente cordiale* but that's the least of Churchill's problems.'

Kane nods. Try as he might, he can't rid himself of the image of Churchill, pink and tubby and naked in Eleanor Roosevelt's precious Rose Room.

'Are you with me here, Kane?'

'I am, sir. Yes.'

'So what's on Churchill's mind?' Donovan asks.

'The rest of the Navy,' Kane hazards a guess. 'Anything left the Brits haven't sunk?'

'Exactly. And where do you think that might be just now?'

'Toulon?' Kane's gaze returns to the map beside Donovan.

'Double tap, Kane. You're good at this. Concentrate a little harder and I'm guessing we might get along.' He turns to the map again. 'Three battleships. A bunch of heavy cruisers and destroyers plus all kinds of other stuff, all of it tied up in Toulon. The Germans, of course, are aware of this and they keep an eye on the port, but the real key – and Churchill knows this – is Darlan. He's still Vichy, very much so. Some days you might even take the guy as some kind of fascist, quietly pro-Nazi, but he's also corrupt, loves money, and he's smart, too. This is a man who sniffs the wind, knows which way the war is going. The Brits still in the fight? The Americans tooling up? And no sign of the Russkies throwing in the towel on the Eastern Front? Mr Hitler has a very big problem and the good admiral wants no part of it.'

Kane nods, at last understanding the story that's beginning to take shape. Then a stir of wind outside brings an especially pungent gust of burning flesh into the office and Donovan checks his watch.

'Dunno about you, Kane, but that smell makes me damn hungry. You eaten yet?'

They go to a fancy restaurant Downtown on Donovan's tab. America's new Intelligence Chief is partial to milk-fed veal. Kane opts for a thick T-bone that overlaps the plate, fries on the side. The '35 Château Margaux, Donovan assures him, will do the food more than justice. While the waiter departs with the order, Donovan wants to know more about Kane's assignment out on the West Coast.

'You had a hand in busting that Hollywood counterfeit ring. Am I right?'

Kane nods, describes the bare bones of the operation, many months of chasing down leads, feelers extended into the darker corners of the LA underworld, then weeks of patient surveillance, all capped with a flurry of carefully synchronised pre-dawn arrests that had drawn the attention of Lou Mahoney.

'How many?'

'Three that mattered. A handful more to thicken the indictments.'

'And these three guys had history? Career crims? Seriously bad dudes?'

'Not at all. That was the surprise. The guy behind it all took off for Mexico. He had plenty of history. But the guys that made the bad dollars, all three of them, had college qualifications. One in particular had taken his technical prowess to the absolute max. They were artists, really, just a bunch of dreamers with hands-on skills you wouldn't believe. The product was eye and touch-perfect and would have earned them a fortune, but money stood in line behind something else.'

'Like?'

'*Creating* money from nothing amused them. It was a technical challenge. It called on parts of them they used every day in the studios. Movies I guess are a kind of big-time counterfeit, all kinds of illusion and kidology up there on the screen, and these clever guys turning their hand to banknotes was the same challenge made small. The notes themselves were works of art. Even some of the experts, senior Treasury people, were fooled.'

'Denominations?'

'Singles, fives, tens, nothing too ambitious. Above ten bucks, one of the guys put a peg on his nose. He told me the smell of money made him want to throw up. Too obvious. Too showboat. The smaller notes you could give away if you felt sorry for someone. This was the same guy who wanted to put Robin Hood on the ten-buck note instead of Alexander Hamilton just to see if anyone noticed. These three guys were all kinds of smart but they'd never bothered to grow up. If we hadn't gotten to them first, the badass gangsters would have eaten them alive.'

'You're still in touch?'

'No, but that could change.'

'What kind of time are we talking here?'

'Twenty years. Uncle Sam has no sense of humour when it comes to messing with the dollar.'

Donovan nods. He's ordered pre-meal martini aperitifs and they've arrived in the hands of a waitress he evidently knows well. She studies Kane for a moment and then deposits the drinks on the table and whispers something in Donovan's ear.

'He's a married man, Evie,' Donovan is laughing. 'Ten kids. Two swimming pools. His wife was Miss America three years running. Give the guy a break.'

'You lie, Mr Donovan.' She winks at Kane and departs.

Kane is still thinking about the guys he's put in the slammer for all those years. To the best of his knowledge they're doing their time in state penitentiaries in the wilds of inland California.

'Why the interest, Mr Donovan?'

'It's Bill from now on. I want you to have a think about those guys, and then choose the best one, the one who was technically perfect. We need to be able to trust this guy, and we need him to be able to keep his mouth shut. Meantime, I talk to Justice and see if we can't cut some kind of a deal.'

'To do what?'

'To release your man against services rendered.'

'Care to be more specific?'

'Sure,' Donovan reaches for his glass. 'We need him to produce a thousand $1,000 dollar notes.'

Kane nods, trying to figure out the math, but Donovan spares him the effort.

'A million dollars, Quincy, in counterfeit notes so good everyone's fooled.' He takes a sip from his martini. 'In my little outfit, we call that a bribe.'

Book Two

9

Venice Beach, Los Angeles. Thirteen days later.

Kane arrives on a flight from DC, fifteen hours with multiple refuelling stops and a troubled passage over the Rocky Mountains. A cab takes him from the LA airfield at Inglewood. The driver is Mexican and wears a *Thwack the Japs* armband. The freewheeling Los Angeles Kane remembers from last year has surrendered to a succession of checkpoints, patrolled by armed troops.

'Looking for Jap saboteurs,' the driver grunts. 'They're vermin. They're everywhere.'

The cab drops Kane three blocks back from the ocean at Venice Beach, an untidy sprawl of food outlets, bars, amusement arcades, and cheap lodging houses. Gus has moved recently and has told Kane to look for an outfit called Hollywood Reptiles. Kane spots it towards the end of the street, a three-storey building in faded pink stucco. The reptile shop occupies the ground floor and Kane turns his back to the driving rain, peering in through the window. He makes out a snake in the big glass tank, an inert curled-up boa constrictor with the girth of a fire hose. Three other tanks, smaller, dirtier, are all empty. Either business is brisk, Kane thinks, or reptiles in wartime are hard to come by.

'Both,' Gus Leaman is standing in the doorway of his top-floor apartment. 'Shop belongs to a Chinese guy. Customers cleaned him out over Christmas and he's been taking fresh orders ever since. People used to buy dogs for security. Now it's reptiles. Rattlesnakes are favourite, I guess because they come with a soundtrack. Think about it, Quince. Dark night. Someone scary at the door. What else would you ever need?'

Gus laughs and steps aside. Kane has lingered in the shop downstairs for a moment or two and brings with him the rank mustiness of the reptiles for sale, but imagines that Gus is used to the smell.

'Nice…' Kane is looking at the line of carefully framed images on the wall of Gus's living room. In one, FDR is pictured with a hook nose and a Jew yarmulke. In another, Eleanor is giving Joe Stalin a blow-job.

'And this?' Kane points to a drift of smoke over a town reduced to rubble.

'Guernica,' Gus murmurs. 'Who says we were never warned?'

Guernica is a town in the mountains of northern Spain. Kane knows that German bombers did Franco a favour by destroying it, one of many atrocities – both fascist and republican – during the Spanish Civil War.

'That was five years ago,' Kane points out. 'You're out of date. You're living with history.'

'You're right, but I guess old habits die hardest. The image is everything in this town, as you probably remember.' Gus nods at FDR, at his wife. 'And people here like a laugh, too. Think cartoon. Think bad taste. Hollywood tried understatement once but it never caught on.'

'So what do people want? Just now?'

'Revenge, *mi amigo*. Dead Japs. The death stink. War hereabouts was never going to be pretty.'

Kane nods. He's liked Gus a great deal from the moment they met years back when Kane was first assigned to the LA field office, and nothing's changed since. He loves his sheer intelligence and the fierceness of his occasional anger. He loves the hinterland this man has made his own, a busy interior world peopled with books in five languages. He's nothing to look at – pale, thinner than most agents, sad eyes, terrible dress sense – but he has a brain the size of a planet and takes a raw pleasure from the madness of Southern California. Kane remembers at least two women who happily described the way that Gus had talked them into bed. Both would have been more than happy to stay longer but Gus has a mistrust – in his own words – of getting his needle stuck in someone else's groove. If in doubt, he always tells Kane, move on.

Just now, he wants to know about Bunker Hill.

'You've found me a place?' Kane asks.

'Yeah. Third-floor apartment on North Figueroa Street. Shit neighbours, zilch facilities, no view, trash everywhere, just the way you say you want it. Cheap, though, and I guess safe as long as you keep the door double-bolted. Listen, Quince, smart people are always on the move in this town. They go away on business or extended vacations and they have nice places. The rent's OK if you come recommended and I can sort you a penthouse in Santa Monica, ocean views, no problem. Bunker Hill? Are you serious?'

'Always. An address is all I need, and a key would be useful.'

Gus has both to hand but for the first time Kane has noticed a glass tank on a low table in the corner. A tablecloth has been draped over the tank, a cheerful pattern of scarlet whorls against a light blue background.

'Is that what I think it is?' Kane has crossed the room for a closer look.

'Sure.'

'You mind?'

'Go ahead.'

Kane lifts one corner of the tablecloth, then folds the whole thing back. In contrast to the bareness of the tank in the shop window downstairs, Gus has borrowed a trick or two from Hollywood and has recreated a dense green smudge of the Matto Grosso, complete with leaf litter, a tangle of vines, something fibrous that looks like speckled moss, and a glimpse of running water. No sign of a snake.

'It's a rhinoceros viper and he can be kinda shy. He bores easy, hides himself away, and likes taking folks by surprise. We bonded at first sight.'

Kane is smiling at the sight of a Welcome 1942 button fixed to a corner of the glass.

'You celebrated the New Year together?'

'Yeah. Early evening, we listened to *Tristan und Isolde*. Later I and a bunch of LAPD dumbfucks got wasted downtown. Reptiles everywhere. Depend on it.' Gus nods at the tank. 'His name's Parsifal, by the way. Homage to Wagner. If you're wanting a look you'll get old waiting. He sleeps during most days which is why I keep the tank covered. You haven't mentioned that woman of yours, *hombre*. We're talking history, already?'

'No.'

'She's still in town? Still writing? Still in training? Still fighting?'

'Sure. But we need to talk, you and me.'

Gus holds his gaze a moment, then disappears briefly before returning with a couple of beers.

'Tell,' he says.

There are three chairs in the room, two of them newly upholstered, the other a relic from the beach. Gus settles in the latter while Kane repeats the bare bones of his assignment. Reviving the counterfeit scam. Getting young Hans Meier out of the pokey, then setting him up again to work the same magic, this time for Uncle Sam. Meier was the lead artiste in charge of the coloured pens on the drawing board. Worked at Sunrise Studios.

'You manage to run him down?' Kane asks.

'Sure. Turns out he was in Lincoln Heights for a while to knock the edges off him. I talked to the watch boss yesterday and he checked the detention records. Meier's in a coop in the Central Valley just now. You want me to sort a car?'

Kane nods. The essence of this assignment, he says, is his own preparedness to vanish. No trail of reservations. No fancy pad in Santa Monica. Nothing to juice the slightest interest from any passing stranger. Agent Kane, in short, has become the submarine from DC, totally submerged in the ever-darkening underbelly of wartime LA.

'No Mahoney?'

'No Mahoney.'

'You mean that?'

'I do. For now. Afterwards, maybe, we all get a little richer, though I haven't given that possibility serious thought.'

Gus nods, frowns, then gets up to put a disc on the phonograph.

'*Tannhauser*,' he mutters. 'You won't know it.'

'And the snake? Your viper?'

'He's a big fan. Sound is all vibrations. Snakes are lucky that way and it turns out he can't get enough of Wagner.'

The music begins, softish footsteps at first, slowly thickening. Kane has his eyes on the tank. Nothing happens.

'You're working for J. Edgar now?' Gus asks. 'This is a federal job?'

'I'm working for the Treasury. Nothing's changed.'

'You're lying, Quince. I've been trying to figure this thing out. No way is this Treasury. Since when did our masters authorise fake bills?'

Kane smiles, shrugs, takes a sip of beer, says nothing. Still no movement in the glass tank.

'You've seen her at all?' Kane asks at last. 'Mahoney?'

'Why would I?'

'That wasn't my question.'

'Then the answer is no. I've got a name for you, though. I thought it might be...' Gus is frowning now, '...helpful.'

'To who?'

'You, *hombre*. And that woman of yours. His name's José Cuesta, half-Mex, half-LA. He's been mobbed-up for years in Tijuana and nothing's changed since. These reptiles are crowding us good guys out. The Japs were still bombing Pearl Harbor when they caught the stench of what's coming. War is always an opportunity and this one won't be no different. Number one, you need to stay alive, and number two you need to be richer afterwards. Reptiles like Cuesta know that, which is something else you need to think about.'

'Why?'

'Because the man's just become Mahoney's agent. We're talking boxing in case that long flight's got to you.'

'You're kidding me?'

'Sadly not.'

'And she knows he's mobbed-up?'

'I've no idea. If she does, that makes her stupid. If she doesn't, it could be even worse.'

Kane nods, drains his beer, his gaze returning to the glass tank.

'You've got a photo of this guy? An address, maybe?'

'Of course.'

Gus is on his feet again. Kane has counted three bookcases. The top shelf of the biggest is home to a line of dictionaries. He lifts the most battered of them, the worn Cyrillic characters on the leather cover almost invisible, and seconds later Kane is looking at a photo of a tall Hispanic emerging from a bar. He's wearing a dark suit. His eyes are hidden behind a pair of sunglasses. His hair is neatly parted and his black shoes are gleaming after a recent shine. He might be any number of things, including an undertaker.

'You took this yourself?'

'I did, Quince. Yesterday. A little moving-in present.'

'For me?'

'For you and Fightin' Flo. I admire loyalty, Quince. In some folks' lives it rhymes with faith. I'm under-persuaded by either.'

'What the fuck does that mean?'

'Go figure.' Gus nods at the photo. 'Appearances lie, *hombre*. This is a guy who thrives on chaos. He's here to make all kinds of killings and my advice is to take him seriously. Fightin' Flo is a meal ticket. The fight's next week, by the way, Wednesday evening. Take Wilshire Boulevard west. When you get to Highland Avenue, turn right. You're heading for a place called Hegarty Autos. It looks like a fancy car outlet but that was a while ago and they never got to change the sign. Out back they have an entertainment space. You should be there by seven latest. If you want me there, you only have to ask.'

'You mean that?'

'I do. Your woman is shitting in high cotton, Quince. She thinks she's got it made but she's wrong. This town does ugly better than any place on earth and she should have wised up by now. Cuesta is one of the meanest guys I know and he wants to be the top face in town. This war is changing everything, Quince. It's a script with legs and no obvious ending and here's where it parts company with Japs and Heinies and Eyeties. The gloves are off, *hombre*. Cuesta is fluent in help-yourself. He has an eye for the main chance and understands the blessings of applied violence. You're getting my drift here?'

Kane nods, says he's grateful. Then he gets to his feet and crouches beside the glass tank. *Tannhauser* is building to a decent finish and Kane catches the tiniest movement before the snake parts a curtain of heavy greenness and slithers into view. Gus is right. Kane has never been partial to snakes but this one is truly beautiful. Bluish-green markings run the length of its body, scrolls of diamond and hourglass shapes. Another black diamond badges its head as it moves easily towards the glass. In the light Gus has just switched on, it seems to shimmer.

'See the horns on its little snout?' Gus has joined Kane in front of the tank. 'That's why they call it the rhino viper. My guess it it's the only specimen in town. Cost me twenty scoots, a while back. Worth every cent.'

Twenty dollars, Kane thinks. What kind of secret agent spends that kind of money on a recluse? On the Greta Garbo of the snake world?

'It bites?'

'Only if you give it a good reason.'

'But it can kill you?'

'Sure, big time. There's an antivenom but it's hard to find and by that time you're very dead.'

'You've got some of this stuff?'

'No way. We're buddies for life.'

Kane's gaze returns to the tank. The viper has come to a halt just inches away from the glass and appears to be entranced by its owner. If reptiles could smile, Kane thinks, we'd all be in a better place. Trust. Love. Forbearance.

'You know the *Parsifal* story?' Gus again.

'Nope.'

'It's about a guy who sets out to look for the Holy Grail. That's all you need to know.'

'And he finds it?'

'He finds himself, *hombre*. So I guess it's about redemption in a wicked world,' Gus kisses his finger, holds it briefly against the glass, and then rocks back on his heels. 'Think about it...' he's still gazing at the snake, '...and then despair.'

10

Despair.

Gus takes Kane to Bunker Hill. He drives a beaten-up old Chevvy with rusting dents on three corners, a ride much in keeping with his contented take on the rest of his life. There's a hole somewhere in the exhaust system and the car slows as it chug-chugs up the shallow incline towards Bunker Hill. This is one of the oldest parts of a city so new it can hardly keep up with itself, and Kane remembers once briefly living here and trying to resist the pressures of near-daily reinvention. Is LA the sunshine and glamour capital of the world? Or a postcard from the near future? Or seventy plus suburbs in search of an agreed name?

Bunker Hill is choked with early evening rush-hour traffic, drivers homeward bound from the downtown grid of offices, doing their best to ignore their immediate surroundings. Bunker Hill is the city's greasy collar, lately fingered by immigrants of every description, by Angelenos down on their luck, and by folks with pretty much nowhere else to go.

Just occasionally, as the traffic crawls forward, Kane glimpses a hold-out property owned and still lived in by somebody who cares: fresh paint on the window frames, a mailbox unstuffed with fliers of every description, and the tell-tale shine of a buffed brass knocker on the gleaming front door. But these clues from a lost inner LA are rare and the glum press of surrounding properties tells a very different story. According to Gus, this is where Los Angeles took a break from the carefree optimism of year-round summer and began to scratch itself to death.

'Not too late, Quince.' Gus has stopped outside a three-storey building. The property is visibly distressed. In the world of Hollywood, thinks Kane, this would figure as the prime location shoot for a bunch of misfit psychos dropping their pants and mooning the future. Drawn grey curtains at every window. Crumbling mortar between ancient bricks. A drift of broken bottles paving the way to the front entrance.

'Not too late for what?'

'For Santa Monica. Brentwood. Even La Jolla. You're on the Treasury dollar, *hombre*, if I believe you. Bunker Hill breaks people fast. Even giants like you, my friend. Get serious. Santa Monica is forty minutes away, even in this car.'

Kane shakes his head, extends his hand for the keys to the room, promises to get in touch.

'Soon, yeah?'

'Sure. When I've got something to say.'

Kane is travelling light. Back in DC, he packed for maybe a fortnight of hiding away from the rest of the world. A big canvas duffel bag that had once belonged to his brother Danny has given him room to spare. An easy carry, he hoists it on one shoulder, grunts a goodbye and heads for the front door. Inside, there are no lights. In the thick darkness the place smells of fried food, rancid cooking oil and over-cooked cabbage, lightly underscored with the sourness of old urine. Twice, moving carefully up from landing to landing, Kane hears a stir of movement as his new neighbours cock an ear to movement on the stairs, and once – when a door cracks open an inch or two – he pauses to make out the faintest oblong of face in the gloom. A man? A woman? Kane has no idea.

'Hi,' he murmurs. 'Cold out.'

Silence, except for the sound of the door closing and the double scrape of bolts top and bottom.

Kane's apartment is 3D, a number he interprets as a portent. Getting away from the flatness and superficiality of this absurd town. Giving it a little volume, a little dimension, a splash or two of extra depth. Will this assignment of his open the doors that really matter? Can he somehow revive a counterfeit scam he spent months helping to break? And is Donovan, with his eye on his own future, really serious about a million-dollar bribe for a French admiral about whom Kane knows so little?

In truth, Kane hasn't a clue. The good news about 3D, when he finally manages to turn the key in the lock, is the fact that the overhead light – a single bulb hanging from the ceiling – works. Not so welcome is the room itself.

Bare is a word that realtors never use and now Kane understands why. A single bed with a tangle of grubby sheets plus two thin blankets, one a faded plaid, the other ex-Army with a pattern of stains in the middle. A stand-up wardrobe leaning towards the window, hands raised in surrender to the general slant of the room. A collapsible table, thin steel legs likewise afflicted. On the bare wooden floor beneath the table is a two-ring electric stove, the top covered with heat-baked spills, the much-repaired lead snaking away to a wall plug hacked into the skirting board.

Aside from that, nothing. No chest of drawers. No

pictures to brighten the damp-blotched walls. No curtain on the lone window, mapped with greasy fingerprints. If rooms had moods, Kane thinks, this one would have opted for total disclosure. I am what you see. I am a muttered apology for a room, the best possible reason for backing towards the door and getting the hell out.

Kane hasn't noticed the envelope on the table. Now he picks it up. It carries a single capital letter – K – and inside he finds a scribbled note from Gus. He's enclosed an article ripped out of some magazine or other. The article includes a full colour photo of a snake Kane recognises, the goddam rhino viper, and further down the page the note recommends an expedition to the john.

Intrigued, Kane steps into the tiny closet and finds a bottle of Jim Beam in the cracked hand basin. The water from the dripping tap, when he tries it, tastes OK but he elects for a glug or two straight from the bottle, making a mental note to buy himself a glass and maybe other stuff before the room assigns him to terminal depression. The bourbon is doing its work already. It scorches down his throat and warms his belly, making him feel a whole lot better. Mahoney, he thinks at once.

Gus again. In the car driving over he'd offered directions to the nearest telephone. Turn right on the street and look for a speakeasy called Blind Mickey's two blocks down. The guy behind the bar midweek will volunteer the house phone against a modest deposit. A nickel or two will buy you all the conversation you'll ever need.

Kane finds the speakeasy, no problem. Half the people on the sidewalk are all-day drunks. The rest avoid his gaze or demand change. Kane has an arrangement with Mike Reilly back in DC. He can patch calls through one of the District Sixteen White House numbers, making it seem like he's calling from the East Coast.

Mike Reilly, when Kane finally gets through, is gruff, blaming overwork. FDR, he says, has become borderline impossible.

'That's because he's missing me.'

'You might be right, buddy. You brighten all our days. You gotta number for me?'

'Sure.' Kane recites an LA number from memory. This sparks a bark of laughter from Reilly who's copped a look at Steve Early's file on the *LA Times* article.

'That's Mahoney,' he says. 'You want to kid her you're still in DC? Is there no one in this world you can be straight with?'

Very good question, thinks Kane. There comes a burst of static on the line while Reilly works his magic, then Kane is listening to the trill of Mahoney's home phone. She answers almost immediately and Kane realises how much he's missed her.

'Me,' he grunts.

'Eight days,' she says at once, 'and counting. So what does a girl have to do for conversation?'

Kane laughs. Two more fingers of Jim Beam from the guy tending the bar are taking the sharper edges off his day.

'Conversation is everything,' he tells her. 'A hundred years ago, I'd be riding an ox cart west for a year or two to pass a message. That guy Edison put the glue back in relationships. Think about it.'

'I do. All the time. How's that little sister of yours?'

'She's due back home any day now. Last time I checked, they were getting her room ready for her.'

'She's better?'

'She'll never be better but her breathing's fine and now she has to learn to walk.'

'She'll cope with that?'

'We all will. One way or another.'

'We're talking money here?'

'Sure. And I guess we're talking Sis. That little girl can't work out what's happening. She thinks she'll wake up one morning and everything will be right again. FDR says he went through the same thing.'

'Denial?'

'Blind faith. Let's talk about something else.'

Mahoney wants to know what he's been doing, who he's met, the fearless steps he's taking to keep God's Republic safe.

'You've been drinking,' Kane says.

'If only. Everything's a big secret these days so here's mine. I'm back in training. I run with the dog every night. He's off the sauce as well.'

'This is Dolores?' Kane tries to keep the tone of the conversation ultra casual. A passing interest. A fond enquiry. Nothing more.

'Sure. Dolores and I have a date. Wednesday, if you've nothing better to do over there in DC.'

'You've met her again? Had a conversation? Kissed and made up?'

'No need. These days a girl has an agent. As in entertainment. As in Hollywood. As in the big money coming my way. My agent does the talking. I do the earning. That's a direct quote, by the way. Him, not me.'

'You've really got an agent?'

'I have. Mr Thirty Per Cent. For a cut like that I'm expecting serious fame and a ton of money.'

'He's got a name, this guy?'

'Of course he does. Everyone has a name. What's it to you?'

'Curiosity is all. I might give him a call. Compare notes. Earning's one thing. Yearning's quite another.'

'There's money in women's magazines, Quince. Language like that you might try your hand.' Mahoney snorts with laughter. 'Why making love at long-distance phone rates is a bust. How Mr Edison never quite managed to close the gap. You think this might fly? Make us both rich?'

'Nice idea. You're really fighting the black girl again?'

'I am, Quince. Wednesday, like I just said. I'll send a plane for you, put new sheets on the bed, hire a violinist to play sweet nothings under our window. In the meantime I tell Dexter we have to run faster and faster and he's definitely tuning in. Eats like a horse these days, prime steak mostly. That makes us best pals, Quince.'

'You and Dexter?'

'The three of us. You, me and the dog. That fight of mine is big news already, thanks to this agent guy. He managed to sneak a letter into that paper of mine. Outraged of Pasadena. Women fighting women? A black woman in against a white woman? Where does all this stuff lead? The guy's a genius, Quince. He tells me tickets are going five times face value.'

'And will you win?'

'Sure. No question. This agent guy has a pro-trainer buddy. Name of Tyrone. He's come to watch me sparring at the gym. My own trainer Billy-Jean doesn't like that much but I tell her we have to ride with it because this Tyrone knows Dolores, knows the way she fights, reads her mindset, and he's given me a hint or two about how to plan the first coupla rounds, how to frustrate the hell out of her before finishing up. It's my turn this time, Quince. It's all in Sun Tzu, but I'm guessing you'll know that.'

'Try me.' Sun Tzu was a Chinese military general from way back.

'Know thyself?' Mahoney suggests. 'Know thine enemy? The man was so, so right. You win a fight before you put the gloves on. Does that make any sense?'

Kane grunts, says nothing. He can see this woman of his. He can taste her.

'This pro-trainer guy, he's in your corner on the night?'

'No way, Billy-Jean would never allow it, but here's the twist. Tyrone trains Dolores, too, which is how he knows so much about her.'

'So he's in her corner? Is that what you're saying?'

'Sure. It's the fight game, Quince. Smallest world you'll ever know. Especially in this town.'

'And you're telling me that's no problem? Backing both women?'

'I'm telling you to relax. You know what's gonna happen next? After I win on Wednesday night we'll have one scalp each. The decider's the star prize. Tickets twenty scoots and climbing. Can't fail.'

'So Dolores throws the fight?'

'No way. You get to meet this woman, you'll know that's impossible. She's a machine. She eats other fighters, chomps them up and spits them out. I'll beat her fair and square because I'm fitter than her, and stronger than her, and all ways round better than her. And you know why?'

'Dexter?'

'Wrong, Mr Kane. It's because of you.' She blows him a kiss on the phone. 'And us.'

Kane says he's flattered. When Mahoney tells him that's old-man speak, he elects for something a little earthier. She counters with a proposal of her own, partly remembered nights together, partly a promissory note to be cashed in the next time they meet, and he tells her he can't wait.

Changing the subject, he wants to know about the Japs out on the West Coast, all the stuff he's been hearing about mass arrests and internment behind the wire. Mahoney says it's all true. LA just now is where no Jap would ever want to be. The older generation, the Issei, have no rights at all. The younger guys, their kids, have been born in the US and are therefore American citizens but just now no one is taking any notice. War fever, she says, has become Jap fever, and with luck she's going to expose the whole sick racket.

'How come?'

'Because there are guys on the paper that have fallen in love with Mrs Roosevelt. Much the way I've done.'

'And?'

'They see advantage in pointing out the obvious, that we're fighting a war for democracy, for freedom. Even J. Edgar gets it.'

Kane nods. According to Mike Reilly, J. Edgar Hoover has been banging on FDR's desk in the name of constitutional propriety. The younger Jap generation could be a national asset. They could be wearing uniforms. Why piss them off?

'You'll write about this?' Kane asks.

'Already done. This story moves at pace, Quince. I'm negotiating access to Camp Harmony as we speak.'

'Camp what?'

'Harmony. Everything's up for grabs in this war, and it starts with language. Harmony happens to be the slang for a camp they're building up near Seattle. There are others much closer to home. They're calling them assembly centres and no one's wasting a cent making them fit to live in. Think earth pits to shit in, Quince. Think a bunch of straw to fill your mattress. Think a paper tag round your neck to remind you who you are, and a coupla bucks a week to get fed. The Nazis do something similar but call them concentration camps. Spot the difference, Quince. Shame you can't make the fight.'

The conversation comes to an end shortly afterwards. Offered another Jim Beam at the bar, Kane checks his watch and shakes his head. Gus has arranged for a car to be delivered to Bunker Hill first thing tomorrow. Donovan has fixed a meet with Meier at a penitentiary in the Central Valley. And so Kane settles up with the bartender before nodding towards the phone booth.

'Thanks for that, buddy,' he grunts.

'Pleasure, sir.' The barman is smiling. 'Any time.'

||

Kane sleeps. Jim Beam stirs his darkest thoughts, about the night-long ravages of bed lice, about the ceaseless advance of armies of cockroaches, and he surfaces into the pallor of a grey dawn, wondering about the lightest whisper of footsteps outside in the corridor, and the scrape of something metallic pushed under his door. Investigation reveals an ignition key in an envelope. The California plate number scrawled on the envelope belongs to a battered '39 Ford Sedan parked across the street. Gus, once again, has been more than kind. The car even has a radio that works.

The worst of the morning rush hour is over by the time he leaves downtown LA and heads east. An all-over cold-water wash has restored his faith in what his father has always called 'Indian living'. The latter boils down to the basic courtesies of life, the chief of which is never to impose your smell, or your mood, on others, and by the time he's bullying the Sedan around the steeper corners of the road through the San Gabriel Mountains, Kane is enjoying a peace he hasn't felt for years.

Wild Bill Donovan, doubtless from the best of motives, has insisted on this disappearing act and it helps Kane a great deal to realise that he's perfectly cast in the role. A life without baggage is a fantasy he's cultivated for years, and his squalid roost in Bunker Hill has been the ideal accomplice. Whoever believes that a life without hot water and a carpet on the floor to be nine-tenths impossible is plain wrong. Jim Beam, he thinks, and that taunting voice on the phone from barely forty minutes' drive away.

The other side of the mountains, listening on the radio once again to the tally of European colonies falling like ninepins to the marauding Japs, Kane realises just how hungry he is. The first breakfast he spots on the road to Barstow has a half-empty car park and the promise of a full-American breakfast swinging gently in the late morning breeze. He parks alongside a huge truck, lingering for a moment to finish up with the radio. Then, with his hand reaching for the ignition key, comes the news that the Japs have been dropping leaflets over US troops defending the Philippines. Surrender, they're pointing out, would be a wiser alternative to certain death. Very true, Kane thinks, glad to be waging a very small corner of this war on his own terms.

At the counter, he eats eggs easy over, waffles dripping with maple syrup and thin rashers of streaky bacon crisped to perfection. The radio high on the wall returns Kane briefly to the catastrophe in the Far East before the hefty trucker on the next stool catches the eye of the woman serving coffee.

'Enough of this Jap shit,' he grunts. 'You mind putting some music on?'

The woman does his bidding. The trucker offers her a nod of thanks for the Andrews Sisters and then turns to Kane and asks where he's headed.

'Las Vegas,' Kane tenders the money for breakfast.

'Feeling lucky, bud?'

'Always.'

*

Half an hour later, the road east to the Sweetapple Penitentiary takes Kane past a big roadside plot that recently housed some kind of rodeo. Stoop labour, mainly Hispanics and blacks, are busy erecting lengths of chain fencing strung between concrete posts while a smaller gang follows behind. The men are wearing thick leather gloves with extended cuffs while a guy with sergeant's stripes on his Army uniform issues a string of oaths as they try and top the installed lengths of fencing with loop after loop of barbed wire.

Kane pulls off the road to watch, wondering whether this might be one of the assembly centres Mahoney had described on the phone last night. Beyond the fence, he can see a fleet of big flatbed trucks offloading hutments in various stages of disrepair and, as he watches, one of these instant barracks snags on the trailer's edge as the crane driver gets it badly wrong. One of the end doors caves in first, then the roof begins to sag as the thick canvas straps fail to keep the structure intact, and seconds later Kane is looking at a mess of tarpaper walls among the drift of tumbleweed and dried-up mesquite shrubs.

This, he thinks, is yet another consequence of Pearl Harbor, a slow-motion collapse that owes nothing to high explosive but plenty to the ungoverned rage of folk unused to being under attack. Jap phobia, Jap fever, Jap enemies within, gnawing at the very foundations of American life. Mahoney, Kane decides, is right. No matter how understandable this response, months or even years behind that wire will never be pretty.

Over an hour later, Kane finally makes it to the penitentiary. First as a cop, later in the Secret Service, Kane has been to plenty of prisons and this one looks no different, a sprawl of low-rise buildings contained by yet more fencing, with barbed wire strung between sturdy watchtowers. America has always been spoiled for space, and a glimpse of convict working parties in the far distance, miniature figures in drab grey fatigues, serves to make the point. The leavings of America, Kane thinks, consigned to oblivion behind yet more barbed wire.

Donovan has equipped him with false ID, plus supporting papers, a blessing when Kane pulls the car to a halt at the office set back from the main entrance.

'Mr Eli Loveless? Do I have that right, sir?'

'Perfect.'

The official nods, pleased with Kane's ready deference, and consults a schedule of expected visitors.

'And you're here to meet with Mr Meier?'

'Hans, yes.'

'You have legal representation? Anyone else we might expect?'

'No. Just me.'

The official nods again, then something catches his eye.

'You've been granted a room of your own for this meeting, Mr Loveless.' He looks up. 'You know how unusual that is?'

'I do, yes.'

'Can't help me out at all?'

'I'm afraid not.'

The official's eye settles on Kane's proffered ID. 'That's a DC address you're giving me here.'

'It is, yes.'

'Then I guess I should quit wasting your time, Mr Loveless.' He lifts a phone, mutters something Kane doesn't catch. Then he's stamping Kane's entry pass, checking his watch and entering the time by hand.

'Will three hours be enough, Mr Loveless? Or should we be planning on offering you supper? It's grits and mash and gravy tonight. I'm guessing you might fare better on the road.'

Kane is escorted through the headquarters building. A sequence of barred steel gates surrender to the gaoler's keys but there are no other clues this might be a prison. No inmates. No sense of menace. None of the normal tell-tales Kane has gotten used to.

Hans Meier is waiting in an office at the very end of the long central corridor. He sits alone at a bare table, his back to the harshness of the afternoon light flooding through the unbarred window. He has a notepad and a sharpened pencil at his elbow and he's been doodling what looks like thunderclouds trailing heavy rain. He's rendered the diagonal fall of rain in a series of dots and dashes that look like Morse code.

Kane hasn't seen this man for nearly three years, not since he accepted the transfer to the White House, and, if anything, Meier seems even younger than Kane remembers: an open, unlined face, the quietest of smiles, plus a talent for bridging the gap with any stranger that Kane had always found truly remarkable. Like Gus, with whom Meier had also bonded, this young guy had used his fierce intelligence to leverage a series of job offers, the last of which had taken him to one of the more nimble Hollywood studios. Executives had recognised his potential within days of starting out, first as a gifted set designer with an unusual palette of camera-ready styles, and latterly as the go-to guy for the trickier challenges involving close-up props.

Hans Meier, it was generally agreed, could conjure authenticity from the most unpromising materials, especially in the field of fake documentation, including numerous currencies, a talent that had later opened the door to a fortune beyond his wildest dreams. The last time Kane had been face to face with Meier, his trial was over and he was facing a twenty-year sentence. Unusually, after piecing the counterfeit scam together, Kane had wanted two things to happen. The first was to say goodbye and good luck. The second was to ask him the straightest and simplest of questions: why did you do it?

'Easy.' That smile again. 'I was bored.'

At the time, Kane had believed him and now he believed him even more. The trappings of Hollywood, even at a studio as bold and creatively hip as Sunrise, had never been enough. The money. The opportunities. The mad whirl of pool parties and beach barbeques. His name up there on the screen. Nods of recognition from folk who seemed to matter. All those baubles had played to the second-generation Berliner with his special knack of so easily making friends. But it had never been enough and when his design for pre-war Austrian banknotes in a limp Viennese drama attracted comment for their sheer authenticity, Meier began to toy with the real thing.

The real thing, fake US dollars, had proved an altogether easier ride than he'd ever expected. The right design skills, the right inks, the right paper, a working knowledge of the tricks the US Treasury pulled to defend the currency, and Meier was looking at a set of near-perfect scoots. There followed an introduction to a specialist print guy with infinite patience, iron nerves and a lively sense of humour, and within a month

Meier had created enough money to last him the rest of his life.

Not that gain or greed had ever figured in the masterplan. On the contrary, Meier was giving most of his beautiful banknotes away to a series of deserving individuals down on their luck. Building a network of the saved, joining the dots between lives and families salvaged from penury or worse, had been one of Kane's early investigative breakthroughs and he still remembered a conversation with an out-of-work steel welder, originally from Pittsburgh, who'd had the good fortune to cross Meier's path when his access to five- and ten-dollar notes was literally bottomless.

'This stuff ain't real?' he'd asked, fingering one of Meier's rare twenties. 'Who the fuck says?'

At the time it had been a very good question, all the more pertinent to the investigation when Kane and Gus and the rest of the team had difficulty finding experts prepared to put their reputations on the line and attest that Meier's masterpiece currency was fake. This, in turn, had led to long evening sessions in a handful of bars across LA when Gus would lead philosophical debates about what – exactly – separated good money from bad.

They were, after all, still within touching distance of the Wall Street crash of 1929, a catastrophe that had closed hundreds of banks across the country. Millions had seen their life's savings swallowed up by that same collapse, and Gus had been unsparing in his analysis of what was really going on.

There was no such thing as bad money and good money, he insisted. Instead, there was only money, a means of exchange, plus the motives of people who wanted to pile it up and piss it away for their own ends. Think outside the box, he said, and the only things that mattered were greed and venality and the rank odour of wise-guy bankers who'd pretended that everything was fine when they knew for sure that the whole fucking economy was going down the tubes. Those vermin, and there were lots of them, cared jack shit about the little people whom Hans Meier and his two buddies were trying to tide over, and, even years later, Gus still held a candle for those three guys. The other two were a fellow German called Marcuse and a Sicilian, Luca Esposito. All three were serving out their time in separate penitentiaries.

Kane wants to know whether Meier's still in touch.

'Sure. We write. We correspond. We compare notes. Most times the letters get past the censor. Some don't.'

'And?'

'They're doing their time. Twenty years can be half a life. Math like that can make you seriously unhappy.'

'And you?'

'I do the same math, the same computations. How many Christmases to go. How many chances left to maybe father a family.'

Kane nodded. Exquisitely put, he thought.

'You've become a Quaker? Have I got that right?'

'I have, yes. Under the circumstances, I guess it comes as no surprise. Quakers understand silence. They tend to have very low blood pressure. That helps, believe me.'

'Inside?'

'Sure, and outside too in the real world. People should try it for size, see how it fits. You're never too old to surprise yourself. Folks have forgotten how to listen. Quakers know how to deal with that.'

At Kane's invitation, Meier described some of the prisoners who'd shunned his company in the early days – too bookish, too naïve, too willing to ride the usual shit that comes everyone's way – but slowly it had dawned on some of them that this was a guy who weighed his words carefully, who had no interest in bull, and who could offer seriously useful advice when it came to addressing the chaos of their private lives. Word had spread, he said, within the penitentiary, and he'd recently been elected a kind of unofficial spokesman for everyone else. Life inside was a non-stop battle against injustices, both real and imagined, and it turned out the young counterfeiter on a twenty-year stretch had a talent for negotiation, for listening to rival parties, for plotting a way through.

'And the people who run this place? They listen to you?'

'Always.'

'Why?'

'Because it's a whole lot better than shooting people, and a whole lot cheaper, too. There's trouble coming for the Japs. All you have to do is to tune into the turnkeys. If they're wise, and a lot of Japs I know are, they'd be wise to turn Quaker too. Except that most of them are Shinto, which is Quakerism, and plenty more. Like I say, all you have to do is listen.'

All you have to do is listen. Kane nods. This man has always impressed him, and nothing has changed.

'OK,' he says, beckoning Meier a little closer across the table. 'Here's the pitch.'

'Pitch?'

'Sure,' Kane smiles. 'All you have to do is listen, OK?'

Meier nods, says nothing. If anything, he seems unsurprised.

Kane explains that a situation has developed. It requires someone with the right skills to counterfeit a thousand $1,000 bills. Meier has exactly those skills and Kane has no doubt that he can meet the challenge.

'You still work for the federal government?'

'I do, yes.'

'And this has their backing?'

'One hundred per cent.'

'So what do I get in return?'

'Your freedom.'

Meier nods and stares down a while at his notepad. Then he's back with Kane.

'Does that mean an official pardon? Only there's an important difference.'

'I'm afraid not. We'll set you up in a new life, new name, new ID, new place to live, new everything. You'll have money, prospects, everything you need to start over. How does that sound?'

'We're talking a million dollars here,' Meier is deep in thought. 'Am I allowed to ask where that money goes?'

'No.'

'Is this some kind of federal scam?'

'Kinda. You might blame the war but believe me it's best we leave it there.'

'Sure, and what about all the stuff I'd need. Paper? Inks? Some secure place to work? Access to the right printer?'

'All taken care of.'

'By?'

'Uncle Sam.'

'And you guys know what you're doing?'

'We do, Hans. We're good. That's why you're inside.'

'Too true.' That smile again, this time a little rueful.

A silence develops but Kane is happy to wait. At last Meier reaches for his pad and scribbles two names. Marcuse and Luca.

'They go free, too,' he says. 'And they get the same deal as me. Otherwise, it's a no.'

This ultimatum, so final, so gently tabled, brings the conversation to an end. Meier gets to his feet, extends a hand, says it's been a pleasure. Then he crosses the room and knocks lightly on the door, evidently a signal that he wants to return to his cell. Moments later, he's gone.

Kane waits for the turnkey to take him back to reception. To his surprise he finds himself looking at a DC number he recognises. Wild Bill Donovan.

'You're welcome to use the phone in there, Mr Loveless,' the official nods at the adjoining office. 'I gather it's urgent.'

Kane steps into the office, shuts the door, makes the call. Mr Donovan isn't available but has left a message. He'll be in LA by mid-afternoon tomorrow. He and Kane need to meet. Four o'clock at the downtown Secret Service field office. Be there.

12

Kane is back in LA by mid-evening. Mahoney has pricked his conscience about Sis, and he walks to Blind Mickey's and spends half an hour on the phone to his brother, rerouting the call once again through DC. Danny's take on the family has always been the one Kane trusts most, and he's relieved to discover that Sis has made it back home.

'Still breathing OK?'

'She's breathing fine, Quince. It's the inside of her little head that needs attention. She thinks there's a wiring problem, messages not getting down to those legs of hers. Tell her different, and she won't accept it. Paralysis isn't a word she can cope with. What she wants is the magic pill that will put everything right. It's a fairy tale, Quince, and I guess it's our job to come up with a happy ending.'

When Kane asks about money, Danny confirms that getting her mobile again won't be cheap. She'll need regular physiotherapy and access to a swimming pool. Then she'll be fitted with specially designed steel braces, and a second pair when she gets taller. Add the many extras required around the house – grab rails, adaptations in the bathroom, regular massage for her dead limbs – and the family will be looking at thousands of dollars, money Kane's father simply doesn't have.

'I guess we should be thinking about some kind of loan,' Danny says. 'Unless you can figure a better way out.'

Kane is noncommittal, says he'll sleep on it. Maybe, when he gets back to DC, he'll ask Eleanor Roosevelt about sources of financial help. Anything to get Sis back on her feet.

The conversation over, Kane collects a beer from the bar and returns to the booth to put another call through to Gus.

'I'm still on the Treasury tab,' he says. 'Have you eaten yet?'

They meet at a Chinese restaurant Gus favours in Santa Monica. Kane passes on Meier's best wishes.

'You're right,' Kane adds. 'The guy's become a Quaker. He always had something of the saint about him. Now I guess it's official.'

'Sure. And look where it got him.'

'We put him there, buddy. You're telling me you regret that?'

Gus ducks the question, grabs the menu, insists Kane tries the chicken in black bean sauce. Kane wants to talk about printers.

'We busted Meier's guy, right?'

'Sure. He's in the pokey. Like the rest of them.'

'And the printing press? I recall we seized it, had it condemned. It was off to the breaker's yard. Abuse of the currency. Conspiracy to defraud. Capital offence.'

'That was the plan.'

'You're telling me different?'

Something in Gus's face suggests to Kane this story's far from over. The printing press had done service throughout the thirties. Working at Sunrise, Meier had gotten to know the printer. Klaus was a fellow German, and Meier had used him on a number of studio jobs. The relationship had deepened and by the time Meier turned his hand to producing real money, Klaus had been happy to go along with the scam. Klaus had a second family thanks to a lengthy affair with an impoverished Danish ex-model, and trying to feed two families during the Depression had frightened him. Who'd ever say no to free dollars?

'So?' Kane ignores the hovering waitress.

Gus is looking irritated. 'Nothing goes to plan in this town. Not now, not then. You know that.'

'And the printer guy? Klaus?'

'Klaus goes down on all counts. We seize his equipment. DC is insisting on destroying it, so that's what we do.'

'Except?'

'Except it somehow gets intercepted en route to the breaker's yard. No one to my knowledge has pieced this thing together but the way I read it at the time, the bad guys got in the way, worked a switch to a pile of junk no one wanted, and presented the certificate of destruction exactly the way we demanded. The paperwork looked clean, Meier and his bunch of other guys were away for a very long time, and we all moved on to the next job. This stuff happens, Quince. Defending the currency was never for the faint-hearted.'

'You're telling me the printing press still exists?'

'I assume so.'

'Assume so?'

'Yeah. I got word a year or two later from a guy finking out the scrapyard scammers. He gave me an address.'

'And you went to check?'

'I didn't.'

'Why not?'

'Better stuff to do. Passage of time. Am I covering my arse here, Quince? Of course I fucking am. We put those guys away. We did the job good. We saved the goddam currency. You want bells and whistles?'

Kane holds both hands up. Gently, gently. Gus is a good friend and just now that matters because he's the only ally Kane has in this town. Trouble is coming down the track. Kane can smell it.

'You've still got that address?'

'Somewhere. Sure.'

Kane nods. Reaches for the menu at last. Shares his plan for tomorrow afternoon. A guy's arriving from DC for a conference. For whatever reason, he's demanding they meet at the Secret Service field office. Maybe Gus might have the address by then, if only for old time's sake.

'He has a name, this guy who needs a meet?'

'William Donovan.'

'Donovan?' Gus is staring at Kane. 'Wild Bill?'

'Yep.'

'You're working for OSS? Spook Central? You're off the reservation?'

'For now, yes.'

Gus holds his gaze for a long moment, then shakes his head.

'Shit,' he says softly.

The news about Donovan changes everything. Gus is demanding the full story – how come? why? what next? – and Kane finds himself on the back foot. The operation, he says, is top-level deniable. In the way of these things, he knows enough to handle his part of the jigsaw and no more. Breathe a word to anyone, even Gus, and his career is history. Along with everything else that makes him get up in the morning.

'So how come Donovan dare show his face on our turf?' Gus can't believe what he's hearing. 'How fucking subtle is that?'

'I've no idea. Except that these guys are forever fighting wars of their own. Donovan's one of them. Hoover's another. They're dogs, Gus. They leave their scent everywhere, they piss on other people's lamp posts.'

'Like ours?'

'Like yours.'

'You're serious? Am I hearing this right? He's stolen your heart?'

'For now, yes.' Kane shrugs. 'Afterwards, who knows.'

'You're looking for advantage here? Skin in the game?'

'Game is good,' Kane nods in approval. 'You haven't lost it, buddy.'

'Lost what?'

'Your sense of humour. One last favour, eh? I'm guessing you know the name of that printing place.'

'You're right.'

'And?'

Gus studies him for a long moment, then pushes the menu away and gets to his feet.

'Look for Ink Inc.'

'Just that?'

'Just that. Ink Inc. It's off Alameda Street.' He nods towards the door. 'Talk nicely to the guy on the desk here and he'll call a cab to get you home.'

13

Kane is in Alameda Street next morning. He's wearing jeans, a pair of scuffed work boots and a whiteish singlet under a chequered lumberjack shirt. He finds Ink Inc. towards the end of the street, wedged between a hardware store and a sorry looking deli specialising in Italian sausage. The sight of a fan of sliced mortadella stops Kane in his tracks. He hasn't eaten since yesterday's counter breakfast, having mislaid his appetite for chicken in black bean sauce.

The print shop is open, but no one appears to be around. Kane stands at the counter. The walls are hung with New Year's calendars, each with its bespoke heading. Segundo Antiques. A timber business. O'Grady Haulage. A Santa Monica art gallery specialising in Far Eastern woodcuts. In short, a rich selection of LA commercial come-ons, most of them smallish enterprises.

Idly, Kane flicks through a calendar advertising a chain of candy stores. When he gets to December, someone has gotten there first. Sunday 7 December, the morning the Japs fell on Pearl Harbor, features crosshairs on a carefully drawn circle. Curiosity takes Kane to another calendar, and then a third. Same date. Same message. Downtown LA has drawn a bead on the sons of infamy.

A door opens behind the counter and Kane finds himself looking at a girl in her late teens. Jet-black hair, oval face, slight figure, very pretty, with an Asian slant to her brown eyes.

Kane asks to see the print shop's owner.

'That's my dad.'

'He's around?'

'Ten minutes. Maybe fifteen. Can I help any?'

'Thanks, no. I'll be back.'

Kane retreats next door to the deli, orders a mortadella sandwich with pickles. The deli owner is Italian and confirms that Ink Inc. has been around a while.

'Tough, though,' he says, declining to go any further.

Kane eats the sandwich in the sunshine out on the street. He's debating a second helping when he spots a figure hurrying around the corner at the end of the street. His blue overalls are spotted with dark stains and he's carrying a brown paper bag. Asiatics age at a different rate from white Americans but Kane guesses north of sixty. The newcomer pauses briefly outside the print shop and nods at someone across the street before pushing the door open and stepping inside.

Kane follows him. The shop, once again, is untended and the newcomer is about to disappear out back.

'Mr...?'

'Takiwa. And you are?'

'My name's Loveless.'

'Can I help you any?'

'Yeah. A conversation would be good.'

The girl has reappeared.

'You want something to drink, Mr Loveless?' Takiwa is inspecting the contents of his bag. 'Coffee maybe?'

Kane says yes. Takiwa dismisses the girl with a wave of his hand. Then Kane gestures at the calendars on the wall.

'Business OK?'

'Used to be.'

'Until?'

'Work it out, Mr Loveless. A face like mine, a name like mine, don't pull custom any more. People you thought you knew, folk you used to trust,' he shrugs, then gazes at the bag. 'Three weeks ago we got lunch delivered every day. Now I join the queue like everyone else.'

'That must be tough.'

'Sure it's tough, but what do you do? This war of ours is still a baby, can hardly crawl, needs its ass wiping. God knows where it all ends.'

'Sure.' Kane nods at the bag. 'Don't let me hold you up.'

Takiwa shoots him a look. 'You're some kind of cop?'

'I'm curious is all.'

'About?'

'About the printing press I'm guessing you have in there.' Kane nods at the door behind the counter.

'You want to buy it? Make me an offer maybe?'

'I want to know where it came from. You bought this place? The print press was already here?'

'Sure I bought this place. Nineteen thirty-five. The press I had then was old, kept breaking down, made in Chicago, no one knew when. Spares were impossible. Something broke, you had to make a new part from nothing, start all over.'

'And then?'

'Then I got an offer. Guy took it off my hands, sold me a new one, maybe not new but plenty loved, plenty looked after. You know anything about the letterpress, Mr Loveless?'

'Try me.'

'It's a Koenig & Baur. Beautiful the day it arrived, and

nothing's changed since. Guy said it printed up a storm and he was right. Never let me down. Not once.'

'You mind if I look at it?'

'Why?'

'I need sight of the serial number. And I need you to tell me where to look.'

'You are a cop.'

'No, Mr Takiwa. Happens I'm on your side, which I guess might be unusual these days.' Kane pauses. He's been around enough small enterprises to recognise the smell of an empty order book and impending doom.

Takiwa thinks about Kane's interest in the serial number for a moment or two, then shrugs as the girl reappears with the promised coffee. He mutters something to her in a language Kane doesn't recognise. Japanese, he thinks. Has to be.

The girl puts the coffee on the counter, then leads Kane into the back of the property. The smell hits him first, the pungent tang of hot ink, and machine oils, and rolls of paper. He'd lived with this smell for a week or two when the Secret Service counterfeit operation was visiting print shop after print shop in every corner of LA, checking out leads. The girl is offering him a pencil and a scrap of paper.

'You want to write it down, sir?'

Sir. This girl, he thinks, has drawn the same conclusion as her father. Respect, especially now, is a precious commodity in this town and it costs nothing. Kane, in other words, is definitely some kind of cop.

She's clambered over a roll of paper and is peering at the back of the letterpress down near the concrete floor.

'You ready, sir?' She calls out three letters and a bunch of numbers and asks Kane to read them back. 'Perfect.' She has a lovely smile.

Back in the shop, Kane is after a name.

'Like who?' Takiwa, munching on a leg of chicken, is more guarded now.

'Like the guy who sold you the press.'

'Guys, plural. I misspoke. I haven't got any names.'

'So how much did it cost you?'

'A lot.'

'More than a hundred?'

'Much more.'

'A thousand, maybe?'

'Nearly.'

'That's serious dough, Mr Takiwa. You're telling me you handed over a sum like that to a bunch of strangers?'

Takiwa appears to have lost interest in the conversation. He mutters something about means and ends and how the new letterpress triggered a flood of orders, and how he'd repaid the borrowed money within six months. Know your trade, recognise a bargain, and the business looks after itself.

'Until now.' Kane is watching him carefully.

'Sure. But Pearl Harbor came out of the blue. Even you guys had your pants round your ankles. You know anything about Shinto, Mr Loveless? Disaster can be like the weather. When it rains you get wet, and when that happens you deal with it.'

Kane nods. One last question.

'That machine,' his gaze settles on the door behind the counter. 'Still as good as ever?'

Takiwa permits himself the ghost of a smile, then he's talking to the girl again. This time she doesn't have to disappear. Instead, she opens a drawer and produces a brown envelope, much fingered, and hands it to Kane.

'Take a look, Mr Loveless.' Takiwa again.

Kane shakes a single piece of paper from the envelope. Inside is a colour print that has to be taken from a photograph. At first glance, Kane has no idea what he's looking at. The object, perfectly lit, looks like some kind of vegetable. It has the texture of a head of broccoli but is grey in colour. When Kane takes a closer look, some of the whorls are veined with thin scarlet threads, perfectly captured, perfectly rendered, but what dominates the image is a gash in the very middle of the object, something violent beyond explanation, and the edges of the gash are seeping a pinkish liquid with a strange sheen.

'You know what that is, Mr Loveless?'

'Tell me.'

'It comes from an autopsy. In one of the city morgues. It's a human brain. A single blow to the head caused that. Probably a lump hammer or maybe an ice pick. Bang—' He drives a bunched fist into the palm of his hand. '*Sayonara*.'

'So where did you get it?'

'One of the guys who sold me the press, Mr Loveless. I guess he was sending me a message. He gave me a good price. I paid it. No more questions, eh?'

'But this was printed on your press?'

'Sure. Before I even owned it. You think it looks like a photograph?'

'It is a photograph.'

'Wrong, Mr Loveless. It's an engraving. Some young guy I never met. Worked in Hollywood for a while.' He nods down at the ruined brain. 'Worked a kinda magic and worked it good.'

Kane checks out the print a final time, then nods. A message, he agrees. Once for Takiwa. And now for me.

By the time Kane makes it to the meeting with Donovan, it's gone four o'clock. The Secret Service field office in LA is a secured unit in the Bank of America building on West Pico Boulevard, and Kane knows it well. Present yourself at the front desk, ride the elevator to the fourth floor and follow the corridor around two corners until an eye in the peephole of an otherwise anonymous door lets you in.

Kane finds Donovan in the roomy central workspace. To his surprise, the empire builder from Spook Central is deep in conversation with Gus.

'You're late, Kane.' Donovan looks him up and down. 'And since when have you been working in a timber mill?'

'Needs must, sir. Your call, not mine. You write the script, I wear the costume.'

'Just kidding, son.' He glances back at Gus. 'We need a little privacy here.'

Gus takes them to one of the interview rooms, and then disappears. Oddly enough, Kane and Gus had conducted the final interview with Hans Meier over this same table. What goes round comes round, Kane thinks.

'Gus tells me you've tracked down the printing press.' This from Donovan.

'Gus is right.' Kane explains about the failing business on Alameda Street, and tables the serial number of the machine. 'It's a Koenig & Baur, sir. And I'm guessing it'll check out.'

'The owner's Japanese, you say?'

'First generation. A son and a daughter live over the shop.

His wife, too. She's white American, an Angeleno. He was born in Nagasaki.'

'Takima? Guy's got a Christian name?'

'Jisuke.'

Donovan makes a note and then looks up from his pad. 'And the machine's still working?'

'So the guy says. I only have his word for it.'

Donovan nods. Gus has clearly spoken to him first about the scrapyard scam and now he wants to know what happened to Meier's engraved plates.

'They all went back to DC.' Kane says. 'I took them myself, handed them over to the Treasury. If you're thinking we can use them again, sir, the answer is no. Meier's insisting on starting over. The thousand buck note features Grover Cleveland, for starters. He says it also contains lotsa booby traps.'

'But he thinks he can do it?'

'He knows he can do it. You want a guess on how long this thing might take?'

'Sure.'

'Three months for the engraving. Double that to get a perfect finish.'

'Half a year? As long as that?'

'Yep. We have to trust this guy. We're in his hands.'

This prospect doesn't please Donovan at all. Kane can see it in his face.

'I'm assuming he can work on the plates anywhere. When it comes to getting the notes done, how secure is this Jap print shop?'

'It's a regular business and that makes it the last place you'd be looking for a million dollars. We can put in extra security, lock it down, no problem.'

'And this guy…' Donovan's gaze drifts down to his pad, '…Takiwa?'

'He's good. He showed me some evidence.'

'But he's a Jap, Kane. How the hell do we deal with that?'

'We ride with him. He knows the press. He's lived with it for years, tended it, nurtured it. You want the best job, he's the guy.'

Donovan nods, says nothing. Then he asks again about Meier.

'He's up for the deal?'

'Sure, but only if we cut his other two buddies free. Same deal, same terms.'

'Otherwise?'

'He stays inside.'

'You're kidding me? This guy's some kind of martyr?'

'He's a Quaker. It's probably worse.'

'Hell, no. No way.' Donovan shakes his head. 'The guy's pulling our pecker, fooling around, playing hard to catch. Double the money.'

'It's not about the money, sir. It's about his buddies.'

'Really? I'm not hearing this. He's on a twenty stretch. He's done three. As I understand it, the current deal is no remission, so we're making life sweet for him. He could be out the moment the President talks to Justice. He could be a free man. He gets a new life, all the money he needs. It'll be like the counterfeit scam all over again except Uncle Sam has his back. What else could a guy in his position possibly want?'

'No idea, sir. I'm sure he'll sign up, just as long as his buddies get a bite at the same apple.'

Donovan shakes his head again, visibly perplexed. Free

money makes the world go round, especially in this town, until some goddam Quaker has second thoughts.

'You think you can make him see sense, Kane? Apply a little pressure?'

'Like what, sir? He's inside already, seventeen years to go. Short of a threat to kill him, what kind of options do we have left?'

'Killing him wouldn't be smart,' Donovan is frowning now.

'You're right, sir. The last thing we need is a dead genius.'

'Might be worth a mention, though.'

'I doubt it.'

'You won't even try, Kane? That disappoints me.'

Kane shrugs, says nothing. Donovan gets to his feet and prowls up and down beside the window, throwing troubled glances at the rush-hour traffic below. Finally, with a sigh, he returns to the table. For someone at the head of the nation's new spook agency, he's a lousy actor.

'Then I guess it's over, Agent Kane.'

'It or me, sir?'

'Both. You're the one with the relationship with Meier. You say nothing will shift him, and you won't even try, so I have to believe you. I guess we have no option. We throw in the fucking towel, we quit, we call the referee to stop the fight. Not good on your sheet, Kane, and not good on mine either.'

This, Kane knows, is a stand-off. First to open his mouth again loses and so Kane says nothing before getting to his feet and checking his watch.

Donovan asks where the fuck he thinks he's going. Kane looks down at him.

'Moving out's no big deal, sir. I can be gone from my little hutch in five minutes flat. There's a red-eye to DC tonight I can easily make. Back at the ranch before they've even missed me.'

Donovan gazes up at him, then gestures abruptly at the vacated chair.

'I guess I talk to the President,' he says, 'about restructuring the deal. Wish me luck if you're still interested.'

'Sure,' Kane manages a cold smile. 'One favour, sir?'

'Name it.'

'Tell him Sis is out of the hospital.'

'Sis?'

'My kid sister. Polio case. The President's been there. He'll understand.'

14

For the next four days Kane hunkers down at Bunker Hill, waiting for word from Donovan. The cold January days are long and he lies under the blankets on the wreckage of his bed, wishing for the first time in his life that he'd become a smoker. Anything to break the monotony. Any way of kidding himself he's still in charge of his fate.

The silence of the house is hardest to bear but then Kane begins to listen properly, to detect the slow drag of footsteps past his door, repeated every hour, or the distant hacking cough of some consumptive upstairs, or an occasional groan from the latest John Doe being serviced by the fat whore across the corridor. Connect these dots, he thinks, and you're looking at an America untouched by the fabled New Deal.

Would Donovan understand any of this? Would he even bother to try? Could FDR himself imagine the life that awaits the distressed, and the inadequate, and the abandoned? By now, he's given the building a name. He calls it by its street number, 115, and those three digits begin to serve as the code that unlocks his most private thoughts. His brief exaltation at abandoning even his name has faded, and the journey he's making is proving way more of a test than he'd ever expected. Close-up glimpses of the darkness at the heart of the American dream have begun to depress him – wasted lives on permanent hold, the inadequate and the deranged abandoned by the cartoon fantasies of this showboat town – and his only regret is that he has no one to share them with, no one to help explore the real implications. 115, he thinks. Welcome to the Land of the Free.

For light relief, he permits himself the occasional excursion to the local corner store for supplies, and afterwards he sits in the beaten-up Sedan across the road and listens to the radio. The news – and he tunes to nothing else – is always bad. The Japs wading into the Dutch colonies. The Japs swarming all over the Philippines. The Japs eyeing Singapore over the Straits of Johore. None of this does anything for his peace of mind and on the second evening he walks to Blind Mickey's to put a call through to Mahoney, but his timing is bad and he finds himself talking to Virgil.

'Out running?' Kane says. 'Again? Is there anything left of this woman?'

'Plenty, my friend.'

'And you're telling me it's every night? Rain or shine?'

'Set your clock by it, buddy. Seven to nine. Run to the gym. Work out. Run back. Hot chocolate and a big fat salad afterwards. Could life be any sweeter?'

Late on the third afternoon, Kane surrenders to his baser instincts. The patter-patter on the filthy window at 115 tells him it's still raining. He grabs a Senators baseball cap from his duffel bag, pulls on a leather jacket and heads for the door. An afterthought brings him back to the bag and a rummage finally produces a pair of sunglasses he knew he'd packed. He checks his watch. He needs to be across town by half-six, latest, parked up somewhere safe. An hour and a half? Even in rush-hour traffic? Easy.

Kane knows his way to Mahoney's condo by heart. She

lives in a modern apartment block on the seafront at Santa Monica, and Kane has lost count of the early mornings he's awoken to the growl of the surf through her open bedroom window. She's always telling him how much of her monthly pay cheque is eaten by the rent, but this is a woman who rarely settles for anything but the best. What she'd make of 115 is, mercifully, beyond his imagination.

The route to Santa Monica delivers Kane to the ocean front by a quarter past six. Parking in the high season can be difficult but the rain is even heavier and the beach in the last of the dusk is empty except for a lone surfer eyeing the frothy whiteness of the messy breaks offshore.

Kane parks with line of sight to Mahoney's ground-floor condo. Her little roadster appears in the rear-view mirror shortly afterwards and Kane ducks his head as she drives past, signals right and disappears into the car park to the rear of the building. From fifty yards, Kane has a brief glimpse of her profile at the wheel. A recent haircut, brutally short, gives her a slightly masculine look but she's wearing the black cashmere dress they'd shopped for back in the autumn. They'd slipped into a changing booth together with an armful of alternatives and Kane still remembers her lingering smile when she'd first tried the cashmere.

'Mine,' she'd murmured to the watching face in the long mirror.

Kane reclines his seat a little, closes his eyes, and asks himself what he's doing here on a wet night in Santa Monica staking out the woman he loves. Wouldn't life be easier if he simply crossed the road and walked to her door, gave her some bullshit story about a sudden posting to LA, and left the rest of the evening to sort itself out? Hadn't the essence of their times together always depended on reckless, impromptu moments that had turned their lives inside out? The answer to both questions is a big fat yes, accompanied by the glow her presence always radiates, but Kane also knows that times have changed. He's working to a very different set of rules now. He's promised to submerge, to do his best to make himself invisible, and he'll stay that way until the job is done.

But there's something else, too, that matters a great deal and he wonders whether he'll be clever and honest enough to give it a name. Kane has rarely been in the business of kidding himself, but he recognises raw appetite when he comes across it and knows that this primal urge has always been Mahoney's special gift to the world. It governs everything she does, every conversation that comes her way, every next story she's assigned to investigate, every challenge she has to meet. The latest appears to be a black fighter called Dolores but when, on the phone, Mahoney dismissed the possibility of another beating, Kane believed her. Why? Because Mahoney is willpower incarnate. Who would even dream of running on a night like this?

And so he settles deeper still in his seat behind the wheel, the peak of his cap low over his eyes, the sunglasses ready on the passenger seat beside him. For once in their relationship, he tells himself he'll be in total charge, the invisible presence, unseen and unexpected. The thought of being able to watch her every movement as if they'd never met, begins to stir him. This, after all, is a town where make-believe has pitched its gaudy tent. Where better to fantasise a little?

She appears late, a darting presence under the streetlights. She has Dexter on a long lead, thin, eager, sniffing the wind off the ocean, and they cross the road together before pausing on the sidewalk to stare into the windy darkness. For a long moment Kane curses his luck. He's blown it. They'll be running on the beach, way out of sight, then Mahoney bends to the dog, gives it a pat and maybe a word of apology for the rain, and Kane is watching them set off along the gentle curve of the promenade, dog and owner casting shadows that shorten and lengthen in the throw of light from lamp post after lamp post.

Kane gives them a head start and then stirs the old engine into life. He's wearing the sunglasses now and he has to concentrate to keep them in view. This time in the evening, the Santa Monica traffic is still homeward bound, and Kane is thankful for the succession of cars that overtake. Mahoney, he knows, has the eyes and instincts of a she-wolf when any kind of threat hangs in the air, but on a night like this she's oblivious to the kerb crawler forty yards back.

The Santa Monica promenade gives out a couple of miles to the north. Dexter sets a fast pace – a steady nine miles an hour according to Kane's speedo – and Mahoney has no difficulty keeping up. Kane watches her moving easily, sidestepping the bigger puddles, occasionally turning her face to the darkness offshore. He can imagine her enjoying the salty kiss of the driving rain, the raw buffet of the gusty wind. Happiness, she'll be telling herself, tastes of the ocean. Then, without warning, owner and dog come to an abrupt halt at a traffic intersection.

The lights are red and Kane is number one in the queue. Reflexively, he pulls down the sun visor and slows the wipers, watching the windscreen pebble with raindrops. Then he flicks his headlights, an invitation for Mahoney and the dog to cross the road. When Mahoney lifts her hand, he acknowledges the gesture with a little wave of his own. Go well, he thinks. Take care. I love you.

But Mahoney is already on the move again, running alongside another major road heading inland. Kane settles for the same forty yards as the houses on either side get smaller. Ahead is a bunch of shops he remembers from way back – Lewis Drug Store, Saba Plumbing, A&P Fresh, plus a Record Mart where Kane had once found an old album of Bessie Smith songs for Mahoney's birthday. She'd played 'Nobody Knows You When You're Down and Out' again and again that day, and Kane knows she's still word perfect on the lyrics.

Beyond the shops, Mahoney increases the pace a little, maybe a clue that the journey's nearly over, and Kane suddenly recalls a modest sports complex off this highway that was always changing hands. In summer the place used to attract young college jocks working out ahead of the new football season, and Kane suspects that this is where Mahoney is headed.

He's right. The complex has been rebadged yet again since he was last here, but the car park is nearly empty and he pulls to a halt beside a black Mercedes limousine, the curves of the bodywork gleaming under the floodlights, the fabric of the folding roof stretched tight. The car park is puddled with standing water, pink neon reflections dimpled with the falling rain. Under the canopy over the entrance to the complex, Mahoney copies Dexter and shakes the water from her hair. Moments later, they've disappeared inside.

Kane wonders how far to push his luck. His memories of the gym are vague. He's been here to work out on a couple of occasions, but he can't remember how easy it might be to hide. He's still wearing his timber yard outfit, unfamiliar to Mahoney, but venturing inside, he decides, is a risk too far. Instead, he steps into the rain, adjusts his leather jacket, pulls the peak of his baseball cap lower still, and sets out on a circuit of the building.

His luck is in. Out back of the complex is a grassed area with swings and a mini roundabout for the kids. Big picture windows, unscreened and lit from within, offer a perfect view of the gym area. A wet January night has pulled barely a handful of clients to the weights, and wall bars, and thick rubber exercise mats, and as Kane watches from the darkness Mahoney appears, blowing a cheerful kiss to a much older woman doing step-ups on a wooden bench. They have a brief conversation, and then Mahoney heads for one of the exercise mats and does a series of stretches. The tightness of her green T-shirt is dark with sweat from the run.

Kane gazes at her. He knows every inch of that body, the swell of her breasts, the little knots of muscle around her shoulders, the flatness of her belly. This is someone he'd love to think he's made his own, yet watching her he knows that this will always be an impossibility. The magic, the lure, the irresistible pull and suck of this woman depends on something else he's only just beginning to understand. That she is, in the end, beyond reach. Does that make her any less hot? Will he ever stop this mad crusade to somehow possess her? Never.

Mahoney has abandoned the exercises now in favour of a session with the hand weights, bringing each up to her chest, a blur of movement. The muscles in her upper arms are in impressive shape and sweat is beading on her face again as she breaks off. A black guy has appeared, medium height, forty or older, not a pound overweight. He's wearing an unmarked black track top over a pair of baggy pants, also black. Mahoney gives him a long hug, and under his supervision Mahoney leaves the exercise mat and adds an extra weight to both ends of a barbell before test-hoisting the bar above her head. Back on the mat, she squats with the weights across her shoulders, then eases herself into the standing position.

'Again,' the black guy is plainly in charge now. The window is an inch or two open and Kane can hear the growl of his voice. This might be Tyrone, Kane thinks. Of Billy-Jean, Mahoney's regular female trainer, there's no sign.

Mahoney does his bidding, back to the squat, tense, rise, hold the weights, then down again.

'Again. Make it smoother. Feel the burn.'

Mahoney nods, beginning to visibly suffer but never giving in. Kane does this same routine himself and, watching her, he can feel the flood of hot lactic acid in his own thighs. Tyrone has gone but Mahoney carries on, her legs beginning to wobble, her gaze fixed on some infinite point where all sensation vanishes into a wilderness of pain. Then, quite suddenly, she steps forward, letting the weights crash to the mat behind her. The impact turns heads across the gym, and she acknowledges the applause with a weary lift of her hand.

Tyrone is back with a pair of lightweight sparring gloves. He waits for Mahoney to mop her face with a towel before lacing the gloves and accompanying her across to a black punchbag hanging from a hook in the roof. For Mahoney, if Kane is any judge, this will be the highlight of the evening's workout, the chance for her to focus what energy she has left on a single target.

She dances on the balls of her feet, loosing combinations of punches into thin air, circling an imagined opponent before closing on the punchbag and extending a gloved hand in mock greeting. This is a make-believe Dolores, Kane thinks, certain now that the black guy has to be her trainer.

By now the rain is beginning to ease a little. Kane can feel trickles of water down his back and chest but his concentration on Mahoney is total. To date, he's had to rely on Gus and Mahoney herself for word on what the world of boxing has to offer, but the solo performance playing out in front of him is for real.

Mahoney is hard at work now, flurry after flurry of blows, first at head height, then lower body shots, intricate combinations scored by the watcher in black. Tyrone is acting as the conductor of this one-woman orchestra, calling changes in pace and rhythm, urging for more attention, more precision, to Mahoney's left hook, trying all the time to maximise the impact of all that exercise. Mahoney does his bidding and seems totally at ease with him, acknowledging his advice with a nod of her head or a brief grin before unleashing another volley of blows that make the punchbag shiver. For the first time, Kane understands Mahoney's choice of ring name. Flo perfectly captures the way she fights, one sustained moment of violence folding seamlessly into the next. Not Flo, but Flow.

Tyrone has a watch in his hand and is timing Mahoney out. Four three-minute sessions, Kane thinks. Just like the real thing.

Finally comes another sweaty hug and the session is over. Mahoney grabs a towel and mops her face again before heading for the open window and a lungful of fresh air. This is Kane's cue to leave and he steps deeper into the darkness, oddly content with his night's work. Yet another glimpse of the woman he loves.

Back at the car, he slips behind the wheel, aware at once of movement in the neighbouring Mercedes. The guy is wearing a dark suit and is smoking what looks like a thin cigar. He looks across and acknowledges Kane's presence before opening the driver's door and stepping out into the thin drizzle. Then, uninvited, he's making himself comfortable in Kane's passenger seat.

'Something I can do for you?' Kane enquires.

The stranger says nothing for a moment, then expels a thin plume of blue smoke and nods at the view through the windscreen.

'Pretty wet out there, yeah?'

'Sure.' Kane has seen this face before.

'So why not watch all that action from inside? Why hide away in the dark like that?'

'You were out there, too?'

'I was. No booze in the gym. No smoking, either. Mind me asking a question?' Kane shrugs. Go ahead. 'You some guy from Dolores' neck of the woods? Checking out the opposition?'

'I might be.'

'And?'

'Your girl's good.'

'She's exceptional. You want to earn yourself a few extra clams, *amigo*? Fifty at odds you won't believe.' He reaches into his inside pocket and offers Kane a card. 'Any time, buddy, day or night. The longer you leave the call, the worse the odds. You follow what I'm saying?'

The conversation is over. The stranger gets out of the car and heads for the gym. Kane waits until he's gone, then puts on the vanity light to examine the card. José Cuesta. The mobbed-up Mexican, and now Mahoney's agent.

15

Kane phones Gus the following morning. He's in a diner three blocks down from 115, having just ordered breakfast. Still no word from Donovan.

'You're telling me you met Cuesta?' Gus barks.

'Yep.'

'Where?'

Kane won't say, not at first, doing his best to sidestep a flurry of questions. Gus is good at this, always has been, offering plausible suggestions designed to trap him in a lie. He'd gotten an address from somewhere? Shown up out of the blue? Or maybe he'd hung out by the Dolores fight venue hoping the guy might make an appearance?

Weary of this game, and running out of dimes, Kane owns up to following Mahoney to the Santa Monica gym.

'She saw you? You've met? You're back in touch?'

'No way.'

'What?' He appears to be astonished. 'You're telling me you staked her out? Took a covert peek at what she's up to? Who she might be seeing? *Hombre*, that's way beyond bad manners, that's flat-out irregular. In fact it's goddam creepy. Juice you any? Get you hot?'

Kane tries to ignore the tidal wave of insults. Gus doesn't believe in innuendo, mainly because he doesn't have to.

They've been reading each other for years, they're word-perfect on every shared chapter of their lives together, but now there's someone else in the room and everything's changed. Gus was never on first-name terms with forgiveness, but this is the first time Kane's been on the receiving end.

'This is about Donovan, isn't it,' Kane says heavily.

'Of course it's about Donovan. That man will be the end of you. You heard it here first and that saddens me, *hombre*, because you should have maybe looked a little harder at the man when you first met. *Caveat emptor*. It worked for the Romans, buddy, and nothing's changed since.'

Caveat emptor. Buyer beware.

'OK, let's say you've got a point, let's say Donovan's leading me astray. "The end of me" sounds terminal. Living at 115, you get a feel for lives hitting the buffers. The place is a train wreck and I'm not talking about the wallpaper. So how come you chose it?'

'I didn't, *hombre*. Donovan did. I got a message from DC. I assumed it was from the Treasury guys. 115. No name attached. Now I figure it had to come from Donovan and that's barely charge one on the fucking sheet. I'd love to tell you he's got your best interests at heart but one of those scary rules I try and keep is never to screw folks who matter to me. That included you.'

'Past tense?'

'Nothing's immutable, buddy. Everything can change and we both know it. But you've got to get your head out of that steamed-up ass of yours. Take a look around. Go figure.'

'Go figure what?'

'Just where he's taking you. And why.'

Kane drops his last dime in the slot and signals the woman cooking his breakfast for more. She wipes her hands, opens the till and gives him change.

'You want that I wait the eggs?' she asks.

Kane nods. Ignoring Gus's last, he's just enquired how Donovan knew about 115.

'Christ knows.' Gus sounds angry now. 'Maybe he was a bum himself one time. Maybe he lived there. Maybe he found God and hauled himself all the way from here to DC. That town of yours is full of hucksters. Put "politician" in your passport and you're halfway to damnation no matter how many prayers you say.'

'You think Donovan's on the take? You think he's off the reservation?'

'It's worse than that, buddy, way worse. I think he's incompetent. I think he's feathered a little nest for himself over there in DC, and given it a fancy name, and clawed his way up FDR's ass. Guys like him are operators. They pretend knowledge they haven't got. Guys in authority, people like FDR, are kids when it comes to the spook world. They take the goods at face value and never bother to check them out. Why? Because it's all so secret. No one must know. No one must hear even a whisper. That buys them cover. They become unaccountable. They can do whatever they want, which is a lovely place to be, not just from FDR's point of view but from Donovan's, as well.'

'OK.' Kane is following the logic. 'So Donovan's incompetent. 115 was a bad idea. What happens next?'

'You should expect him to come back to you. I've talked to the guy, remember. I know he's trying to keep you in line because he practically told me so. When it comes to tactics, he's crude as hell. He's betting you're as obsessed by glory as he is. So first off you need to give yourself a fighting chance.'

'I'm listening.'

'OK. Number one, get out of that rats' nest on Bunker Hill. I'll find you somewhere better, somewhere you can get a proper night's sleep, somewhere with a telephone, for God's sake.'

'When?'

'Now. Today. This afternoon, maybe. Donovan won't like it at all but you gotta realise he needs you a whole lot more than you need him. We were the guys who put Meier and his buddies away, remember. We were the guys with the inside track, and I still am when it comes to reading this town.'

'We? You want in on this? Co-shares?'

'I want that you don't end up as dog meat. Cuesta has a neat little trick that features a power saw and lots of brown paper bags that end up in trash cans around town. He's done his apprenticeship. He's plenty practised. By the time he fires up the saw you're calling for your mother because he operates mob-handed and not even you can get the better of those odds. It doesn't have to be that way, *hombre*. Just pay me a little more attention.'

Kane nods, feeds the first of his reserve dimes into the slot. In the interrogation room, Gus always knew how to command attention and nothing's changed.

'Tell me about Cuesta,' Kane says. 'Start with the Mercedes.'

'That fucking showboat limo? It's exactly the same model that Hitler uses. The roof folds back. You can stand up and listen to the acclamation of the masses. Big phrase, *hombre*, but it matters in certain quarters. A Jew producer, someone big in MGM, bought it in Germany and had it shipped over. It must have cost him a fortune but I'm guessing it was his way of telling the fascists that money conquers all. Then Cuesta laid eyes on it and told himself he was owed. Had to have it. The provenance. The Hitler smell. Those fabulous running boards. So the producer guy, Manny Raab, named a silly price and Cuesta paid it and put the Merc in his own garage, drove it everywhere, played the gangster who knew a thing or two about style and the grand sweep of European fucking history. Only one problem. The Jew had screwed him for far too much money and other people knew it. That was a big fat mistake, and you know what happened next?'

'The power saw? The brown paper bags?'

'Sure, and then some. Cuesta had a party that night, intimate friends only, turned the whole thing into a movie shoot. Happens I've seen the fine cut. Revolting doesn't do it justice. Evil would come closer. Plus he laid a music track against the action, which I guess was an ironical nod to Hollywood. Good taste is maybe the issue here, *hombre*. Any guesses?'

'You mean the music?'

'I mean the music.'

'The "Horst-Wessel"?'

'Neat idea but no banana.' For the first time in the conversation Kane hears him laughing. 'Check out Fred Waring and his Pennsylvanians. You can catch it on Movietone News. Land of the free and home of the brave. Yep, the star-spangled fucking banner. We're all patriots now, pardner.'

On the phone, Gus's laughter dies. Then he's gone.

★

Pardner. Gus is at Kane's door in 115 three hours later. He brings with him a cable, high priority, despatched on the secure OSS line from DC.

'Donovan?' Kane enquires.

'The man himself.'

'You've read it?'

'Of course.'

'What does he say?'

'What do you think he says? Had a conversation with FDR. Roosevelt says he'll talk to Justice about Meier's two buddies, just to keep the record nice and tidy. That means the answer is yes, all three walk free. Home of the brave, baby.' Gus looks round. 'Must break your heart, leaving this shit hole.'

They drive in convoy to a big colonial-style house in Beverly Hills. From the road, Kane can see white pillars framed by a frieze of tall evergreen trees. The entrance to the drive is heavily secured, two men behind a new-looking iron gate. Kane watches them bending to Gus's car. They obviously know him, and when he gestures back towards the Ford Sedan, they nod and step away to let both vehicles through before shutting the gates behind them. In the world of LA according to Gus, this is woodsy swank. To Kane, already, it looks a whole lot closer to a fortress.

Kane follows Gus and parks on the hardstanding outside the house. The property is even bigger than Kane had thought, the stairs to the front double doors in deep shadow under the semi-circular portico. In one of the tall upstairs windows he catches a brief glimpse of a woman's face before she steps back.

'Here's the deal,' Gus has gotten into the front of the Sedan. 'The estate belongs to a lady who calls herself Prosper. Is that her real name? I doubt it. She's made a pile of money in skin flicks, largely by breaking all the rules. She's someone you'll never have met before. She comes out of Bumfuck, Oklahoma. She's seen more in her life than anyone in Hollywood could ever invent but most of it she never talks about. She was a suspect in a major tax fraud case with Treasury implications, which is how I met her. She keeps most of LA at arm's length and if you're asking the obvious question, I'd trust her with my life. Or even yours. A couple of hours ago she told me she might have space for Meier if he comes recommended, which will be useful because her kind of money buys the best security. She has a little suite of rooms with a lock on the main door connecting with the rest of the house which sounds exactly what we're after. Good luck, *hombre*. Sleep well. Keep notes. Phone me.'

Gus extends a hand across the front seats, pats Kane on the shoulder, opens the car door, leaves. Kane watches his ancient Chevvy disappear down the drive in a cloud of grey exhaust, then gets out of the Sedan to study the house. From this angle it's even bigger than he'd anticipated from the road, and his gaze drifts up the first floor, wondering exactly where Meier might find the security he'll be needing.

'Prosper?' The name sits uneasily on Kane's tongue as he fingers the bell on the big front door. The door takes a while to open but then Kane's looking at the woman he recognises from the upstairs window. She's tall, nearly as tall as he is. Her tan face is unlined, not a trace of makeup, and there's a hint of American Indian blood in the fall of jet-black hair and the high cast of her cheekbones. Her gaze is steady and she's not smiling. Forty? Maybe a year or two older? Kane can't be sure.

'You're buddies with Gus?' Deep voice, almost male.

'I am.'

'Then you're welcome.'

She holds the door open, steps aside, nods for him to come in. She's comfortable in a simple shift, belted at the waist, that belongs to a warmer season, and she wears silver toe rings on her bare feet, but what catches Kane's attention is the tattoo on her left wrist. He's looking at an 'S' shape, indigo and scarlet, and it takes him a moment to recognise the figure of a snake rearing up in preparation to strike. He thinks at once of Gus, and his cherished rhino viper.

'It's Cherokee. You like it?'

'Kinda.'

'You wanna see another one? A bunch, maybe?'

Kane shrugs. He's come here to move in, to take advantage of the kindness of a stranger, not to browse American Indian tattoos.

'You have bags?' She's looking beyond him at the Ford Sedan. 'Luggage? Possessions? Some kind of life?'

'I have a bag.'

Kane fetches the canvas duffel bag from the Sedan's back seat.

'That's all?'

'That's it. That's me.'

'Wonderful. I mean it.' She nods in obvious approval. 'And so rare, too. Gus told me you were different.' She looks him up and down. 'Welcome, Mr Kane.'

She leads him into the big hallway. The floor is polished marble. Trophy art hangs on the wall, huge American landscapes rendered and ribbed in layers of thick oil paint, mountains and rivers of frozen ice a blind man could appreciate beneath his fingertips.

Kane wants to touch it, asks whether she minds any.

'Go ahead.'

Kane extends a hand and then stands back from the canvas. This is a wide-screen study of the Rocky Mountains by Albert Bierstadt. The accompanying brass plate is telling him so. A raw chunk of America, he thinks. Set out from New England, head west for a new life, wake up with a view like this and you'd probably quit trying. Except that tens of thousands roused themselves every morning on the trail, drank cold coffee from the previous night's dregs, backed their horses or their oxen between the shafts of their wagons, clambered atop their family's meagre store of possessions, took a peek at the next mountain range and dared the landscape to break their will. This is Gus again, his favourite pioneer fantasy. Make it through the Adirondacks, across the Great Plains, and finally wrestle the Rockies to the mat, and you've flat earned the rest of your life.

'Gus tells me Oklahoma,' Kane murmurs, still gazing at the deft savagery of the brush strokes.

'Sure. You've been there?'

'Never had the pleasure. Born and raised?'

'Born, certainly. Raised never came easy.'

'Care to tell me why?' He turns to ask the question. He can feel the heat of her body beside him.

She studies Kane for a long moment and then nods at the door at the end of the hall. More to show him, more to see.

He follows her down the hall, past fresh glimpses of the American wilderness, and then through the door at the end.

This must be the grandest room in the house, and Kane at once scents the smell of death. Death by over-accumulation, death by clutter, death by the painstaking recreation of an age that has gone. This might be a movie set, carefully pieced together to mimic the heart of a French chateau. Heavy furniture, opulent, over-polished, oppressive. Not one but two chandeliers, hanging from the ornate ceiling. Falls of gathered damask at every window, ready – no doubt – for the evening blackout. A huge, gilt-framed mirror hanging over the giant mantelpiece.

The corner of the room furthest from the throw of light through the window is dominated by a grand piano. The gleaming top is propped open, sheet music readied on the stand.

'You play?'

'Never. Someone good, I listen.'

'But this is your doing? This room?'

Kane's question raises the ghost of a smile.

'Mine? No. Like you, I'm a guest.'

'In this house?'

'Sure, and maybe in this city. If you're wise you never stop moving. The house belonged to a very good friend. We buried him last year.'

'We?'

'His wife and me. His name was Manny Raab. Afterwards, in December, Esther made her way to Israel. Once he'd gone, she'd lost everything. None of this mattered any more.' She gestures round at more fine art on the walls, at the cabinets showcasing porcelain and glass, at the eyeless head sculpted in white marble. 'Jerusalem on Christmas Eve? What better time to arrive, Mr Kane.'

'Quincy.'

'Quincy.'

'So you own this place now? Is that what you're saying?'

'I own nothing. The place exists. It has a life of its own, but only just. Everything Manny brought, everything he collected, was a boast. This is a Hollywood set. His wife spent Manny's money and got fatter by the day. I looked after the rest of him.'

Kane nods. 'Oklahoma,' he says. 'Tell me more.'

'I was a kid. My father died, and my mother also, and I ended up with a bunch of cousins and an uncle who had a farm, ran cattle, grew stuff, but then the money ran out and the weather changed and the dust and the soil kept blowing away. Hot summers out west we licked our own sweat and stank like mules and then one night there was a bang and it was all over.'

'Some kind of accident?'

'A shotgun. My uncle took his life. I was fifteen by then, half-girl, but mainly woman. I had Indian friends, Cherokee. I asked them to look after me, take me in.'

'So how did that work?'

'I was a kept woman. The tribe liked me, protected me, shared me.' Her fingers find the tattoo. 'You want to see the rest? Take a shower maybe? See where this conversation leads next?'

Kane smiles, shakes his head, says no. She touches him lightly on the arm, no offence.

'There's someone else in your life?' she asks.

'There is.'

'You're married?'

'No.'

'Lucky woman. Care to see what you're missing?'

The shift is buttoned loosely at the top. Within seconds she's naked, studying herself and Kane in the mirror over the mantelpiece. She has the body of a woman half her age, full breasts, flat belly, legs that descend forever, and it's hard to find a square inch of flesh that hasn't been tattooed. Her long fingers drift from motif to motif, and most of them to Kane look American Indian. Ancestor references, Kane thinks, tepees, warriors on horseback, the shapes of birds and bison, a living diary of indelible memories and keepsakes in indigo and burned ash brightened, she explains, with the essence of various herbs, an entire history that will be with her forever as her body slowly ages.

'You're sure, Mr Quincy?' Her right hand has tracked south across her belly. She eases her legs apart and begins to finger herself, reflective, at peace, beyond reach.

Kane watches her every move. This is an act, a performance, and they both know it. She must have done it hundreds of times before, in front of countless men, and the luckless owner of this tomb was probably one of them. It has taken a while, far longer than it should, but Kane is – at last – beginning to figure the latest episode of this woman's story.

'The guy that owned this house worked for MGM?'

'He did. Manny was a nice guy.'

'Big executive?'

'Yes.'

'And a friend of yours? Or maybe a client?'

'Both. I kept a little fuck-pad in Hollywood. Five-minute drive from MGM.'

'And?'

'We met regularly. I gave him what he wanted, as often as

he wanted. There were other clients, too. Rich men. Men of power. Different tastes. Different action. Manny was a Boy Scout compared to some.'

'He drove a Mercedes? Imported from Germany?'

'Sure.'

'And that car got him killed. Am I right?'

'Yes. He wanted too much for it. That was his only weakness.'

'Greed?'

'Miscalculation. He sold it to a guy called Cuesta. That man's no Boy Scout, believe me. Manny never saw that. He screwed him for too many dollars and paid the price.'

'Like Cuesta killed him?' Kane suggests. 'Chopped him up?'

'You know that already?'

'I do.'

'Gus told you?'

'He did.'

She nods, evidently surprised by the extent of Kane's knowledge, and then picks up her shift.

'Cuesta got the Mercedes,' she murmurs. 'He wants the house next but Gus has other ideas. He's another guy who says no,' she gestures at her still-naked body. 'Which makes you both very unusual.'

16

It's dark by the time Kane catches up with Gus. He finds him at home. Back when Kane was working alongside him at the LA field office, they had a code for when matters were getting out of hand. Four raps on his door signalled urgent. Tonight, Kane makes it five.

'Something up?' Gus is wearing a towel round his waist in the open doorway. Apart from that, on a chilly evening, he's buck-naked.

'We need to talk.'

Gus takes a second look at his face, tells him to wait a coupla minutes. Kane hears voices, the beginnings of an argument, then he's looking at a woman in a fur coat and high heels who can't wait to leave. She pushes past him in a cloud of expensive scent and clatters down the stairs without a backward glance.

'Shame,' Gus has thrown on a pair of track bottoms and a heavy sweater. 'So what's so fucking important?'

Kane wants to know about the woman with the tattoos, about the dead owner of his new lodgings, and about exactly when he might expect Cuesta at the door. He very seldom allows anger into his life but tonight is different.

'He's spooking you? Our Mexican friend?'

'Not at all. I just want to know where I belong in this script. Nothing happens by chance in this life of yours, my friend, so tell me about Prosper. Her real name might be a useful place to start.'

'It's Keaton. Her mom had a thing about how moody Buster could be. Changed her name after watching some of his early movies.'

'Christian name?'

'Babs.'

'And Oklahoma?'

'Totally kosher. Parents dead. Adopted by an uncle. Ended up with the Cherokee. She told me recently it was a homecoming. You've taken a good look at her? The face? The cheekbones? The hair? She thinks her real father was off the reservation, bummed a life in the city, made good. It may be true. It may not. Either way she weathered the bad times with the folk who knew best how to cope. Shit weather and no food was how most Indians started out. Happily they'd learned to live with it, generations back. These people have long memories. Either you make friends with want, and bad water, and all the rest of it, or life on the plains kills you. The Whities headed for the coast. The Cherokee stayed put, mainly because they had no choice, maybe even prospered. Leaving the farm was a smart decision on her part, *hombre*, and in my book it set her up for life. She'd signed up for the dreamcatcher thing. Deal with the bad guys during the night, and in the morning the world looks a whole lot better. Circle of life? She tell you about that?'

Kane nods. He's heard of the dreamcatcher, the feathered disk you hang above a bed to capture evil spirits, and now he remembers how often this same motif recurred among this woman's many tattoos.

'The circle and the feathers are everywhere,' he says. 'On her breasts, especially.'

'She showed you?'

'She did.'

'And the red hands across her belly? Like the lousy palm ID you have to do again and again?'

'You got it.'

'And she explained about the hands? What they've done for her? Why they're there?'

'No.'

'Easy, *hombre*. The dreamcatcher keeps her safe. The hands keep her childless. No babies. Not ever. No matter how many men she screws.'

'Right,' Kane nods again. 'So why Hollywood? After the reservation?'

'Easy pickings, *hombre*. She came here to make money and it worked. She started in skin flicks, did wild stuff that took even this town by surprise, figured out she'd make more by cutting out all the slimebags who were taking a slice. That worked, too, though she needed protection.'

'So where did she find it?'

'Guy in the PD. Top guy. Almost the toppest guy. She's been screwing him every which way for years and still does. They're a very happy couple, though some of his tastes haven't helped him any. He loves it up the ass and she's happy to oblige.'

'How?'

'How?' Gus laughs, fetches a couple of beers. 'This is a woman with the world's biggest collection of dildos. Ask her nicely and I'm sure she'll show you. Her Indian friends taught her to hand-carve and polish, mainly cedar wood, and she learned good. The kicker here is the blessings they carry. She's great at Cherokee-style carvings, real artist, and women I know say they do the job every time. They tell me they come like an express train and feel great the rest of the day.'

'And the LAPD guy?'

'He gets it up the ass. She does strap-ons, works out a lot, great abs. The abs are apparently the key. Perfect control. Big finish. Wild applause. You getting the picture here, *hombre*? About your new friend? One foot planted in the spirit world? The rest of her making so much money she sends most of it back home?'

'Back home?'

'To the reservation. She calls them her people, and why the hell not?'

Kane takes a mouthful of beer. He's thinking about Cuesta again.

'This movie,' Kane says. 'The one where the guy gets sawn up.'

'Manny Raab?'

'Sure. The movie exists. Cuesta has to be in it. That suggests evidence to me. So how come no cop's turned up to arrest him?'

'Great question, *hombre*. This is Prosper again. She has a fuck-pad, like everyone else in this town, and that's where she services the PD guy. She also called in a coupla favours and had a movie camera installed next door, specially blimped, doesn't make a sound. A lot of the movies feature the PD honcho and she tells me her Cherokee friends love them. A white guy getting screwed up the ass by one of their own? The Injuns celebrate big time, crack another quart of bourbon, dance on hot stones, all sorts, but that's not the point.'

'Of course it's not. The point is Cuesta.'

'And?' Gus wants Kane to do the work here.

'My guess is she's sold him the PD footage for a lot of money. One way or another, our top cop will know that. The footage is Cuesta's insurance against arrest. Big time.'

'And that's why they won't move against him? On the Manny Raab job?'

'Exactly. And you want to know how much she screwed out of Cuesta for the footage? Before he chopped the guy up? Half a million dollars, but it won't end there, *hombre*, because Cuesta hates being taken for a sum like that. Hurts his pride. Gets him talked about for the wrong reasons. Same with Manny Raab and that silly auto. Cuesta takes stuff like that personally and it might have paid Prosper to think about the consequences.'

'Like...?'

'Like it's Manny and the Mercedes all over again. This time Cuesta wants the house. He calls it payment in full. Happens that the two sums kinda level out. Four hundred thousand for the property plus more scoots for the contents, against the half mill he's already paid Prosper for the fuck-pad footage.'

'But who owns the property? Has to be the wife, the widow, doesn't it? Esther? Or are you telling me different?'

'Esther's in line for most else of what he had. Stocks, investments, a fat slice of various movies, lotsa other properties.'

'And Beverly Hills? That house of Manny Raab's?'

'He gifted it to Prosper. Services rendered.'

'She told me otherwise. Said she travels light, owns nothing.'

'That's true because most of it goes back to her Cherokee brothers and sisters. But she showed me the deeds to the house one time and her name was on the line that mattered.'

'Right,' Kane nods, determined to wrestle the last piece of this jigsaw into place. 'So tell me something I don't quite figure. How come Cuesta's got under your skin? What is it about the guy's worth all this trouble?'

'Aside from being a scumbag piece of shit, you mean?'

'Yeah.'

'And a two-bit sadist?'

'Yeah.'

'With a taste for watching other people die?'

'Yeah.'

'Simple, *hombre*. Because he's desperate to fuck your Mahoney. And she keeps telling him no.'

17

My Mahoney. Kane is in bed but emphatically not asleep. Prosper has given him a perch in the first-floor corner of the mansion assigned to Meier. It has two bedrooms, a shared bathroom, a tiny kitchenette, and a sitting area Kane has earmarked as a joint working space for both of them. It has a view of the garden, plenty of space for a drawing board, plus a telephone and – as promised – a lock on the connecting door to the rest of the property.

In every respect this suite of rooms is perfect for a spot of freelance counterfeiting and tomorrow Kane will make contact with Meier and tell him where to come. By then he'll have badgered Donovan for a modest budget to furnish whatever Meier needs in the way of specialist equipment for the all-important engraving process.

But for now Kane has to contend with Cuesta. He's met the man in person for no more than a couple of minutes, but that's hardly the point. Gus has given him all the evidence he'll ever need that the man is a nightmare. For now, he has to assume that Cuesta knows nothing about his link to Mahoney. He'll have talked to Tyrone, the black trainer, he'll know that Kane's presence in the enemy camp is a fiction, but with luck he'll assume his presence in the darkness outside the gym was down to a sad man taking a peek at goods he'll never be able to afford. Look, don't touch. Save up the images for later.

Kane shakes his head on the pillow. Time, he knows, isn't on his side. The Dolores fight is barely days away. In situations like these, his instinct has always favoured the front foot, and he remembers a saying that his grandfather once taught him. The quote comes from Napoleon: *On s'engage, et puis l'on voit*. Give the enemy a shake and see what happens. Might this be wise? Or should he be plotting something a little more subtle?

He drifts into sleep, the questions unanswered. Aware of Cuesta's interest in the house, he's taken the precaution of parking his car around the back of the property. Should Cuesta pay a visit, the Sedan he'd seen in the gym car park will be invisible. Beyond that, for now, he can do no more.

Next morning, early, he telephones Donovan, knowing calls to his office line are rerouted to his home phone. It's still dark in DC, barely five in the morning, and Donovan is pissed to be woken up. He has difficulty grasping why Kane has abandoned 115 but Kane invents an altercation with one of his neighbours, a fight that left the guy unconscious on the stairs, and then presses for the release of funds. Donovan, still groggy, wants more detail but finally tells Kane to extract whatever he needs from the Secret Service field office on the assurance of repayment from DC. In every respect, it's a beautiful outcome, and Kane spares a nod to Napoleon. Give the enemy a shake, he thinks. And look for the right opportunities.

He's kept Cuesta's card, waits until the start of the LA

business day. Downstairs in the huge kitchen, Prosper is gazing at a half-empty cup of coffee and nods wordlessly at the pot on the stove. To Kane's relief, he's spared both tattoos and conversation and returns upstairs with the coffee before lifting the phone and dialling the number on Cuesta's card.

'*Si?*' Cuesta answers after the second ring.

'I've been thinking about laying a few clams on that fighter of yours.'

'And you, my friend, are who?'

Kane offers yet another false name – Steve Kennedy – and reminds Cuesta of their brief meeting in the gym car park. There follows a lengthy silence before Cuesta returns to the phone. He apologises for the interruption, blames someone at his office door. Kane knows it's a lie.

'You remember me?'

'I do, my friend. Shit little Ford. You're telling me you've got the money to place a bet?'

Kane says yes. Reminds Cuesta of give-away odds. Cuesta laughs, offers Kane an address.

'Come over,' he says. 'Let's talk it out.'

Talk what out? Cuesta has hung up. Kane checks his watch. A quarter after nine. Every rule in the book tells him to be careful, to phone Gus, to seek back-up. Instead, he gets to his feet and heads for the door. He has thirty dollars in his pocket. More than enough.

The address, which Kane had been half expecting, is Hegarty Autos, the venue for Wednesday's fight. He follows Gus's directions across town and parks a block away. Hegarty Autos is a single-storey building, white render over brick, with big metal-framed windows, all of them screened by interior blinds against the low morning sun. Once, Kane suspects, the space out front would have been home to a fleet of cars for sale. Now a single Mercedes is parked beside the building's entrance, the roof retracted.

Kane pauses briefly beside the car. The sleek polished metal is already warm to his touch and he stares down at the leather seats, the perfect stitching, the promise of 120 mph on the speedo recessed into the dash. He's trying to imagine Mahoney in the car, hoping she'd be under-impressed by the coarseness of a trophy like this, new money on old wheels.

'Kennedy?' Cuesta has appeared from nowhere. No Mister. No courtesy. No respect. He's wearing his undertaker suit and doesn't bother to offer a handshake. Instead he nods at the entrance door, now open.

'Go ahead,' he says. 'You know how to count? Third door on the left.' Kane ignores the invitation. 'You hear what I said?'

'Sure.'

'You want that we talk here?'

'Why not?'

Cuesta is looking round.

'You walked, buddy? Took a trolly?'

'There are no trollies. I took a cab.' Kane nods at the building. 'This is where the fight happens?'

'Yeah.'

'Care to show me?'

Cuesta studies him for a long moment. He wants to say no but something in his eyes suggests that Kane has caught his interest.

'You still want that bet?'

'Sure. At the right odds.'

'And you're coming Wednesday?'

'Of course.'

'You've got a ticket?'

'No. That's something else we need to talk about.'

Cuesta nods, says nothing. Then he's leading the way round the building. Towards the back is an access bay to the rear of the building. A gaudy placard in faux brass – the Downtown Arena – is a mere gesture to extending a proper welcome, thinks Kane. It still looks like the entrance to a garage.

Cuesta has stepped into the gloom of a bigger space than Kane had been expecting. The smell of engine oil and rubber still hangs in the air. Cuesta reaches for a wall switch and the space is suddenly bathed in a hazy white light. Kane is looking at a raised square platform in the middle of dozens of round tables. Cuesta flicks another switch. The white light dims to be replaced by three spotlights, harsh, unforgiving, that settle on the platform's bare canvas.

Kane is looking hard at the canvas. In the closest corner he can see an irregular patch of staining.

'What's that?'

'Blood.'

'This is the boxing ring?'

'Yeah. Weekends we run all kinds of entertainment. No need for ropes. They'll be back for Wednesday.'

Kane wants to know more. Entertainment?

'All sorts, my friend. Magic shows for the kids. Music. Decent crooners. Late-night adult stuff. Vic Hegarty used to think the money was in autos but he was wrong. Keeping people happy is bigger bucks.'

Kane nods, says nothing. Mahoney won't leave him alone. First the Mercedes, now this sad arena. He's counting the tables. He makes it thirty-one, with six seats at each table.

'Tell me about Wednesday,' he asks. 'How many do you expect?'

'Six hundred. Minimum.'

'So where do they sit?'

'Come Monday we're building bleachers in back, over there, all round.' Kane follows the vagueness of his gestures. 'Think atmosphere. Think excitement. We're gonna pump up the evening and sell it hard. You're serious about getting a ticket, now's the time to say. Those two women are the hottest item in town.'

'How much? For the ticket?'

For the first time, Cuesta permits himself the ghost of a smile.

'For you? Twenty dollars. And that's a steal, believe me.'

'Twenty dollars is what I'm putting on the fight. And twenty dollars is all I've got. You're giving me odds, here?'

'2/1 Dolores wins. 5/1 Mahoney goes the distance. 10/1 she wins. 40/1 she wins by a knockout.'

'You don't think she'll make it?'

'You've seen her. You've watched her. What do you think?'

'I think she's great. But punch bags don't fight back.'

'Exactly, my friend. This is a tough game. Dolores is a pro, takes no fucking prisoners. If that Roosevelt had a brain in his head he'd put her in uniform and point her at the Japs. You wanna get rich? Give me your twenty clams on a Mahoney knockout. It might just happen. I've seen crazier things in this town.'

'Sure. And the ticket?'

'If she puts the black girl down, I'll take it out of your winnings. If she doesn't, you owe me twenty bucks, plus fifteen per cent on the vig.'

Three dollars on the house commission? Kane nods, counts his wad, hands it over.

'I get a slip, here?' He's nodding at the stained canvas. 'Proof I laid the bet?'

'No, my friend. You trust me. All you have to do is turn up on the night and watch. Is that too much to ask?'

18

Kane meets Meier next day outside the Amtrak station in Little Tokyo. The one-time convict's ridden the Greyhound from Bakersfield, and freedom – he tells Kane – is going to be the taste of stir-fried glass noodles.

'*Pad woon sen*?' Mahoney, who's a great fan of Thai food, has shared her passion for this dish with Kane.

'You got it, Mr Kane. In Korea they call it *japchae* but it's great in any language.'

They go to a little place Meier knows in Duccomun Street. He looks round as if he's never left, draws a handshake from the guy at the door, then a hug from a pretty Asiatic girl dispensing bottles of sake who asks him something in what Kane assumes is Japanese, and then bursts into laughter.

Afterwards, Meier heads for a vacant table.

'You speak Jap?' Kane asks.

'Yes.'

'And?'

'She asked me where I'd been. I told her. That's why she was laughing.'

'A twenty-year sentence is funny?'

'She asked about the food. I told her the cooks in the penitentiary are the baddest guys of all, deserve a life sentence.'

They settle into conversation. Kane wants to know what the world looks like after three years in the slammer.

'Noisy,' Meier says at once. 'And folks feel different.'

'Different how?'

'Different on the inside, I guess. They look worried, most of them. That's the clue. Guy and his wife on the Greyhound coming to LA had given up on Iowa, never had enough dough to farm, never had enough dough to put a chicken in the pot. I told him money never settled anything. When he said I was crazy I told him about all the money we made, all those beautiful notes, all the doors it opened, all the empty spaces the other side. That made for a conversation, believe me, but his wife never believed a word I said. By the time we got off, she thought I needed medication.'

Kane nods. His plan is to devote the rest of the day to setting Meier up in Beverly Hills and the good news is that Meier has drawn up a list of everything he'll need. Copper plates and acids, a range of pens, specialist expertise, infinitesimal attention to detail, and above all time.

'You know where to get this stuff?'

'I know who to ask. Just as long as they're still around. Most of them are buddies from the studio. You got wheels?'

'Sure.'

Kane is watching the pretty young waitress. Someone on the sidewalk outside has caught her attention, and already she's retreated behind the counter. Then the door opens and Kane is looking at an overweight guy in his twenties, jeans and a grease-stained jersey, savage haircut, three-day beard. It's early in the day to be drunk but his tiny eyes are bloodshot and he's having trouble making the counter in a straight line.

Meier, who scented trouble the moment the guy appeared, is already on his feet.

'Gotta help out here,' he nods at the Asian girl, and moves to intervene.

Heads turn at other tables. By now, Meier has put his skinny frame between the drunk and the counter. He tells the Asian girl not to worry. He says he's here to handle the guy. Then he looks up at the drunk, asks him to step away, suggests they maybe have a little talk, straighten one or two things out.

The drunk can't quite believe what's happening. He stares down at Meier, shakes his big head, then hunches a grubby fist and drives it into Meier's face. The force of the blow throws Meier across a neighbouring table. A woman screams and Kane, on his feet by now, watches the drunk as he lurches round the counter and heads for the kitchen out back. The Asian girl has disappeared through the same door.

'You OK, buddy?'

Meier's hand is cupping the remains of his nose. Blood everywhere.

'The girl,' he says thickly. 'Her name's Youko'

Kane nods, tosses Meier a handkerchief, makes for the door behind the counter. The heat of the kitchen hits him first. Through the steam he can make out the bulk of the drunk. He's confronting one of the cooks who has a kitchen knife while Youko has retreated to the big stove that dominates the kitchen. Pots of various sizes are bubbling on the stove. The girl looks terrified.

Kane takes the drunk from the back, locks a chokehold round his throat, whispers in his ear, tells him to take it easy. The cook is grinning now, watching the drunk trying to tear himself free, then Kane catches the girl's eye, nods at the biggest of the pots, motions for the cook to stand aside.

For a second, the girl looks puzzled, then the drunk starts struggling again and tries to make a lunge towards her, and she reaches for a spatula, and scoops a helping of noodles from the boiling water, and Kane, his arm still locked, ducks as she throws the noodles into the drunk's face. Then comes a bellow of pain, laced with anger, and she does it a second time before he goes limp in Kane's arms.

For a moment, nothing happens. Kane lowers him to the floor. His flophouse stench fills the kitchen and he's clawing at the noodles on his face and then the door opens and Meier appears. One look at the drunk on the floor and he's talking to the Asian girl again. She fills a bowl with cold water, finds a towel, and gives them to Meier who kneels beside the drunk and begins to attend to his face.

One of Meier's hands is still cupping his own nose and from time to time drops of his blood splatter the drunk's ballooning face, but Meier's other hand is gentle and deft, swabbing away the curls of hot noodle, and Kane watches, shaking his head in wonderment.

A Quaker on the front line, he tells himself. What a way to go to war.

19

Prosper makes Meier very welcome indeed. One look at his busted nose and she disappears to conjure a herbal poultice which she moulds around the worst of the damage. Cherokee medicine, she tells Meier as the nose starts to weep and more blood reddens her busy fingertips. By now, Kane has dismissed the incident at the noodle café as just another flutter in the racing pulse of LA life, some no-good juice hound taken prisoner by the bottle, but Meier has been talking to Youku and knows different.

'The guy's been following her everywhere,' he says. 'He's crazy about her. He steals flowers and makes her little bouquets. He's even named a tree after her. It's a eucalyptus. Apparently he's carved her name in it.'

'And Pearl Harbor?'

'Makes no difference. In fact, the guy came in last week to apologise.'

'For what?'

'He thinks the so-called raid is all pretend, made up, never happened. He told her this country of ours had begun to embarrass him. Plus he loves the food she serves.'

Kane nods. The image of Meier swabbing glass noodles off the love-struck bum's face will stay with him for a very long time. In the Sedan, returning to Beverly Hills, Meier had warned him about the perils of over-reaction. The guy may be scarred for life.

'Sure,' Kane had conceded. 'But maybe that's the whole point. One look in the mirror, he'll never do it again.'

'Do what?'

'Bust a stranger's nose. Terrify a waitress. Act like the bum he is.'

Meier had snorted with derision in the car and now Kane is watching more blood pink the seams of the poultice. Prosper appears with a pot of herbal tea. Kane says no but Meier sips at the tea and then wipes his mouth before taking the wreckage of his nose to his new quarters upstairs for a lie-down and maybe a nap. After lunch, he promises, they'll make it out to the Sunrise Studios to chase up old contacts. Given the state of his face, Kane has doubts, but Meier's store of surprises is bottomless and by mid-afternoon they're crossing the studio lot at Sunrise and climbing an iron staircase to Meier's old design office beside one of the two big sound stages. To Kane, these magicians are kids, barely out of college, but one of them studies the face behind the poultice and scribbles the address of a name Meier recognises.

'Ivan's still around?'

'Alive and kicking.'

'And doing what?'

'Pay him a visit. Beat on his door. You won't regret it. People find God in this town every day of the working week but how many turn him into serious money?'

Kane and Meier drive across town again. Ivan turns out to be an older man, lank, greying hair gathered into a ponytail, Hawaiian shirt patterned in sunrise shades of scarlet and yellow. Below the waist he wears a thin cotton *longyi*, knotted over the merest suggestion of a belly. He has a face scored for laughter and the sight of Meier at his open door prompts a long hug.

'You're telling me you escaped?' He's looking hard at the poultice. 'The disguise fooled them?'

The question delights Meier. He introduces Kane.

'This is Quincy, my new buddy. He beats up strangers for a living. He likes to call it street justice but he's kidding himself. Guys at the studio tell me you're making a fortune from the Bible. You've sold the film rights? Working on the sequel?'

Ivan laughs. Says he's turning the parables into cartoons for kids. Meier wants to see the evidence, but Ivan won't show him. He says the good news is that most Angelinos have a reading age of twelve and love cartoons. Huge market. Fat profits.

'Profits? Prophets?'

'You choose, buddy. Either way, it's money in the bank.'

Kane is looking round. Ivan's living room reminds him a little of Gus's place out at Venice Beach except there's no sign of a reptile tank. Mexican rugs on the floor, along with a scatter of fat old cushions that evidently serve as chairs. Low-level comfort, Kane thinks, conjured from the tightest of budgets.

'Meier's back in the counterfeit game,' he grunts. 'Ask him nicely, he'll show you his shopping list.'

'You've got money, you guys?'

'We've got a deadline. Maybe it's the same thing.'

'So how can I help here?'

Meier rattles through the items he needs. Ivan makes

himself a list, looks up, his eyes drifting from face to face, finally settling on Meier again.

'This is like last time? Singles? Fives? Tens? Maybe some twenties?'

'Bigger.'

'C-notes?' He's looking impressed.

'Bigger still.'

'Shit, man. You're missing the penitentiary already? Can't wait to get back?'

'Can't wait to please Mr Quincy here. I'm a man of peace, buddy. You guessed it all along and you guessed it right. But wars have their uses, as I'm starting to discover.'

Ivan scratches his belly and scowls.

'Someone got your back on this one?' Ivan turns to Kane. 'You're a peeper maybe?'

Some kind of PI? The thought amuses Kane. Mahoney had once asked him the same question: why didn't he quit working for the government and become a private investigator?

Kane shakes his head. Nice try.

'Some kind of cop, then? Working the odds? Playing both ends against the middle?'

'Nope.'

'But am I getting close? A yes is all I need. In this town, nothing is as solid and real as it looks. A guy I know loves the way we live. In fact he's writing a novel about it. Buildings? People? Trust? Cops? Everything's negotiable, everything has a price. So far he's done the first ten pages and he started a while ago, but like I told him last night he needs nothing but the title he's dreamed up. Care to take a guess?'

'Tell me.'

'The Big Flimsy. LA nailed to the floor in three words,

in four goddam syllables. I can see it on the shelf. The Big Flimsy. A must-read book for the beach. LA laid bare.'

'The place is getting to you?'

'Happened long ago. I love it here and that's the whole point, my friend, intact and entire. LA is an exercise in expectations. Lower the bar any further and we'll make like limbo dancers and be flat on our backs like a bunch of kids. Unless, of course, the war doesn't get to us first.' His eyes drift to his list. 'Gimme a couple of days, Meier, and maybe a number I can call.'

The next two days, LA flirts with an early version of spring. Women with Hollywood legs parade in beach shorts and every next car is suddenly a convertible. On Wednesday, Kane is due at the Dolores fight and devotes a little time to Meier. Prosper has parked him on the property's ample patio like a winter houseplant starved of sunshine and serves him with a variety of herbal teas until they settle on turmeric laced with something that tastes, to Kane, of old socks.

Kane is wary that his tame counterfeiter may be losing momentum, back in the excitement of LA. Home comforts, plus the sight of Prosper sprawled semi-naked on a blanket on the lawn beside the patio, are no friend of the painstaking work Kane knows must go into the thousand-dollar bill but he needn't have worried. Since picking up with Ivan, Meier has been working the telephone and both days see a succession of visitors turning up at the property delivering packages of various sizes. All of them are collected at the front gate by Meier himself, and as far as Kane knows, no money changes hands. Quite how Meier is working this latest trick remains a mystery but when Kane checks on the second evening, he finds him bent over the newly delivered drawing board.

'Direction of travel is all, Mr Quincy.' Meier nods at the board.

The sketch is in pencil, a faithful rendering of a photo of a thousand-dollar bill Meier has also acquired. The photo is taped to a corner of the drawing board and Kane takes a proper look at the progress Meier has made. The bold proclamation of unimaginable value trailing across the bottom of the note. The boxed figures – 1,000 – in both corners. The emerging face of President Grover Cleveland, the oval frame supported by laurel leaves, dead centre.

Meier's rendition is barely half complete, heavy grey shading here, lighter tones elsewhere. He's paid a great deal of attention to the US Treasury's intricate tango of lines and whorls, and already Kane can sense the strange magic of a piece of paper worth a thousand dollars emerging from the blankness of Meier's pad. In time, once complete, he must repeat exactly this same exercise, weave exactly this same magic on a sheet of copper, scribing the lines with an engraving pen, but the degree of concentration Meier is bringing to the image speaks for itself.

'You find it easy? Picking this stuff up again? Getting into every little detail?' Kane asks.

'I never stopped, Mr Quincy,' Meier is attending to Grover Cleveland's whiskers. 'In the pokey, any time day or night I might pick up a pen, see where it took me. Twenties were my favourite. Drove the turnkeys mad, all that money lying around.'

'And now?'

'Now is different. You want the truth? When you first

explained the deal, I thought it was bullshit. Spreading the love to the other two guys told me different. Now it's kind of addictive. If a man's looking to get better fast…' he briefly touches the end of his nose, '…he can do no better.'

20

Wednesday is Dolores Day. Wednesday, Kane senses, is the moment when he and Cuesta stop playing games with each other and declare their real interests. Wednesday will be the baying of the crowd and the clanging of the bell for the opening round. Lights down. Seconds out. Just the merciless throw of the three follow-spots from which there will be no escape. What's coming for Mahoney, thinks Kane, is also coming for me.

Bring it on.

Kane arrives early at Hegarty Autos. The temptation, as ever, is to pick up with Mahoney where they left off, to find the locker room, to put his head round the door, to tell her that he made the coast-to-coast flight with seconds to spare, that he's come to watch her win. But that, in this showboat town, is just another fairy tale.

Instead, he'd phoned her last night, listened to the tally of hard miles she and the dog had put in since their last conversation, agreed that the fight game was altogether brutal in ways unwise and maybe impossible to describe, and pledged that one day very soon would find them in a safer space. The latter thought, explored for a brief minute or two, had brought the conversation to an end, and when she said goodbye Kane had detected a catch in her voice he'd never heard before. Maybe, he told himself, Lou Mahoney has had a closer look at the recipe marked 'Showtime' and tossed it in the trash. Shame, he thought, and far, far too late.

The arena, even with forty-five minutes to go, is already packed. The premium tables around the forbidding square of canvas are still unoccupied because the sixty-dollar ask buys you the right to arrive late but the same rule doesn't apply to the bleachers. Tier after tier of plain wooden planking climbs up towards the ceiling of the garage, and bottles of Budweiser, sold by a small army of semi-clad girls, pass from hand to hand. These girls are also toting vinyl records for sale, the same face featured on cover after cover. A single glance confirms that this is none other than José Cuesta himself, and a brief conversation with one of the girls explains why.

'Guy's got a great voice,' she's giggling. 'You're telling me you've never heard him?'

'Never. Anything else on the bill? For afterwards?'

'Sure. There's a weird act with a couple of black dames and a live snake if you're in the mood. Otherwise, mister, I guess it's an early night.'

Indeed. Kane buys a beer and finds himself a space on the third tier, wedged between a fat old guy with mustard on his fingers and onions on his breath, and a younger woman who's already drunk. She tells Kane that her current squeeze hasn't turned up, cheating bastard that he is, and that she's glad for company. She has greedy eyes for Kane's beer but he's in no mood for either conversation or sharing. Not that his new pal pays any attention.

'You seen the white dame before?'

'Pardon me?'

'The white gal? Flo?'

'No.'

'They say she fights good. She's game, brave as hell. A bit of a looker, too. Tell me, why risk all that?'

'Dunno.'

'Care to guess?'

Kane shakes his head, looks around for somewhere else to sit, knows the quest is probably doomed.

'Money, maybe?' he suggests.

'Sure. Me? You'd have to pay in gold fucking bars and I mean that.' She offers Kane a vigorous nod, two chins and a third on the way. 'Don't get me wrong. Women fighting women is kinda weird, but it turns men on, women too. You married?'

'No.'

'Ever?'

'No.' Kane lifts the bottle to his lips, then hands it to the woman. 'The rest is for you. Keep the seat for me?'

He gets to his feet and makes his way past dozens of spectators, mainly men. All the spaces have gone but he spies a gap at the very top of the bleachers and clambers slowly upwards. The gap lies beside another woman. She looks Hispanic, proud face, dark eyes, stylish jacket, and she has a pair of opera glasses in her lap. When Kane pauses beside her she looks up at him, happy to make space on the rough wooden plank. As far as Kane can gather, she's also alone.

'Why boxing?' he asks. 'And why this fight?'

'Me?'

'You.'

She seems startled by the question and Kane apologises at once for the intrusion, only to find her hand on his arm.

'No problem,' she says. 'I guess it's a fair ask.'

'So?'

'I happen to be Spanish, and here and now that matters. Fighting, spectacle, it's in the blood. This is *corrida*,' she nods at the sea of bodies descending towards the ring. 'It's very crude, very noisy, but maybe hard to resist.'

'And two women?'

'Makes no difference. Back home in Spain I always thought women would make the best *matadoras*.'

'More graceful?'

'More instinctive, more subtle. Women understand pain. Men understand only death, and death can be the easy bit.' She extends a hand. 'Carlotta.'

'Quincy.'

'You bring any glasses, Quincy?'

'Afraid not.'

'Here.' She reaches for the clutch she's stowed between her feet, produces a second pair of glasses.

'You always carry two?'

'Sure. One for me. One for a good friend. His eyes are even worse than mine.' Her smile is luminous. 'Dolores or Flo?'

'Flo.'

'You've put a little money on the fight?' she asks.

'I have.'

'And?'

'Flo by a knockout.'

'You kidding me? You never saw the first fight?'

'I didn't. Help me out.'

'Flo's a novice. Moves well, knows how to mix the punches, but Dolores is another class.'

'That might change.'

'In a coupla months? That would be a miracle.'

A miracle. It's a fine word, perfect for Mahoney, and Kane stares down at the distant square of canvas for a moment, before turning to Carlotta again. Confession time, he thinks.

'I know this woman, I know her well, I know what she can do.' He nods, comforted by the thought. 'You know something?'

'Tell me.'

'Surprise is a gambling man's best friend.'

Cuesta appears in the ring shortly afterwards. From the top of the bleachers, he's a tiny figure in a tux. He has a microphone in his hand and he prowls the ring, moving from corner to corner, acknowledging waves from the tables that have now filled up. Then, on his cue, the music starts, brass and drums, fiercely martial, and then he puts the microphone to his lips like he's sipping a drink, and launches into 'The Battle Hymn of the Republic'.

The crowd are silent now, respectful, then one of the guys at a table down beside the ring motions his buddies to their feet, his other hand clasped flat to his chest, and there's a scraping of more chairs, as more bodies rise, not just around the ring but in the bleachers, too, and the reeking dankness of the one-time garage fills with hundreds of voices, all word-perfect.

'*Glory, glory, hallelujah...*'

If Cuesta is surprised by this sudden gale of patriotism, it doesn't show. Kane tracks him through the glasses as he moves easily in time to the onward march of the anthem, one hand for the microphone, the other conducting the crowd. He has a lightish voice but hits the notes without any seeming effort and he draws a roar of applause as he urges yet more volume for the big finish.

Then comes a stagey bow and a thank you for a list of sponsors that have made the evening happen. Kane recognises none of the names but knows it doesn't matter. This gaudy event, as it turns out, isn't about the rematch at all. It's about José Cuesta, LA's newest, biggest thing.

Carlotta is impressed. She nods down at the crowd, eager, vocal, bonded by the nation's favourite hymn.

'*Duende*,' she murmurs.

'*Duende*?'

'Passion. Spirit.' Her hand bunches into a tiny fist. 'Belief.'

Duende. A recorded blast of trumpets announces the arrival of the two fighters. In shorts and singlets, they follow an Amazonian starlet holding a placard as they make their way between the tables to the ring. The placard reads 'The Spirit of '42' and draws another roar from the crowd. White hands reach for the fighters as they close on the ring. Neither woman is smiling, neither acknowledge each other, and through the glasses Kane watches Mahoney as she mounts a pair of wooden steps and eases herself between the ropes before heading for her corner.

Waiting is a woman in a pink tracksuit who Kane assumes to be Billy-Jean, her trainer. Dolores, meanwhile, is on her toes in the other corner, jogging up and down, easing the tension in her shoulders and neck, listening to last-minute instructions from Tyrone. Once again, the two women have their backs to each other, alone in this cauldron of noise.

The referee calls them to the centre of the ring. He briefly checks the lacing on their gloves. Mahoney, Kane notes, has gone for scarlet while Dolores favours black. At last the two women are eye to eye, and Kane finds himself looking at a stranger.

The training, the anticipation, the event itself have plainly gotten to her. Like Dolores, she's on the move, easing left to right, half listening to whatever it is the referee has to say, holding the dead gaze of the woman she's come to beat. Alone is the word she uses more and more on the phone when she talks about the fight game, and for the first time Kane knows exactly what she means. Nothing can help her now. Nothing but effort and pain and more effort stand between her and the next twelve minutes.

Kane feels the lightest pressure on his arm. Carlotta. She, too, is watching through the glasses.

'*Mano a mano*,' she murmurs. 'Good luck to your friend.' *Mano a mano*. Hand to hand.

The referee has finished. The women retire to their corners. When the bell clangs, they advance to the middle of the ring again, exchange curt nods, briefly touch gloves, then begin to circle each other.

Mahoney lands the first blow, a looping left hook that grazes Dolores' temple. Kane last saw this opener in the gym at Santa Monica, Mahoney teaching the punchbag a lesson or two, but Dolores – as calm and watchful as ever – merely shrugs it off. Then, abruptly, the two women are toe to toe, Dolores planting a combination of body shots, using her momentum to crowd Mahoney into a neutral corner.

Kane swings the glasses right, beyond the bright cage of the ring, to focus briefly on the eager upturned faces in the shadows. One guy is smoking a big cigar, the other has his arm round his trophy starlet, and by the time Kane is back with the action Mahoney has somehow danced free.

'Good,' Carlotta is saying. 'Much better than last time.'

This, to Kane, offers a little comfort but Dolores has

taken the measure of her opponent, recognised where the training has made a difference, and adjusted her game plan accordingly. This time there's no role for the neutral corner. Instead, she half drops her guard, and beckons Mahoney closer. Mahoney falters, confused maybe, and that split second is enough for Dolores to step inside and land three shots in a blur of leather, two of them to Mahoney's face.

Through the glasses, Kane can see pain, and then just a hint of panic as Mahoney slips the fourth shot and tries to counter, but Dolores is already out of range, her eyes narrowed above her gloves, trying to assess the damage she's done. In she comes again, closing the gap with a series of left-hand jabs. Mahoney rides them on her gloves and upper arms but already Kane can see swelling around her left eye. Then comes a left hook from Dolores, followed by an uppercut that drives clean through Mahoney's guard and leaves her open-mouthed, desperate to suck in air.

The crowd are on their feet. They know she's in trouble. They want her to hang in there, to fight back, to march to the fife and the drum, to shout hallelujah and teach the uppity black dame a thing or two, and Mahoney nods, ups her rhythm, starts dancing again, acknowledging the roar of the crowd with a tiny shiver of a raised fist.

This time it's Dolores' turn to hesitate, and Mahoney steps inside, turning a fight into a brawl, slamming hard at whatever she can reach, face, upper body, anywhere. This is what the crowd have paid for, this is what Cuesta has promised them, raw violence, woman on woman, hand to hand. And so the first round continues, both women fighting for breath, trading blows, feeling nothing but the raw bite of adrenalin, an excitement shared across the bleachers.

Then, out of nowhere, comes the bell and the women slow before stopping, glancing across at the referee as if robbed.

'*Ay, caramba!*' Carlotta sits back against the roughness of the garage wall. 'This is war.'

She's right. Kane has his glasses trained on Mahoney's corner. Billy-Jean, bent over her charge, blocks most of the view but brief glimpses of Mahoney reveal a sponge pressed to her left eye and a series of nods as she takes in fresh instructions. Kane guesses that a wise trainer will tell Mahoney to cool it, to slow the pace, to leave time and space to get back to proper boxing. Wrong on all counts.

The bell brings both boxers out for the second round. Dolores looks fresh, untroubled. She even has the beginnings of a smile on her face as if she knows something her opponent doesn't. This is catnip for Mahoney. On this night of all nights, Kane senses that she's not putting up with any shit, any hint of disrespect, and so in she goes again, a maddened, crazy Ferris wheel of a woman, riding high on the baying of the crowd, throwing all caution to the wind, landing blows wherever she can. A couple of them, probably lucky shots, draw blinks of surprise from Dolores, and one in particular – towards the end of the round – stops her dead for long enough for Mahoney to land another left hook on the point of her jaw.

The bell goes again. By now the two women are entangled, a pact of mutual exhaustion, and the referee has to physically separate them before despatching them to their respective corners.

'Some woman, your friend.' Carlotta again, nodding down at Mahoney's corner.

Kane knows she means it as a compliment but this time he has the glasses trained on Dolores. Tyrone, her trainer, has his face inches from hers. He keeps nodding back in the direction of Mahoney. Dolores has also sustained damage around her eyes and Tyrone smears Vaseline on a tiny cut. Then he reaches for some kind of nasal spray and gives her a short burst up both nostrils. Dolores blinks, lifts a glove to wipe her face, nods at a fresh volley of instructions, and gets to her feet for the final round.

Another touch of glove on glove, then the tempo drops briefly, exploratory jabs from both women, before Dolores frowns, and lifts a glove briefly to her face before sidestepping a fresh onslaught from Mahoney. The crowd are on their feet again, willing an end to the fight, sensing something wrong with the black girl, wanting Mahoney to step in for the kill. Tuned in to the building crescendo of noise, Mahoney does their bidding.

By now, Dolores has come to a halt. Her gloves are down and she seems to have lost her bearings, and Mahoney closes the distance between them, awaits the perfect moment, and then unleashes a torrent of violence that makes even Kane flinch. Blows to Dolores' unprotected face, a left hook, a stabbing right jab, another left, and finally a vicious uppercut. Dolores' unprotected head snaps backwards, her legs buckle, and the fight is over.

Mahoney stares down at her body as if she doesn't quite believe the evidence sprawled on the canvas. Then her hands go up, a Roman gesture of triumph, and she starts to circle the ring, bathed in the breaking waves of raucous glee that wash down from the bleachers. The richer guys, meanwhile, are on their feet. Some are punching the air. Others simply applaud.

Some of them are reaching for their wallets, awaiting the moment when this white goddess brushes past them on her way back to the locker room.

Kane is watching Tyrone bringing Dolores to her feet. Walking unaided appears to be beyond her, and so Tyrone half carries her to the waiting stool. At this point Mahoney crosses the ring for a consolatory word, but Dolores simply gazes up at her, as if she doesn't know the hell who she is. Mahoney stares down, shakes her head, returns to the waiting referee. By now, Cuesta is back in the ring, his microphone trailing a black lead. Ignoring the drama in Dolores' corner, he announces Mahoney as the undisputed winner by a knockout. Moments later, the referee raises Mahoney's ungloved hand and the arena erupts.

'Phoney,' Carlotta says, shaking her head. Kane, disgusted, can only agree.

Book Three

21

Two days later Kane is still looking, without success, for Cuesta. In the meantime, he's been trying to contact Mahoney, but Virgil says she's flown to DC for another meet with the nation's First Lady.

'How's the eye?'

Virgil says he hasn't a clue. Never met Eleanor Roosevelt in his life.

'I meant Lou.'

'You were at the fight?'

'I was.'

'She knows that?'

'No.'

'You want that I tell her?'

'No. When's she back?'

'No idea, *hombre*. Not long. Could be the weekend.'

'OK,' Kane pauses. 'I never phoned. We never talked. You OK with that?'

Saturday morning, Kane at last finds Cuesta at his office. In three busy days, he's become the toast of the town. Even the *LA Times* has run an item on Wednesday's fight.

'Missed the big fucking headline, though.' Cuesta is sitting behind an enormous wooden desk, mahogany with all the trimmings, inlaid on the top with slightly scuffed leather in a pleasing shade of dark green. The *LA Times* story lies open in front of him, complete with a photo of the proud impresario with the two fighters.

'So what did they miss?'

'The decider, my Spring Special. One fight each? Can't fail.'

Cuesta opens a drawer, sorts through a bunch of envelopes, tosses one in Kane's direction.

'Count it later, my friend. You're talking to a busy man.'

Kane fingers the envelope. He's done the math already. Eight hundred bucks.

'You've taken the seat price and the vig?'

'Of course I have. You don't get to sit behind a desk like this otherwise.'

Kane nods, gazing at the framed black and white photos already on the wall. Dolores and Flo snapped from every angle. Cuesta's passport to the big time.

'That fight was thrown,' Kane says softly. 'It was fixed. Your white girl did well, no complaints, but I'm guessing Dolores might be wondering what went up her nose before that last round. None of this is subtle so the question I want to ask is who else might have noticed?'

Cuesta shrugs. 'I'm not hearing this,' he nods at the envelope on the desk. 'You're sitting on seven hundred bucks and you've got some kinda beef with the result?'

'We're talking fraud, and there's no way you don't know it.'

'We're talking showbiz, my friend. You're some kind of cop? Or a peeper maybe? Just who do you fucking represent? Who's paying you to make trouble? It was a great evening.

Those women were stars. Everyone says so, and the next one will be a smash.'

'Dolores' trainer was in the gym that night with Mahoney.'

'You mean Flo?'

'I mean Mahoney. Next time I see him, he's sending Dolores into battle. The first coupla rounds she does OK, weathers the storm. Round three, Mahoney's fighting Madam Rubberlegs. No one ever connects the dots in this town but I'm guessing you offered 40/1 on a knockout to a whole bunch of guys you wanted to impress, and then laid off the bet to cover yourself. I'm getting warm here? Just a nod will do.'

'You think I wanted to impress you? Who the fuck do you think you are?'

'I think you wanted to buy me off, keep me quiet. Didn't work, *amigo*. I'm back in that face of yours and I ain't going away.'

Cuesta stares at Kane for a long moment. Outrage has given way to something more sinister. He leans forward over the desk, steepling his fingers, Mr LA Cool.

'Beat it...' he says very quietly, '...whoever you are. Get the fuck outta here. You know the trick in LA? Rule numero uno? Never ask questions if you don't know the answer else people might get the wrong idea and come calling. You're hearing me?' He nods at the envelope again. 'Seven hundred scoots? Count yourself lucky and fuck off. I've no idea where you're calling home just now but you might take a detour to Bunker Hill. You get that for free, by the way. Take it easy, my friend, else the rest of LA will be up your sorry ass.'

Kane gets to his feet, stares him out. Turning for the door, he spots another framed photo hung on the wall where

Cuesta can see it from his desk. A tall figure stands beside a yellow biplane. He's wearing a heavy aviator jacket, and a leather flying helmet, and his face is half hidden behind a big pair of sunglasses, but it's recognisably Cuesta.

'That's yours?' Kane nods at the photo. 'The plane?'

'Yeah,' Cuesta nods. 'Know anything about aeroplanes? It's a Stearman. God's gift to California. Comes with the territory, mister. Up in that baby you're with the angels. Nobody can touch you.'

Kane studies it a moment longer and then leaves without a backward glance. Soon, maybe very soon, he may have the satisfaction of settling his accounts with Cuesta more directly, but that time has yet to come. For now, he needs to check out Bunker Hill.

A twenty-minute drive through thin weekend traffic takes him downtown. 115 lies on the south side and the moment the property swims into view is the moment he realises the true weight of the message Cuesta is sending. For the time being Kane can only guess how, but one way or another LA's latest success has managed to link him to the pitiful third-floor rathole where Kane did Donovan's bidding and so briefly pitched his tent.

115 is no more. The building is a shell, burned out from the ground floor upwards, charred wooden frames around empty windows, a mess of tossed-away wreckage among the weeds out front. Kane parks the Sedan and gets out. He can smell the sour taint of wet ashes and charred timber from the other side of the street and when he starts to rummage among the leavings in the weeds he recognises the bottle of Jim Beam Gus never quite managed to finish.

There are other items here from other lives: a half-burned

slipper with holes in the rubber sole, a battered photo frame with the sepia curl of a woman's smile still inside, someone – Kane guesses – younger, prettier, less abandoned. Nearby, he finds a biscuit tin with a bunch of postcards from Des Moines, Iowa, inside. The cards have suffered in the heat of the fire but Kane sorts through them, tries to decipher messages on the back but gets no further than a single line accompanied by a scrawled kiss. 'Love from your Mom', someone has written, 'Take care out there, my baby'.

Take care out there?

Kane steps back, gazes up at the ruin of 115. Barely a couple of generations ago, this property with its turreted corners, and high ceilings, and respectable neighbours, would have been a fancy LA address. Decades later, unthinkable to those families who once lived here, the area has become a battlefield disfigured by poverty, and empty lives, and dreams long abandoned after that first giddy rush to the coast.

'Help you at all, buddy?'

Kane turns to find himself joined by an old man who looks familiar. He's wearing a beaten-up old trench coat, tan, unbelted, far too big for his skinny frame, and his face has been hollowed out by exhaustion and a lousy diet. Room on the ground floor, Kane thinks. Plus an ancient wooden rocker he'd position on the big front porch to catch the first taunting rays of the LA spring.

'So what happened?'

The old man frowns, sucks his teeth, and Kane knows at once that this will be a story he's already told a thousand times.

'Middle of the night. Maybe two, three in the morning? Big whoosh. Gasoline. You could smell it. Me? I'm outa bed like a three-year-old. Grab the dog, tell the mutt everything's going to be Yankee Doodle, then we're heading out. The place is burning around me. Folks screaming upstairs. Some jumped, some made it, some didn't.'

'How many didn't?'

'Fifteen? Twenty? More? I guess they're still counting. This is a fire someone laid, buddy. Do I have the proof? A face or two? No way. But I know the smell of gasoline and no one here had the money to buy the stuff. You get my drift, buddy? Know what I'm telling you?'

Kane nods, and then reaches in his pocket for Cuesta's envelope. He tears it open. The money is in twenties. He counts out five bills and presses them into the old man's hand.

'That's a hundred bucks.' He can't believe it. 'Are you out of your mind?'

Kane leaves him shortly afterwards, drives back to Beverly Hills. The weather is lousy, thick grey clouds off the ocean with the taste of rain in the air, and Kane finds Meier bent over the drawing board in his bedroom. By now, his first pass at the thousand-dollar bill is almost complete and Kane makes the time to take a proper look. Meier's work with the much-sharpened pencil is faultless, perfectly mapping every square inch of the original design, and when Kane asks whether he's happy with the results, he nods.

'Here and here could be better,' he directs Kane's attention to an area of intricate linework in the bill's top left-hand corner, 'but next time round there won't be a problem. Perfection never comes easy, but I guess you know that already.'

Kane smiles. Then Meier breaks off and gets up from his perch at the drawing board. Prosper, he says, has lent him a couple of hundred scoots he needed to pay off suppliers of specialist equipment. Might Kane be able to settle up with her?

'Sure.'

Kane fetches out Cuesta's envelope again and peels off two hundred dollars.

'You're sure that's enough?'

Meier doesn't answer. He's looking very hard at one of the notes. Then he holds it up against the light before he takes a tiny nibble at one corner.

'Something wrong, buddy?'

Meier is smiling now, examining the rest of the wad.

'Sure. Where did you get this stuff?'

'Someplace else. You don't need to know.'

'Then I'd take it back, if I were you. Return to sender.'

'Why?'

'It's counterfeit.'

'How do you know?'

'I made it.'

22

Gus, it turns out, was also at the fight. Saturday night he makes an appearance in Beverly Hills. He's bought a present for Prosper because he knows she adores early forced daffodils, an out-of-season miracle she still doesn't fully understand. She arranges them in a fluted vase, and Gus leaves her to talk to the flowers in a bid to unlock the brightness of their little yellow secrets.

Upstairs, Kane is trying to wrestle a schedule out of Meier. He's been on to Donovan. FDR is anticipating his next conference with Churchill and badly needs to sustain the transatlantic relationship with *une friandise*, a treat, of some kind, and FDR thinks a million pounds' worth of leverage against the slippery Admiral Darlan might do just fine. That way, the French fleet at Toulon might finally fall into Allied hands. But how, exactly, is Donovan planning to tempt Darlan into accepting the bribe?

Donovan is naturally reluctant to expose his hand at the poker table of DC politics but wants the simplest of answers from Kane. Three long-term felons have been granted their freedom. Real money has been spent, risks taken, reputations put on the line. Now he wants to know when he can first lay sight on a thousand-dollar bill that will fool the French admiral.

Meier, as ever, treats the question with his own brand of measured respect. The key challenge, he says carefully, is the preparation of the engraving plates. After that will lie technical mountains that only a trusted printer will be able to scale. The right man with the right equipment will take at least a month to set up his press, adjust for a trillion tiny variations, and finally press the button that will create a million dollars. Meier has met Takiwa, the Jap with the printing shop in Alameda Street, and – more importantly – has talked to other printers in the field. His conclusion? That Takiwa is key to the entire operation.

So far, so good. On Monday, Kane plans to drive Meier to Alameda Street to agree a schedule and tie the Jap printer into a handshake contract with Uncle Sam. A delivery date agreed, Kane will lift the phone to Donovan and pass on the news. In the meantime, he's keen to quiz Gus about Wednesday's fight.

'You were in the bleachers?' Kane asks.

'No way. It pays to have connections in the fight game and mine had a spare ticket at a table. Cops grease everything in this town, and this guy is no exception.'

'This guy?'

'A friend, *hombre*,' a wary smile from Gus. 'Us friends draw the line at a name.'

'But well placed?'

'Exceptionally well placed, fingers in all the LA pies that matter. One of them was also at that table of ours. Guy from the oil business, Armenian-born, married a German movie star and brought her out west. Made a fortune on a couple of lucky gushers a while ago and never looked back. That kind of money, believe me, opens every door.'

'He's in deep with Cuesta, this oil guy? Is that what you're telling me?'

'He ponied the fight purse. A hundred dollars to each girl? A budget to make the venue look kosher? Small change, *hombre*. He thinks Cuesta is a spick loudmouth and nothing he saw on Wednesday night has changed his mind. She's back, by the way. Flew in this afternoon.'

'Mahoney? You've seen her?'

'Took a call. She's back from DC and she's somehow figured you were there on Wednesday night and she's hot for an explanation. She also says she's still wearing dark glasses and hope you won't be put off. I told her I thought that was unlikely. If I'm right, it's not too late to make a call.'

Kane leaves Beverly Hills minutes later. It's dark by now and turning onto the coastal highway at Santa Monica he can't help remembering the last time he was here. Pouring rain, he thinks, and the strange excitement of staking out the woman who's changed his life.

He leaves the Sedan outside her apartment block and crosses the road. He can see lights on in the ground-floor condo and wonders whether Virgil will be the one to open the door. Wrong.

'You.' She's staring up at him. No dark glasses, just the remains of the bruise around her left eye. 'A hug, maybe? Or something stronger?'

He puts his arms round her. She feels smaller, leaner, harder. She lays her head flat against his chest and when she finally looks up at him, her eyes are glistening. By now, the bruises have begun to yellow, with the worst of the swelling largely gone.

'Shit,' she says, wiping away a tear. 'This was never in the script.'

'You were great. Are great. Proud doesn't do it, doesn't

come anywhere close. I was there with you every step of the way. I thought you were due another beating and I was wrong.'

'Yeah?' She forces a wan smile. 'But it wasn't right, was it?'

Kane says nothing. Not at first. When he asks about Virgil she says he's away in San Francisco for a while. New boyfriend. Hot Cuban guy with great hair.

'So?' Kane is still on the doorstep, still gazing down at her.

'What kind of question is that, Mr Kane?' At last she's smiling.

She leads him into the apartment. Dexter is neatly folded on the hall floor outside the kitchen door and Kane remembers exactly the same pose from their days together in DC. Nothing changes, he thinks, looking round.

Mahoney's bedroom is a mess, a bunch of clothes half readied for the laundry in one corner, abandoned gym kit behind the door, the bed unmade.

'You could have brought me flowers,' Mahoney says. 'Brighten the place up.'

'I didn't come for the place.' He's looking at a framed photo of the First Lady, propped against the wall. 'Where did you get that?'

'Chateau Roosevelt,' she grins this time. 'Where else? Scary guy called Steve Early passed it on. I asked nicely and he said yes. Sends his best, by the way. Hopes the new job's working out.' The grin fades. 'New job?'

'It's complicated.' Kane takes her in his arms again, cups her face in his big hands, kisses her. He can feel a shiver as she winds herself around him, and when she turns her head away he knows she's crying again.

'I like complicated,' she swallows hard. 'Or I thought I did.'

They make love, say very little, risk nothing. Dexter appears at the door a couple of times to check them out, then wanders away. Afterwards, Mahoney lies in Kane's arms, her head on his chest. He's never known her so passive, so happy to let Kane make the running, but now she wants to know everything.

'You were really at the fight Wednesday?' she asks.

'I was.'

'Grotesque, wasn't it?'

'Showtime. Your agent's big night out.'

'The man's a gangster, you know that? He's mobbed-up. He's probably killed people.'

'I know.'

'You know?' She's up on one elbow now, staring down at him. 'So why the fuck didn't you tell me?'

Kane tries to gentle her, fails completely. When she asks how long he's been in LA, he tells her a couple of weeks. He's been strong-armed by another of the DC chieftains, put on a different payroll, told to go undercover, tasked with a job he only half understands. His life is no longer his own.

'It never was, Mr Kane. You've always belonged to others. Last month it was Roosevelt. Before that you've never told me. So who's this new guy in your life?'

Kane shakes his head. A little truth here wouldn't hurt. He wants to say Mahoney. He wants to say she matters more than anyone else, more than Donovan, more than FDR, more – even – than little Sis. He wants to tell her that it's time they both got off the roundabout and took a good look at what's happened to the Land of the Free, but something still gags him. Duty? Some twisted notion of self-respect? Or maybe plain fear of the consequences, emotional or otherwise? He doesn't know, but one look at her face tells him that here and now is the time to try.

'I love you,' he touches the remains of the bruise around her eye. 'Can we start there?'

She nods, agrees, kisses the tips of his fingers. She says she feels the same, has done for a while, but was nervous about the consequences. Round one, she murmurs, you keep your hands well up, take few risks, figure out the opposition.

'Opposition?'

'You, Mr Kane.' She kisses him, explores him a little, then moistens a finger and traces one of the many lines in his face. Her sheer physical closeness has an innocence, a simplicity, that Kane has never sensed in her before, and when she whispers his name – Quincy – and tells him that this is serious, that this matters, that being hot for each other is no longer enough, he can only agree.

'You were missing me?' she says. 'When you were holed up down the road?'

Kane nods, then tells her about the wet night when she went running into the darkness with the dog.

'You were checking me out?' She seems pleased.

'I guess I was.'

'Making sure there was no one else in my tidy little life?'

'Making sure you were OK.'

'And?'

'The answer was no. That was the night I met Cuesta.'

'Yeah?' She's back on one elbow, back in the world of stories. 'How come?'

Kane explains about arriving at the gym, about the parked

Mercedes, about watching from the darkness at the back of the gym.

'You were watching me work out?'

'Sure. That was the whole point. You and the punchbag and the black guy, Tyrone.'

'You know his name?'

'Sure.'

'How come?'

'It's what I do for a living, you know that.'

She thinks about the proposition for a moment or two, and then nods.

'So how did I do?' she ducks her head beneath the sheet, 'on that saggy old punchbag?'

They make love again, more eagerness this time, more urgency, back on familiar territory. Afterwards, she turns up the heating in the kitchen, feeds the dog, and directs Kane to a store three blocks away that sells salad stuff and decent bagels. It's nice, she says, to be sharing space once again with the guy who's stolen most of her, certainly the best bits, and before he leaves she tells him not to be spooked.

'By what?'

'It's dark out there,' she reaches up and kisses him. 'But I guess you know that already.'

Kane drives to the store. Glowing is something he's never made space for in his life. It's a word that belongs in women's magazines. It has to do with cheap writing and all kinds of fakeness. It signifies the kind of dumb simplicities he's always done his best to avoid. But tonight is very different. Tonight is the moment he took a proper look at himself and drew the only possible conclusion. That Lou Mahoney, in ways that he's only recently noticed, has stolen all of him.

The store is deserted. Kane browses the two aisles, buys bagels, smoked salmon, a lemon, a bunch of salad stuff, a jar of dried dill and a bottle of Napa Valley Sauvignon. Back outside, he's about to open his car door when his view of the store is curtained by three figures. A fourth appears, slightly taller, wearing an open raincoat and a much shorter haircut that doesn't suit him.

Cuesta. In the undertaker's suit.

'Put the wine in the car,' he nods at the bottle. 'The other stuff, too. Be a shame to waste them.'

Kane is looking from face to face. He has no weapon, never thought to bring one, was far too happy to give the possibility of ambush a second thought, and now he knows he must pay the price. The older thugs are always the ones to avoid. You can tell by the eyes, he thinks, by the way they stand, by their readiness for the unexpected. Two of them have produced saps, weighted with lead. The third totes a baseball bat. Trapped against the Sedan, Kane knows he has nowhere to go and so he does Cuesta's bidding and leaves the food and wine on the driver's seat.

'Well, my friend, you ready for this? It's gonna hurt, hurt bad, and that's a promise.'

Cuesta nods at the guy with the baseball bat and steps aside, a spectator at the gourmet feast to come. Kane crouches, hands up, protecting his face, but knows already that the odds are impossible. The baseball bat swings in the dazzle from a nearby streetlight, full force, perfectly aimed, and Kane hears his upper arm explode. The pain is intense, shooting across his shoulder, across his chest, everywhere.

For a split second he's thinking of Mahoney in the ring, toe to toe with the black girl, and he kicks out and tries to claw his way towards Cuesta but it's far too late. The other two guys are busy with their saps now, taking their turns on his face and ribs, working methodically, leaving their mark. A lunge at one of them brings Kane within biting distance of his busy hand, and he chomps down, tasting blood and raw flesh as the guy gasps with surprise. The baseball bat again, this time on the side of Kane's thigh, same result, more pain.

Dimly, Kane can see Cuesta. He's playing the referee, keeping the violence at arm's length, nodding with pleasure and approval as more blows go in. Kane can taste his own blood now, and fragments of a tooth that must be his. He's alone in a wilderness of pain but knows, at all costs, that he has to stay on his feet. Flat on his back in front of guys like these and he's probably a dead man.

Then, suddenly, it's all over. He can hear soft laughter that has to come from Cuesta, and he feels strong hands on either side of his sagging body. They drag him across the sidewalk and then comes the sound of a car door opening and a rough push sends him backwards across a bench seat. He can smell expensive leather laced with a hint of cigars. The Mercedes, he thinks.

Outside, the brief growl of a conversation before a hand reaches into his pocket and extracts the keys to the Sedan. Kane is groaning now, trying hard to sort the pain into manageable chunks, failing completely. Then the Mercedes is on the move and briefly he gives up the struggle, swamped by a darkness that is more than welcome. When he comes to again, he thinks he can hear the rasp of distant surf but he's not sure. The Mercedes glides to a halt. A door opens. The hands again, pulling him bodily into the chill of the evening, ignoring his gasps of pain.

They lay him face-up on the ground. By now it's started to rain. Kane's eyes are beginning to close but he can see an apartment block climbing above him into nowhere. More conversation, and then the clink of a bottle and a sudden pressure, very light, on his groin.

'OK down there, buddy? Hope so, else next time we'll cut the fucker off.'

It's Cuesta, his raincoat now draped around his shoulders. He might have stepped out of the theatre. He might be en route to some other pressing social engagement.

A playful kick in Kane's ribs, and Cuesta has gone. Then comes the muted peal of Mahoney's doorbell before the shadows vanish and Kane catches the low burble of the Mercedes pulling away. His grasp of time, of circumstance, of the immediate future has gone, but he knows exactly where he is, and why. A message, Kane thinks, for Mahoney.

Her door opens and there's a moment of absolute silence before her face appears, inches from his. She wants to know what hurts and where. She wants to know whether he's still alive.

'Sure.' Kane slurs the word, tries to get up, but moving is too painful. Then the pressure on his groin has gone and Mahoney is back on the very edge of his vision, holding something in her hand. With an enormous effort, Kane gestures her closer. He wants to know what she has in her hand. He squints, fighting to bring the object into focus. No good.

'It's a pair of scissors,' Mahoney is looking down the road at the lights of the departing Mercedes. 'That bastard was never subtle.'

23

Mahoney drives Kane to a retired physician in Santa Monica. His name is O'Hagan and three generations ago his family were living in Skibbereen, in Southern Ireland, which Mahoney knows well. This last year they've bonded over plates of Irish colcannon, and now she leads him to her car where Kane has adopted the foetal position on the back seat.

O'Hagan has a torch. He examines Kane's face, eases his mouth open, tut-tuts about the damage to his jaw and the ridges of bone around his eyes, but what worries him most is his arm and his thigh. Both, he says, will have to be fully checked out in case of breaks to the underlying bone.

'Who did this?' He's finished with the torch.

'It doesn't matter.'

O'Hagan gives Mahoney a look, and then shrugs. LA, he mutters, can be unforgiving, and here's the proof. Mahoney nods. What she really wants to know is whether her retired doctor can help out with painkillers and maybe a stitch or two. Painkillers, he says, will be no problem. He has some heavy-strength Demerol, a recent substitute for morphine, and whoever did the damage has been careful not to break the skin so nothing in the way of stitching needs to be done. Kane, he says, would be wise to find a good dentist as soon as possible, and he can recommend a private hospital where his arm and leg can be X-rayed.

'You figure they're broken?'

'I figure we need to find out.'

O'Hagan steps back into his house and reappears with three packets of Demerol and a bottle of Jameson Irish whiskey.

'Triple-distilled,' he gives her the bottle. 'That's the least I can do for him.'

Mahoney drives Kane back to her condo. Kane has been dreading the moment when he must get himself out of the car but he's swallowed two tablets already, washing them down with two scorching gulps of Jameson's, and by the time Mahoney is parked at the kerbside, he's feeling a whole lot better.

'Numb,' he says when she's bent over him again, asking how he feels, and he reaches for her hand with his good arm when she tells him everything will work out just fine.

Getting inside the apartment is the work of many minutes. Supported by Mahoney, short of breath, eager for another mouthful of whiskey, Kane finally makes it into the bedroom. His mouth and nose are still bleeding, and Mahoney tends to him with a damp flannel.

'Your sheets,' he mutters. 'The pillow.'

'Fuck my sheets. Just behave, Mr Kane. My lovely agent left the shopping outside the door. Bagels might be an ask too far, but smoked salmon? If I cut it up for you? Maybe a little Sauvignon?'

'Whiskey,' Kane says thickly. 'Let's run away to Skibbereen.'

'And then?'

'You marry me.'

She gazes down at him, gives his mouth another dab with the flannel.

'Any time, Agent Kane. Your job here may be done.'

The thought plagues Kane for most of the night. He drifts in and out of consciousness, reliving every moment of the beating, trying to work out what else he could have done to limit the damage. He's faced violence on countless occasions, mainly as a Boston cop, but these were messy fights, most of them in bars, mad Irish violence fuelled by booze and imagined insults, easy to cope with.

LA, on the other hand, elevates that same violence to an art form, trusting its application to a bunch of experts, well-paid artists in the field who know exactly how to injure in less time than it takes to boil an egg. Three minutes, Kane thinks, exactly the length of a round in the boxing ring, and as he feels for Mahoney's hand in the bed he wonders what other specialists Cuesta might have on his payroll. When Mahoney jerks awake, asking him how he feels, Kane is able to muster a smile in the darkness.

'It could have been worse,' he says. 'He could have turned up with a chainsaw.'

Next morning, Kane asks Mahoney to phone Gus, get him over.

'For what?'

'Council of war.'

'You have to be kidding. Look at the state of you.'

'But that's the point. He's a lovely guy. Big on reptiles. Cuesta's gonna love him.'

Gus turns up mid-morning, appears with Mahoney at the bedroom door.

'Shit,' Gus says.

'Quite.'

'And Cuesta did this?'

'He watched. Left the business to his paid help.'

'So how is it? How are you?'

'Not great.' Kane nods at the bottle on the bedside table. 'You got time for a Jameson's?'

Gus declines. When he asks Mahoney what she's done about finding a hospital, she mentions a clinic that happens to be in Beverly Hills, much favoured by Hollywood's finest.

'You'll need money for that,' Gus says at once. 'Lots of it.'

Kane says Meier will take care of it. Just give him a couple of months. Gus laughs.

'You pay the medics on the nail, *hombre*. Otherwise nothing happens. You want me to talk to Donovan? Send him a photo maybe?'

Kane ponders the suggestion.

'You're serious?' he says at length.

'I am. Your job ain't done, ain't even half done. We both have a connection to Meier but I'm guessing yours is best. That's why Donovan asked for you. In my book that's the only sane thing he ever did. We're at war, now, buddy, and this has nothing to do with the Japs. Cuesta's dug a trench for himself. He wants you out of here, out of this bed. He wants a clear run and what that creep wants he generally gets. He also wants the Prosper house and he doesn't plan on paying for it. So the movie's rolling on, and we're all wondering about the big finish, even fucking Cuesta, and so here's the only question that matters: what the fuck do we do next?'

Mahoney's gaze settles on Kane. She's taken to Gus, he can see it in her face. She likes the whiff of anarchy he's brought into her apartment. She likes how direct he is, and how much faith he still has in Kane. What she doesn't like is the suggestion that she's still wide open to Cuesta, and she tells him so.

'But you are,' Gus says. 'It might be an ugly place to be, but you have to get inside this slimebag's head. He's made you. He owns you. He's your fucking agent, for God's sake. In his world, that gives him rights and one of them starts in that bed.'

'And me? Do I get a say here?'

'Of course you do. But take a look at Agent Kane. That's what LA does to decent folk who should know better. DC might be the centre of the free world but it turns your brains to mush. There are different rules here, people take liberties and a whole lot else, help themselves to whatever or whoever they fancy, not a trace of conscience or restraint. LA exists to make them fat and happy and very very rich.' He turns to Kane. 'Am I right, *hombre*? Shouldn't you have been taking just a little more care last night? I can think of a million reasons for running the odd risk, but smoked salmon and dried fucking dill isn't one of them. *Comprende*?'

Kane has no answer. Neither has Mahoney.

'So what do we do?' Kane asks at last.

24

It takes the rest of the day to make the arrangements. Kane contacts Donovan in DC and outlines what's happened. His new boss, to Kane's relief, asks none of the obvious questions and appears to assume that the injuries have been sustained in the line of counterfeiting duties. He takes the name and contact details for the Beverly Hills Medical Center and promises to have the bill for all treatments settled out of his operational budget. When Kane enquires about additional dental treatment, Donovan confirms that these expenses will also be met.

'So who did you upset out there?'

'Best not to ask.'

'And the boy Meier?'

'Counterfeiting as we speak.'

'Good to hear.'

Donovan gone, Kane watches Mahoney preparing to close the apartment up. In a separate conversation, Gus has convinced her that staying alone in Santa Monica would simply act as a come-on for Cuesta. The heavy lifting, he'll tell himself, is done. He's put LA's latest boxing sensation at the middle of every conversation that matters, and he's about to make her rich. All that remains is to cash in and pocket his own winnings.

'You?' Kane enquires.

'Me,' Mahoney nods. 'The guy's medieval. *Droit de seigneur*. Bring the choicest maidens to my castle and leave the rest to me. One day that man will meet his maker and I just hope I'm around to watch.'

'No more boxing?'

'No more Cuesta. Same thing. Did the fight game do anything for me? A bit. Can I still go running, me and the dog? Of course. Will I miss beating the shit out of someone I barely know? Highly unlikely. Life goes on, Mr Kane. Even here.'

That afternoon, after making excuses at the office for her absence, Mahoney drives him to the Beverly Hills Medical Center. On the phone she's already arranged for a consultation and while they wait to be called they settle in a lounge that belongs in a five-star hotel. Kane, a little guilty about getting in the way of her job, asks her how it's going.

'It's going good. My big break was Eleanor. She's very East Coast, and they hate that out here, but I guess she's the closest we get to royalty without bending the knee. She's outspoken, tells it the way she sees it, and they like that. Where they draw the line is over the Jap thing.'

'Internment?' Kane tells her about the camp he saw under construction out in the Central Valley.

'Sure. Eleanor calls it the land of the unfree but that's a phrase that goes no further.'

'And you'll write about it?'

'I will, yes, and soon. I spent serious time with her in DC and briefed her on what's in store if you happen to be Japanese out here. The way it's happening so quickly is sinister. Eleanor should have a word with that husband of hers. This stuff would shame any decent society. Aren't we supposed to be fighting a war about liberty?'

Kane can only agree. When a nurse appears to collect him for the consultation, she's pushing a wheelchair. Just the sight of it puts Kane back in DC, playing the FDR role as his buddies try to bust the magic push to the US Treasury.

'You want me to sit in that thing?'

'I do, yes.' She smiles. Perfect teeth.

Kane insists on getting into the chair by himself and then sits back, using his hands to wheel it towards one of the consultation suites. At every turn in the corridor the smell of money grows thicker, and by the time he's offering the doctor a stiff handshake he's begun to sweat.

The doctor holds him at arm's length, looks him up and down, sniffs.

'Jameson's,' Kane says at once. 'And Demerol.'

'You find they help?'

'Couldn't do without them. Especially the whiskey.'

The doctor nods, says nothing, then outlines the days to come. X-rays first, face, ribs, arm, thigh, with a full review thereafter.

'Go easy on the Jameson's, Mr Kane. When the Demerol runs out, we'll fix you some more.' His gaze drifts to a handwritten note on the bottom of his clipboard. 'The US Treasury are evidently paying your fees. Might I ask what you do for a living?'

'Sure,' Kane tries to ease the pain in his knee. 'I bodyguard the President. Make sure he comes to no harm.'

'Is that right?' Kane has caught this man's full attention. 'And that puts you in harm's way?'

'Only in this town,' Kane shoots him a toothless smile. 'No offence.'

By nightfall, the X-rays awaiting detailed analysis, Kane and Mahoney are back in Beverly Hills. To Kane's surprise, Gus appears also to have moved in.

'This is your idea?'

'Ours, *hombre*. Out here we call it teamwork. The good guys circle the wagons and keep their powder dry. That's us, buddy. Even Prosper agrees, and she knows a thing or two about the fucking Cherokees.'

Prosper herself descends from her bedroom where she spends most of the daylight hours. A nod to Mahoney, and then a hand to her mouth when she sees what's happened to Kane.

'You?' she says. 'Of all people?'

'Me,' Kane agrees.

'Gus here tells me Cuesta. I hate that man.' She's still in the middle of the room, looking slowly from one face to the other, from Mahoney to the wreckage of what used to be Quincy Kane. Kane has no idea about the conclusions she comes to but the next thing that happens is an abrupt nod towards the door, summoning Gus for a private chat. He's back minutes later, shaking his head.

'Jesus H. Christ,' he mutters. 'This town is fucking insane.'

'What's happened?' The question comes from Kane.

'She's on the phone already. She likes you, *hombre*, you know that, and she takes this stuff personally. Maybe it's a tribal thing. Either way she's talking to a guy she knows over in Bumfuck. She wants four young bloods on the Greyhound by tomorrow and she won't take no for an answer.'

'Bumfuck?' Mahoney is lost.

'Oklahoma,' Kane again. 'Back of fucking nowhere.' He turns back to Gus. 'And these guys? They'll do what?'

'Think war party, *hombre*. She named them all. She knows them all. She's probably fucked them all. And now she's calling in all those little debts.'

'But to do what, exactly?'

'Good question, *hombre*. Wish I could give you an answer.'

The Cherokee travel overnight from Oklahoma and arrive in LA late afternoon. Last night, with the assistance of both Gus and Prosper, Kane made it to the first floor where Prosper has assigned him and Mahoney the biggest and grandest of the guest bedrooms, but this afternoon he's examining details on the completed pencil sketch of the thousand-dollar note when Meier calls from the window.

'C'm here,' he says. 'Unbelievable.'

'Tell me,' Kane is in no state to make it to the view. 'Describe what you're seeing.'

'Hard to,' Meier shoots him a look. 'Just listen.'

This is the moment Kane first hears the drum, insistent, urgent, the same pattern of beats repeated over and over. Four guys, Meier tells him, in a circle around Prosper, one of them with a hide drum under his arm. They're wearing turbans brightened with feathers. Their faces are daubed with paint. They're all bare above the waist, in good shape, young guys who work out a little. And they're dancing, or maybe better stamping, bam-bam, round and round.

'And Prosper?'

'She's dancing, too, but different. They've done it before, she and them, you can tell, and now they're speeding up a little, clockwise, anticlockwise, round and round. Now they've stopped. Boom. They're all looking up. You think it's an out-of-world thing? Addressing the spirits? Shit, they're off again.'

Meier has been joined by the dog. The two of them bonded at first sight, Dexter sniffing at the remains of the poultice on Meier's nose, and now the dog has his paws on the window sill and is peering down at the performance outside.

After a moment or two of silence, the drumming has resumed. Meier returns to the drawing board, shaking his head. He knows Kane is in deep shit because he can see the evidence in front of his eyes, but now he's beginning to tease some sense out of this bizarre series of events.

'You upset someone bad, right?'

'I did.'

'And they beat you up, yeah?'

'Yeah.'

'And now Prosper's looking to get even? Is that the way it might go?'

'You want the truth? I've no idea. Going to war this way was never my plan. I'm Secret Service, right? In LA my job was to take you guys down and that's exactly what we did. Back in DC I now keep the President in good shape, head off the crazies, make sure everything stays nice and tidy. Then the good news is I get to have a stake in this city of yours. You've never met her and I doubt you ever will because we have to keep her out of your business but she's changed my life, buddy, and just now that matters because I ain't in great shape. *Comprende?*'

'Sure,' Meier has coloured up a little. 'You're telling me she's living here?'

'She is.'

'And we'll never meet?'

'That's the plan.'

'Why?'

'Because she works for a big newspaper. Can't help herself when it comes to asking questions. And that, believe me, is the only thing that ever comes between us.'

Meier nods, beginning at last to understand.

'And Prosper,' he asks at last. 'She's OK with all this?'

'Better than OK. She took a look at us last night, me and Mahoney, I watched her doing it. These people outside, Prosper herself, they're different folks entirely. Different rules, different instincts, more generous, more giving maybe. Quite where this ends is anyone's guess, but unpack whatever luggage those guys may be toting and I'll lay good money you'll find all kinds of surprises. Not for us, buddy, but for the guy who did this to me.' Kane gestures briefly at his face.

'Surprises?'

'Knives. Tomahawks. Maybe guns, too. You want to settle a debt, you come prepared. That's why they're here. That's why she's got on the tom-toms and called them over. Old-style justice, buddy. The white man taught an ancient lesson.'

'You're telling me they're here to put the record straight? With whoever beat you up?'

'I'm telling you they're here to help,' Kane is watching

the dog, who's begun to howl. 'Something wrong out there?' Kane gestures at Dexter.

Meier gets to his feet and returns to the window.

'He's upset,' he nods down at the dog. 'Because they've gone.'

25

The story of the next week or so takes everyone by surprise, not least Kane himself.

Some of the news is good. The Demerol, fortified by occasional shots of Jameson's, continues to numb the pain and detailed X-ray analysis of the damage to Kane's arm and thigh shows far less damage than anticipated. Both limbs have swollen but there won't be the need for surgical intervention, and neither will he be in plaster. A protracted visit to a dentist cleans up the worst of the wreckage in his mouth, while yet another X-ray reveals that his jawbone has sustained only a minor fracture, nothing too serious. But this cheerful audit of the damage is barely half the story because mentally, inside the person he once knew so well, Kane is in deep trouble.

Nights are the worst. Mahoney asleep beside him, he lies awake through the small hours, tormenting himself with images that refuse to go away. What went missing that night he drove to the corner store was his judgement: that instinctive talent for recognising a bad situation, for anticipating the consequences, and for dealing with them. He should have been carrying a weapon. He should have used it. He should have taken down at least a couple of Cuesta's goons, and sent the rest on their way.

Consequences? Certainly. But nothing he and his new

boss couldn't have handled. More than a decade of training, learning how to cope with literally hundreds of what Mike Reilly still calls 'situations', should have wised him up about retribution waiting in the shadows. Instead, like some love-struck adolescent, he barely gave disaster a second thought.

Love, he thinks. Mr Invincible. The guy who drives through darkened streets without a second look in the rear-view mirror. The guy who doesn't bother to check out the sidewalk on leaving the store. The Mercedes was parked in plain sight. Spoiled for clues, he'd walked into an ambush with his eyes tight shut. What followed will stay with him for the rest of his life, partly because that kind of pain leaves an indelible scar, but mainly because it should never have happened. How come?

Love, again, he thinks. The sweetness of a wholesale surrender he's never known before, thickened now by the overwhelming simplicity of his immediate physical needs. Early in the week, Mahoney negotiates three days' leave. She changes his bandages. She holds a cup of water to his swollen lips. She mashes up potatoes, adds a spoonful of cream, feeds him like a baby. She helps him attend to his most intimate functions. She even helps Prosper apply a poultice to his upper arm and thigh before flexing the limbs makes the stuff fall off. In truth, Kane rather enjoys the herby smell and the strange, unaccustomed warmth, yet another sign that he's gone soft in the head. Lou Mahoney fell in love with a guy who knew how to handle himself. Now she's looking after a cripple.

The room they're sharing looks like a stage set, a wildly over-decorated boudoir with no concessions to good taste, but that's Manny Raab's doing and not Prosper's, and as long as Kane can avoid the mirrors he's grateful for the space, and for the view of the front garden through the huge windows. After Mahoney returns to work mid-week, he spends the day in an armchair beside that same window, enjoying the warmth of the sun, trying not to think too hard, and when he can spare the time Gus joins him.

Gus brings a board and a box of pieces and they play chess together, a novelty for Kane. Gus has played all his life and Kane is grateful for his patience in explaining the rules, in quietly correcting yet another lousy move, in explaining why the trick is looking way ahead, five moves ahead, maybe more, and as Kane slowly gets the bigger picture, he realises just how much this crazy buddy of his cares.

It's Thursday afternoon and Kane has just lost again. While Gus resets the board, Kane gazes out of the window.

'Cuesta?' he says softly. 'What do we do?'

This is the first time either of them have mentioned the name and for this Kane is grateful. Gus gets to start. A bishop move he's never made before. Already Kane can taste defeat.

'We take him down,' Gus grunts. 'And we do it good.'

'How?'

'I dunno, *hombre*, but I guess we'll figure it out. Life can be kind that way. Think opportunity, think luck.'

Kane has no faith in either, not any more. He moves a pawn to threaten the bishop. An hour ago, under supervision, he'd made it up and down the big sweep of the staircase unaided. Gus led the applause.

'Move your knight,' Gus says. 'Make life tough for me.'

Kane stares at the board. Once again, he hasn't a clue what to do.

'I'm losing it, Gus,' he says softly, 'I don't know who I am any more.'

'I know. That's why I'm here.'

'So what do I do?'

'You get better. You stop feeling sorry for yourself. Both will happen sooner than you think.' He reaches for Kane's knight, moves it towards the bishop.

'And Mahoney?'

'Mahoney is the best thing you've got just now. She's probably the best thing you'll get ever but that's not my call. She loves you, *hombre*. She loves you whole and she loves you broken. That doesn't happen often in this town, believe me.' He reaches across the board, gives Kane a gentle pat on his good arm, and then moves his queen.

'Checkmate?' Kane has run out of options again.

'Fraid so. Take a hint from me, *hombre*. Don't be frightened of getting better. It won't hurt you.'

The following evening, Mahoney returns from work later than usual. Their bedroom empty, she finds Kane sitting alone in the big kitchen, reading the afternoon edition of the *LA Times*. Kane looks up, tells her he made it round the garden three times without stopping.

'With Gus?'

'Without Gus. Just me.'

'And?'

'No problem. I've been a pain in the ass.'

'Who says?'

'Gus.'

'He's right,' she kisses him. 'But it's a lovely ass.'

She peels off her coat, collects two beers from the fridge. She says she's just spent nearly an hour with a guy called Andy. Andy is the sports editor on the paper, runs a big team of reporters, nice guy, much respected.

'And?'

Mahoney pours the beers, settles beside him. A handful of staff, mainly friends, had been to Wednesday's fight and compared notes afterwards. They all agreed that something bad had happened to the black girl between the second and third rounds. Two of them recalled seeing her trainer at work with a nasal spray and were wondering quite what he'd had in mind. The sports editor hadn't been present at the fight, but readers had also been making contact with similar reservations. Given the weight of money riding on a torrent of bets, the sports editor – Andy – had called Mahoney in.

'He wanted my take,' she says. 'I told him exactly the way the third round went. I was expecting another catfight and it never happened. Her gloves were down, her eyes had gone, huge pupils, no focus, close up she looked like she'd seen a ghost.'

'Meaning?'

'Meaning I stepped in and knocked her out. That's the deal. That's what you do. Did I take advantage? Never. In the ring it's all adrenalin, otherwise you're history. You're high. You're obeying your worst instincts. You want the truth? I couldn't wait to put her away.'

'And afterwards?'

'Afterwards I went across to make sure she was OK. She wouldn't look at me, probably couldn't look at me. She was jello, she wasn't with us any more. Her eyes were gone.'

'And Tyrone?'

'He told me I'd caught her with a lucky shot. Sent her into dreamland. That was a lie. Start of the round, I hadn't touched her.'

Kane nodded. Mahoney's story exactly matches what he'd seen on the night, every last detail. Now she's offering him a typed list of items which mean nothing.

'They're incapacitants,' Mahoney explains. 'The favourites are based on various plants. Refine them properly and they become psychochemicals. These are from Andy. The way he described it, it's magic stuff that puts you out for a while.'

'Meaning?'

'He thinks there's a fair chance some of this stuff went up Dolores' nose,' Mahoney nods at the list. 'I gather it wouldn't be the first time.'

'She's done it before? Gone jello? Thrown the fight?'

'I doubt it. She's not the type. Andy says it happens a lot, other venues, other fighters. All you need is a pile of money on an obvious winner and the rest is down to chemicals. I thought I won on the night but now I'm not so sure.'

Kane nods, studies the list again. None of the items mean anything.

'So what will Andy do about it?'

'I guess that was the point of us getting together. Like I say, he's a nice guy but journalism's a tough business. He thinks he might be sitting on a page lead, and I suspect he's probably right.'

'He'll need evidence.'

'Of course he will.'

'Hard evidence.'

'Sure,' Mahoney toys with the remains of her beer, then asks whether Kane might be able to handle a little expedition.

'Like where?'

'Tyrone lives in one of those bungalow courts in Hollywood. I've been over a coupla times and I know for a fact that he's never there at weekends.' She smiles. 'You can still figure how to get through a locked door, Agent Kane?'

Mahoney has a home phone number for Tyrone. She rings it mid-morning the following day and gets no response. Kane, barely limping now, sits beside her as they drive out of Beverly Hills. The bungalow court lies in a grid of side streets off Hollywood Boulevard, modest rentals much favoured by extras and walk-on actors hired by the nearby studios. The unit Tyrone occupies, he's told Mahoney, previously housed a Czech-born stuntman specialising in tumble falls from impossible heights, and Tyrone himself has grown to love the edge that a bunch of transient showbiz folk have brought to the area.

The bungalows overlook a long oblong of tended garden, stands of buddleia and dwarf conifers with twin paved walkways down the middle. Tyrone lives in number seven, iron bars on both windows and a solid-looking front door. Mahoney knocks twice, stands back while Kane watches a guy in a recliner at the end of the court. He has a newspaper open on his chest and he appears to be asleep.

'Gone,' Mahoney has knocked a third time, no response.

Kane nods. Thanks to Gus, he has a set of thin steel picks that should open most doors. He tries with one, then another, then a third, shielded by Mahoney. Then the thinnest of the picks finds the spring he's after and a moment later the door is open.

'Tyrone?' Mahoney has followed Kane into the gloom of the tiny hall. 'It's me, Lou.'

Apart from the steady drip-drip of a leaking tap, nothing. Kane knows that he should surrender the lead to Mahoney because she knows this place, but old habits die hard. A quick check behind all four doors reveals nothing but smallish, airless, empty rooms curtained against the early spring sunshine. He turns to Mahoney.

'You wanna take the bathroom cupboards? Just in case?'

Mahoney nods and disappears into the closet while Kane bolts the front door from the inside and pushes into the living room. Tyrone, he senses, has done his best but everything looks just a little worn out: the sagging two-seat sofa, the cigarette burns on the cheap carpet, the patches of damp on the low ceiling. Only a line of framed black and white photos on the back wall hint at a life outside this shadowed retreat.

Kane scans them one by one, tallying the names: Max Baer seconds away from knocking out Primo Carnera, Panama Al Brown, his gloved hand raised by the referee, Max Schmelling at work on an opponent Kane doesn't recognise. These are the faces Tyrone has chosen to live with and only one of them, the genius bantamweight Panama Al, is black.

Kane nods to himself, filing the thought away. The door is still open and he can hear Mahoney emptying the cupboard in the bathroom, just in case Tyrone has been reckless enough to hang on to the nasal spray. The answer, it quickly turns out, is no. Mahoney has stepped in from the hall and is eyeing a battered escritoire in the corner of the room.

'Paperwork?' she queries. 'Maybe he got the stuff mail-order?'

It's a neat suggestion and together they spend the next

ten minutes going through all three drawers, pulling out a mess of invoices and payment reminders, looking for any trace of the names on the sport editor's list of incapacitants. Again they find nothing, except for a bunch of diaries secured by an elastic band. The diaries go back to 1938, and Kane leaves Mahoney to go through them while he tackles the bungalow's single bedroom. One way or another, they need to build a picture of the relationship between Tyrone and Cuesta, and the diaries might offer a clue or two. Just how long have they been in business together? Where did they meet? And what did it take to keep Tyrone in line?

Kane is enjoying this. After watching himself fall apart last week, he begins to feel whole again. Tyrone's bedroom, like the sitting room, could be bigger. A single bed hogs most of the available space. The glass of water on the bedside table is half-full, and a cloth edition of *The Black Mask* lies propped against a tin of biscuits. Kane looks under the pillow, feels inside the case, then starts on the contents of the wardrobe. Tyrone has a liking for plain shirts and dark pants. His taste in jackets runs from scuffed black leather to an off-white cotton but none of the pockets yield anything of any interest. At the bottom of the wardrobe is a scatter of footwear, including three pairs of plimsolls, all heavily worn. Kane carefully replaces every item, then checks around one final time before remembering the space beneath the bed.

The suitcase is as old as the plimsolls. He pulls it out, tests the catches, opens it. Inside, to his disappointment, are the changes of shirt and underwear you might take away for a week out of town, but then, in the catch-all pocket sewn into the top of the suitcase, he spies a brown envelope. He pulls it out, holds it up to the thin strip of daylight parting the curtains. Las Vegas postmark, with a smudged date: 23 December 1941. Typed address, Tyrone K. Smith, 7 West Court, LA zip.

Kane opens the envelope and shakes out the paperwork inside. Two sheets of paper. The first acknowledges an order of 17 December 1941, and acknowledges pre-payment in the sum of $3.50. The second appears to be a tally of instructions. The consignment, as promised, comes in powder form. Dilution with two fluid ounces of warm water is recommended for low-capacity nasal sprays. Extreme care should be taken to avoid accidental ingestion. He blinks, reads the instructions again, then notices another envelope, deeper in the pocket, white this time, and a little thicker. Inside he finds a thousand dollars in fifties, secured with a rubber band. No note.

Kane rocks back on his heels, knowing he's hit the motherlode. The substance is called Hyoscyamine. The order and delivery dates on the paperwork fit perfectly with Wednesday's fight, and an hour in the city's library should reveal exactly what this stuff does.

Kane slips the paperwork back into the envelope and puts it aside, along with the money. Then he closes the lid on the suitcase and slides it back under the bed before returning to the living room. The first hot jolt of triumph has gone but for the first time in over a week he feels utterly normal. Patience, he thinks. Figuring out the hows and the whys and maybe even the what's nexts. And now the sweetest taste of all. Hard evidence.

Mahoney is still sitting cross-legged on the carpet, an open diary in her hands. She looks up.

'He met Cuesta only last year,' she says. 'And told himself to step careful.' She spots the envelope. 'What's that?'

The city's central library lies downtown, a handsome building less than two decades old, the approach flanked by tall green cypress trees. At the front desk, Kane tables the single word Hyoscyamine and asks where he might enquire further. The duty librarian lifts a phone, has a brief conversation and directs Kane and Mahoney to the third floor.

'Botany section,' she says. 'Ellen will be waiting for you.'

Ellen offers a single volume, already bookmarked. Mahoney follows Kane to a table by the window. Hyoscyamine, it turns out, comes from henbane, otherwise known as stinking nightshade. In any quantity, it can kill. Diluted, it produces a range of side effects which are said to last for three or four hours.

'Side effects?' Mahoney asks.

'You ready for this?' Kane is smiling. 'Dizziness, confusion, dilated pupils, dry mouth and blurred vision. It was Tyrone who knocked her out. You were late to the party.'

26

That night, a council of war. Kane, Gus and Mahoney meet upstairs in the big guest bedroom. Kane donates the remains of the Jameson's and proposes a toast to the absent Cherokees. Prosper has acquired an old Army tent big enough to house them all, and they're now camped in one corner of the property's extensive garden. Their spokesman, the smallest guy in the war party but emphatically vocal, draws up a roster for every new day. Gus has buddied with him and knows that the property is in safe hands. Bumfuck's finest, he says, are on patrol day and night and leave nothing to chance. He's supplied them with several photos of Cuesta and told them to scalp the bastard if he ever dares make an appearance.

Up in the guest bedroom, Mahoney wants to take the evidence to the paper, to Andy on the sports desk. It will, she says, be safe in his hands. With countless contacts in Vegas, he knows a great deal about the fight game and he has the experience and the guile to build Wednesday's fight into a really big story. If the intention is to ruin Cuesta, to run him out of town, then a blockbuster piece in the *LA Times* will be a very good start.

'No,' Gus shakes his head.

'No?' Kane can feel Mahoney bristling. Her fight. Her reputation on the line. 'Why the hell not?'

'Because we haven't finished with Tyrone yet. We need to

sweat the guy. We need to confront him. Throwing the fight was Cuesta's doing, not his. It would be nice to have Tyrone confirm that.'

'Why?'

'Because the guy we're taking down is Cuesta. He's the slimebag that matters.'

'Won't work,' Mahoney shakes her head.

'Why not?'

'Because Tyrone won't rat him out. Number one, he's not that kind of man. And number two, Cuesta probably frightens him.'

'Doesn't matter. We're rattling Cuesta's cage. If you think Tyrone might get angsty, I can lay hands on a bunch of Cherokees who might take care of the situation.'

Mahoney frowns. Gus, as ever, is rolling her over.

'You're worried about the paper?' he suggests. 'Losing that big fat scoop?'

'Of course I am.'

'But nothing's lost,' Gus insists. 'We can deal with Tyrone in ways that your Andy guy probably can't. And afterwards Andy gets to keep the exclusive. How's that for a plan?'

Mahoney is thinking hard. Finally she needs a second opinion.

'And you, Agent Kane?'

Kane is gazing at Gus. Opportunity, he thinks. And luck. Just the way he predicted.

'I'm with Gus,' he says. 'We talk to Tyrone.'

It takes a while to make the arrangements. By now, Meier is happy with his preliminary sketch and has started work on

the etching for the thousand-dollar bill. The acids that bite
into the copper plate come in thick glass phials and the smell
fills the room. Meier himself is wearing a mask when Kane
turns up with a handful of fifty-dollar notes.

'Take a look at these for me?'

Meier nods, fingers one of the bills, smiles.

'Yours?' he asks Kane.

'No.'

'Just as well.'

That same afternoon, Mahoney – phoning from her desk
at the *LA Times* – finally gets through to Tyrone. Later, back
in Beverly Hills, she says the exchange was warm, friendly,
matter-of-fact. Tyrone appears to be carrying no baggage
from the fight and has readily agreed to a meet. At Gus's
insistence, Mahoney has suggested a bar in Venice Beach.
Gus says he treats the place like home and there's a private
room in back where the four of them can get together. He'll
also organise for a couple of Cherokee to ride shotgun out
front.

'Tomahawks?' Mahoney enquires drily.

'Guns.' Gus nods at the fading bruises on Kane's face. 'A
time and a place, *hombre*. Am I right?'

The meet is fixed for the following evening. By now, Kane
is driving again but Mahoney takes the wheel, following
Gus down to Venice Beach. The bar is on the waterfront and
some of the pink stucco hasn't survived the winter gales.

Gus leads the way inside. He's taken the precaution of
making two copies of the paperwork lifted from Tyrone's
bedroom and has lodged the original in the safe at the Secret
Service field office. Tyrone has arrived early and is talking to
the barman over a beer.

Mahoney handles the introductions, kissing Tyrone lightly on the cheek. Tyrone raises an eyebrow at the sight of company he clearly hasn't expected but consents to join them all in the back room. The room is baseball-themed. Posters around the wall celebrate the history of the Brooklyn Dodgers, the bar's adopted team, and the display includes a framed shot of a black guy, his bat raised.

Tyrone gives it a long look, nods.

'Jackie Robinson,' he grunts. 'First nigger to play Major League Baseball. Raised in Pasadena.' He's looking at Gus. 'Right?'

'Right.'

They settle at the table. Gus disappears to collect drinks from the bar while Tyrone studies Kane's face.

'Auto crash?'

'Something like that.'

'But you didn't go through the windshield?'

'No.'

'Lucky guy. The rest of you OK?'

'Sure.'

Kane is watching him carefully and concludes that he knows nothing of what happened outside the corner store. This evening, he tells himself, is a chance to gauge exactly how close this man has gotten to Cuesta. According to the diaries, they met a year ago, in the spring of 1941.

Mahoney waits for the drinks to appear before leading off. Gus has mapped the way he wants the conversation to develop.

'You know Andy?' Mahoney is looking at Tyrone. 'Top honcho on the *LA Times* sports desk? You remember me talking about him?'

'Sure. You told me he'd show on Wednesday. Mr Cuesta had a place at a table for him.'

Mr Cuesta? Kane reaches for his beer, says nothing.

Mahoney is apologising for Andy's absence. Another pressing engagement, she says. The curse of top management on a paper like ours.

'I'm sure,' Tyrone nods peaceably. 'So what's this about?'

'Andy's a grassroots guy, always has been. When I told him about the set-up over at the garage he was happy to give me a hearing. Girl-on-girl spoke to him big time, especially me working on the paper.'

'Sure. So how can I help here?'

'He wants to know about what happens next. Am I hearing a third bout? A decider? If the answer's yes, Andy will be more than interested.'

'Interested how?'

'Big feature. Lots of coverage. Maybe a fancier stadium. How does that sound?'

'Sounds good. Me? I'm just a trainer, a pain in the ass on those gym sessions and a voice in the corner on the night. Mr Cuesta takes the decisions that matter.' He pauses, looking at Gus. 'You're writing that down?'

'I am.'

'Why?'

'Because...' Gus shrugs. '...I guess it might kinda fit.'

'With what, buddy? Care to tell me?' Tyrone's wary now. His glass is untouched.

'With where these fights, this garage thing, goes next. Hegarty used to sell autos. Exactly what is Mr Cuesta peddling now?'

'A great night out, I guess. This Andy fella wants the

proof? He should have been there. We did the count later. Nearly a thousand tickets sold. That's a lot of geld.'

'Sure. And the bets on top? The wagers? You gotta figure for that, too?'

'Not my department, buddy. I make the preparations, take the fighters where they need to be. Training is all, fitness, making sure it's all working up here.' Tyrone taps his head and then nods at the Jackie Robinson photo on the wall. 'Any athlete, any discipline, same story. Success is a mountain you gotta climb. Nothing in this town happens by accident.'

Nothing in this town happens by accident. This time it's Kane writing down the quote.

'What's going on here? You mind telling me?' Tyrone is spooked and it shows.

Mahoney catches Gus's eye. A tiny lift of her head is all it needs for Gus to produce one of the copies of the correspondence Kane lifted from Tyrone's bungalow. He lays it carefully on the table. Tyrone stares at it.

'Where did you get this?'

'We took it out of your suitcase, Mr Smith. The one under your bed. And in case you're wondering, we photographed it first, in that goddamn pocket in the lid. In my trade we call that provenance.'

This is a lie but Tyrone's not looking any more. Instead, he's studying the other sheet of paper. Finally, he looks up.

'So what?' he says, shrugging.

'So what?' Gus is leaning forward now, wanting to close the case, a pose – thinks Kane – that wouldn't be out of place in the ring. Kane's carrying a 9mm automatic, first round chambered, and his good hand slips under his jacket, checking the shoulder holster. Gus, he knows, is also armed.

'So what?' Gus repeats. 'We've had this stuff researched, my friend. Too much, and you're dead. A little squirt up the nose, you're flat on your face on the canvas.'

'You think I put her out? Between the rounds? Is that your beef?'

'I think Mr Cuesta told you to do it, and I think you said yes. All you have to do here and now, my friend, is to agree. A nod will do fine.' He stares Tyrone down. When Tyrone shakes his head, Gus produces the other envelope with the money. 'This is something else we found in that suitcase of yours, a thousand dollars in fifties. Care to tell me where they came from?'

'I sold a car,' Tyrone says at once.

'You can prove that? Show me a receipt?'

'There is no receipt.'

'I'm not surprised, and you know why? That money is worthless. It's all counterfeit, bad bills, nicely done but completely fake. That's the world your Mr Cuesta moves in. Smoke and mirrors and little something up the black girl's snout. He cheated on the fight and he's cheated paying you out. The guy's worthless. He's a gangster with fancy ideas but he needs to pay attention to the small print. He likes to play the Big Guy in this town and playing the Big Guy's gonna bite him in the ass. A thousand people watched that fight on Wednesday and I'm betting none of them bought the way it ended. You have anything to say, Mr Smith?'

Tyrone sits back. He's caught his breath, calmed himself. Impressive, Kane thinks.

'You guys some kind of cops?'

'Sort of.'

'You gonna arrest me? Shoot me maybe, get this thing over?'

'We're gonna do a little more work, Mr Smith, not much, and then we're gonna have another conversation.'

'With me?'

'With Mr Cuesta.'

'And what do you tell him?'

'We tell him exactly what we've just told you. We tell him that he's the big guy taking all the decisions here. We do the math on the bets laid and the odds he was offering, and we take one of those educated guesses about how much he made on the side. Oh yeah, and we also tell him about the big favour we just did you. The big reveal, my friend. A thousand bucks in ass-wipe currency.' Gus offers Tyrone a cold smile. 'Does that sound reasonable? Any of it? All of it? You have something to say, maybe?'

Tyrone is getting mad again. Kane knows exactly what he wants to do. Gus first, he thinks, then Kane himself, then maybe even Mahoney, and so he produces his weapon where Tyrone can see it.

'A warning is all, my friend,' he murmurs, 'just in case you have something foolish in mind.'

Tyrone looks first at the gun, then at the money and the documentation. Gus saves him the choice of voicing the obvious question.

'They're yours, Mr Tyrone. The letter is a copy. We have the original under lock and key. The thousand bucks you also get to keep, though in your shoes I'd ask Mr Cuesta for real clams that won't put you in the pokey. Everything has a deadline in this town and here's Mr Cuesta's. He needs to be in touch with me within forty-eight hours. I've ringed the number.'

Gus produces a card and slips it across. Tyrone studies it for a long moment and then sighs.

'And me?' he says.

'We put you to one side for the time being. Maybe we cut you a deal, maybe we don't. Depends how Mr Cuesta's disposed.'

Tyrone nods, gets to his feet, checks his watch. Everyone's looking up at him, everyone's watching, but it's Mahoney who breaks the silence.

'So how's Dolores?' she asks.

Tyrone studies her a moment, then offers a thin smile.

'Better,' he grunts.

Tyrone leaves. The Cherokee close around him in the darkness outside the bar and shepherd him to his car. Kane knows that word of the precautions they've taken – the private room, the carefully baited conversation, Kane's automatic, and finally the muscle waiting outside – will get back to Cuesta, and for that he's grateful. Cuesta's caught him with his guard down once. Never again. Gus shrugs, waves Kane's thanks away. Now, *hombre*, we wait.

Over the next two days, nothing happens. No words from Cuesta. No phone call. Nada. Then, on the Thursday morning, Kane lifts the phone in Beverly Hills to find Mahoney on the other end. She's sounding anxious. She's taken a call at the office, a male voice she didn't recognise. The message, repeated twice, sounds like a tip. Get yourself round to the Hollywood bungalow courts. Number seven. Tyrone Smith's place. As soon as.

'This guy left no name?'

'Nothing. I don't want to go alone, you know what I'm saying? I'll pick you up. Twenty minutes, Mr Kane.'

Kane gets dressed, checks his weapon, collects two of the Cherokees from their tent in the garden. It's hard to put the thought into words, and probably wrong to try, but what's started to happen here makes him very, very happy. He's back in control, able to call the shots, and for now at least he thinks he has the measure of this crazy town. Gus, as ever, was right. Rattle Cuesta's cage and see what happens.

Mahoney is a little late but the sight of the Cherokees flanking the tall figure of Kane puts a smile on her face. They drive east, hit Hollywood Boulevard, park outside the bungalow court. Mid-morning, the place is empty except for a Mexican gardener staring at a mess of weeds.

When Kane knocks on Tyrone's door there's no response. He knocks a second time, same result. The biggest of the two Cherokee offers to kick the door in but Kane has his picks out already and knows exactly which one to use. The spring gives with a tiny click and the door opens to a gentle push.

Kane draws his weapon and steps inside. The tap is still dripping and the curtains are still drawn against the daylight but there's another noise he can't at first figure out. He moves slowly down the narrow hall, heading for the living room. The door is an inch or two open and the noise is getting louder. Then he pauses. The noise is insistent, a buzzing, rising and falling. Flies, he thinks, or maybe bluebottles.

He eases the living room door open with his good foot, the gun steadied in his left hand, and it takes him perhaps a second to recognise the body slumped across the battered sofa. Tyrone's head is thrown back, lolling to one side, a small hole with powder burns in his temple. An automatic with a silencer is still dangling from one hand and the wall behind the sofa is caked with grey brain matter, darkened with dried blood and tiny shattered particles of bone.

Kane steps closer, waving away the cloud of bluebottles, suddenly aware of Mahoney's presence beside him. She's staring down at Tyrone's body.

'Mother of God,' she whispers. 'What the fuck have we done?'

Kane makes the calls. The first goes to Gus, who says very little. The second goes to the LAPD, who tell him to step away from the scene of the crime, lock the front door from the inside and await the arrival of officers. Kane sends the two Cherokee back to Beverly Hills, and a couple of cops attend within the hour, a beefy uniformed sergeant with a thinner detective, an older man in a decent suit who could use a good night's sleep. He takes a good look at Kane's face, and at the limp he's trying to disguise, and then asks for ID. Kane hands him his driving licence, as does Mahoney. The detective makes notes, and then pulls on a pair of gloves and circles the body on the sofa. The sergeant, meanwhile, has developed a serious interest in Mahoney.

'Hegarty Autos,' he says at last. 'I was there. Table by the ring. That was you put the black dame away?'

'It was, yes.'

'And this gentleman,' he nods down at Tyrone. 'He was in the black girl's corner?'

'He was.'

The detective steps back from the sofa. He's heard every word.

'Folks tell me that fight was fixed,' he's looking at the sergeant. 'You have a view on that, officer?'

'Folks are right. Fixed, and fixed good.'

'Ma'am?' He's turned to Mahoney now. 'You mind coming with us to the station? Tell us what happened?'

'In the ring, you mean?'

'No, ma'am.' He looks briefly at Kane, and then nods down at the body. 'Here.'

Mahoney is staring at him in disbelief. Kane asks whether they're under arrest.

'You mind if I do a body search, Mr Kane? Only now's the time to say.'

27

The uniformed sergeant drives to a police station back of Hollywood, Mahoney and Kane in the rear seat. Kane tells her to say nothing without having an attorney present. When she asks in a whisper why he hasn't told these people about his own status – Secret Service – he simply shakes his head.

At the police station, the sergeant hands over Kane's weapon, confiscated at the bungalow. The officer behind the desk writes Kane a receipt.

Mahoney uses a downtown legal practice retained by the *LA Times*. Most of their effort is expended on defending the paper from a variety of suits, mainly alleging defamation, and Kane takes advantage of Mahoney's right to have persons of her choice at the pre-interview brief. The lawyer the firm has despatched is a woman in her mid-thirties, older and plainer than Mahoney. Within minutes, Kane senses that Harriet Wallace has no time for women fighting women.

She makes notes on Mahoney's brief history with Tyrone Smith and has trouble understanding why Dolores' trainer should be offering pre-fight tips to an opponent.

'That's a straight conflict of interest, surely?'

Mahoney says something lame about the fight game. Keeping strange company, she mutters, is all part of the script.

'Script? You're telling me this fight was figured out beforehand? Who wins, who loses?'

Mahoney stares at her, then seeks help from Kane. The events of the past couple of hours, maybe days, have gotten the better of her. She liked Tyrone. She was OK with him, respected his knowledge, doesn't begin to understand why he'd find himself in so deep with a two-bit mobster like Cuesta.

Kane eases his damaged leg a moment, then leans forward. His overwhelming priority is to get them both out of here without a whiff of attached suspicion. The last thing Donovan needs is to have the LAPD all over Meier's revived interest in counterfeiting.

'Tyrone shot himself, right?' Kane says.

'He took a bullet through his head,' Wallace is frowning. 'That's all the police know for sure. I've dealt with Connolly a couple of times before. He's very experienced, very shrewd.'

Connolly is the suited detective who showed up at the bungalow. As soon as Mahoney and Kane are through with the attorney, he'll be asking the hard questions. Separate interviews, no conferring in between.

Wallace wants to know where Kane fits in all this. She's still searching for an appropriate word when Mahoney saves her the bother.

'We're buddies,' she says simply, nodding towards Kane. 'He takes care of me.'

Wallace doesn't like this either, raises an eyebrow, scribbles herself another note. Then she returns to Mahoney. She's playing the cop now, suspecting homicide dressed up as suicide. Every police investigation begins with the issue of alibi. So where was Mahoney these past two days?

'You want a full account?'

'Sure. It may save you trouble later. It pays to get these things clear in your own mind.'

'You think I did it? Killed the guy? Why would I ever do that?'

'That's different. That's motivation. We're dealing with opportunity. If you can prove you were somewhere else, produce a witness or two, we're home safe.'

'Shit.' Mahoney blinks.

'I beg your pardon?'

'I'm sorry.'

Mahoney throws another look at Kane, and then reconstructs the story of her last couple of days. Daytime, much of it happens at work. Nights, she's looking after her buddy.

'Looking after' is an unfortunate choice of verb. Wallace is staring at Kane, at the damage on his face, at the way he cups his injured elbow, much the way the detective did in the bungalow.

'You think I need an attorney of my own, ma'am?' asks Kane.

'I think you're gonna have some explaining to do. A guy appears to have shot himself to death. You were carrying a gun. Your friend here has prior knowledge of the victim. And I'm guessing you've been in some kind of altercation.'

Altercation, Kane thinks. Wonderful. 'You're telling me I've been settling accounts?'

'I'm telling you the LAPD are very straightforward when it comes to coincidence. The guy's dead. You're visibly injured and then there's the issue of the weapon you were carrying. You both have skin in the game. So, yes, an attorney of your own might be a wise precaution. You want to make a call?'

'I don't live here.'

'You don't? Someplace else? Some place close?'

'DC.'

'I get it,' Wallace nods, thoughtful now. 'You mind me asking what you do for a living, Mr Kane?'

'Sure, I mind.'

'That's a no?'

'That's a no.'

'You want me to organise someone?' The frown has returned. 'Only that might take a while.'

'Fine. I get one call from here. Is that right?'

'It is. You want that I organise a phone?'

Kane nods. The moment the attorney leaves the room Kane tells Mahoney to stonewall the detective as best she can.

'Give Connolly only what he needs,' he says. 'And leave Cuesta out of it.'

'Why? The guy wanted to fuck me. That matters.'

'Negative. We both need to be out of here before Connolly figures he's got enough to charge me.'

'For what?'

'For killing Tyrone. You tell Connolly about Cuesta, about how bad he wanted you, and Connolly will have the time of his life cooking up all kinds of fancy motivation. Maybe Tyrone was pimping for his boss. Maybe Tyrone himself had sampled the goods. Anything to turn me into Mr Jealous, the man with the gun.'

'Sample the goods? That's me?'

'That's you.'

'This is sick. What makes you say that?'

'I was a cop once. I know how these things play out. Guys like Connolly count the scalps they take. He's a Cherokee in a decent suit. Means and ends, Lou. Build a case, spin a yarn, and leave the rest to the jury. This is Hollywood, remember. My life in Connolly's hands? An LA jury between me and the chair? No thank you.'

The door opens and Wallace is back. A telephone is available on the front desk. Kane thanks her, offers Mahoney a parting nod, and makes his way back to the counter. The uniformed sergeant is making small talk with the woman behind the desk and Kane is aware of his eyes on the phone as Kane dials Gus's number. Mercifully, Gus is at home.

'Hollywood LAPD,' Kane says. 'Both of us.'

'I know, *hombre*.'

'You've got it covered?'

'Of course.'

Kane puts the phone down, watching the sergeant carefully transcribing the number. When he finally looks up, Kane asks about coffee.

'Sure.' He nods at Kane's face, at his ruined mouth. 'Black guy sure did a job on you, buddy.'

Kane drinks the coffee alone in another interview room, awaiting the arrival of the summoned attorney. He knows he'll have no problem fending off Connolly. His X-rays at the showbiz clinic, plus testimony from the medics, are all the proof he'd ever need that his injuries way pre-dated Tyrone's death, but dealing with Cuesta, settling his personal accounts with the man, have begun to swamp everything.

The moment he saw Tyrone's body on the sofa he knew this was no suicide. On the contrary, Cuesta was sending yet another message. A phone call to Mahoney at work was all it took. Just hurry along and see what you find. Mahoney, a journalist, responds to calls like that and the expression on her face as she stepped into the room and saw Tyrone was – Kane is certain – the work of a sadist. On one level, a chainsaw, the full Hollywood treatment, and a bunch of brown paper bags in city-wide trash cans afterwards. On another, a stranger's voice to summon the woman Kane loves to the remains of an execution.

Kane nods to himself, drains the coffee. On both occasions, Cuesta knew he could walk free and so far LA has made it easy for him, but that kind of liberty, even in this town, will one day come to a messy end. And when that happens, Kane plans to be around.

His summoned attorney has still yet to arrive when the door opens and Kane turns to find Gus stepping into the room. His face is wet from the rain beating at the window.

'Done,' he says.

'Done how?'

'Later, *hombre*. Your lady awaits you.'

28

Gus wants to take them both to a downtown nightclub called Dixie. It's barely five in the afternoon, dusk, rain still sheeting from a grey sky, and Kane isn't clear why they're getting wet when the place will be shut.

'Not to us, *hombre*. Trust me?'

Kane knows he has no option. Gus, he's decided, has become a magician. First, they've both been released without charge or further questioning. And now, he's about to open a door that should be locked.

The vestibule is dark, the desk unmanned. Gus leads them through another door, hits a light switch, gestures at a line of sepia photos from the Deep South as they head for a hanging bunch of beads at the end of the corridor. River scenes from Charleston and Savannah, horse-drawn buggies circling Atlanta's city centre, black musicians swaying along Bourbon Street in New Orleans.

Gus tallies them all, then parts the beads and stands back to gesture Mahoney through. He's dressed like a hobo, thrift-shop pants in a garish yellow that hang on his thin frame, a sweatshirt that could do with an hour in the wash. Kane knows that this is deliberate, a bid to unsettle the opposition, to wrongfoot people who think he's an easy mark, and just now it's a comfort to know that he's probably the best-connected Secret Service agent on the West Coast.

'Now what?' Mahoney has come to a halt. This is the heart of the nightclub. It's dark in here, and smells of carbolic soap, but candles flicker on a distant table. Gus takes the lead, his sandals flap-flapping as they cross the dance floor. They pass the glint of bottles behind a bar, thread their way through a maze of shadowed sofas and half-curtained booths, finally come to a halt. Dimly, Kane can hear the murmur of rush-hour traffic as LA buries another working day. The candlelit table is set for four.

'We're expecting company?'

'We're expecting a drink. My pleasure, guys.' Gus nods towards the bar. Mahoney wants a glass of water. Kane settles for a beer. Gus goes to the bar, hits another light switch, finds his way around. He returns with the water, three glasses and a bottle of Jim Beam.

'Krikorian only does Bud, *hombre*. He's got some crazy deal with the brewery people. I'm saving you getting angry.'

Kane nods. He hates Budweiser.

'Krikorian?'

'He's the guy started this chain. Dixie came to him one night a coupla years back. He was in bad company, bunch of off-duty LAPD. I know that because I was there and they were doing their best to get him wasted. Failed completely because the guy never takes a drink. The first Dixie was in Atlanta, and bombed. The next three were in the Bay Area in Frisco and are making him a fortune. This is his first try-out in LA.'

'Krikorian is the oil guy you mentioned? Got rich on a couple of gushers way back?'

'He is. Same guy. Same focus. Even more geld in the bank.'

'And you know him well?'

'Like a brother. Sharpest dude I ever met. Scary.'

'Scary how?'

'The brain on the guy. He thinks in five dimensions. Tosses out ideas, funds the good ones, puts the rest to sleep. Gimme a moment, *hombre*. We'll need to eat.'

Mahoney watches Gus get to his feet and disappear through a nearby door. The corridor beyond the door is lit and Kane catches the distant clatter of cutlery before the door bangs shut.

'Weird,' Mahoney mutters. 'Weird back with that cop and weirder now.'

Kane says nothing. When Gus returns he's carrying a leatherbound menu.

'Anything you like as long as it's cold,' he says. 'Except for the fries.'

Mahoney has no interest in the menu. She wants to know how come the police let them go. Her session with Connolly had barely begun when his phone rang and it was over.

'Was that your doing?' she asks Gus.

'Kinda.'

'How?'

Gus pours two Jim Beams, pushes a glass in Kane's direction.

'I'm blaming Prosper,' he says. 'She has this thing going with a guy way up the LAPD. The current Chief has a heart attack or some other dumb thing happens, and this is the guy who takes over. He sees a lot of Prosper, and I mean a lot. He's all-over familiar with the lady and Prosper has the evidence to prove it. They get up to stuff together, stuff he wouldn't like the world to share. Crude? Sure. But a phone call is all it takes.'

'You made the phone call?' Kane, this time.

'I did, *hombre*. And our LAPD friend was grateful. He knows I have the pix because Prosper told him way back. I told him about Tyrone, and I told him the time he was wasting talking to you guys. I also told him where else to maybe look. Result? You both get an early pass, and here we are. The fries are sensational, by the way. And so is the Caesar salad.'

'Where else to look?' Kane asks.

'Sure. If I was Cuesta just now I'd be thinking hard about TJ.'

'Tijuana?' This from Mahoney. She's looking at Kane. 'I thought you told me to lay off Cuesta.'

'I did.' Kane nods at Gus. 'But this changes everything. Let Connolly off the leash and, like I said before, he'd have found ways of framing a case against me. Cops aren't fussy about evidence. Juries might like the cut of the Prosecutor's suit and a bunch of other irrelevant stuff. I don't recall shooting Tyrone Smith, but the truth cuts no ice out here.'

'That's harsh, *hombre*.' Gus is laughing. 'Not that I disagree.'

'You mean it?' Mahoney is staring at Gus, then Kane. 'Both of you?'

'I guess we do.'

'That's sick.' She closes the menu.

Moments later, footsteps coming down the corridor from the street. A door opens and shuts to admit two women. One of them reaches for a switch on the wall and the nightclub is suddenly flooded with light.

Kane turns in his seat, reaching under his jacket for his weapon but remembers that it's still at the police station, confiscated after a body search. Then he feels Gus's hand on his arm.

'Steady, *hombre*,' he mutters. He gets to his feet and saunters across to the raised dais that serves as a stage. The older of the two women he clearly knows. They hug and when he gestures back towards the table the woman takes a look and raises a hand in greeting. The other woman is much younger, taller. She's wearing some kind of beach robe, probably flannel, and she's carrying a tightly rolled length of something that looks like cotton.

Kane is gazing round. The shadowy magic of the nightclub has gone. Half a dozen Confederate generals photographed in various settings peer down from the walls, but the rest of the place looks empty and cheerless, a set scored for low lights, heads-together conversation and unlimited quantities of alcohol.

Gus is still looking at the tiny stage. 'The older woman used to be a stripper back in the day, really nice woman, raised a storm every night over in Venice Beach. Krikorian put her on the payroll, my idea, and kinda fell in love with her. Now she handles the entertainment in all his outlets.'

'And the other woman?' Mahoney is watching her unfurl what turns out to be the Confederate flag.

'Dipshit from Paramount. Body like you've never seen before but absolutely dead above the neck. That's Krikorian speaking. She won't leave the poor guy alone. She's desperate for a break and thinks he's the guy to make it happen. This is an audition. She gets one shot in front of the talent boss. Either you look or you don't, your choice.'

Mahoney half turns away but Kane knows she's still watching. The older woman has yet to shed her coat.

She's bending over a turntable on the edge of the stage and moments later they're all listening to 'Dixie Land'. It's a cheerful, upbeat ditty, scored for ukelele and marching troops on dusty roads, with lyrics that set millions of booted feet tapping and tapping.

Away! Away! Away down south to Dixie!

The starlet from Paramount looks blank for a moment, and then steps out of the beach robe, and gives the flag a shake or two. She's naked except for a stripper's thong and there isn't a line in her body that any casting director would ever want changed. Even the older woman is looking impressed.

Whether or not there's any script here, any suggestion of what she might do next, isn't clear but a slightly impatient gesture from the older woman stirs her into action and she tries out a couple of moves with the flag but nothing matches either the spirit or the tempo of the music.

This, Kane knows, is a big ask. There's nothing raunchy about 'Dixie Land' and it would take a great deal of experience to make it work in front of a nightclub audience. The starlet tries a couple of game moves, hopelessly out of time with the music, before coming to a halt. Gus, Kane thinks, is right. The body of a goddess but nothing upstairs to bring it to life.

At this point, Kane becomes aware of another presence beside the table. He's tall and a pound or two overweight. He's sharply dressed – blazer, white shirt, red tie with thin blue stripes, knife-edge creases in his grey pants. The hint of a tan has so far survived the winter, and his jet-black hair is combed back from a high forehead. The contrast with Gus couldn't be more stark.

Krikorian, Kane thinks. And he's right.

Gus does the introductions, offers Krikorian a seat, shrugs when he elects to stay on his feet. He's watching the stage as the starlet takes advice from the older woman, abandons the flag and launches into a whole new routine as the music picks up again from the start.

Krikorian gives her maybe twenty seconds. The starlet has peeled off her thong, snagged it on one heel, and landed on her ass as the music skips away.

'Well?' Krikorian is looking at Gus.

'The answer's no. She's wasting her time, and yours. Drawing classes, maybe. Still life might be more her thing.'

Krikorian nods and draws a manicured finger across his throat when the older woman checks him for a reaction. A minute later, and the pair of them have gone.

Krikorian settles at the table, enquires whether they want food. When Gus and Kane both say yes, he takes their order and departs to the kitchen.

Mahoney wants to know why he's here. Kane knows that the interlude with the hapless starlet has deepened whatever's gotten under her skin.

'Krikorian backs hunches,' Gus says. 'Famous for it.'

'And?'

'One of them was Cuesta. The guy talks a good business plan. Krikorian made the mistake of believing him but I'm guessing that bit of the story might be over, which will be a very big problem for our spick friend. Krikorian backed him with a little money of his own but friends of his underwrote pretty much every other investment. The moment Krikorian pulls out is the moment Cuesta goes under. Maybe this is the time to do us all a favour.'

'Me?'

'You.'

'How?'

'All you have to do is listen. He's like the dentist of your dreams. Full root canal but you won't feel a thing.'

Mahoney holds his gaze for a moment, and then shakes her head. Bad to worse, Kane thinks.

Krikorian reappears from the kitchen. The food will be on its way within minutes. In the meantime, he takes the spare seat next to Mahoney and offers his congratulations.

'What for?'

'Your Wednesday appearance. I was there at ringside and I saw the first fight, too. The black girl could have hurt you very badly. She's good. No offence but she's different class. You took the fight to her and the record says you won.'

'The record?'

'The referee found in your favour. In my book, that's winning.'

'But?'

Krikorian studies her for a long moment. Then he says he wants to know about Cuesta.

'You were happy to have him as your agent?'

'I was flattered. No one was taking much notice of me. Having him on board made a big difference.'

'So what did you think he wanted?'

'He wanted big numbers. That's what he told me. That's the phrase he used. Women fighting women sells tickets. Black on white sells more. On both counts he was right so I'm not complaining.'

'And what did he want from you?'

'He wanted me in shape. He told me Dolores was a class

act. He had a couple of movies, previous fights of hers, two knockouts within the distance, so he was right.'

'Anything else?'

'She'd been fighting forever. She knew all the moves.'

'I meant you…and this new agent of yours.'

Mahoney freezes for a moment, then looks away towards the abandoned stage.

'What do you really want to know, Mr Krikorian?' she asks.

'I want to know…' he shrugs, '…about any pressures he might have put on you.'

'To win, you mean?'

'That, too.'

Mahoney shakes her head, studies her hands, then finally looks up. Kane knows that now is the moment he should intervene, but he also knows that it's far too late.

'He wanted to fuck me, Mr Krikorian. He wanted to do that very badly and he's not the man to keep secrets. I have a say in this kind of stuff and I told him no. That's a word he doesn't like.'

'So what happened?'

'He offered me money. Not some kind of come-on, of course, because he doesn't do free money, but money against future earnings. He called it an act of faith. He called me his investment.'

'How much?'

'A thousand dollars.'

'To sleep with him?'

'To fuck me. I'm not sure this is a guy with much conversation. Are you getting the picture here, Mr Krikorian? Cuesta is an animal. He believed that once he'd fucked me

I'd find it hard not to come back for more. One word would be overconfident. Another might be delusional. Either way, I'm afraid the party's over.'

'Meaning?'

'In the first place I won't be fighting Dolores again. And number two, I'd quite like Cuesta to be the guy that gets fucked.'

All heads have been turned to Mahoney. A polite cough reveals the presence of a loaded tray. The cook leaves the food on the table and offers Krikorian a respectful nod before beating a retreat. By now, Mahoney has drained her glass of water and pushed her chair back.

'That creepy audition,' she nods towards the stage. 'When will you men ever take a look at yourselves? Cuesta belongs in a zoo. I've thought it for a while. But what gets us truly mad is the rest of you. We're women, for God's sake. We have a voice as well as a body. I know I sound like Eleanor Roosevelt but maybe that's no bad thing. Wise up, guys. It's a whole lot later than you think.'

Mahoney gets to her feet, stoops briefly to plant a kiss on the worst of Kane's bruises, and then heads for the door that leads to the street.

The men round the table watch her disappear, and then exchange glances. It's Gus, as ever, who finds the words that best fit.

'Outstanding,' he says. 'She nailed it on the first take.'

Hours later, back in Beverly Hills, Kane finds Mahoney in bed. It's late evening and Kane thinks at first that she's asleep. Then she stirs, opens an eye, reaches out for him.

'No need.' He settles on the edge of the bed. 'Krikorian won't be a problem.'

'You think I'm supposed to apologise?' She's staring at him. 'You don't think I was serious?'

'Of course you were serious. I meant not staying, not listening to the guy, not hearing what he has in mind for Cuesta.'

'So tell me,' she's wide awake now. 'Come to bed.'

Kane strips, eases his knee, climbs in beside her. Krikorian, Kane says, has decided to dump Cuesta. Without the Armenian's backing, his days in the LA limelight are history.

'And that makes you happy?' This from Mahoney.

'Yes. And you?'

'It won't happen. Anyone who thinks that man's gonna take it on the chin, and act humble, and say sorry, and pack his bags for TJ doesn't know him. I do, and so does Prosper. Have you talked to her? Gotten an opinion?'

'No.'

'Then do. Krikorian should have looked harder in the first place but I guess you can say that about any man. One other thing, Agent Kane. That chemical smell and that locked door at the very end of the corridor? The one that Dexter can't leave alone? Whining and whining? Exactly what happens in there? And how come it's so goddam secret?'

29

Next morning, Kane waits for Mahoney to leave for work before taking the key to Meier's suite of rooms. Last night he'd done his best to fend off her questions about the locked door and the dog missing the company of Prosper's live-in counterfeiter. The last thing he needs just now is Mahoney all over an operation as sensitive as this, and although she'd given his story about some precious family archive of Prosper's a cursory hearing, he knew she hadn't really bought it. Keeping Mahoney at arm's length, even in a house this big, was never going to be easy but just now it feels close to impossible. Best to hurry the operation along, and get Meier settled someplace else.

Happily, Meier – thanks to an all-night session – is way ahead of schedule. The engraved copper plate is now ready for a trial run through Takiwa's press, and Kane lets him grab just a little more sleep before running him downtown to Alameda Street. The rain has gone now, and the business district is basking in the LA soup of sunshine and vehicle exhaust.

Kane parks and leads Meier across to the print shop. To his surprise, the big plate windows in the front have been criss-crossed with brown tape, and the moment he pushes in through the door he senses a catastrophe in the making. Both Takiwa and his daughter emerge from the print room in back. The old man looks even more gaunt than usual and the sight of two damaged faces does nothing for his peace of mind.

'Auto accident,' Kane explains lamely. 'Too much rain, guys driving like maniacs.'

Takiwa doesn't believe him.

'Someone hit you?'

'A Cadillac. Last year's model. Christmas present from his wife. Like I said, the guy shouldn't have been driving so fast.' Kane nods at the windows. 'Expecting bombers? Some kind of raid?'

Under the circumstances it isn't the most tactful of questions, and Kane catches Meier wincing. Takiwa looks helplessly at his daughter, robbed of an answer, and the girl steps forward with an explanation. All the neighbouring Japanese businesses have been closed, she says. Whole families have been arrested and shipped out in the backs of Army trucks. The only shop still open is their own, and white Americans in the area are demanding to know how come.

'So what do you say?'

'Say?' The old man this time, very angry. 'We can say nothing. Nothing. Why? Because you tell us, because you say softly-softly, because of that.' He's guessed the contents of Meier's carefully wrapped brown parcel. 'These people, your people, want us out. They come in the evening, every evening. They frighten my wife, my family. They frighten us all. So what we do, Uncle Sam?'

It's a very good question and just now Kane doesn't have an answer. Can Donovan organise protection of some kind? LAPD? A bunch of US Army reservists? Or would that simply make the situation worse? He simply doesn't know, but for now he needs to put Meier and Takiwa together. Kane is impressed by the $1,000 engraving but he's no expert. Only Takiwa can make the judgement call that matters.

The daughter leads them into the print room. It's dusk outside and Takiwa switches on a powerful spotlight before laying hands on a big magnifying glass to examine Meier's work. To Kane's relief, this has a calming effect on the old man. He begins to make small animal noises of what can only be approval, tiny snuffles of appreciation. When his magnifying glass lingers over Grover Cleveland's moustache he's beaming with delight, and he finishes up with a long slow pass over the signature of Henry Morgenthau Jr.

'*Subarashi*,' he murmurs.

'Fabulous,' his daughter translates.

With a low bow, Meier thanks him in Japanese. Friends again, Kane thinks.

While Meier discusses the next technical steps with the old man, Kane takes a stroll down the street. The deli next door is doing slow business for this time of the evening and Kane steps inside to ask the owner about the print shop. This time the guy is guarded. Sure, folks around here are riled up about Takiwa and his family. He's no personal beef with the family next door, nice people, hardworking, but, hell, we're supposed to be at war with the Japs so how come the print guy's still in business? When Kane asks about the possibility of violence, of a crowd taking proceedings into their own hands, of maybe even storming the place, the Italian simply shrugs.

'Might happen, might not. Who knows, buddy? Times like these?'

At this, Kane nods, leaves his card, adds Prosper's home

number, asks the Italian to phone him if there's trouble tonight. Then he leaves the shop, knowing he has to assume the worst and lay plans for the evening. Back in the print shop, Meier has finished with Takiwa. The old man is keen to test-print a sample of the notes, maybe as early as tomorrow. He seems to have forgotten all about white mobs howling for his blood.

Kane shakes his head.

'Wrap it up again,' he nods at the plate. 'And ask if I can use the old guy's telephone.'

Meier gets the daughter to sort out the telephone. Meanwhile, he carefully wraps the copper plate, tapes the brown paper, and secures the package with string, an operation that appears to perplex the watching Takiwa. When he mutters a question to Meier, Kane – back from the phone – asks for a translation.

'He's offering to try a test-run tonight.'

'No,' Kane shakes his head. 'Tonight you're sleeping at a friend of mine's. And the plate comes, too.'

Kane drives Meier down to Venice Beach, where Gus makes him welcome. He says there'll be no problem finding a cushion or two on the floor, and if the guy's really lucky he might score a small-hours sighting of Parsifal.

'You like Wagner, *hombre?*' He's looking at Meier.

'*Tannhauser?* Sublime. Listen to it forever. The later work? Not so much.'

Gus stares at him, for once taken by surprise, but Meier pats him on the arm, a gesture that indicates no offence meant.

Quakerism in action, Kane thinks. Peace and resolution and the hand of friendship. Just what this crazy nation needs.

'Tomorrow, buddy,' Kane tells Meier. 'And good luck with the snake.'

Gus accompanies him downstairs and out into the street.

'Cuesta's gone missing,' he says. 'According to my cop buddies.'

'You know why?'

'There's a warrant out for his arrest. Our LAPD friend listened hard to what we all had to say last night and drew the right conclusions. Mahoney needs to take care. Cuesta on the lam is something she'd be wise to avoid.'

Kane drives back to Beverly Hills. As he's cleared by security on the gate, he's puzzled by the absence of Mahoney's car in the drive. She should be back by now, he thinks. He parks and lets himself into the house. Upstairs, he unlocks the door to Meier's secured quarters and cleans up the remaining traces of his work before Mahoney gets back. Dexter joins him within seconds, moving from room to room, hunting for his beloved Meier. Kane has bought slices of salami for the dog from the deli next to the print shop and tempts him downstairs to the kitchen. Prosper is drinking coffee at the big table and wants to know why Mahoney is so late. Kane says he doesn't know.

'Cuesta,' he says. 'You know him. You've dealt with the guy. Tell me the worst.'

Prosper doesn't answer. Instead, she goes to a cupboard and fetches out a bottle of bourbon, not Jim Beam. She pours three fingers, adds a trickle more, and sets it down on the table.

'Water?' Kane enquires.

'No water.' She raises her coffee mug. 'To that lovely woman of yours.'

Kane doesn't move, doesn't touch the bourbon.

'Cuesta's on the run,' he says. 'What happens next? What will he do? What's he feeling right now?'

Prosper studies him for a while.

'They're really after him?' she asks at last.

'They are.'

'Then it depends, I guess.'

'On what?'

'On what's gone down.'

Kane tells her about Tyrone Smith. About setting Dolores up for the fall. About the big money in a third fight. Then he tells her about Cuesta's thousand dollars riding on Mahoney saying yes.

'That's the guy. A price on everything.'

'So when she says no?'

'He'll double it. And maybe double it again if he has to.'

'He didn't. Not according to her.'

'Then he's decided to find another way. That won't be a problem. This is a man who knows no limits. Did his mom never smack him right? Did he even have a mom? Life has a way of dealing with people like Cuesta, and maybe this town is the perfect example. In the end they get trodden on. They get crushed. Same used to happen back home on the reservation. Guy – and it's always a guy – is a pain in the ass. Does bad things. Then very bad things. Then the worst of things. Then you wake up one morning and go out into the sunshine and there he is, pegged down in the dew, knives through his hands and feet, buck naked, unzipped, ripped open, just alive, and folks just pass him by. The last thing he sees are folks ignoring him. These are people he knows, people he sees every day. That hurts plenty. That kills.'

Unzipped. It's a wonderful image. Kane at last reaches for the bourbon.

'You're telling me he needs the attention?'

'Of course. He's a man-child. He needs the attention, and he needs the applause, and he needs to have people step aside for him in the street. He needs to make a noise. He's a kid that way, and he's never stopped because noise matters. That maybe puts him alongside most folks in this town but Cuesta was born different. He never figured the truth about pain and pleasure, where one stops and the other starts, and that's maybe because they both feed from the same trough. This can be kinda confusing, especially if you happen to be a woman. Cuesta can look after you good. He can make you laugh. He can buy you fancy presents. He can even quote Spanish poetry, though women who know better than me says he makes it up. But that doesn't matter because you're opening the door to a guy who will figure out just how best to juice you.'

'You know this?'

'I do.'

'Care to tell me?'

'Why?'

'Because it matters.'

'To you? To Lou?'

'There's no difference.'

'That's nice. That's good. That makes you one lucky man, Mr Kane.' Prosper nods, impressed.

'So?' Kane gestures around. 'He came here?'

'He did.'

'Daytime? After dark?'

'One afternoon.'

'You'd met him before?'

'Plenty. He'd seen my movies. He told me I'd given him an idea or two. This is a guy who doesn't do impressed but I guess I came close. Back in the day when they shot those movies I could do some wild things. I thought he wanted some of that and I was wrong.'

'So what happened?'

'He wanted to fuck but he wouldn't kiss me. No foreplay, no smoochy-smoochy, *nada*. He knew from the movies I liked oral, doing it, having it done. Me? The mood's right, I go along with anything. So we're next door, down on the carpet, with a cushion under my ass, and I'm thinking he might start low, an ankle maybe, work north, and that's what he did in a way, but quick, real quick, like he was parked illegal, needed to run down the road and get back behind the wheel. I juice easy. I'm wet as hell and wanting him bad and he knows that because I've made plenty of room for him, opened wide, and he keeps taking a little peek up at my face, seeing how I'm doing, where I'm at, and then he's there, on time, on schedule, and he's good, little flicks of the tongue, a teaser, a guy who knows his way around, and then it's the full tour, his tongue everywhere like he hasn't eaten for days, and all of a sudden I'm burning up a storm, pain like I can't describe, real fierce, deeper and deeper, worse and worse, and I've pushed him away, and rolled over, and tried to make the pain go away. Tears in my eyes, Mr Kane. And that's only happened once in my life.'

Kane nods, studies the bourbon, reaches for the glass.

'So what happened next?'

'He started laughing. He was on his feet now, buck naked, he was standing over me, he was getting an eyeful. Not of someone he wanted to fuck. But of me hurting.'

'That's what turned him on?'

'Sure. I guess the word is control. He wanted a celebration, a scalp, not a fuck, and I guess that's what I gave him.'

'But how did he do it? What made you burn?'

'Raw chillies. He chomped a couple before he arrived and I never knew. Later I heard it's an old Mexican trick spicks play on whores they don't like.'

'In Tijuana?'

'Sure,' Prosper reaches for her own glass. 'And here, too.'

The phone goes minutes later. It's the Italian who owns the deli next to the print shop. Kane can hear the bellow of a crowd in the background. The print shop, the Italian says, is under attack. He thinks the mob want to burn it down. He's phoned for the cops but so far nothing's happened. Some of the guys outside are mashed. He's seen chains, baseball bats, a coupla guns. Kane tells him he's on his way.

'You'll need help, *amigo*. You gotta gun, too?'

Kane has no weapon. He should have claimed it back from the LAPD but he hadn't. Cursing himself, he limps as fast as he can to the Sedan. The bourbon has topped him up. He's brimming with anger, with something close to wrath. LA, America's bright future, is darkening around him. Mahoney, he thinks. Takiwa and his family. Truckloads of Japs, arrested and corralled and run out of town to spend God knows how

long behind the wire. Dolores in recovery, wondering what
on earth happened to her. Cuesta running neat rings around
a bunch of LA's finest. And then Mahoney again. How come
she hasn't made it home? Where is she?

Kane drives to Alameda Street. The print shop lies half a
block away and, turning off Alameda, Kane can suddenly see
the mob ahead. There must be hundreds of them. They're
washing back and forth, the way crowds do, a human
concertina, pausing to suck in air for another volley of
obscenities. Kill the Japs! Remember Pearl Harbor! Death
to Tojo! Then he spots a curl of smoke coming from beyond
the mob and his blood freezes. They're in, he thinks. They've
smashed the windows, stormed into the print shop itself, set
fires with all that spare paper. He glances up at his rear-view
mirror, wanting whole fleets of LAPD response wagons, cops
with nightsticks, serious civic intent, but all he sees are the
shadows of yet more protestors, keen to volunteer for this
grubby little pocket of the nation's war.

Kane abandons the Sedan and begins to run as fast as his
injuries will allow. Getting through the crowd is a nightmare
and in the end he backs out and takes advantage of tiny gaps
around the edges. Not having a weapon, he realises, is the
dumbest thing he's ever done. Say he gets inside the print
shop? Say he has to deal with a scrum of drunks and psychos
and crazed racists? Does he talk nice and point out the error
of their ways? Does he do the Quaker thing and rely on
silence and good faith?

'See what I mean, buddy?'

It's the Italian from the deli. He's standing square in
Kane's way, pointing at the print shop. Kane was right about
the windows, right as well about the mob wanting to destroy

everything, to burn the place down, to warm its hands on the embers of what's left.

'Takiwa? The girl? The rest of the family?' Kane is watching a guy emerge from the shop with an armful of groceries.

'They fled earlier, right when the trouble started, they'd had enough, don't blame them.'

'So what's next?'

'They'll torch the place. I know some of these faces. They're scum. They come for a night out.'

Kane nods, knowing he can do precisely nothing. Then something else happens, something he'd least expected, a glimpse of a face he knows only too well.

Mahoney.

She's maybe twenty yards away, an impossible distance in a mob like this. She's animated, bent over her shorthand pad, trying to hold the attention of the big guy beside her. She's the reporter from the *LA Times*, summoned to explore the snarl on the face of this great nation, to map its uglier moments, and to record whatever happens next.

Kane pushes hard to close the distance between them, fails completely. He can smell smoke now. Fireworks? The blaze catching at the print shop? He has no idea but then comes a huge surge, a wave of movement transmitted from body to body, and Kane nearly falls as a stranger catches his wrecked thigh. Kane gasps with pain, recovers, finds Mahoney again. For whatever reason she's further away, buoyed by the crowd. Her interviewee has disappeared and she's started on another guy, smiling her smile, rolling her pencil the way she does, readying a new page on the shorthand pad. Kane shouts her name, shouts louder. Nearby heads turn, ask what the fuck he's doing, tell him to take it easy. He ignores them, turns briefly to check on the Italian, but the man has vanished. Mahoney, he thinks. Before this thing gets out of hand.

From nowhere comes the bright dazzle of a firework, then another, someone lobbing them from the back of the crowd. For a moment, Kane has lost touch with Mahoney but the heads in front of him suddenly part and he sees her. She's still asking questions, still scribbling, still squeezing strangers as hard as she can to see what might come out. Then, just a glimpse, another face, male. He's close by Mahoney and when heads crane back for sight of yet another firework he doesn't move. Kane can't be sure, not yet, but now something else is happening. The distant howl of police sirens grows louder and louder and suddenly the end of the road is full of LAPD riot wagons, plus a couple of fire tenders. The noise is deafening and the full beams of the headlights settle on the besieging mob.

Kane is still looking at the face. Even the presence of the LAPD doesn't distract him. He's feet away from Mahoney now. She has her back to him and she's stuffing her pad into her bag. Then he reaches for her. He has something in his hand that Kane can't see, and when she struggles to turn – far too late – to investigate, he sees the panic in her face.

José Cuesta.

Book Four

30

Gus and Meier are listening to music when Kane makes it to Venice Beach. Gus insists he come upstairs, fails to realise what Kane badly wants to say. Meier is flat on his back on the carpet, staring up at the reptile tank, his long fingers keeping time with the music in the late evening chill.

'*Tristan und Isolde*,' Gus is looking down at Meier. 'Our third go at the prelude. Halfway to heaven already. Ever think what awaits us up there, Quince? Ever give it a thought? Hell and damnation? Wall-to-wall Coke and fries? Our friend here is thinking the big silence but I guess all Quakers count on that.'

'Cuesta,' Kane says. He's looking at the disc going round and round. The wind-up phonograph has developed a squeak.

'Yeah?' Gus, at last, is tuning in.

Kane brings him up to date. Mahoney, he says, has been abducted. The print shop, last time he checked, was still on fire. The Jap family made it out OK but he's guessing the machinery out back is in ruins.

Meier rouses himself, steals across the room and lifts the needle from the disc. No more talk of the afterlife.

Gus is already bent over the phone, dialling a number, shielding the mouthpiece.

'You got the time it happened?'

'Gone ten. You're talking to the cops?'

'Will be. Once the guy picks up.'

'Tell him the cavalry had just arrived. They'll have it on the log.'

'What else, *amigo*? Cuesta had wheels? A plate number maybe?'

'No idea. It was a crazy night. A mob like that, you've got no chance.'

'But he walked her out? Found a way? That's what you're saying?'

'Yeah. The cops broke everything up. Enough nightsticks and you're looking to go home. I was trying to find the Mercedes but...' he shrugged, '...*nada*.'

'He could be driving anything. Even Cuesta wouldn't risk showboat wheels on a mission like that.'

Gus finally makes the connection on the phone. He briefly explains what's happened and then reaches for a pad and a pen. Lots of nodding. A brief, mirthless laugh at the end, then the conversation is done.

'That was...?'

'Buddy of mine on Homicide, name of Vic Kosch. Happens he's on the Cuesta job, excellent guy, we couldn't have done better. That car of yours still outside? *On y va*, Quince. *Muy pronto*.'

They drive to the Hollywood precinct station where Kane had left his gun. Kosch has given up on an early night and meets them out front. Gus says Vic is one of the top detectives in the squad, just promoted Senior Leader, which sits oddly with his looks. He has the body and the face of a choirboy. Mid-twenties, Kane thinks. Max.

Kosch takes them inside and negotiates the release of Kane's weapon against his signature. Privacy comes in the shape of an airless cubby-hole with a door that barely fits but Kosch has sole occupancy. There are scabs of dried glue on the wall where the previous owner hung his posters, and Kane briefly inspects the family photo on Kosch's desk. The woman has a melting smile for the camera but *three* kids? Hard to believe.

Kosch has produced a thick file from the safe in the corner of his office. Aside from a steel cabinet, this is the only item of furniture in the room. Kane has seldom sat in a chair so uncomfortable.

'We've listed addresses of interest,' Kosch is looking at Gus. 'You're welcome to help yourself.'

'I can take it away?'

'Of course you can't, buddy.' He finds a pad and pen, and slides them across the desk.

Kane watches Gus get to work on the list. Each address is accompanied by a name or names, and where appropriate lists of previous indictments.

Kosch wants more detail on the riot outside the print shop. Kane does his best but knows he can offer nothing to move the enquiry forward. No witness statements. No vehicle details. Not even a confirmation that Mahoney was taken at gunpoint.

'Likely, though?' Kosch asks.

'Your guess, buddy. Might have been a blade but a scene like that a gun would be favourite. Something small, something neat and tidy. Snub-nose, maybe. All she has to do is see it. You've profiled Cuesta?'

'Not me personally. There's a whole bunch of stuff in here

but I only just picked up the file from Connolly. He sends his best, by the way. No offence intended.'

'None taken. Guy has a job to do.'

Kosch nods. Close up, Kane thinks, he looks a whole lot older.

'Secret Service?' Kosch asks. 'Am I right?'

'Yeah.'

'DC? All that Precinct Sixteen shit?'

'You got it.'

Kane goes no further, happy to leave Donovan out of the conversation. When Kosch enquires what he's doing in LA, Kane sees no point in playing games. These guys, after all, take motivation very seriously.

'I guess you could call it a vacation. The lady's name is Mahoney.'

'Wife? Girlfriend?'

'Partner.' Kane offers the ghost of a smile and then scribbles the Santa Monica address and hands it over.

'And this is where we'll find you?'

'Afraid not.' Another address, this time in Beverly Hills.

Kosch nods, impressed, wants to know more, and so Kane tells him about Cuesta, about his obsession with Mahoney, about the Dolores fights, spells out the entire timeline until he's gotten to the corner store and a small armful of shopping.

'They jumped you, right?' Kosch is looking at Kane's face. 'How many of them?'

'Four, including Cuesta.'

'You were carrying?' Kosch's hand strays to his shoulder holster.

'No.'

'No? How does that work?'

Kane's gaze drifts to the family photo on the desk.

'Good question,' he mutters. 'And one I've lived with ever since.'

Kosch has the eyes of a good detective. Stony when it matters, warm when it matters more. Just now, he's smiling.

'How about I write "vacation",' he nods at the pad. 'And leave it at that?'

Gus and Kane are on the road within the hour, heading back to Venice Beach. Gus has been through Cuesta's file page by page and has a bunch of notes to prove it. Tomorrow, he says, Kane might put in a call to Donovan. With the print shop trashed, and the Takiwa family probably en route to internment, the counterfeit caper will have to be cranked up all over again, but Meier's the one best placed to find another printer. In the meantime, Gus and Kane can settle their account with Cuesta.

'He'll be in touch,' Kane says. 'I guarantee it.'

'How come?'

'The guy's a psycho. Weird and sad and dangerous. He's very particular the way he gets his kicks and something tells me he's only just started. He's gonna tie us up tight and yank us every which way, me especially. You piss the man good, and you're in for the worst time. Lou knows it already, and so do I.' Kane touches the worst of the bruising around his eyes as Gus brings his car to a stop outside the reptile store.

'You figured it all out already?' Gus says with just a hint of admiration. 'Got it flat down there? No creases? No smudges? Ways to go?'

'Not me, buddy. Prosper.' Kane smothers a yawn and fumbles for his car keys. '*Mañana*, eh? Can't get any worse, says me.'

31

Kane passes a long night in Beverly Hills. No Meier. No Mahoney. Just the low murmur of small-hours conversation through the open window from the Cherokee tent in the garden. Dexter pays him a visit shortly before dawn, sniffing Mahoney's pillow, and for once Kane is glad of the dog's company.

Prosper brings him coffee an hour or so later. She also drops a letter on the blanket. Kane studies the envelope. The clue is the letter 'K', thick, black capitals.

'Left at the front gate in the middle of the night.' This from Prosper. 'Young guy in some kinda uniform. Left no name. You want that I leave?' She's looking hard at Mahoney's side of the bed.

Kane has yet to tell her about last night but decides this is the time. She sits on the bed, listens hard, strokes the dog. At the story's end, she nods and tells him to maybe open the envelope.

'Why?'

'Because there'll likely be more of them, more envelopes, and in that case we might take an interest in who's doing the deliveries.'

Kane nods. Sound advice. Inside the envelope is a photograph of premises he recognises. Hollywood Reptiles. Venice Beach. He turns the photo over. On the back is a message in the same black ink. Four in the afternoon, two days ago. Paid with a C-note.

Kane looks at the photo and closes his eyes. It's a rattlesnake, poised to strike. Prosper hasn't moved.

'Well?' she says.

'Lou hates snakes. They're the one thing in the world that terrify her. Cuesta must know that.'

'How?'

'Either she told him, because she never kept it a secret, or maybe he read it in the paper. She did a piece back in the summer last year. Mid-August, slow news month. She took a trip to the Grand Canyon one time and came face to face with a rattler. Nothing bad happened. She backed off and the snake was gone but the sound, that rattle, never left her. We were in a circus back of Redondo Beach last year and there was a flamenco band. The lady with the castanets? Lou was out of there in seconds.'

Kane takes the photo to Venice Beach, shows it to Gus. Gus pulls a face – bad shit coming – and together they go down to the reptile shop. Gus and the owner are big buddies. Coupla days back? Late afternoon? Sales just now are slow to non-existent and he has no problem finding the entry in the ledger.

'Rattlesnake,' he looks up, grinning. 'Real beauty. Prime condition. Young male. Vicious as hell.'

The news ices Kane's blood. Lately, for whatever reason, his subconscious has become his worst enemy and now he's fighting images of Cuesta taunting Mahoney with a snake like this. He'd have taken her somewhere safe, some nondescript hideaway in the vast sprawl of LA. He'll have neighbours with locked doors, and curtained windows, and not an ounce of curiosity. With a rattlesnake and God knows what else, he can rely on time and maybe despair to make Mahoney do his bidding. Time, Kane thinks. Another enemy.

Kane limps back upstairs. Overnight, Gus has been checking the Cuesta file and has drawn up a priority list of leads. Now Kane picks up the phone and makes contact with Donovan. The news about the riot is far from welcome. FDR, he says, is beginning to have second thoughts about entrapping Darlan with fake dollars. For the time being, Donovan is still tight with Roosevelt and wants to keep it that way. He knows every move in the DC playbook and he knows as well that momentum is all. Nothing oils the wheels of the federal government more quickly than hard evidence, and evidence doesn't come harder than a thousand-dollar bill.

'You hear what I'm saying, Agent Kane?'

'Sir.'

'So when?'

'Just as soon as I can, sir, but we need to tread careful here. Equipment is one thing. Finding the right guy to take care of it, sir, quite another.'

'Sure. Keep me looped, eh?'

Kane puts the phone down. Gus has heard most of the conversation, figured out the rest.

'You know what I'd do?' he says. 'If I was Dumbfuck Donovan?'

'Tell me.'

'I'd have Meier take another look at that engraving of his, plant a couple of deliberate mistakes, and then hand the rest of the job to government printers, one of the outfits on the Treasury-approved list. That would get you a bunch of notes for I'm guessing a specific operation, and no blow-back if the shit hits the fan because the booty is just fake enough. This is abroad? Am I right, *hombre*? A come-on of some kind? Or maybe a little *douceur* for some daisy-crazy German guy wants to tell us everything?'

'Something like that.'

'Perfect. Everything fucking leaks in this town and we know Cuesta's still living off Meier's bad bills from last time round. Do the printing here, and half of LA will be queuing up next morning.'

Kane nods. Like most of Gus's ideas, it's near perfect, but for now he needs a reason to be in LA.

'Maybe later, buddy. When we've put Cuesta away.'

Midday, Kosch puts a rummage team into Hegarty Autos. They find the filing cabinets empty, the company records gone, even the pictures on the wall removed for safer keeping. A Honduran cleaner confirms that Cuesta was last around a couple of days ago and handled most of the removals work himself. The boxes, she says, went into a white van with one of the headlights smashed. The only trace of Hegarty Entertainments left is a single envelope in one of Cuesta's desk drawers. Once again, the single letter 'K'.

Kosch, keeping an eye on the search by telephone, drives over to take a look. He pulls on a pair of gloves and opens the envelope. Inside, he finds a single red chilli.

The search has been coordinated by the junior detective on the squad.

'K?' he queries.

'Kane,' Kosch grunts. 'Has to be.'

'And the chilli?'

'Maybe he'll tell us.'

Kane complies. Thanks to Prosper, he knows exactly where Cuesta likes to share his taste for hot bird's eye chillies. By now the hunt for Cuesta has an operational codename – *Barbour* – which no one seems able to spell properly but Kane knows this is a good sign. Every investigation he's ever been part of relies on access to a decent pot of money and Kosch is happy to reassure him that, in this respect, *Barbour* is blessed. Every next lead they're turning up confirms a web of contacts, intimate and otherwise, that stretches deep into various corners of the LA establishment. The currency of power in this town has always been information and, in the person of José Cuesta, Kosch and his squad have hit the gusher.

Gus is amused. He's worked his many LAPD contacts for years in anticipation of a moment like this. State police and the Secret Service have never been the closest of buddies in the on-going turf wars that plague law and order, but Kane has plenty of skin in this game, maybe too much, and Gus has had no problem using his buddy to leverage access to leads and a shared pool of what he terms 'intelligence shit'. The reptile shop is the perfect example and Kosch already has a detective en route to Venice Beach to statement the owner and make further enquiries.

That afternoon, Gus and Kane drive to a smallholding in the dusty sprawl of rising land in the foothills of the San Gabriel Mountains. According to Kosch, the spread belongs to a fellow Mexican who was one of Cuesta's early contacts back in the days when he came north from Tijuana to make it in LA. The guy calls himself Luis Desantos. Years ago he was importing women from Mexico and Central America for, in the dry prose of the court summons, the purposes of prostitution. He supplied a number of downmarket brothels that catered for LA's booming Hispanic community of largely single men, thus attracting the interest of both the immigration authorities and the LAPD. In court, he pleaded guilty to all charges and served a four-year sentence in an upstate penitentiary. Since then, says Kosch, he's become the go-to guy for horses.

Kane knows little about horses, never trusted them. They've found the smallholding and parked up. The last of a sensational sunset throws long shadows across the wooden fence around a scrubby paddock. On the far side of the paddock are a couple of barns and a scatter of outhouses. Farther still, at the end of a dirt road, is a sizeable bungalow with a white van parked outside.

No horses.

'He breeds them?' Kane grunts. 'Rents them out? Races them? How do they pay their way?'

'Fuck knows,' Gus is rereading his notes. 'Better ask him.'

In the flesh, Luis Desantos turns out to be a low-slung guy with thinning grey hair and huge hands. He's wearing jeans, leather chaps, heavy boots and a thick patterned shirt. His Mexican face has become a breeding ground for moles the size of black buttons and he's spent far too much time in the sun.

He meets them in the yard out front of the bungalow. Wants to know their business. Gus shows Secret Service ID, Kane, too.

'How come?' An old man's voice, cratered by smokes. Kane can smell bourbon on his breath.

'Just some questions, Mr Desantos. You mind if we go inside?'

They talk in the main room. Bare, thinks Kane, would be a kindness. A table. An assortment of chairs. Ashes in the grate. A scabby dog licking its balls under the dim single light bulb hanging from the ceiling.

'You live here alone, Mr Desantos?' This from Gus.

'Yeah.'

'No wife?'

'Nope.'

'And the horses?'

'Who said anything about horses?'

'We understand you keep them, house them, feed them…' Gus shrugs. '…whatever.'

'You're doing the IRS some kind of favour? You wanna see my tax returns?'

'I'm asking you about horses.'

'Sure. You wanna know the deal here? The studios get through a whole bunch of horses and don't know what to do with them after. Shooting Westerns eats horses alive. I might give them a feed for kindness' sake and there's the odd horse that might make a ride for kids but most of them go down the road for dog meat. It's called business, buddy, and if you're asking whether it pays well, puts fillet mignon on the table, the answer is no.'

Kane ducks his head, hides a smile. From Hollywood fame to the knacker's yard with the briefest pause on these gloomy acres.

Gus has produced a photo of Cuesta, wants to know

whether Desantos can put a name to the face. Desantos barely spares it a glance.

'Nope,' he says.

'You're sure?'

'Of course I'm sure.'

'The guy's name is Cuesta. José Cuesta. Way back you gave him house room, bed and board, maybe here, maybe some place else. He was fresh in from Mexico. I'm guessing you knew the guy back home. You wanna take a little time to remember? Maybe take another look at the photo?'

Desantos is wary now. Gus reaches out to walk him to the window where the light is better, but he pushes his hand away.

'You think I can't see good?'

'I think you want us gone.'

'You're right there, buddy. A million things to do and none of them can wait.' He lifts his head and his bloodshot eyes track slowly from face to face. 'You guys get wages? Regular cheques? One of them nice pensions maybe, for later? The answer is yes and you know something else? It shows. On your way, gentlemen. In this house time is money. Don't bother me again.'

Gus doesn't move, just stares him out.

'We've come about Cuesta,' he says at last. 'And you haven't answered the question.'

'Sure.'

'So?'

'Yeah, I knew a guy looked like him once.'

'And?'

'He blew through, like they all blow through.'

'What does that mean?'

'He knocked on my door, told me he needed a place to stay, rest up. I said yes, is all.'

'You knew him before? Back in Mexico?'

'A little, sure.'

'Like how?'

'I had a bar, kinda nightclub. Rough end of the waterfront in TJ. Gave it a fancy name. Hired pretty women. Lowered the prices. Never fails.'

'It had a name, this bar?' Gus has his pad out.

'Sure it had a name. You're asking me to remember it? Ask all you like, buddy. Some things a man can't argue with and one of them is age.'

'Describe it.'

'Cheap. And busy as hell. That face of yours was one in a million, two million, who's counting? I sold up and headed north.'

'When? Give me a date.'

'I can't. I just told you.'

Kane watches Gus's pen race across the page. Desantos is looking even harder. His entry to the States, that drive across the Rio Grande, will be in the court papers, Kane thinks. Subtract a month or two and you're maybe looking at a sale date on the bar.

'So how long did Cuesta hang around?'

'Too long. He was a cross we had to bear, that kid. Big mouth on him. Got sauced too often.'

'We?'

For the first time, Desantos is wrong-footed. He frowns, annoyed with himself, mutters about some hooker or other who'd also moved in.

'Name?'

'Fuck knows.'

'Back then you did time for importing women, right? Hispanics? Running them into LA? Do I hear a yes, Mr Desantos?'

Desantos says nothing, just stares out of the window, red-faced, baleful, losing what little patience he ever had. Gus hasn't finished.

'So maybe you helped yourself a little here, and maybe Cuesta did, too. Pick of the crop? Free board and lodging for services rendered? Happens, Mr Desantos. You wouldn't be the first.'

'Wash your mouth out, son. Cuesta wouldn't have known one end of a hooker from the other. Mummy's boy, fresh from the fucking egg.'

'Really? So I guess you got to know him pretty good?'

'I threw him out, showed him the fucking door.'

'And since then?'

'Since then I got older, wiser. The slammer does that to you.'

'And Cuesta? How old would he be now?'

'No idea. You work it out.'

Gus starts into an elaborate pantomime, counting his fingers, putting a frown on his face, starting over again, finally coming up with a figure.

'Late thirties? Ball park? Maybe a year or two older?'

'Could be.'

'And did you recognise him after all those years?'

'Like when?'

'Like when he came and knocked on your door coupla weeks back.' Gus nods towards the window. 'Tell me I'm wrong, Mr Desantos. Just look me in the face and tell me.'

'You're wrong, buddy. You're letting that skinny ass of yours do the talking. Now do me a big favour and get the hell out of here.'

Gus is writing on his pad again. Desantos, Kane knows, is close to losing it. He's broad across the shoulders, volatile, full of anger. Kane asks him where to find the john.

'Out back.' Desantos waves vaguely at the window.

Kane leaves the room. Down the corridor are two doors. One opens into a bedroom, bare except for an unmade bed, two empty bottles on the floor and a big chest missing one drawer. On top of the chest is the sun-bleached skull of an animal, possibly a horse, and an ashtray full of stubbed-out butts. The air is stale, heavy with the reek of alcohol.

Kane goes quickly through the other drawers, finding a mess of clothes, nothing washed, nothing ironed, more gusts of sweat and booze. Uncertain of what he might find, but sure that Desantos is lying, he quickly searches the bed. Neither pillow smells of Mahoney.

The other door is across the corridor. Inside, Kane finds himself in a tiny bathroom. This time his search is systematic, painstaking. He kneels beside the bath. The stained enamel is ringed with a scum line that looks recent, and he runs his finger around the plughole, searching for stray hairs. He finds two of them, both grey. Desantos, he thinks.

Next, the cracked hand basin, same routine. A bar of cheap carbolic soap lies in the bottom of the basin. He lifts it out, turns it over, finds nothing. There's more hair knotted in the sluice. He does his best to disentangle it but once again it seems to belong to Desantos. The closet has no lid, no seat. He peers into the murky water. Pebbles of hardened shit and the sodden remains of a sheet of torn-up newsprint. *LA Times?* He doubts it.

Kane steps back from the sink, eyeing himself in the mirror. The mirror used to be oblong but one corner's gone missing and his image is fuzzy and black around the edges where the silvering has fallen off. Picturing Mahoney in surroundings like these isn't something Kane does lightly. Like Gus, he smells a lie in Desantos' gruff denials but it's an evidential jump to try and tie Mahoney to surroundings like these. Desantos is a drunk. He nurses multiple hates. He appears to live alone and Kane can think of a thousand reasons why.

He can hear voices now down the corridor, Gus and Desantos trading insults, but before he leaves the bathroom Kane opens the cupboard beside the sink. At the back, behind a big bottle of aspirin, he spots a pack of rubbers. They look brand new and come in fives. He fetches them out, counts them.

Four.

Kane leaves the bathroom and joins Gus and Desantos in the gathering darkness outside. Desantos is making a final effort to play nice, now that he's got them out of the house. When Gus enquires about the van, how long he's had it, he tells them he bought it from a guy who had cows on a farm down by the arroyo.

'Old milk van,' he says. 'Guy used it to run churns to the dairy.'

Gus nods. Asks what kind of difference it's made out here in the middle of goddam nowhere.

'Makes every difference. Takes two horses in back if you know what you're doing. Other stuff, too. Never let me down. Not once.'

32

Kosch joins them that night. Gus has in mind a plate of grilled prawns with a little garlic and a bottle or two of chilled Chardonnay at a place he knows down the coast in Playa del Rey. This time of year, he assures Kosch, the restaurant will be empty.

Kane feels uneasy taking time off like this but knows that Gus has matters well in hand. Kane describes the life Desantos leads out on his smallholding and agrees with Gus that he saw most of their moves coming and ducked. Challenged by Kosch, he thinks it likely that the two Mexicans have gotten together recently but has no proof. The one loose end that still troubles him is the missing rubber in the bathroom cabinet. No woman in her right mind, he says, would ever entertain the likes of Desantos in the same bed. This draws a laugh from Gus.

'We're in LA, *hombre*. Show me a woman in her right mind.'

Gus gives Kosch the detail on the place Desantos ran in TJ. Rough end of the waterfront. Big and busy enough to buy Desantos a new life across the border. Sale of the place probably agreed a month before he entered the States.

'Place?' Kosch is making notes.

'Bar during the day, nightclub after dark. I get the feeling he liked women and drink and made money from both. The guy's a goner now, up here…' Gus taps his head, '…but everywhere else he's still a proposition. Either way, you might get someone down to TJ.'

Kosch nods. Every cop, Kane knows, loves the challenge of turning a hunch, the merest suspicion, into hard evidence. He's done it himself, hundreds of times, and never underestimates the chore of looking, and then looking harder, and then looking harder still. Muster enough of the dots, arrange them every which way, and in the end comes a pattern that speaks for itself.

Gus wants to know how the rest of the investigation is going. Kosch shrugs, more tight-lipped than he need be. His squad have fanned out across LA, he says, mainly downtown leads in the fight game. What they've found is a grudging respect for Cuesta's handling of the white girl, Fightin' Flo. None of these guys much like him, and all of them swear he'll never make it as a singer, but neither are criminal offences. Questioned about his taste in women, most have declined to speculate, though one guy, an ex-fighter himself, described Cuesta as a one-night wonder.

'Bores easily,' Kosch says. 'Mate and move on.'

Mate and move on. Kane has no doubt that it's probably true but wonders how it applies to Mahoney. For reasons he understands only too well, this is a woman that has gotten under Cuesta's skin, first in the training gym, second over a drink or two, then in whatever conversation led to his offer to take charge of Mahoney's career. To Cuesta, this would probably have qualified as courtship and the slow realisation that his new prospect very definitely had a mind of her own would have simply raised the stakes. Mute compliance can take a man only so far. One day, even Cuesta was going to find someone he couldn't talk or bully into bed. Hence everything that has followed.

The food arrives. Kosch eats sparingly, drinks very little. He's talked more than enough about his squad out on manoeuvres and now he wants to know where Gus and Kane are headed next. Kane takes a pass. Gus, he suspects, has a plan and for once he's prepared to share it.

'Cuesta?' he grunts. 'We need to tempt the guy out. Having detectives up his ass must be a nasty surprise because he thought he'd covered that angle, but nothing lasts forever in this town. He thought he'd taken one of your bosses to the mat, bought himself a lifetime's cover, but it turns out he's wrong. He won't stop trying, stop pushing to get this whole thing closed down, but in the meantime we gotta make all that effort on his part worthwhile.'

'How?'

'By turning him into a movie star. By putting him in the middle of the action. And here's the kicker: the movie is about him, his story, TJ grifter made good, the guy who takes LA by storm and keeps the change. We've got it to script stage already. It's a rough draft but it's a diamond in the making.'

'We?' This from Kane.

'Me and my good friend Virgil. You've met him? Lou's roommate? Guy's a piece of work, watch your ass, but he puts it all out there on the page. Everything best in this town starts with a title. Virgil's called the movie *Angel*. It's heavy on the irony but that's studio-hot just now. *Angel* is the story of a guy fighting the odds on every front, of a guy making out in the toughest, brightest, most wicked town on the goddam continent, of a guy who charms money out of the oil biz and gets his way. This is a movie that will never get made but the script does the work. Cuesta takes one look at the first page, reads on and creams himself. Our thanks, ladies and gents, to Mr Virgil Standfast.'

Kane visits Virgil the next morning, driving down to Santa Monica and knocking on Mahoney's door. He's never met Mahoney's roommate face to face and is surprised by the depth of the tan. Tall, with a wild explosion of blond curls and a marquee smile, he's wearing a pair of satin pants and a white singlet straight out of the box. Barefoot and lightly muscled, he belongs on a commercial for vitamins.

'It's summer in Frisco?' Kane enquires.

'Wrong town, buddy. Wrong fucking country. Think Cuba. Sunshine for the body and food for the soul. You ever catch any of that salsa jazz? Jungle music, baby. Changes your life.' He pauses, looks harder at Kane. 'And you are?'

Kane introduces himself, already feeling twice his age. Virgil opens his arms wide, enfolds Kane in a hug as light as cotton candy. Then he holds him at arm's length. He smells of an hour in the bathroom, and Kane recognises a hint of the perfume Mahoney uses on special occasions.

'C'm in,' Virgil extends a hand Kane doesn't take. He steps into the apartment, his candle guttering in the storm-force winds that blow around this man. Kane knows that Mahoney first met him on a protest march demanding a clean-up of LA's many tar pits. Within an hour, she said, she'd visited every corner of his busy, busy head and within a week she'd agreed rent for the spare bedroom.

In the lounge, Virgil has set up a typewriter on a table

beside the window. A pile of foolscap lies beside it, and the waste basket is full of discarded sheets of carbon paper.

'You're a movie star,' Virgil is attending to specks of dust on bare shelves of the bookcase, 'Lou told me plenty.'

'Movie star?' Kane is lost.

'Bodyguard to Mr Roosevelt. Keeping us all safe. Your buddy Gus, too. He used the word outstanding about you, which is nice. I guess he's smitten, and I can see why. Shame about your face. You headbutt the mirror?'

'Worse. I made a coupla wrong calls. They came back and bit me in the ass. Don't get excited, buddy, it's just a phrase.'

Virgil abandons the duster and blows him a kiss. Kane is beginning to get the measure of this guy, beginning to understand why Mahoney would find him fun to have around.

'May I?' Kane has picked up a handful of the manuscript.

'My pleasure, Mr Quincy. We're talking first draft. You'll see daylight through the holes but I'll do a little darning later. That lovely buddy of yours, Gus, wants the opening, the curtain coming up. All the real fun happens after, but I'm guessing he knows what he's doing so the first scene's what I'm gonna give him, both pages, buddy, depend on it.' He pauses, frowns. 'Poor Lou. What do you think?'

'I think we'll find her.'

'And the guy Cuesta?'

'I'll probably kill him.'

'Quickly? That'd be a shame. Guy deserves to suffer. Treat him like the devil's child he is. Murmur sweet lullabies in his ear and find some way to make him really hurt. He came here once and I met him. He had a dog with him, huge thing, German shepherd. We had to take poor Dexter upstairs.

Guys like me read the signs real quick. He was playing the gentleman that morning but his eyes told you more than you'd ever want to know. And that divine auto? What a waste...'

Kane is scanning the first page. Tar pits again. Fancy angles making the most of a moody dusk as the opening titles roll.

'Why tar pits?'

'Because tar pits tell us everything. Put your fingers on the pulse of this tormented fucking town and what do you find? Oil seeps up along the Sixth Street fault, sweats in the sunshine, turns into asphalt. That whole mess sucks in animals, horrible, and then the bigger guys happen by, easy kill, but the tar eats them, too. Been happening a while. Millions of years. Dig a little deeper and you're looking at the history of everything. A whole mess of bones and the same old story. Dog eat dog. Welcome to LA.'

Kane nods, returns to the script, picks up the title page.

'Angel?'

'Sure. Light in our darkness. Gus tells me I'm cooking up a little plate of something special here. It has to catch the attention of our spick friend. It has to tease him, play with him, tempt him. Angel is the woman he's pursuing. Angel is redemption and the night of nights in one irresistible package. She's a geologist. She knows about old rocks. He's a playboy developer, riding waves of his own making. He wants her bad, needs her even worse. They meet at the La Brea site. He's planning a big leisure development, kinda educational, telling folks the real story with saunas and fine cuisine and king-size beds attached. All I have to do for now is write that first scene, make it credible, not to you and me, baby, but to Mr Dumbnuts. Bait the line good, says Gus, and we sell him the movie. Do that, and we arrange for a test shoot on the first scene. That way he's tempted to show up. Everyone's got a fatal flaw and his is vanity. Can't resist the exposure, and I'm guessing that's the moment you and Dumbnuts get to meet. Sounds like a plan, Mr Quincy?' He steps closer. 'Want a little Vaseline for those wounds?'

Kane is gone within the hour. Getting Cuesta to break cover was never going to be easy, and he's enjoyed Virgil's take on the Hollywood bullshit, but he senses that even this man isn't fully convinced that Gus is in his right mind. The only ammo he's supplying in this vicious little war are words on paper, and though Virgil turns out movie scripts for a living, this one's gotta be different, bolder leaps of the imagination, loud primary colours, pushy grabs for Cuesta's attention. What he's done so far, he admits, is no more than a cry in Lou Mahoney's wilderness, and more work will make it better, but success in Tinseltown rarely comes easy. Gus, it seems, has a way of getting the opening scene to Cuesta. Will it work? It has to, Kane tells himself. Else that lovely woman is in even deeper shit.

He has yet to get back in the little Sedan. It's a beautiful LA morning, no wind, the sunlight dancing on the deep blue of the offshore ocean. Off to the right Kane can see the stubby jut of the Santa Monica Pier, and the cluster of amusements on the landward end. The last time he was here, high summer, he and Mahoney had strolled to the end, paused, gazed down at the tide nibbling the barnacles on the pier's iron supports. Back then, he was only beginning to sense where this relationship might lead. Besotted is a word he's never used in his life but the conversation with Virgil, once he'd calmed down, has confirmed that she, too, had lost her bearings. That lovely woman, he'd said. More right than he can possibly know.

A ten-minute drive takes Kane to Venice Beach. Meier is still in residence in the apartment above Hollywood Reptiles and directs Kane to a breakfast bar where Gus goes for waffles and maple syrup. They meet late morning.

'Cuesta's guy's been shopping again,' Gus wipes his mouth. 'Bunch of scorpions this time, whole family of the critters. Should I be telling you this, *hombre*? Probably not.'

Kane isn't interested in scorpions. He wants to know about Virgil's script. How will Gus get it to Cuesta?

'Krikorian,' he says. 'Our Armenian friend. He never got rich by getting people wrong but Cuesta's the exception, the blemish on his otherwise perfect record. Cuesta's faked him out, done a job on him. Krikorian says he was never really fooled but he's talking to himself. Fact is, Cuesta lied, and lied good. Now Krikorian wants a little restoration.'

'You mean his money back?'

'Money's the least of it. His reputation matters more. Other folks bankrolled Cuesta on Krikorian's word. In this town, Armenians understand money. If Krikorian says Cuesta is good for a mil, then no problem. Turns out it's a big fucking problem. Cuesta has blown up in mid-air and it's other people's scoots all over the prairie. That hurts, hurts bad, and Armenians are shit at forgiveness.'

'But he's still talking to Krikorian? Is that what you're saying?'

'Sure. And that's because he has to. Word's gone round already. Cuesta's on the death slide but guess who's hanging in there?'

'Krikorian?'

'Exactly. And you know why? Because he wants to do the Armenian thing. He wants to bide his time, and have Cuesta come begging, and then finish the job. Virgil gives me a pitch for *Angel* plus the opening scene, I give it to Krikorian, and then he passes it down the line to Cuesta. Major studio already on board. They want Cuesta up there on the big screen, starring in his own movie. They've seen him at work on fight night. They've listened to him crooning. The guy has presence, looks, chutzpah, the whole deal. They've bought into him. They can take him to every movie house coast-to-coast. All they need is evidence that he can act, can deliver a line or two, can hold an audience.'

'And the cops? The LAPD? Do they have a say here?'

'Kosch has handled that. That insurance Cuesta bought himself? The Prosper footage? It's come good again. At the very top, LA's finest are backing off. Guy gets a free pass. Again.' Gus devours his last waffle, calls for the cheque, abandons the stool at the counter. 'Be honest, *hombre*, look me in the eye. It ain't us busting our balls looking for Cuesta, it's Cuesta looking for us. Can life ever come sweeter than that?'

33

Back in Beverly Hills, Kane tries to take stock. Years of working alongside Gus have taught him how artful, how devious, how frankly impossible he can be. Show him the mountain, and the trail he blazes is always his own, never anyone else's. He breaks every rule, defies every reasonable expectation, turns every lazy assumption on its fat head. This trademark impatience with mainstream thinking scored result after result in countless Secret Service investigations and put a smile on Treasury faces back in DC. Gus is no more biddable now than he ever was, and Kane knows that. He also knows that Mahoney matters to him, and that he's laid his plans accordingly. On the face of it, no sane person would go along with Virgil's script but that, maybe, is the essence of the scam. As Gus pointed out in the windy sunshine outside the breakfast bar, Cuesta is a fruitcake.

'This came for you.' It's Prosper. She's holding yet another envelope, manila this time, same black 'K'. Prosper thinks it might be important.

'Front gate again?'

'Yeah.'

'When?'

'Six in the morning. That's when the guys have a shift

change. Someone's been watching. They left it on the watchhouse step.'

Kane opens the envelope, shakes the contents into his hand, finds himself looking at a rubber, used this time. He shakes his head, disgust salted with rage, aware of Prosper watching him. They're talking in the kitchen, Prosper stirring a big pot of lentils for the Cherokees out back.

'That's exactly the reaction the guy wants,' she murmurs.

'Sure. I get that. What I also get is that it's a lie.'

'Meaning?'

'Meaning Lou would never say yes. And meaning that Cuesta is way too proud to stoop to rape. He's helped himself to a rubber from Desantos' bathroom and he's sent it to hurt me, not Lou. Has it worked? Am I disgusted? Yes. Do I buy her presence in his bed? No way.'

Prosper nods, agrees he might just have this thing right.

'Anything I can do to help here?' she asks.

'You just did. Listening doesn't come easy in this town.'

She smiles, lays a hand briefly on his, tells him to stay strong.

'Cuesta's a child,' she says again. 'I guess the word is spiteful.'

That afternoon Kane thinks long and hard about Virgil, about Krikorian, about Gus, and above all about Mahoney. He's mindful of his buddy's efforts to entrap Cuesta, and there's part of him that admires the brilliance of the plan no one else could have dreamed up, but success rides on the psychology of the guy, whether he's as easy a mark as Gus seems to believe, and something tells him that Dumbnuts – in Virgil's phrase – might not be the whole truth. And so, by the time dusk has darkened the view from his bedroom window, Kane has decided to take another initiative, alone this time. *On s'engage*, he tells himself. *Et puis l'on attend.*

Prosper has lent him a couple of torches and a handful of tools. He has a spare clip for his weapon, and more rounds if he needs them. He waits until past midnight before slipping behind the wheel of the Sedan and following the curve of the drive down towards the gates. One of the security guys bends to his window and hands over yet another envelope.

'Came half an hour ago,' he grunts. 'We tried to lay hands on the guy but he was gone.'

Kane is fingering the envelope. Something hard and boxlike inside. He lays the envelope among the tools in the passenger footwell and thanks the guard.

'Pleasure, buddy. Take care out there, you hear.'

Desantos' smallholding is an hour east. Kane drives through downtown, pausing on Alameda Street and making a brief detour to check out Takiwa's print shop. Tarpaulins cover the worst of the fire damage, and the windows and front door have been boarded up. Police No Entry signs deter prowlers, though Kane is aware of movement in the shadows beside the fire-blackened stucco. Mahoney, he thinks again, remembering her face in the crush of the mob, trying to boil down the mad chorus of protest to a page or two of printable quotes. That someone, anyone, a woman for God's sake, should be brave enough to risk violence on this scale defies belief. That it should be Lou Mahoney fills him with pride.

He drives on through thinning traffic until the road east is empty. A mile or so from Desantos' place, he slows to find somewhere to park the Sedan. A scatter of darkened houses looms up from time to time, and he finally comes to a halt beside a turn-off that appears to lead nowhere. He reverses the car into the narrow track and bends for the tools in the footwell. The envelope, he thinks.

He switches on the smaller of the torches and grips it between his teeth. Inside the envelope is a matchbox. When he shakes it, he can hear something moving inside. He shakes it again. Same result. Very slowly, he begins to inch it open, then stops. The poisonous barb at the end of the black tail, shiny in the torchlight, is unmistakeable. He stares at it for a moment, then shuts the matchbox. Scorpion, he thinks, courtesy of Hollywood Reptiles. The temptation is to throw it into the darkness, or – even better – stamp the bastard to death, but instead he slips the matchbox into his pocket.

Minutes later, nearly two in the morning, he's within sight of Desantos' bungalow. He lingers on the edge of the paddock. There are no lights on inside the property, nor can he see any sign of the white van. Following the line of the fence, he reaches the tyre-gouged dirt at the mouth of the drive and heads for the bungalow. The wind is gusting from the south, hints of somewhere warmer, and a full moon lightens the darkness. He pauses from time to time to check for movement in or around the bungalow. Nothing, and no trace of the van there either. Desantos, he concludes, may be away for the night. Here's hoping.

The scatter of outhouses lies to the right of the property, where an open gate offers access to the paddock. There are two barns, one with a sagging roof, and a low line of what he imagines must be stables, half-doors closed in the silver throw of the moonlight.

He starts on the individual stables, one after another, stepping inside, closing the upper half of the door, then sweeping the torch right and left, looking for signs of recent occupation. The first half-dozen stalls are empty, no straw, no scent of anything animal, but further down the line he at last finds himself staring at the skinny shape of a horse lying on the bare earth. The animal stirs in the beam of the torch but Kane, no expert, senses at once that it's sick. Heaped in a corner of the stall is a pile of filthy straw, clotted with horse shit. In another corner, a tangle of discarded leather tack, scuffed and worn. Kane stares at the tableau for a long moment, trying to imagine how lives can ever come to this level of neglect, then the horse stirs again, sighs, and begins to cough. Kane moves on.

The stables done, he moves to the bigger of the two barns. There are more horses here. None of them will ever grace a movie or become a treasured ride for some family's kids, but they appear to like the comfort of being together. Kane's arrival brings them to their feet and they plod across the barn to the nest of hay bales stacked beside the door. The beam of Kane's torch moves from animal to animal as they approach. I should have brought offerings, he tells himself, some apples maybe, or sugar cubes, or whatever else you offer a horse in its dotage, but in their absence he extracts handfuls of hay and watches the horses trying to cope. Some of them appear to have no teeth. Others poke at the hay with their huge nostrils, a blankness in their eyes. Either way, it's pitiful.

Only the smaller of the barns remains. This time there are no horses, not even the warm, distinctive animal smell. Instead, Kane scents the sharp tang of petrol. The beam of his torch finds a line of three drums immediately inside the door. A hand pump is attached to one of them, and all three drums carry the same stencilled ID. Avgas? Kane frowns, wondering for the first time whether the paddock might also serve as a landing strip. Any incoming plane could refuel here, and then be on its way again. The Stearman on Cuesta's office wall, he thinks. The precious biplane, yet another LA toy.

Kane steps deeper into the barn. The space beyond the fuel drums has been subdivided into wooden booths, and he begins to check them one by one. Most have been used for storage, decades of broken tools, discarded equipment, hessian sacks of miscellaneous junk, the leavings of a life parcelled out on these bare acres.

Booth by booth, the story deepens. An abandoned suitcase, the lid hanging by a single hinge, the faded brown leather badged with a patchwork of destinations, most of them in Mexico and the Caribbean. The remains of a child's bicycle, entangled with the metal frame of a swing. The frame has been hastily assembled, the uprights crudely welded, the metal scabbed with rust, and Kane begins to wonder where a woman might figure in this saga. Did Desantos have kids down in Mexico? Did he bring them and the leavings of their youth with him when he headed north for a new life? And, if so, how did they make out when he disappeared into the slammer for a couple of years?

In truth, Kane has no idea but he's into the last booth by now and here, for the first time, his pulse quickens. No refuse, no tools, no reminders of a life thrown into the trash.

Instead, Kane is looking at a thickish layer of straw on the floor and a sturdy wooden stake driven deep into the beaten earth. He looks hard at the straw, trying not to kid himself. It's difficult to be certain but he thinks he can make out the imprint of something long and heavy in the straw.

He kneels, then reaches for the wooden stake and tries to give it a shake. It doesn't move, doesn't even tremble, stuck fast in the earth. He gets closer still, runs his forefinger down the grain of the wood, finds abrasions – areas where something has rubbed – maybe a foot above the straw. He rocks back on his heels, thinking hard, then takes an even closer look. He hasn't imagined the abrasions. A whole area of the stake, chiefly on the sides, has been rubbed back to reveal fresh wood.

Someone's been here recently, he tells himself. Someone's lain on this straw, probably handcuffed, and then chained or roped to the stake. He lies full length on the straw and tries the pose for himself, reaching over his head for the post, feeling the newly roughened wood. It fits perfectly, the whole story. Lie here, a prisoner of the handcuffs and the stake, and this is exactly what you'd do, hour after hour, trying to saw your way through maybe three inches of seasoned wood. Any chance a fit man might make it through? None. Any chance Mahoney, even with her gym-honed muscles and limitless self-belief, might somehow engineer a miraculous escape? Again, zilch, *nada, rien*.

Kane is on the move now, on his hands and knees, sifting carefully through the straw of the mattress. He's looking for something, anything, that will cement the link with Lou Mahoney. It might be a piece of jewellery, maybe one of her jet earrings. It might be a strand or two of hair, any tiny shred of evidence he can take back to Kosch, to Operation *Barbour*, anything to bring this waking nightmare to an end. But time and again, reaching ever deeper into the straw, he finds nothing, except an old hide stretched tight beneath the straw. Then, from far away, comes the slow beat of an engine. It grows louder and louder until the driver changes gear, and slows, before stabbing the throttle again. Desantos, Kane thinks. Back with the van.

He follows the pool of light across the barn, kills the torch, hauls the door open a foot or two, peers out. The white van is approaching the bungalow, moving slowly, weaving a little. One headlight is out and the effect is strange: the one-eyed monster with a life of its own. It finally judders to a halt in front of the bungalow, maybe thirty yards away. The single headlight fades, the engine manages a final cough and then dies.

In the silence that follows, Kane can hear a voice, the old man's voice, Desantos' voice, low, threadbare, as ruined as everything else. Then comes a growl, followed by a furious barking. A door opens on the passenger side and a dog leaps out, nose to the ground, moving left and right. The scent of a stranger, Kane thinks, pocketing the torch and easing his weapon free.

The dog isn't the ancient mutt he's seen before on his last visit but a German shepherd, big, probably young, certainly game. Aggression, Kane thinks, will come with the neighbourhood, with being around the old man, with ingesting his impatience and his anger.

First the dog heads for the stable block in the moonlight, then it pauses, confused by a returning scent in another direction, and Kane hears the long splash of the old man pissing into the dirt of the courtyard. The dog is on the move again, heading for the bigger barn but then it changes its mind and comes bounding across to the tiny sliver of open door where Kane is standing. Kane is slow in getting the door shut or perhaps – he thinks later – it's simpler than that. After everything that's happened, he's very happy to take charge.

The dog is on him now, jumping for his throat, missing as Kane lashes out. The dog tries again, this time going for his left arm. Kane feels teeth through the thickness of his shirt, then he puts the muzzle of his gun between the dog's yellow eyes and squeezes the trigger. The dog goes limp and falls at Kane's feet. Kane gives it a kick and puts another bullet into its chest. Out in the yard, the old man has finished pissing. He comes stumbling across the yard, cursing the dog, enraged by the gunshots, making blindly for the figure by the door, and Kane realises that he's mashed, that an evening's drinking, or a whole day sucking on the bottle, has gotten the better of him.

He comes to an unsteady halt in front of Kane, staring down at the body of the German shepherd.

'You just shot that fucking dog,' he says thickly.

'You're right. Maybe you should have taught it some manners.'

'Yeah?' The old man comes closer and Kane can smell an overwhelming gust of alcohol and piss where he's wet his jeans. 'You think that makes anything good again?'

This is a stand-off but Kane knows exactly what has to happen next. He fetches out the torch and shines it in the old man's eyes. Desantos lunges at him. Kane steps aside and Desantos ends up beside the body of the dog, on hands and knees, not quite believing what he's seeing. One thick finger pokes at the dog, trying to stir it into action, trying to remove this troublesome stranger from his life, but all he hears is Kane telling him to get up.

'Get up or what? You're gonna kill me? Go ahead. See if I fucking care.'

Kane looses off another round. The dog's body jerks with the impact.

'Shit.' The old man looks shocked. 'You're killing him twice?'

'Get up,' Kane says again, 'else the next bullet is for you. One promise, my friend. It won't kill you but the rest of your goddam life won't be worth a cent.'

Desantos blinks, farts loudly, struggles to his feet.

'What's this about?' he asks.

Kane hauls him into the barn and turns him round. 'Just walk. Last booth.' Kane's torch finds it. 'You hear what I'm saying?'

Desantos has stopped in his tracks.

'No,' he grunts.

'I said move.'

'No. Just tell me what you want, what you're doing here. You came before, right? You and that other guy.'

His voice has nearly disintegrated, a mess of broken syllables, but Kane can hear alarm now, and maybe something close to panic. Don't stop, he tells himself. Keep pressing before booze, or maybe a bullet, closes him down.

'The dog belongs to Cuesta, yeah?'

'The dog belongs to me. Used to.'

'But Cuesta has it sometimes, yeah?'

'Cuesta fester, Cuesta bester, Cuesta mester.' The old man's grip on real life, on now, on Quincy Kane, has slackened. He's started dancing in the gloom of the barn, a slow clumsy jig. Once, in a former life, he might have pulled this off but no longer. Grotesque, Kane thinks. A burned-out lush trying to hide himself away, act crazy, duck the questions that matter.

Kane pushes him roughly towards the end stall, feels the dead weight of his body, of his sodden liver, of his no-good memory. Finally, they both make it to the stall. The torch again, playing on the straw, on the wooden stake, before returning to the old man's face. He lifts a tired hand, tries to shield his eyes.

'Whoever it was,' he says slowly, 'beat you up good, yeah?'

Kane ignores the jibe. 'Tell me about the woman,' he says. 'Her name's Mahoney. You'd have known that. Cuesta will have told you. He brought her here? Special delivery? Sign on the dotted line? Maybe drove her over? Maybe flew her in? He asked you, told you, to keep an eye on her, to save her for later? For when he was ready? For when he'd come back to pick her up? Is that how it went?'

'Nothing went. Nothing. You want the real story about that boy, mister?'

'What boy?'

'Cuesta.'

The old man totters backwards into the stall and then collapses on the straw mattress. Kane very badly wants him not to go to sleep.

'What boy?' he repeats, standing over the old man, the beam of the torch still on his face.

'My boy.'

'Your boy?'

'Sure, José Desantos, my boy. He changed his name, see?

334

He trashed it, just like he trashed everything else. You want that we talk about that?'

Kane is trying to get the measure of this conversation. Maybe the old man is faking but two decades in the field tells him that alcohol rarely lies. This is the truth. José Cuesta is Desantos' son.

'So where's Mahoney? Where's the woman he kidnapped? Where's the woman he brought here?'

'Fuck knows. And that's the truth.'

'I don't believe you.'

Kane is on his knees now, beside the old man, the gun pressed to his forehead.

'Just here or some place else? Here will be quicker, which is a shame.'

'Help yourself. Go ahead.'

'So where is she?'

'I told you. I don't know.'

'I don't believe you, so let's try again. Where's that boy of yours?'

'Dunno.'

'Try harder. You have to know.'

'Why? You mind me asking, mister?'

'Because that boy of yours has checked out of the rest of the human race. Probably years ago. Probably longer than you can remember. He's the most disgusting piece of shit I've ever met and you're looking at someone who's spoiled for choice.'

The old man's eyes have closed now. Then a tongue appears, coated with white spittle, and he's licking his lips.

'You're right,' he says.

'Right? How does that work?'

'It doesn't. We loved the boy back when, we probably spoiled him, bruised the apple, squeezed the fucking plum, whatever. Our fault.'

'We? Our?'

'Me. And her.' His eyes briefly flick open. Glassy, Kane thinks. Booze? Fear? Remorse? Regret? Kane has no way of knowing. No way of bothering time for a replay to check the details.

One more try, Kane thinks. One more chance to get to the old man's failing brain before it checks out for the night.

'You know about the movie producer?' Kane asks slowly. 'The guy from MGM your boy chopped into bits with a chainsaw?'

'Sure,' Desantos nods. 'He told me. Twice.'

'And all the other stuff? What he does to women? The little tricks he plays? Anything to keep himself amused? Anything to keep the upper hand? He mention any of that?'

'Sure, it's a boast. Loves the sound of his own voice. Always did.' He nods. 'Makes him feel good.'

'And that's some kind of excuse? Makes things better, lets him off the hook?'

'Sure. No. Yes. Dunno. Always wanted his own way, that boy, famous for it, and now rich, too.'

A trace of a smile plays on Desantos' thin lips. When he begins to snore, Kane tries to shake him awake, and when that doesn't work he slaps his face. The old man's eyes open again. He looks hurt, slumber disturbed, unfair.

'Yeah?' he says, yawning.

'One more question, just one. Who sent me a used rubber today?'

The old man stares up at him, trying to focus. He shakes his head, says he doesn't know, but the smile spreads and spreads until Kane eases his leg, and steadies the gun until it's inches from his face.

'Open your mouth,' Kane says.

The old man nods, does his bidding. Stained teeth. Two missing in the front.

'Now tell me where she is.'

'Go fuck yourself.'

'One last chance.'

'You want another rubber, mister? You want them all?'

Kane freezes, knowing he has to kill this man, knowing the time has come to level the score, to put a bullet through his sorry brain. For Mahoney's sake. And for his own. But then he figures the consequences, trying to explain a corpse of his own making, pleading his case with Kosch before the dead hand of law and order kicks in and he parts company with Operation *Barbour*.

Slowly, he withdraws the weapon, returns it to his holster. Another way, he thinks. Infinitely sweeter.

In his jacket pocket is the matchbox. He tells the old man that he has no more questions, that he can sleep now, that he'll leave him in peace. Desantos nods, smiles again, begins to snore.

Kane waits a moment or two until the old man's breathing has settled down, and then he shakes the scorpion onto his face.

'Help yourself,' he murmurs, struggling to his feet.

34

What's left of the night gifts Kane a sleep deeper than he can remember for many months. Not a trace left in the warren of his subconscious of Desantos, of his doomed German shepherd, of his homicidal son, even of Mahoney. Kane awakes to a familiar figure at the bedroom door. Meier has arrived in Beverly Hills with, he says, a small present.

'For you,' he says. 'It's just a test print but I guess I'm asking you to keep the faith.'

'*Semper fidelis?*' Kane is looking at a $1,000 bill. The paper is wrong, the weight, too, but in every other respect, through Kane's barely opened eyes, it looks perfect. Meier is telling him that it's simply another step in the agreed direction. A contact from one of the studios had it printed on a special press in Culver City. Both the studio contact and the printer are sworn to silence and Meier says he trusts both with his life which, to Kane, sounds like a dangerous pledge.

'Show it to whoever matters in DC,' Meier suggests. 'Get them off our backs.'

Kane intends to do just that. The Secret Service field office downtown operates a secured courier service back and forth to US Treasury's headquarters in DC, and there's no reason that an envelope marked for Donovan's eyes only won't find its way to Spook Central.

Gus, arriving in Beverly Hills hours later, agrees that Meier has done his bit to debauch the currency. He's watched Meier at work on his engraved plate these last few days, but this is the first time he's seen the finished product.

'A thousand bucks?' he ponders aloud. 'Four of those babies and you can buy the house of your dreams. Pool. Palm trees. Nice view. The works.'

Indeed. Meier gone, Kane tells Gus about last night, about Cuesta being Desantos' wayward son, and about the scorpion. For the second time this morning, Kane thinks, Gus is seriously impressed. Desantos, on the strength of a single encounter, isn't his favourite person.

'Is the guy dead?' he muses. 'Probably not. My guess is the scorpion did the sensible thing, made his excuses and left. In the wild, most critters settle for an easy life. Same with snakes. Aggression is something only we bring to the party.' He looks up at Kane. 'So what do we do next, *hombre*? You know Desantos. You've looked into his eyes. Let's assume he's still alive. What now?'

'He's got a phone. He contacts Cuesta.'

'For sure. And then what?'

'I put a call through to Kosch in the middle of the night once I'd gotten back, brought him up to speed. He arranged a stake-out at the Desantos place on the spot in case Cuesta comes looking for his dad.'

'Why couldn't Desantos get the hell out? Just drive away?'

'I immobilised his van. Four slashed tyres and sand in the fuel tank.'

'That's showboat, *hombre*.' Gus is amused. 'Two tyres would have been plenty.'

'Sure, but there's something else. There's a whole lot of

Avgas in one of the barns. Cuesta is a pilot. He's got a plane. He probably flies into the paddock.'

Gus frowns at the news. Kane wants to know about Virgil's script.

'I took it to Krikorian this morning,' Gus says. 'He's waiting for Cuesta to get in touch and says it's just a matter of time. He's hung the guy out to dry, spread the word. Cuesta's run out of money and the rest of LA doesn't give a damn.'

Kane nods. This is good news. One way or another, the odds now point to a reckoning with Cuesta. The Mexican's still depending on Krikorian, has to do his bidding.

'So what now?' Kane asks.

'We wait, *hombre*. Hard, I know, but we just have to hang in there.' He touches Kane lightly on the shoulder. '*Semper fidelis*, yeah?'

Images of Mahoney crowd the days that follow. Mahoney that first night in the Mirador hotel in LA. Mahoney over the lazy evenings and nights that followed, Kane discovering someone who seemed – without any visible effort – to mirror exactly his own take on life. How crazy it could be. How unforgiving. And how, if you were very lucky, it might one day deliver a relationship like this: impossibly perfect, implausibly whole, a marriage of appetite, laughter and deep, deep respect.

Then comes an urgent message from Gus. Krikorian, he says, has been in touch. Cuesta has agreed to attend an evening shoot at La Brea Tar Pits. MGM are supplying a skeleton crew with lights and camera equipment. The call time for the shoot will be noon for the crew and three o'clock for the actors. Krikorian will be bringing Cuesta and if all goes well the location should be wrapped by mid-evening.

'He's read Virgil's script? Cuesta?'

'He's read the first scene.'

'And?'

'Loves it. He's got four lines. I counted them. Even he can make it through to the end if he tries really hard.'

'And the woman? Angel?'

'Girl from MGM. As fame-hungry as Cuesta.'

Kane nods. Weird, he thinks. Some stranger playing Mahoney.

'So Krikorian drives him over? And then?'

'Endgame. The scene gets shot and then Kosch takes care of everything else. He's giving us a quiet couple of hours to sweat the guy. That should take us to Fightin' Flo.'

'And you've got that scripted, too?'

'Not me, *hombre*. Mr Reptile.'

Kane can do nothing but go along with it. A caper like this belongs in the outer edges of Gus's imagination but Kane has been proved wrong on more occasions than he can count by underestimating the guy's genius and so he does his best to hide his reservations. Late afternoon, he tells himself. La Brea Tar Pits plus a page of Virgil's dialogue and an undiscovered starlet from MGM. He nods to himself, smiles at the prospects. Mahoney, he thinks yet again.

The pits lie inland from Santa Monica in the Hancock Park area of LA. Thin traffic on Wilshire Boulevard slows as drivers take a look through the fence and glimpse the blackness of the pond through a scatter of trees. This time of year it

looks trackless and desolate, with a background of abandoned
oil derricks and the dark swell of the mountains beyond.

Gus is at the wheel of his car. What follows, Kane senses,
will belong to him. He's dreamed this thing up. He has faith
in Cuesta's vanity, in Virgil's dialogue, in Hollywood briefly
waving its magic wand over these forlorn acres. Cuesta's
hunger to get himself back in the LA spotlight, he tells Kane,
will deliver them the sweetest of outcomes. A reunion with
Mahoney is only hours away. Believe me. Trust me. Just
fucking relax.

Kane would love to believe it, to relax, can't. A gate in
the perimeter fence lies open, two guards in attendance.
Beyond the gate lies a wilderness of scrub and pockmarked
soil. The biggest of the pits is closest to the road and a bunch
of technicians, maybe half a dozen in all, have erected a loose
semi-circle of three big lights on metal stands, cables snaking
away to a battery cart. Through the open window, Kane
watches one of the crew munching on a hot dog. La Brea,
he thinks, smells of a garage forecourt on a hot LA day, the
sharp tang of gasoline laced with asphalt.

Gus bumps to a halt beside the vehicles from MGM.
The guy he knows is called Mossman, a young second unit
director charged with bringing this brief audition home. Gus
has talked to him on the phone, understands the way he's
organised the shoot. Now he introduces Kane.

'Buddy from the same outfit,' he says simply.

'Secret Service?' Mossman extends a soft hand. He's small,
eager, keen to please. 'You know Virgil?'

'I do.'

'Great dialogue. Every word counts. That's rarer than you
might think. Quester?'

'On his way,' This from Gus. 'Should be here by now.'

Quester? Neat. Kane is looking at the plaid blanket laid on a patch of tired winter grass in front of the lights. A woman in her early twenties is sitting cross-legged on the blanket, studying the two sheets of dialogue. She's wearing a woollen jacket against the late afternoon chill, with folds of a silk scarf around her neck, but nothing can hide her beauty. She has a face Kane last saw in a copy of *Collier's*. Gene Tierney, he thinks, perfect bones, full mouth, huge eyes, perfect everything. Her life, Kane guesses, is a constant stand-off between the stillness of a face like this and something a little pushier. Just now, the pushiness wins.

'You wrote this?' She's on her feet with the script, brushing her skirt with the other hand, looking at Kane. 'Is that what I'm hearing?'

'No ma'am. Someone else.'

'But you're involved?'

'I am.'

Involved. Kane shakes his head, tries to think of something sensible to say, fails completely. Gus comes to the rescue.

'The script comes from someone we both know,' he says, 'Quincy much better than me. You want to talk motivation? Quincy here can help you out.'

Gus leaves them to it. He's back with the young director, checking his watch, eyeing the open gate.

'I'm Corinne,' the actress extends a hand. 'Quincy's your family name?'

'Kane. Call me whatever.'

'Sure. Quincy's fine with me.'

She offers a melting smile and then lifts a word from Gus. She wants to know about motivation, and about what made the script happen. The latter question is a very big ask so Kane settles for the first thing that comes to mind.

'I guess you're young, pretty...' Kane nods down at the script in her hand, '...ambitious.'

'I've got a job? A career maybe?'

'Sure. And you're good at it. The job matters to you. It's important.'

'So what is it? What do I do?'

'Let's say you're making it in a man's world. Does that help?'

'It helps lots.' That smile again. 'But what do I do?'

'Your call. It could be the movies. It could be finance. It could be something in entertainment. The key here is men. No one's really got to you so far. No one's made the right kind of moves.'

'Meaning?'

Kane is in deep already, and he hates it. Gus's fault, he thinks.

'Meaning no one's taken your eye,' he says lamely. 'Until now.'

'And the guy on the page – Quester. This is my Mr Right?'

'He might be.'

'I'm hedging my bets?'

'You're reserving judgement.'

'Judgement? That's a big word.'

Kane gazes at her, shakes his head. Corinne is studying him with renewed interest.

'What's the matter, Quincy? I said something out of turn? Offended you, maybe?'

'Not at all. Far from it.'

'You mean I'm on the money?'

'I mean you're thinking just like the person Virgil scripted, the women he knew.'

'Knew? Past tense?'

Kane ducks his head, turns briefly away. When the conversation resumes, she wants to know about her fictional job again, like it matters to whatever performance she's planning.

'Just tell me,' she says. 'Just give it a name.'

'You should be a journalist,' he tells her. 'Why? Because you're nosy, because you're impatient, and because you never leave a question unanswered.'

'And these are some kind of clues?'

'They might be.'

'Good,' she's smiling again. 'I can ride with all that.'

They gaze at each other for a moment, then Mossman approaches with another blanket, draping it around Corinne's shoulders.

'Mr Kane help any?' he asks.

'Mr Kane helped lots. Probably more than he intended.' She shivers, and then gathers the blanket a little more tightly. 'So when do I get to meet my beau?'

The answer is that no one seems to know. Short of sending a messenger to the nearest telephone, there's no way of establishing whether Krikorian has even left home. Gus volunteers to make the call, returning in minutes with the news that Krikorian isn't answering, and must therefore be en route.

By now, the crew are getting fretful. As dusk falls, they fire up the lights and the director asks Gus to stand in as Quester for a couple of read-throughs. The rehearsals, as far as Kane can gauge, go well and Mossman is effusive.

'Much better,' he tells Corinne.

'I got it wrong before?'

'You got it righter this time.'

'That's down to Quincy,' her eyes find Kane in the gathering gloom. 'He gave me the clues I needed most.'

'Like?' Mossman sounds genuinely curious.

'Like nuance. Like motivation. Like truth.'

Kane acknowledges the compliments with the briefest nod. Miles away, he can hear the steady cackle of an aircraft engine. He steps away from the group by the lights, looking up into the grey of the dusk. The aircraft is getting closer, the noise louder, and finally he sights the faint outline of an aircraft against the last of the daylight out to the west. Moments later, the shape has resolved into a yellow biplane, the pitch of the engine changing as it begins to lose height, the blur of the big prop revealing a helmet and a pair of goggles easing the aircraft down.

Mossman has seen it, too. He touches Corinne lightly on the arm, directs her attention west. Gus shoots a look at Kane. Something about to happen, *hombre*. Something bad.

Kane agrees. Cuesta is a pilot. He flies a Stearman. He's seen photos on Cuesta's office wall. The aircraft is yellow. Just like this one.

The plane is close now, close enough to make out another figure in the rear cockpit, maybe a hundred feet up. Mossman orders the cameraman to start filming, and the crew turn the three lights onto the incoming aircraft. Then, abruptly, the plane flips onto its back, flying inverted, still fifty metres short of the tar pit, and in the glare of the lights a shape – something human – leaves the rear cockpit and falls diagonally down. The pilot's judgement is near-perfect. On a bombing run, he'd be claiming a bull's eye. The body hits the surface of the tar pit with a lazy splash as the plane rights itself and climbs away with a dismissive waggle of its wings.

For a moment, no one says anything. Then Corinne starts to scream, her hand to her mouth. The body has surfaced. Tiny movements, just visible in the gloom, suggest it's still alive. Kane is first into the tar pit, wading out, joined by one of the technicians. It's deep now, and Kane – way out of his depth – begins to swim. He can taste the harsh chemical foulness of the water, feel it reaching for the faintest abrasions in his face and neck. He tries hard not to swallow, swimming hard, the body in the blackness of the water getting bigger and bigger. Under the glare of the redirected lights, he finally makes it, breathing hard, turning the body over, trying to check for a pulse. It's there, but only just. Krikorian, he thinks.

'Hang in there, buddy,' he gasps, starting to haul him back towards the dazzling semi-circle of lights. Krikorian's face has ballooned from an earlier beating, damage around his mouth and both eyes.

The technician has caught up now, and together they take turns with the dead weight of the body until Kane feels the stony texture of the bottom beneath his feet and starts to stagger backwards towards the shoreline.

Only when he and the techie are carrying Krikorian up the beach does he realise that the unit cameraman is still filming this entire episode. Kane lays Krikorian on his back on the blanket. The camera swings round, the lights, too, greedy for the smallest details. Kane feels for a pulse again. It's gone, briefly returns, fades. He tells the techie to start pumping on Krikorian's chest, opens his mouth. His front teeth have been broken, and Kane feels more damage further back in his mouth. He cleans out some of the gunk Krikorian's half swallowed, watches tiny bubbles of air surfacing through what's left, then puts his own mouth to Krikorian's and sucks. The taste is beyond foul. Kane turns his head and spits the stuff out. Again, he thinks. Force yourself. Make it happen.

He wipes his mouth, tries again. More gunk. This time Kane has no option but to vomit noisily into the gathering darkness. By the time he returns to the body, Krikorian is dead.

Kane rocks back on his heels. A hand on his shoulder. It's Gus. From somewhere he's found a bottle of water. Kane sucks at it, spits it out, does it again, then a third time. By now, the last of the daylight has gone. Perfect, he thinks. Perfect timing, perfect altitude, perfect speed. An audition has become a news story and Cuesta has won the golden prize of his wildest dream. For days, thanks to the efforts of the MGM cameraman, his will be the lead story in Movietone newsreels across LA.

35

Gus takes Kane to the hospital downtown. Corinne wants to come too, but Kane won't have it. Just you, he mutters to Gus.

Kane finds himself in the hands of a youngish emergency physician. He administers an emetic, encourages Kane to bend over a bucket and void the contents of his stomach, and offers slightly dark advice to avoid smoking.

'Otherwise,' he says, 'you may still explode. Keep belching. Let's get rid of this stuff.'

This stuff? Kane doesn't need Gus to remind him of the ironies bobbing in the wake of Krikorian's death. That a businessman who made his money from oil ends up choking his life away in the black stuff. And that the new focus of LA's attention flies away untroubled by the long arm of law and order. Neither Kane nor Gus have the slightest doubt that it was Cuesta at the controls of the Stearman, that it was Cuesta who never had any intention of turning up for the audition, and that it's Cuesta who is still in charge of the script. Gus, for once, has the grace to admit he's been taken for a sap.

'I guess I got the guy wrong,' he says simply. 'That's the way this town can get to you.'

Kane has no idea what the latter comment means. Has Gus been carried away by the giddy reach of Hollywood? Has the fame virus infected his own bloodstream? Either way, he's contrite, something Kane has never witnessed before, though Mahoney feels as beyond reach as ever. Assuming she's still alive, there has to be a way of finding her but Gus is taking a break from fresh initiatives and it falls to Kane, back in Beverly Hills, to try and tease the beginnings of a path forward from the wreckage of the tar pits.

Fact: Cuesta has fled in the Stearman. Fact: the aircraft has a range of nearly 500 miles on a full tank of fuel. Fact: that could put Cuesta anywhere within – or 300 miles beyond – the greater Los Angeles area. The Stearman is a robust aeroplane. It's engineered to cope with the roughest fields. The Movietone newsreels will alert tens of thousands to what's happened, and to what the aircraft looks like, but the fact remains that dozens of strips across the region could have been Cuesta's destination. Wheel the aircraft into a hangar or a barn, and it's gone, disappeared, swallowed up by the near-desert of Southern California.

Next day, Kane attends an Operation *Barbour* meet summoned by Kosch, whose thinking, overnight, has mirrored Kane's.

'No more Hollywood showboating,' he promises. 'This is a homicide investigation, plain and simple. We bust the guy the way we've always busted these people. We get out on the ground. We do it systematically, working outwards from the tar pits, and no detail is too small to matter. This guy has no protection any more, certainly not from anyone within this force. Krikorian has gone, and that means Cuesta's money has gone, too. That gives us just an edge because Cuesta has no place to go.'

Kane lifts a hand. He wants to know what's stopping

Cuesta flying over the Mexican border, back to his buddies in Tijuana. Why stay in LA? Why bother California with his presence when safety is two hours flying time away? How come he wouldn't have flown direct to Mexico from the tar pits?

'Good question,' Kosch concedes. 'Based on advice I trust, the guy would have needed a proper flare path to make a landing at night. Three problems. One, you have to find the airstrip. Two, you have to be sure the flare path is there to be lit. Finding your way home around LA is simpler. It was a moonlit night. He knows the area, the major roads, the spread of the suburbs. From where I'm sitting, a landing around LA is favourite. It won't be Desantos' property. He's too canny for that. He must guess we're watching. So it has to be someplace else. That's one of the points we need to agree.'

Heads nod around the room. Men exchange glances. Kane knows detectives, knows the way they operate. A search on this scale guarantees a bucketful of overtime. Christmas all over again, he thinks.

A hand goes up, an older man, the daddy of the squad.

'Your other problem, chief?'

'My other problem is this,' Kosch is playing with his pen. 'My take on Cuesta suggests unfinished business.' He turns to Gus. 'Care to explain?'

Gus nods, and Kane settles a little deeper in his chair, curious to find out what might follow. Gus has a great deal of ground to make up, and he appears to know it.

'The guy is anal,' he grunts. 'He attends to the smallest detail. He has a mouth the size of the Grand Canyon and a heart smaller than a raisin. A raisin is a dried-out grape. You're getting the picture here, guys? Guy's a performer, sure, but he's also psychotic. Stuff that matters to you and me is cotton candy to folks like Cuesta. No boundaries, no restraints, no sense of right and wrong, not a whisper of compassion, and absolutely no role in his sorry fucking life for the merest flicker of conscience. Guilt is a word he'd have to look up in the dictionary. On paper, that makes the guy a bit of a proposition. In real life, I'm astonished he's still alive.'

'Something we might attend to?' the daddy of the squad enquires.

Kosch ignores the ripple of laughter around the room. He wants Cuesta alive, and he wants that to happen soon. He looks to Gus again.

'You haven't finished,' he grunts. 'Where's the weak point? What keeps him here?'

'There's a woman called Lou Mahoney. You all have the briefing notes. He abducted her the night of the riot in Alameda Street. She's stayed abducted ever since and you don't need me to remind you that kidnap is a capital offence. Find the guy, make the case stick, and he's a dead man. But that, says me, makes no difference because this is Super-Cuesta, the guy that gets his way, gets the woman who's juiced him up, whatever risk he has to run. Bear in mind the Stearman is designed to be a trainer. And that, gentlemen, means two seats.'

Super-Cuesta. The name strikes a chord in the room. Kane watches one detective after another make a note, nodding in approval, maybe trying to imagine Super-Cuesta spiriting this woman south in the ride of his dreams, and then he catches Gus's eye and draws a finger over his own throat. Enough, Kane is saying.

*

Over the next week, Operation *Barbour* inches forward. Kane checks in every day while keeping an eye on Meier's efforts to secure a new printing deal. The latter keep hitting a brick wall, mainly because a supply of plausible thousand-dollar bills opens the door to all kinds of LA mischief, and the news from Kosch isn't much better. The *Barbour* squad are doing his bidding, checking lead after lead as they appear, but getting nowhere fast.

Krikorian's wide-screen death, meanwhile, has been front-page news in papers across Southern California, and movie theatres are reporting queues even for lousy films because folks have come to catch the footage from La Brea Tar Pits. The evidence to nail José Cuesta is up there on the screen. He's become talked about state-wide in ways that he can never have imagined. Yet still no one has any idea where he might have holed up.

Kane feels the weight of these early spring days. So far, he's clung to the conviction that Mahoney is invincible, that her spirit, the sheer pluck of the woman, will somehow get her through. Whatever pressure Cuesta brings to bear will make no difference. Whatever he wants, demands, forces upon her, she'll refuse. Why? Because that's her nature, because that's the way God wired her, because submission to someone as crass and ugly and altogether lightweight as Cuesta is unthinkable.

And yet. And yet.

Kane is aware of Prosper watching him, keeping an eye on him. A couple of times she tries to sit him down, to open him up a little, to take a look around and maybe try and help.

Kane is grateful for her friendship but doesn't want to talk. Solitude, he's decided, is the safest option just now. Then comes the morning when he wanders into the kitchen and finds the youngest of the Cherokee sitting in the kitchen with Prosper. He's barely hit his twenties, a thin, slight figure in jeans and a decorated buckskin shirt that is way too big for him. His name is Huyano, which Kane understands is Cherokee for 'Water after Drought'. Huyano is a deaf-mute and Prosper communicates in a blur of sign language.

The boy wants to know why Kane is so sad. He has an open face that reminds Kane just a little of Mahoney. It's a face that radiates curiosity, that reaches out for conversation, a trait – Kane assumes – that Huyano must find deeply frustrating.

'What's he saying?' Kane asks through Prosper.

The boy's fingertips touch his eyes, his mouth. His shoulders slump, a cartoon piece of body language that makes Kane laugh. At this, the boy grins. See? He seems to be saying. Life isn't as bad as you think.

Kane loves people who live on their nerve ends, who intercept the subtlest of signals and turn them around and weave them into interesting pathways forward. Gus has been doing it most of his life. Mahoney's world class. It speaks of a preparedness to watch, to listen, and to pitch your tent in someone else's head. It turns witness and attention into an art form. And it makes for great company.

That morning in the kitchen Kane stays more than an hour with Prosper and the boy, getting to know him a little, learning about ways the tribe closed around his deafness, acknowledging another mysterious gift from the spirits, not a handicap at all but a blessing.

Prompted by Prosper, Huyano signs about a particular Ghost Dance, a collective communion with long-dead elders, a ceremony scored for feathered headdresses and a particular pattern of facial paints. His fingers dance over his face again, stripes of ochre-red here, saffron-yellows there, and with encouragement from Prosper he gets to his feet and clump-clumps around the table, swaying on his thin legs, his eyes half closed. After the third circuit he pauses beside Kane and takes his hand and gestures him upright, and to his own surprise Kane, too, is stamping round the table, feeling the grain of the wooden floorboards beneath his bare feet.

When the boy brings the dance to an end, he embraces Kane, a brief clinch that Prosper later describes as a mark of respect. Huyano likes Kane, trusts him, wants to help. You don't need to listen, she says, to be someone's friend.

That morning in the kitchen leaves a deeper mark on Kane than he likes to admit. The same afternoon, he pays a visit to the Cherokee tent and invites Huyano to walk with him in the garden. There's no Prosper this time, no interpreter, but Kane is a quick study and the rapport between the two men swiftly thickens. A raucous crow in the big sycamore tree, bossing every other bird in the garden. A fleeting glimpse of a hedgehog in the green wall of shrubs down by the road. The boy has the eyes of a hawk and Kane begins to understand the way that deafness and life on a reservation returns a man to nature. The four Cherokee, he thinks, are here to protect Prosper, but they belong somewhere very different and Kane warms to the notion of a friendship undiluted by the mad clamour of LA.

★

Then comes the morning of 9 February 1942. Radio stations are reporting the overnight fall of Singapore. For Kane, who has just woken up to turn on the radio, this is an abrupt return to the world of war. According to CBS, the British are shuffling into captivity in their tens of thousands, much to the quiet delight of many Americans, including – Kane suspects – FDR. Roosevelt, while happy to give Churchill every support as well as limitless time, has never been a fan of the British Empire and Kane suspects that tonight's Children's Hour in the White House might be even more cheerful than usual.

Kane reaches across and mutes the radio. It's still barely eight in the morning and the rest of the day yawns before him. His check-in calls with Kosch these last few days have become more and more sporadic, partly because there's never any news, and partly because Kane himself feels increasingly useless. Kosch is a good cop, shrewd, honest, always nailing the smallest details, and he's taken care to recruit like-minded detectives. Cuesta has been a very public embarrassment to the LAPD and the bosses have shovelled a great deal of money into Kosch's budget. In short, given the sheer reach of Operation *Barbour*, there's very little that Kane can bring to the party. Or so he thinks.

A light tap on the door brings Prosper into the bedroom. She's looking anxious, an expression Kane has never seen before.

'We have a visitor,' she says carefully, 'at the front gate. I've gotten our friends to take care of him.'

'Friends?' Kane asks. Prosper nods, gestures at the window and the garden beyond. 'You mean the Cherokee?'

'Sure.'

'Why?'

'It's Cuesta. And he's asking for you.'

Kane is staring at her. Some kind of joke, he thinks. Gus
at his most playful. Some newspaper guy after an exclusive.

Prosper can see what's playing out on Kane's face.

'I mean it, Quincy. I've been down there, taken a look. I
know the guy. I know him good. It's him, Cuesta.'

'What does he want?'

'You. He's talking about a little ride, just the two of you.'

'No bullshit?'

'None. Believe me.'

Kane gets out of bed, pads around, checks his weapon,
loads two extra clips, prepares to get dressed. The prospect
of seeing Mahoney again is suddenly very real, but what does
a man wear for a meet like this? With a guy like Cuesta?
With a face in every LA paper? In the end he goes for the
hobo outfit from his days at 115: jeans, lumberjack shirt,
heavy boots. For reasons Kane can't explain, it feels wholly
appropriate. Rejoin the ranks of the dispossessed, he tells
himself, and you're probably immune from disappointment.

About to leave the room, he becomes aware that the jeans
no longer fit properly. He must have lost weight, he thinks.
He checks himself in the full-length mirror. He's right, the
jeans are sagging, and when he looks hard at the leather belt
he finds that he's already on the last of the holes. He's still
wondering about hunting for something to make a new hole
when Prosper is back. She taps her watch. Cuesta is getting
impatient.

Kane finds him waiting at the gate. He's wearing his black
suit, black tie, shiny black lace-ups, and he's surrounded by
the Cherokee. Like Prosper, they're uncertain how this scene
may play out. They've come armed, two rifles, a fire axe, a

knife each, and they're looking to Kane for some kind of lead. Prosper offers a curt nod of greeting and then looks at Huyano before gesturing at Kane's sagging jeans.

The boy nods, understands at once what Kane wants. He removes his own belt, leather in a light tan with strange markings, and he offers it two-handed the way you might present a treasured gift. When Kane's hand touches his own chest, saying thank you, the boy briefly lifts the belt to his lips before Kane swaps it for his own. He feels better now with his jeans secure, and he turns to find Cuesta deep in conversation with Prosper. He's telling her it's been a long time. He's telling her he's still interested in the house. And he appears to be totally untroubled by the watching Cherokee.

Kane, meanwhile, is studying the limousine parked at the kerbside. It's an undertaker's hearse, black, the perfect fit for Cuesta. In the back lies an elaborate coffin topped with an explosion of fresh blooms and someone's given the vehicle an all-over shine this very morning.

'Yours?' Kane is looking at Cuesta.

'Sure. The ride of your dreams. Drives like an angel.' He lets the last word hang between them, smiles his undertaker's smile, nods towards the hearse. 'Shall we?'

'Shall we what?'

'Get on our way, *amigo*. Lou can't wait to see you and that's a promise.'

Lou.

Kane gazes at him, counts his options, recognises how smart this guy is being. Batter him, tie him up, unleash the Cherokees, even shoot him dead and Mahoney remains beyond reach.

'Where is she?' Kane asks.

'Come with me and I'll show you.'

'She's alive?'

'Big time.' A taunting smile, close to a leer. 'You with me, *amigo*? Or do I drive away?'

Kane bides his time. He wants proof that Mahoney is alive. Cuesta agrees that sounds reasonable. From his jacket pocket he produces a photo, hands it over. Kane stares at it. Mahoney's face, intact, unmarked. Mahoney's smile. She's holding a copy of the *LA Times*, showing it to the camera.

'Check out the headline, *amigo*.'

Kane returns to the photo. *Singapore Close to Surrender*.

'This is yesterday,' Kane points out.

'Sure. I can't invent magic tricks that don't exist. I got a print off the negative last night. Best we could do.'

'We?'

'Me and Lou. You coming, Agent Kane? Rude to keep a lady waiting.'

Kane looks away a moment, then tells Prosper to contact Gus, tell him what's happening here.

'And these guys?' Cuesta is nodding at the Cherokee.

Kane has another word with Prosper. Stand them down.

The Cherokee have been following this exchange with interest. Now, nursing their disappointment, they shrug and head back towards the tent. Huyano is the last to leave. He smiles at Kane, his hand to his chest.

Cuesta is already stood beside the hearse. With a sweep of his arm, he opens the passenger door and invites Kane to take a seat. Moments later, Cuesta behind the wheel, they're pulling away.

Cuesta wants to talk, or maybe boast. Kane can sense it. Make it easy for him, Kane thinks.

'Was that you over the tar pits?' Kane asks.

'Sure. You really think I'd ever buy all that Hollywood movie shit? Make it so easy for y'all?'

Kane says nothing, marvelling at the way the rush-hour traffic parts for the passage of a hearse.

'And afterwards? That evening?'

'I headed out of town. Somewhere private. In my game, *amigo*, a man is wise to plan ahead. I bought a ranch a while back, different name, untraceable money.'

'Bad bills?'

'You got it. That boy Meier?' He shakes his head in admiration.

'And now?'

'Now you'll get to see the place for yourself. You know how many house guests I've had over? Just two, and you're the second.'

'And Lou?'

'The first.'

'She's still there?'

'No. Just now she's someplace else. Which is why we have to fly.'

By now, they're through the downtown area and heading south towards Bunker Hill. Cuesta slows when 115 comes into view.

'You did that?' Kane is looking at the blackened shell of the building.

'Me again, something TJ gets to teach you. Know how old I was when I burned my first house down? Favour for a buddy in all kinds of shit? Fourteen, *amigo*. Gasoline's an old friend of mine. Oil, too. Just ask Krikorian.' He smiles his mirthless smile and glances across at Kane. 'You know the story with that guy? He had it coming to him, he truly did, trussed me up good, assumed I was some spick fucker didn't know his way around a balance sheet. The poor sap got me badly wrong. Me and figures have been best buddies for years. Hegarty Autos? Everything that went down before? Slam dunks, my friend.'

'So where next?'

'I told you. Out to the ranch.'

'I meant after that.'

'After that?' Cuesta reflects on the question, then a hand disappears into the pocket of his suit and moments later Kane is looking at Mahoney again. 'Keep it, *amigo*.' The smile again. 'Get yourself in the mood.'

Kane ignores him. This area of Bunker Hill is still home to the deranged, the infirm and the dirt-poor, and block after block they remove their caps and stand bareheaded on the sidewalk as the hearse sweeps by. Cuesta occasionally acknowledges them with a derisive lift of his hand: imperious, beyond reach. As the traffic begins to thin, it occurs to Kane for the first time that the coffin in back might not, after all, be empty.

'You got anyone else on board?' Kane jerks a thumb.

'Not that I know, *amigo*. I borrowed this from a buddy. The flowers are for show. He's buried most of the people who've gotten in my way and appreciates the business. That's what talks in this town.'

'Dying?'

'Getting buried right. Appearances matter, even after you're meat on the slab. You need a card to contact the guy? I've got plenty. Took a stake in the business.'

Forty minutes further south, and they've left most of the

traffic behind. Fresh building lots by the roadside have been fenced by the developers. The ground has yet to be sold and broken but a couple of Mexicans are busy adding to the forest of 'For Sale' signs. In a couple of years, thinks Kane, most of this entire region will be one vast suburb. The sheer weight of bricks and mortar will capsize Southern California and let the ocean in. Is that something that concerns him any more? Kane thinks not.

Cuesta's ranch lies in the foothills of the Fuente Hills. The similarity to Desantos' place is remarkable. The same gruff nod to home comforts in the shape of an ugly four-square bungalow, the same scatter of semi-derelict outhouses and barns. Is this affection for the worn and the shabby buried deep in the Desantos gene pool? Passed on from generation to generation? Or has Cuesta adopted seeming poverty as a ploy to throw the rest of LA off the scent?

Kane has no idea but now might be the moment to find out.

'I met your dad,' he says. 'He lives in a place just like this.'

'I know. He says you tried to kill him.'

'And did it work?'

'I guess not. He was certainly on his feet this morning. Sends his best, by the way. And the dog, for the record, was mine.'

'The German shepherd?'

'Yeah, Fritzy. Dad butchered him good. Passed him off as horsemeat so I guess that's in the genes, too. No one looks too hard these days.'

The loss of the German shepherd doesn't appear to disturb Cuesta. He brings the hearse to a halt outside the biggest of the barns.

'Gimme a hand here?' he grunts.

Kane gets out, looks around. As far as the eye can see, no trace of neighbours, not a single For Sale sign.

'Shit soil.' Cuesta has a gift for reading his mind. 'And too goddam hot for most folks.'

Cuesta takes a key to the big padlock on the barn and gestures to Kane to help him push both doors open. Inside, Kane can see the outline of the biplane he last saw over the tar pits. The Stearman, he thinks, egg-yolk yellow, huge radial engine, fat tyres. Cuesta gazes at it for a moment and then wants to know whether Kane is armed.

'Of course.'

'Gimme.'

'Why?'

'You think I'm crazy?' He nods towards the plane. 'You're in the back, buddy. Do I want a gun to my head? Will that get us back on the ground in one piece? You still want to see her, right? Then give me the fucking gun.'

This, Kane knows, is the real Cuesta: abrupt, peremptory, never to be crossed. The point about Mahoney is well made. He unholsters the weapon and hands it over.

'Now spread your arms. And relax, *amigo*. Like I say, this is for both our sakes.'

Kane feels Cuesta's hands patting him down. The body search is thorough, professional. Cuesta, finding nothing, climbs onto the lower wing of the biplane and tosses a leather jacket and a pair of goggles to Kane.

'Gets cold up there.' He nods at the jacket. 'Should fit.'

The jacket is thin, belongs on someone smaller. Maybe Mahoney's worn this, Kane thinks, left her scent. The moment he pulls it on, he knows he's right. He can smell

Mahoney, imagine her in the rear cockpit, Cuesta's trophy passenger. Another tiny touch from the master sadist.

Cuesta is still on the lower wing, reaching deep into the front cockpit to release the parking brake. He has an aviator jacket. It looks brand new, tan, fur-trimmed, and back on the ground he puts it on.

'Get behind the left wing,' he says. 'You push where you see the black arrow.'

Kane circles the aircraft, finds the arrow, applies his weight, beginning to sweat at once in the warmth of the barn. Cuesta is on the other wing, grunting with the effort. Slowly, the aircraft begins to move out of the barn until Kane feels the heat of the midday sun on his face.

'OK?' The plane has come to a halt.

Cuesta shoots Kane a look, then swings the prop a couple of times and clambers onto the wing again before lowering himself into the pilot's seat. He concentrates for a moment on the bank of switches around the dashboard, and then hands down the crank to help start the engine.

'Fits in the hole ahead of the left wing,' he says. 'You crank clockwise. Be careful not to step backwards when the engine catches else you're ground beef.' He gazes down from the cockpit. 'Shoulder and lap straps on your seat in the back. Make sure the buckle fits tight, listen for the click then test it with your weight. You done this before?'

'A coupla times.'

'Sure, buddy. You want me to go through it again?'

'No.'

Kane takes the crank handle, finds the port, slips it in. Goggles and a leather flying helmet have transformed Cuesta. The funeral director has become a fighter pilot.

'OK?' he calls.

Kane works the crank with his good arm. It's tougher than he expected. He can feel the weight of the engine, of all the cylinders, pushing against him. Nothing happens, and so he does it again, and then a third time. By now, sweat is pouring down his face.

'You wanna take a break?'

Kane nods. He's hyperventilating. He feels a little dizzy. Then he reaches for the crank and has another go, more effort this time, getting a feel for the way it works, and on the next turn of the crank the engine coughs a couple of times and then fires. The force of the backwash from the spinning prop comes as a relief. He steps forward, limps around the wing, clambers awkwardly into the rear seat.

'You still got the crank handle?' Cuesta shouts.

'Yeah.'

'There's a couple of brackets on the left of the cockpit. The handle fits just nice. You got that?'

Kane nods, secures the crank handle, makes sure it's a tight fit.

'Now strap yourself in. Goggles on the floor. Tell me when you're all set.'

Kane wriggles into the straps, one over each shoulder, another around his waist.

'Tight?'

'Tight.'

The growl of the engine falters a moment and then becomes a roar as the aircraft begins to move. With the Stearman's nose in the air, Kane is looking up through the tiny wind deflector and can see only the blue of the California sky beyond Cuesta's black leather helmet. Apart from loosening the straps and reaching forward to give his shoulder a tap, there appears to be no means of communicating with Cuesta. Kane has been open-cockpit flying before. But never has he been cut off like this.

They're bumping past the parked hearse now, and Kane wonders why Cuesta hasn't bothered to drive it into the barn. The barn doors, too, are still open to any passing stranger. Odd.

Cuesta taxis the length of the field, weaving left to right to keep on track. Looking down from the rear cockpit, Kane can see flints and stones the colour of chalk among the worn patches of grass, but the big Stearman takes the field in its stride. At the end of the taxi run, Cuesta brakes and makes a 180-degree turn to align the aircraft for take-off. The wind is from the north, a light breeze, nothing more.

When Cuesta guns the engine, Kane feels the biplane shudder and then comes a pressure in his back as they begin to roll. Seconds later, the pale greens and browns of the field are beginning to blur and the Stearman, eager for flight, is taking little exploratory skips into the air, fighting off the suck of gravity. The tail comes up, the end of the field suddenly in view, and then the bumping abruptly stops and Kane watches the joystick between his knees come back as Cuesta urges the plane into a climb. Easy, Kane thinks.

The dashboard in the back carries a replica set of instruments and Kane watches the needle on the altimeter settle as Cuesta levels off at 1,500 feet. From here, Kane can see clear down to the hazy line where Southern California ends in the ocean. Webbed by the safety straps, he's beginning to relax, enjoying the view and the oily blast of the slipstream sluicing back past the cockpit. Mahoney, he thinks to himself. Anticipation smells of burned gasoline and hot engine oil.

Kane gives the straps a precautionary tug, then scans the instrumentation on the dashboard. The speedo is showing 85 mph, the altimeter 1,600 feet, and the fuel tank is full. All morning, Kane's been wondering where Cuesta will be heading. Will he fly south? Towards the Rio Grande and the Mexican border? Put the LA manhunt behind him? That would be logical, the sanest course of action, but it seems not. The compass is showing a north-easterly heading, up towards the brown hump of the San Gabriel Mountains. Why head north, deeper into California, when you've got half the LAPD up your ass?

Kane knows he's in no position to figure any of this out. The noise of the big radial engine is deafening. There's no way of checking with Cuesta. Like it or not, he's totally in this man's hands, trussed up like a turkey, helpless as a babe in arms, the prisoner of a killer he has every reason to hate. Did he have any option, back in Beverly Hills, when the man came calling? Sure, he had plenty. He could have shot the guy or have the Cherokee rope him to the nearest tree. He could have put a call through to Kosch and waited for Operation *Barbour* to call round and pick him up. But what of Mahoney? And the rest of their lives together?

Kane shakes his head, knowing deep down that he's not the prisoner of circumstances, nor even of José Cuesta, but of his own neediness. Everything begins and ends with Mahoney and has done for a while. End of.

That final? Kane hopes not, wants to believe not, but he's been around far too long to count on the blessings of mere assumption. Whatever happens next, simply happens. *Que sera*, he tells himself, settling deeper in the seat.

Movement in the front cockpit. A gloved hand pointing ahead and down to the right. Kane rouses himself and does his best to follow the pointing finger. He can see another property, similar to Cuesta's ranch, a fenced paddock, a rudimentary landing strip and an untidy scatter of outhouses, but no bungalow, no milk van parked out front. The outer reaches of LA must be full of these places, he thinks. No wonder Kosch had a major search on his hands.

Cuesta has dipped a wing now, and the joystick between Kane's knees pushes forward as Cuesta eases the aircraft into a shallow dive. There are two tiny figures in the very middle of the paddock, and as the altimeter unspools Kane realises that one of them is a woman. Her hand is shielding her eyes against the glare of the sun and she's wearing exactly the clothes Kane remembers from the riot outside Takiwa's print shop. Then she waves and Kane's heart skips a beat. Mahoney. Has to be. Alongside the stocky figure of Desantos.

Kane lifts a hand, waves back. Crazy times, he thinks. Crazy, crazy days delivering a sight, an image, like this. He wants to wave forever. He wants to be up here, in the blast of hot air from the engine, with the plane in a shallow dive, and with Cuesta preparing to land. He wants the sweet anticipation of the moment when the wheels touch, and the speed comes off, and the bumping stops, and Cuesta lets him free, and guns the engine again, and flies away. He wants to wrap his arms around Mahoney, to know that she is safe, and whole, and his.

The altimeter has steadied at 100 feet. From this height, looking down, the paddock is a blur. Mahoney and the old man flash past, an all-too-brief appearance, and then the joystick comes back, deep into Kane's belly, and he feels his stomach dropping into his boots as the aircraft powers upwards.

At exactly the same moment comes a new noise from under his seat, metal parting company with metal, inexplicable. This sudden departure from the script fills Kane with dread. Something broken, he thinks, something very wrong. He tugs on the straps, feels them give, ends up with a mess of webbing in his lap. He stares now at the shoulder straps, and the belly strap. Nothing will restrain him any more. Nothing is connected. Nothing will keep him in this aircraft.

Krikorian, he thinks. This is what happened over the tar pits, the night Cuesta slipped in from the west. Drop a wing, invert, fly upside down, give the aircraft a shake, and Kane is a dead man. Do it from height, where the plane is headed now, and he'll be nothing but a tiny dot falling and falling, getting bigger and bigger, until he explodes like a ripe fruit at the feet of the woman he loves.

Kane is looking around the narrowness of the cockpit, searching for handholds, for anything to grab onto, desperate to find a way of maybe wedging himself tight against the pull of gravity for when Cuesta turns the aircraft upside down. Just now the force of the climb is keeping him safe but very soon, at God knows what height, Cuesta will be levelling out and after that Kane will be doomed.

He shuts his eyes, forces himself to concentrate, to think, to pluck a move, any move, from the onrushing certainty of his own death. He's been here before, he tells himself, both times in Boston, and both times he somehow emerged intact.

Luck? Judgement? The hand of God? Now is the time to trust all three. Then, faintly, just a hint, the faintest whisper, of redemption. Huyano, he thinks. And his leather belt.

His fingers find the belt around his waist. He pulls it out through the loops of his jeans. Back on the ground, he'd already discovered the bar that adjusts the seat back and forth. It runs the width of the seat, feels solid, and now he slips one end of the belt beneath it, and then reconnects with the buckle. Now he has something to hang onto, a loop of Cherokee leather inset with mysterious symbols. The spirits of the Elders, he thinks. The Ghost Dance, he thinks. And the slight figure of Huyano, his body, hand clasped to his skinny chest.

Cuesta is at the top of the climb now, the altimeter showing 1,600 feet when the joystick briefly centres. Kane grabs it with his right hand but it's disconnected from active control and no input on his part can make any difference. Then, very slowly, Cuesta drops a wing, just the way it happened over the tar pits, and moments later they're flying upside down. Kane hears the thunder of blood rushing into his head, feels the beat of his racing heart, knows that any moment his brain may explode, but he has both hands clamped around the loop of Huyano's belt, and so far it's holding.

Everything in his body wants to surrender to gravity. He's still upside down, still hanging on. The muscles in his arms are burning up and he can no longer feel his hands. Twelve stone of Agent Kane, he thinks grimly, at the mercy of the Elders. It's at this point, impossibly, that he realises he must somehow stay low in his seat, hunkered down against the giant tug of the earth below, invisible in the mirror mounted in the front cockpit. Only that way can he fool Cuesta that he's dropped away, left, gone. Otherwise Cuesta will simply fly inverted until Kane gives up, falls out and dies of exhaustion.

Then, suddenly, the joystick flops to the left and the plane is back where it should be, back upright, and Kane is slumped low in the seat, his hands still clamped around the belt, his head down, everything in his body on fire. His palms? His arms? The mess that used to be his elbow? His shoulders? All he can feel is pain. But pain is good. Pain is a blessed release. Pain means he's still alive.

Cuesta has throttled back. The needle on the altimeter has just gone through 700 feet. Kane daren't take a look out, daren't show himself in Cuesta's mirror. Instead, very carefully, he releases the belt from the metal bar beneath the seat and runs the leather between his throbbing hands. He's trying to visualise the shape of the aircraft on the ground, the distance between the rear and the front cockpits, and as he does so he realises that it might, if he gets the timing exactly right, just be possible.

Cuesta is preparing to land. The engine is idling, the speedo indicating 50 mph. Then comes a bump from the big main wheels touching down, and the nose slowly rises as the tail wheel reaches for the paddock, and the aircraft begins to slow under the bite of the brakes.

Wait, Kane tells himself. Wait until the plane comes to a complete halt. Wait until the taxiing is over, and Cuesta is seconds away from hitting the release buckle on his seat belt. He'll be in the mood to celebrate, Kane thinks grimly. Another body. Another scalp. Another nuisance despatched to oblivion.

At last, the aircraft is at rest. The engine coughs and dies.

The propeller comes to a halt. Cuesta is shouting to someone nearby, someone close, and Kane hears Desantos' answering growl. Enough, he thinks.

The belt stretched between his hands, he stands erect in the rear cockpit. Cuesta feels the aircraft moving under Kane's weight and is puzzled by his father's warning shout but by then it's far too late. Kane is oblivious to everything except the black helmet in front of him. The distance between the two cockpits is greater than he'd thought but he reaches forward, pushing his body to its limits, and loops the belt around Cuesta's neck, then pulls and pulls, one hand on each end of the belt, his upper arm throbbing as Cuesta tries to claw free.

The ghosts of the watching Elders, Kane thinks savagely as Cuesta begins to choke. Kane ignores the pain in his upper arm and hauls the belt ever tighter, feeling Cuesta's resistance beginning to flag, then the figure in the fancy aviator jacket sags for a brief second before Kane abandons the belt, crooks his elbow beneath Cuesta's chin, and yanks hard, upwards and backwards, to break his neck.

Kane has killed men before. It's often been easy and it's never been a pleasure but this time he feels nothing but a scalding jolt of something wholly primitive. Joy? Glee? Satisfaction? None of the above. For Prosper, he thinks. For Mahoney. For Gus. For Huyano and the Ghost Dance and the Elders.

Kane is looking down now from the cockpit. Desantos is limping away towards the nearest of the barns but Kane has eyes only for Mahoney. He's been anticipating this moment for weeks but now that it's come he can only shake his head at how normal everything feels. Mahoney looks no different from the way she's always looked. The same teasing smile. The same wry delight at one of life's bigger surprises.

Kane hauls himself slowly out of the cockpit, loses his balance on the wing, jumps clumsily to earth. Mahoney is there to steady him, to break his fall, and he wraps his arms around her.

'Impressive, Agent Kane,' she murmurs, her head on his chest. 'What took you so long?'

Desantos is back. He's carrying a watering can. He gives it to Kane and tells him to empty the contents onto his son. Kane can smell Avgas. The smell, like the invitation, is overpowering.

Back on the lower wing, Kane takes the can from the old man, pours the gasoline over Cuesta. Held upright in the seat by his straps, aside from the strange angle of his head, he might be still alive.

Kane looks down at Desantos.

'What happened to my seat belt up there? Help me out at all?'

'The boy had a way of messing with it. Same thing with the oil guy. How did it work?' He shrugs. 'Search me.'

The old man has fashioned a long spill of rolled newsprint. Kane gets down from the wing again, dips the end of the spill in what's left of the Avgas, and borrows Desantos' lighter to set fire to it. Avgas is everywhere around the cockpit, the metal wet and shiny in the brightness of the afternoon sun. Kane motions Mahoney and Desantos away and then tosses the burning spill into the cockpit. A whoosh, and scalding flower of flame, and Cuesta is alight.

Desantos nods in approval. His ancient mutt has appeared from nowhere, staring at the bonfire in front of him.

'Should have happened years ago,' the old man grunts. 'The boy burns good.'

36

Mahoney and Kane travel back to LA, with Desantos at the wheel of an ancient Ford that has replaced the milk van. The old man, evidently happy at the despatch of his son, wants the rest of the business over and done. Cuesta has led him a dance these past few years, and he evidently views his imminent arrest as a chance to relax.

Kidnap? Conspiracy to murder his own son? The likely charges make no visible impact, and Kane realises that Desantos has developed the beginnings of genuine affection for Lou Mahoney. He can see it in the way the old man glances up at the rear-view mirror, checking her out on the back seat, huddled against Kane. In his gruff offer of a cigarette from the crumpled pack in his shirt pocket. Is Kane surprised by this plot twist? Not at all.

Kosch, at Operation *Barbour*'s headquarters, listens to Kane's account of the surprise meet with Cuesta at Beverly Hills, of the journey out to the ranch in the undertaker's hearse, and of Cuesta's bid to kill him.

'He'd have flown to Mexico after,' he says. 'Probably with Mahoney. He had the fuel and one of our guys in TJ says he's expected tonight.'

Mahoney disputes this account. She's spent interminable days with either Cuesta or his dad. From the start she'd made it very plain that neither of these men frightened her, nor would she ever have any intention of sharing their sad lives. The old man, she says, never laid a finger on her and was sometimes minded to apologise for his son. As for Cuesta himself, he certainly did his best to coax her into bed but ended up settling for a kind of arm's length friendship. Psycho? Definitely. A man who loved inflicting pain? Yes. A guy who fell in love with a Hollywood version of himself? Again, yes.

'So why didn't you get out of there?' Kane asks. It's dark now, and they're back with Prosper in Beverly Hills.

'Where's there? You mean the old man's place? The barns? The horses? The paddock? He had a hidey hole, a cave, down beneath one of the stalls. I spent days and nights in there. He fed me, he kept me gagged, but in a strange way I trusted the guy. He was completely shot, wrecked. I felt sorry for him and I felt even sorrier for his liver.'

'And Cuesta?'

'Different challenge. I learned to humour the man. He'd never grown up. He was a kid at heart. Blow smoke up his ass and he was very, very happy.'

'So why didn't you leave? Use the phone? Get in touch?'

'Cuesta watched me constantly or had me watched. He also had a dog until you shot it. Nice work, Agent Kane. That dog terrified me.'

'Maybe he thought you'd go to Mexico with him.'

'In his dreams. After you took care of the dog they moved me out. I guess Desantos' place was too hot. Cuesta lived an hour away.'

'But you talked about it? Mexico?'

'Of course we talked about it.'

'And?'

'I said yes. Every time. That's what you do with psychos. That's how you handle them. You give them everything you can short of bodily fluids and hope to God they can live on a promise. Me? I never stopped believing in you, Mr Kane. And you know what? Come here.'

After two of Kosch's men have spent most of a day taking a full statement from Mahoney, Kane passes the next week in her apartment in Santa Monica. Virgil has the tact to move out for a while, and they have their lives to themselves. Slowly, day by day, Kane realises that Mahoney – deep down – has been way more damaged than she'll ever admit by the kidnapping. Her first instinct was to downplay everything, to pretend that the days and nights at the mercy of two strangers, both crazy, had been nothing more than an extra gust or two of wind in the choppiness of her life in LA.

She thrived on challenges. That's why she'd taken up boxing. She loved the wild unpredictability of where the next story might lead. That's how you made a name for yourself in big-time journalism. But Cuesta turned out to be LA in the major key, and from the moment this agent of hers stuck a gun in her back in the middle of a full-scale riot, she feared for the worst. She could still hold her own, still keep him at arm's length, but stamina is everything out on the coast and, by the time Cuesta had decided for sure on Mexico, she was beginning to fear the worst. He'd told her twice that he'd kill her rather than lose her, and both times she'd believed him. Not that she'd ever admitted it. Giving Cuesta that kind of satisfaction was exactly what you'd never do but all the same, the fear was there, and inside she was a mess.

'Still?' Kane murmurs.

'Still.'

'Any way I can help?'

'You help big time, Mr K. You help by being here. You help by listening to me. You help by not believing easy endings. That's just three reasons for loving you, and killing that man is another, but life here is altogether crazier than I ever thought and if you want the truth I'm not sure what happens next.'

'Us? Do we happen next?'

She looks at him, runs her finger down the deepest scar in his face, kisses him softly.

'We are what we are, Mr K. And I love you for that, too.'

Not believing in easy endings. Kane knows exactly what she means and for now he also knows that he has no option but to wait for time and God knows what else to take Mahoney to some inner destination maybe a little safer. Getting there may take a while, but when he tells her he's OK to wait, she says she's glad.

'Glad's good,' she adds. 'And don't confuse it with grateful.'

Kane is happy with the distinction, and happier still when word comes from Kosch that the old man turns out to have a stash of saved money, all of it kosher, not a single bad bill.

'So what's this to do with me?'

'It's not,' Kosch tells him. 'It's to do with that lady of yours.'

That night, still living together in the Santa Monica apartment, Kane breaks the news to Mahoney. Desantos has a whack of money he wants to gift Mahoney. Call it conscience. Call it a late Christmas present. Call it whatever you like, it's still a sizeable sum.

'Like how much?'

'Like twenty thousand dollars.'

'Where did he get that kind of money?'

'Nobody knows but Kosch has seen it, counted it, put it in his personal safe until you turn up to collect it.'

Mahoney nods. Frowns. Shakes her head.

'Not me,' she says. 'Not mine. Yours. For Sis. Out here we'd call it karma. All kinds of bad stuff happens, then God's in a better mood and the sun comes out. You mind if we take a trip east? Turn up in Boston with a bundle of LA money?'

By now, in any event, it's time for Kane to strike camp and return to DC. Meier has taken the counterfeit scam as far as he can and is awaiting instructions from Donovan. The Cherokee have returned to Oklahoma. The day they left, Prosper threw a party and Huyano insisted on Kane keeping the belt that had saved his life. Kane, honoured, pledged to diet forever to give it a permanent home around his waist and the boy coloured up with pleasure.

'The Elders will look after you,' he promised, 'and your lady, too.'

The following day, Kane has a final meal with Gus and then takes the red-eye to DC. Gus makes a point of driving him to Inglewood for the late-night departure, and they get drunk at the airfield bar. Gus rarely lets booze write the script but the last month or so he says he's grown to feel pretty special about Kane, and getting mashed is the only way he can admit it. He also has some news from Donovan.

'The guy figures this is only the first reel,' Gus says.

'Meaning?'

'Meaning he loves us. Wants us. Thinks we're pretty special.'

'You're drunk.'

'No kidding, *hombre*. When a man has to spend the night in his car, you know he means it.'

'Means what?'

'Tell you in DC.'

'But you live here.'

'Did once.'

'You're leaving?'

'Sure. Everything comes to an end, *hombre*. Even LA.'

Kane stares at him, then decides that he was more right than he knew. Gus is well and truly mashed.

In DC, Kane reports to Donovan out at Navy Hill. Spook Central's manic boss is as busy as ever, and in between phone calls in his corner office Kane gets the impression that the counterfeit scam is in serious jeopardy. For one thing, FDR's doubts have appeared to harden, and for another current intelligence out of Vichy suggests that Darlan has been subject to credible death threats.

'From?'

'You name it,' Donovan growls. 'We're dealing with the French here. They're too goddamn busy fighting each other to bother with the Germans. They also think we're in the business of tearing what's left of their empire apart, which is awkward because it happens to be true. FDR is wondering whether we're in the right shape to try any kind of landing, and if so who might watch our back once we've got boots on the ground. Any thoughts, Agent Kane?'

Kane has nothing to contribute. He went to LA to organise a million dollars in counterfeit bills, and he's more or less delivered. As a side order to the main course, he got himself in deep shit with a psycho gangster, was beaten once, and nearly dropped from 1,600 feet weeks later. For now, he tells Donovan, he'd appreciate a little peace and quiet.

Donovan looks up. He isn't used to honesty on this scale.

'Am I hearing this right? You wanna go back to the White House? Babysit FDR?'

'I do.'

'That might not be an option, buddy. You never got this from me but I'm guessing Roosevelt may have other plans.'

Two weeks later, after resuming his duties under Mike Reilly and the rest of the agents in Precinct Sixteen, Kane takes three days' leave and heads north to Boston. He meets Mahoney off her plane at Logan airfield, and they take a cab back home. Kane's mom and dad are there, as is his brother Danny. Kane introduces Mahoney, and knows at once that she'll fit right in. His dad can't take his eyes off her. Her mom is curious about the name. Skibbereen? Does she have that right? Coupla generations back?

At this point, Kane's dad disappears upstairs, reappearing minutes later with Sis over his shoulder. Mahoney gets to her feet, abandons the sherry, kisses Sis. Sis's eyes are bright. Mahoney's arrival has been kept a secret. Who is this woman?

For Kane, the rest of the evening passes in a blur of Guinness, laughter, and brimming plates of colcannon. Kane breaks the glad news about Mahoney's windfall and an exchange of glances across the table confirm that

$20,000 will pretty much put Sis back on her feet. Not the way she was, not altogether perfect, but secure for the rest of her life. Danny gives Mahoney's hand a squeeze beneath the table.

'You're a generous woman,' he murmurs. 'Welcome home.'

Ignoring the bedroll on the floor, Mahoney and Kane share the tiny spare bedroom that night. Mahoney is thoughtful, reflective, the only one still sober. She says she's glad about the money, and gladder still to have been briefly part of the family. Tomorrow, she says, she must fly back to Southern California, to her desk at the *LA Times*, and to whatever the news agenda next has in mind for her.

Kane asks about meeting again, about him flying out, or her making it to DC, or about maybe a week in Chicago to let their hair down and take in a little hot jazz, but Mahoney shakes her head. For now, she says, it's best that they don't bother each other with regular calls. She needs just a little peace and quiet, a chance to maybe draw breath, and she hopes – knows – that Kane will understand.

Kane doesn't understand, not really, and he presses her for more details about her days and nights with Desantos. At first she's reluctant to revisit the paddock and the squalid little bungalow and the falling-down barns, but then she admits that maybe it's best to share this stuff, rather than let it fester.

'Fester? That bad?'

'Worse. You want the truth? You want to know the way it really happened? He was ready for me. That was the first shock. Cuesta had guys at the riot. We all drove over to Desantos' place, me in the back with a gun to my pretty head. It was Cuesta that took me to the barn with the wooden booths. One of those booths was for me. That was the one you described, the one with the straw and the wooden post.'

'He tied you up?'

'Yes.'

'Cuesta?'

'Yes. And he said he'd be back when I was ready.'

'Ready?'

'Guy lived in his head which is no place for anyone half-sane. Nothing matters except possession. After you're his, the rules write themselves.'

Kane nods, shakes his head.

'Bad?'

'Horrible. He went away that night, they all did except the old guy. In his way Desantos did his best, looked after me, fed me, kept me watered. I probably got better treatment than the horses but that buckskin hide under the straw stank of abattoir when it got warm during the day and the rope made me cramp up and after a while everything went crazy.'

'Crazy how?'

'It turned out there was a sort of cave under the booth. Get rid of the straw and the buckskin hide beneath and you're looking at a wooden trap door. Rickety old steps, Mr Kane, going down into the darkness. Desantos told me it came from the bootleg days, kind of cellar, place where you stored all your booze. Desantos had a flashlight, played the host, took me down there. It was tiny, a cell, rough walls, no plaster, chunks of soil falling out. Nights it was freezing and pitch black. Days it was hot. That's the only way you keep track, figure out what time of day it might be. Desantos gave me the flashlight but there were no more batteries so I mostly saved it. Noises, Quince. Buzzing, Quince. Insects dancing on your face and something bigger I was too frightened to name, always moving around. It might have been in my head, I had no way of knowing, and that was even more scary. Desantos would come with stuff to eat, bread, water, rotten leftovers he must have been keeping for ever, and sometimes he'd let me back up, back onto the straw roped to that goddam post and a filthy gag round my mouth tied way too tight, but then it was back down those steps again, back into the dark, and because I couldn't figure any pattern, any reason for the coming and the going, that only made it worse. Turned out the one thing that scared Desantos was his son. Cuesta would phone up, make a call, give him his orders, sometimes once a day, sometimes twice, sometimes every hour. He had us both hog-tied, that man. Control was everything and the worst of it all was Desantos coming to and fro from the house, obeying his son's fucking orders: put her underground, bring her up again, let her rest, give her a shake, get inside her head.'

'You were down below most of the time?'

'To begin with, yes, until Cuesta took me to his place, but underground was the worst. You play games with yourself. I've no time for shit metaphors but there was a whole lot of reasons that hole under Desantos' barn became LA. Dark as hell. Full of menace, threat, crazy stuff you couldn't figure, didn't want to figure. The moment you realise you're both in the hands of a true psycho, both me and the old guy, both being jerked around by someone who wants – maybe needs – to hurt you, that's the moment you start listening hard for the next page turn, the next plot twist, maybe footsteps on the boards at the top of the steps, maybe something big and furry with huge teeth prowling around God knows where, maybe the biggest spider you've ever seen who badly wants to be your friend. Anything, Quince. Anything that can pitch its sorry fucking tent deep in your brain and invite you inside. This stuff drives you madder than you've ever thought possible, which I guess is the whole point. Cuesta wanted my compliance, he wanted me to say yes, and little boys that sad and that wicked get their way in this world. Shit.' She shakes her head, looks away.

'You coped? You fought him off?'

'I kept him at arm's length. I think I told you already.'

'How?'

'I played games. Games in my head. I'd lie there in the darkness, just me and a thousand insects, critters, tarantulas, scorpions, God knows what else. I'd go for runs in my head. I'd lift the phone and talk to friends. I'd remember parties, nights on the town, big stories I'd cracked, folks being nice to me. Often I was in the gym, working out. Sometimes I was in the ring, one of those two fights, faces watching from all those tables, just me and Dolores waiting for the opening bell, but mostly it was the runs beside the ocean, the getting out in the fresh air, the breathing deep and steady, that way you hit your rhythm, on and on, mile after mile, outdoors stuff. You ever smell the city after a big rainstorm? The clouds gone? The leaves all shiny in the sunlight? You ever smell the fog on the beach on winter nights? Like now? The chill? The damp? Tiny little waves at your feet? The ocean being polite? Or maybe one of those freezing Santa Ana days with the wind blowing down from the mountains? That kept me sane, Quince. And something else, too. Santa Monica Pier. Summer, mostly. Night-time again. All the coloured lights on the blackness of the water, rippling and rippling. And you, Quince, big and grown up and smelling wonderful, and always making me laugh.' She pauses, gropes for his hand under the blanket. 'You really came to that barn? Found the straw? The post?'

'I did.'

'Shame I wasn't there.' She's reached for the switch on the bedside light and turned it on, and now she's gazing at him, trying to summon a grin, or maybe the hint of a smile. 'I'd have guessed,' she says softly, touching his face. 'I'd have known it was you. I'd have tidied up down there, maybe baked a cake. I did none of those things, Quince, but now it's maybe good you know the way it really was.'

Kane nods, understands only too well. Hollywood Reptiles, he thinks. And the guy whose shopping list extended to a single item.

'You want to tell me about the rattlesnake?' he says softly.

'You know about that?' She's looking briefly startled.

'We made some enquiries, figured it out. You don't have to do this. It's just a question.'

Mahoney looks at him for a long moment, finally shrugs.

'This was later at Cuesta's place. He'd tied me up and driven me over there. He kept the snake in a glass cage. Wherever I was in that house of his, the snake was there. He carried it from room to room. He'd give the cage a shake when the snake was asleep, rile it up, get it angry, tell me the snake was mad at me, tell me what a horrible death it would be, pain like I couldn't imagine, and then not being able to breathe any more. Death by suffocation. Death by snake. The top of the cage lifted off. There was a padlock. Cuesta had the key.' She looks away, shakes her head. 'He knew snakes terrified me. All I had to do was say yes, just the once, and I'd never see the fucking rattler again.'

Just the once.

'And?'

'I couldn't do it. I couldn't say yes. Better a rattlesnake than Cuesta on my belly. You understand, Quince? Just say yes.'

Kane nods, says nothing. He can feel her trembling beside him.

'I'm guessing it got worse,' he says at last.

'Yeah?'

'Yeah. I'm here for you, Lou. That's all you need to know.'

Mahoney closes her eyes. There was another cage, she murmurs, much smaller. Bunch of tiny mice inside. Every time she said no, Cuesta fed the snake another mouse, made her watch what happened next. He said he'd starved the snake for weeks, getting ready for when he might need it.

'And?'

'The snake killed the mouse. Devoured it. Me? I was the mouse. He put the glass case real close, made me watch every detail, every last second. Crude but effective, Mr K. What that man wanted was consent, compliance, me saying yes, and the word no was the one thing I had left, the one thing that kept me whole.'

'So why didn't he rape you? Just get it over and done?'

'Because it would taste much sweeter if I said yes, then he could kid himself we'd fallen in love or some other dumb fucking thing. It's called control, Mr K. And one day, I told myself, it would end up killing him.'

'It did. And you were there.'

'Sure.' Kane feels the lightest spread of her fingertips on his face. 'And I meant to say thank you.'

★

Next day, Kane takes her back to Logan, tries to tempt her with a little breakfast at a counter by one of the big picture windows, but she settles instead for coffee she doesn't touch, staring out of the window, out beyond the scatter of parked aircraft, out to the far horizon with its tumble of clouds. Beyond reach. Kane thinks. Nothing to say. Nothing to suggest they'll ever meet again. When the flight is called, he accompanies her to the door that leads out to the tarmac. They're last in line, and he watches the straggle of passengers making their way towards the plane.

'Ma'am? Sir?' A stewardess offers them a bright smile. 'Are you flying with us this morning?'

Kane shakes his head. He badly wants to say a proper goodbye but knows it will never happen.

Mahoney turns to him. She looks pale and thin. Back at the house, the cab waiting outside, little Sis had still been in bed.

'Say hi for me, Quince?'

'Of course.'

'And take good care of her?'

'Sure.'

Mahoney nods, holds his gaze a moment longer, and then she puts her hand briefly on his before turning away and stepping into the brightness of the sunshine, careful not to risk a glance back. He watches her cross the tarmac, hesitate for a moment at the foot of the steps, then climb towards the open cabin door. At the head of the steps, thinks Kane, she'll pause, look back, raise a hand, maybe blow him a kiss.

Nothing.

Kane can't believe it, fights the image, watches the door close, the props begin to spin, the plane inch slowly away. No face at the window, no wave of farewell, no voiceless lips shaping the message he so badly wants to hear.

'I love you, too,' he murmurs to himself, 'and now you've gone.'

Outside the terminal building, he returns to his car. Bent over the driver's door, trying to figure out the key, he feels the lightest touch on his shoulder. I've become an old man, he thinks, overtaken by events I'll never understand.

It's Gus. He's still dressed for LA but doesn't seem to care.

'What the fuck are you doing here?' Kane manages.

'That lady of yours,' Gus extends a steadying hand. 'She seems to think you might need someone sane around.'

Afterwards

Fedala, Morocco, 8 November 1942.

Nine months later, alerted by DC, Kane is watching one of the spearheads of Operation *Torch* from the flat roof of an empty house half a mile back of the beach at Fedala, close to Casablanca. The previous evening, a bid to silence Vichy guns had been foiled and French fire pours into the bent ranks of the oncoming Americans. Kane watches the toppling bodies, weighed down with heavy packs, marvelling at how seeming allies – Americans, French – can be killing each other. The invasion of this part of North Africa is led by a hard-driving major general, George Patton, who – as far as Kane can tell through his borrowed binoculars – doesn't make a personal appearance in the heavy surf. The Fedala beachhead, littered with wreckage, is secured by mid-afternoon, by which time Kane has made himself scarce. Of events at the other two landing zones, he has heard nothing.

By arrangement, he meets Gus a couple of days later at a deserted bar in the backstreets of Casablanca, once the fighting has died down. The bar is owned by an Arab he's gotten to know well and somehow Tareq's managed to lay hands on fresh eggs to go with the thick roundels of unleavened bread that constitute breakfast. Gus, who's been at the wheel of an ancient Citroën all night, wants bacon to go with the eggs. He looks, to Kane, even more wrecked than usual.

'Oran?' Kane ignores the bid for bacon.

'Surrendered yesterday. The French fought like monkeys but it was all over by last night.'

'Algiers?'

'Different story. There was token opposition in the port itself, but they were waving the white flag by nightfall.' Gus signalled for more coffee. 'Ask me about our man.'

'Darlan? You're telling me he was there?'

'Sure. He says he was passing by on some private visit but that's his story. I'm figuring something different. I'm figuring he knew what was coming and wanted to be around when it happened.'

'And?'

'And nothing. Murphy put him in the slammer with another guy and did his best to get them to see it our way but Darlan wasn't in the mood. The local cops sprung them next day and Murphy had another go. This time it worked. Giraud had cooked his own goose so the whole deal fell into Darlan's lap. FDR's given him a fancy title – French High Commissioner in North Africa – and handed him the keys to the kingdom. That's why it's gone so fucking quiet.'

Robert Murphy is FDR's stake in the North Africa game, an experienced diplomat from Wisconsin who has been despatched by Roosevelt as resident Consul to knock French heads together. Henri Giraud, brave but hopelessly naïve, is the toast of the infant French Resistance. Admiral Darlan has obviously outflanked both of them.

'He's the go-to man?' Kane asks.

'Completely. He told his precious countrymen in this

benighted place to behave and that's exactly what they've done. Downed weapons and waved the flag. FDR can't believe it. Sure we've lost a bunch of men getting here but that's one of the pleasures of war. No one expected this so soon, and that's Darlan's doing. The guy's walking on water. FDR says so and Eisenhower can't believe his luck. It's Day Four, for Chrissakes, and we're home safe.'

'And the Krauts?'

'No sense of humour. Hitler's occupied Vichy and threatened Tunisia with fire and brimstone. There's also a fuss in some of our papers but this stuff writes itself because we've done a deal with the devil. Darlan the Nazi puppet. Darlan the collabo. Darlan backing both ends against the middle. You know the guy. You've broken a little bread with him. He's clever and he's very French and for my money he's made exactly the right call. Why is Hitler so pissed? Because Darlan's taken a long hard look at what's on offer and decided that we're gonna win. Play the game right, and he'll be smelling of roses. That's what hurts the Krauts. That's what makes them so mad. It's not Darlan himself, it's the judgement he represents.'

'So Darlan's on the team. Is that what you're saying?'

'Darlan is the team. There's no one else in sight. All we have to do, *hombre*, is keep him alive. And that comes direct from FDR.'

Kane rocks back in his chair, letting the bar owner pour more of the thick gritty coffee that – just now – is keeping Gus awake. Then he pushes his own glass forward for a refill.

Kane knows that the covert posting to this Godforsaken place has put him back together again. Donovan had been right about FDR. After months of bullying from Churchill, his new pal, Roosevelt has finally conceded to landings in North Africa, a chance at last to take American might to the edges of occupied Europe and kick down Hitler's door. But before GI boots hit North African soil, the man in the White House was looking for people he personally trusted, people with the right language skills, plus unquestioned loyalty, to bed themselves in, take a good look round and report back. That job should have fallen to the Office of Strategic Services but FDR wanted to keep his own counsel. Wild Bill Donovan was busy building an empire of his own. Kane and Gus Leaman were Roosevelt's personal pick.

With the help of Gus, over a busy month and a half, Kane has managed to make just a little sense of the French surrender to the Nazis and of the rich pickings of colonial rule in North Africa. With his rusty Québécois accent he's made lots of contacts but few friends. By and large, the French *colons* in North Africa have wanted no part in this crazy war. They preferred the Brits to stop fighting, do the sensible thing, and to see the new peace in Europe Hitler's way. Most of them are Vichy, which is French for realist, and have never fathomed either Churchill or the haughty General de Gaulle's passion for continued resistance. But now, in the shape of the three Operation *Torch* landings, they face not only the Brits but the Americans as well. Irritation is giving way to alarm. Where, *mon Dieu*, will all this madness end?

Kane has written a number of reports ahead of the American invasion for FDR's eyes only and has been glad to say goodbye to Donovan's outfit. He still thinks constantly of Lou Mahoney, of opportunities lost, but Gus assures him that the wound will, in the end, crust over and heal. For now, more pressing business awaits.

'We're here to keep Darlan alive?' Kane asks. 'Is that what I'm hearing?'

'You, buddy. You're here to keep the guy alive. You did it just fine with Roosevelt. He appreciates that. Now it's Darlan's turn, for just as long as he stays useful.'

'And you think he's really under threat?'

'I do. There are people here who want to kill him.'

'Sure. Plenty of folks tell me that but just now he's all they've got. FDR loves him. Eisenhower, too. Darlan will keep the lights on. The French adore a strongman. Otherwise it's chaos. *Anarchie.*'

'Who said anything about the French?' Gus is toying with his coffee. 'Take a little care is all I'm saying. This goddamn place is a bunch of snakes. You're allowed one mistake.' Gus eyes Kane for a moment, then swallows the rest of the coffee in a single gulp and looks for Tareq. 'Does this guy have a bed to spare?'

And so, over the days to come, Kane makes it his business to once again get alongside Darlan. The man is the new French High Commissioner in town, but this isn't easy. Darlan has, after all, dictated the shape of Kane's personal war. It was to bribe the French admiral that he'd conjured the thousand-dollar bill from the engraving pen of Hans Meier. It was to François Darlan he owed that troubled stay in LA. And it was thanks to the wily Frenchman that he'd gotten so tantalisingly close to another human being. Ironic, really.

Nothing in life comes for free and after all the bids to bribe Darlan, to lure him into a trap with a million counterfeit scoots, Kane has been suddenly handed another task. Keep the man alive. At whatever cost.

That Churchill still wants to rip the heart out of François Darlan is common knowledge, but now, given what Gus drily describes as 'political circumstances', the wretched man is FDR's best hope of keeping otherwise hostile French *colons* in check. The price of American blood is Admiral Darlan, and confirmation – if Kane needs it – comes in the shape of a summons to Robert Murphy, FDR's presence in North Africa.

They meet, briefly, in Murphy's office in Algiers. By now, the *Torch* landings are over and done, and more than 50,000 American troops are safely ashore, but Murphy is reaching the limit of his patience with the French in North Africa and it shows. He's lost weight since he and Kane last talked and the burden of trying to shield his GIs from the sharper edges of their assignment is beginning to show in other ways. Normally, Murphy carries himself well. He has the nose of a boxer and a certain brisk charm, but now he looks harassed. He looks gaunt. He looks as though a return to DC might do him good.

'You've met Darlan. Am I right, Kane?'

'You are, sir. We've met twice, once to say hello, the second time to properly check each other out over a meal. He seemed to think I was more important than I am. He loves all this FDR off-the-reservation shit.'

'So what do you make of him?'

'Make of him?' Kane lets the question settle, gives it the time and space it deserves. 'I think he has little time for anyone but himself, his own interests,' he says at last. 'He's turned opportunism into a way of life and who else around here can say he's wrong?'

Murphy gives this assessment an impatient nod of the head. Evidently, it isn't the answer he wants.

'Do you like him?'

'Like him? What is there to like?'

'It's a question, that's all. Man to man, do you detect, have you detected, any areas of...' Murphy shrugs, '...common interest?'

'That implies I've gotten close to the man. So the answer has to be no.'

'But you speak French.'

'I do.'

'Doesn't that help any?'

'Not at all. We just get to the end of the conversation more quickly. Darlan thinks constantly of Darlan. He's clever, don't get me wrong. He knows we need someone like him.'

'Meaning?'

'A man with his fingers on the right buttons. In a way he's a genuine patriot and there was a time when the Brits might have figured Darlan as the leader of the Free French. He could have been de Gaulle with better manners but he stayed a Vichy man and turned up in Berlin instead, playing footsie with the Heinies. Churchill has never forgiven him but I'm guessing you know all this.'

Murphy nods, says nothing. Kane, in turn, bites his lip. He's here to get his marching orders and he's curious to know where Darlan really stands with the new masters in North Africa.

'Churchill is a very big problem,' Murphy grunts at last. 'He thinks Darlan is a liar and a crook, not proper French at all, not Churchill's kind of French...' he pushes back his chair, '...and this conversation is for our ears only.'

The exchange is virtually over and Kane leaves minutes later. Murphy says he's checked out Kane's Secret Service record and confirmed that he's an accredited bodyguard. He has FDR's personal assurance that Kane was one of the best at Secret Service District Sixteen, and that the current assignment fits him like a glove. Pressed by Kane, Murphy confirms that the Donovan bribery scam is dead in the water. Darlan has finessed himself into the top position in North Africa and it's in everybody's interests that he stays there. Kane's job, in short, is to keep the man alive.

Kane shares this with Gus, who appears to have known most of it all along. Gus has an apartment overlooking the Bay of Algiers, his deeply personal stake in this curious world that FDR is determined to briefly make America's own. The apartment runs to three first-floor rooms and Gus has furnished it with his usual contempt for both fashion and comfort: beaten-up furniture bought for a song in the local souk, a poster of FDR dressed as Father Christmas, threadbare rugs left for collection by the previous owner. Half close his eyes, and Kane could be back in Venice Beach.

'And Darlan? You've told him about the bodyguard thing?' Gus asks.

'I have. Murphy insisted I went right round and what Murphy wants, Murphy gets.'

'And?'

'Darlan thinks it's a joke. He says he's well protected, French guys he knows and trusts, and what the hell should he make of little me?'

'And the answer?'

'It got nasty. I told him the offer wasn't up for negotiation. Like it or not, he has to make room for us Yanks. Not just the odd briefing meet to keep DC happy but in his private life as well. That means the full deal, twenty-four-hour cover, everything.'

'And?'

'He just laughed. Remember, this guy is slippery as hell. Only last year he was offering Berlin French military heft against the Brits. That never happened but only because the Heinies don't trust him. Now the man is eating on our tab and helps himself to the best of everything.'

'So what happens next?'

Kane would love to answer the question but can't. 'Next', in this country, is an impossible ask. Will the *colons*, the French who have largely gone native, continue to do Darlan's bidding? Are they, like the new High Commissioner, momentarily signed up behind the Americans and the Brits? Will the untested GIs be able to do the business against German and Italian troops in neighbouring Tunisia? And will Darlan himself stay in one piece through this war of dancing shadows?

The latter thought has already occurred to Gus and he has no hesitations in voicing it.

'So where, *hombre*, does that leave us?'

Kane shrugs. FDR has personally sent them ahead of the American invasion to scout the territory and work out where the going will get toughest. With American boots at last on foreign soil, Admiral Darlan has abruptly turned everything on its head. In truth, whichever way Kane frames the question, the answer comes out the same.

'Our problem, Gus, will be the Brits. But where the hell are we supposed to start?'

Gus holds his gaze for longer than is comfortable. Then comes one of his trademark grins before he reaches for the stone-cold coffee pot.

'Wish I knew,' he offers the pot to Kane. 'Here's to Christmas, *hombre*.'

Within hours, Kane is back with Robert Murphy, the irascible Consul and one of FDR's most important voices in North Africa. Since the successful landings, Darlan has done exactly what the Americans wanted. Casablanca, Oran and Algiers are safely in Allied hands at the cost of a little showboat resistance, enough to warm hearts in Vichy but over now. This is old ground to both men but Murphy is keen to dispel any trace of ambiguity, which is a big ask in North Africa. Every French *colon*, he says, can park his weapon, hold his head high and devote himself anew to the task of making yet more money.

For Murphy, the cost of acceptance is Admiral Darlan. FDR's deal has raised angry voices all over the alliance but for the time being having a collabo in the camp doesn't matter. Another day not watching our backs, as Murphy insists, is another step towards neighbouring Tunisia and the German reinforcements pouring in. That, after all, is the whole point of the exercise in the first place. With the Brits in the east and the Yanks out west, Rommel and his Afrika Korps will soon be caught in the jaws of the nutcracker. And after that, the Germans will be gone. In the meantime, Kane's priority is to keep an eye on Darlan.

'That make any sense, Kane? Or shall I go through the whole pantomime again?'

And so Kane does Murphy's bidding and turns up at the Hôtel Palais d'Été where Darlan has a desk in a suite of offices on the first floor. The little admiral operates behind a screen of French people he's known forever. By far the most important is a tall, trim ex-officer from the French Navy called Pierre Ancille. He occupies a role in Darlan's life midway between guard dog and social companion. Darlan's arrogance, coupled with a reluctance to trust anyone, has left him at the mercy of a tiny bunch of disciples and Kane realises at once that getting on with Ancille will be the key to his own role.

To that end he makes it his business to be as frank as he dares. In his quaint Québécois French, he draws Ancille to one side, sits him down in the hotel bar, orders coffee, and establishes the rules of engagement. Number one, Darlan has been happy to fall into the lap of the Americans. Number two, the tasking – Kane in charge of his security – is non-negotiable. Between them, as minor actors with walk-on parts, he and Ancille have to make that work.

Ancille, if anything, is amused. He has a cautious smile.

'How well do you know this country?'

'Not at all. You?'

'I've lived here a couple of years now. One day it might make some kind of sense but for now, my friend, North Africa is the enemy of everything you've taken for granted. The place is a shithole. And I mean that.'

'But your shithole. No?'

'No. Arabs? Tuaregs? Berbers? French Resistance? Vichy? And now your lot and Boche spies under diplomatic cover?

Mix those colours and you need a very big canvas, as well as a sense of humour. The first time I landed here, the first couple of weeks, I loved it. The views, the people, even the food. I was wrong, my friend. North Africa is our punishment for being French.'

Kane is impressed. He thinks he can hear Darlan's voice in his merciless dismissal of everything North African and he can readily imagine the two men together. To date, he's got absolutely nothing from the new High Commissioner, but he's determined to build some kind of rapport with Ancille.

In terms of the smallest print, this is remarkably easy. Kane has simply transferred a long list of responsibilities for FDR's wellbeing to Darlan. He needs unquestioned access. He needs to know, well in advance, the shape of every working day. He needs a list of the people with whom the admiral is dealing, where and how often he meets them, and who might represent a problem. Above all, he needs to win a little response, a little warmth, from Darlan himself. They are, after all, on the same side, with the same war to win. Fair?

'Perfectly. I can attend to all that except the last. You won't expect detail but his Excellency isn't the easiest man to share time with.'

'That's your take on the guy? His Excellency?'

'The admiral's. He takes his promotion seriously, as he must. Winning promotion in this country is one thing. Getting people to take notice, quite another. Shouting isn't his style. Words matter.'

'His Excellency,' Kane muses. 'Thanks for the tip.'

'A pleasure. You'll need a room of your own here. You want me to organise that?'

The offer takes Kane by surprise. Hidden microphones, he thinks at once, or maybe some kind of other bug, an obvious move in a situation as complicated as this. The French would love to eavesdrop on Kane's reports back to DC.

'No need,' he watches Ancille begin to lose interest. 'I'll do it myself.'

The room is on the top floor, far from ideal. It's tiny, with a mustiness that speaks of unopened windows, and way too many cigarettes. Access to Darlan's suite of offices is via a creaky lift that takes an age to arrive.

Kane looks round, asks for something on the first floor. The attendant from reception shakes his head.

'Everything booked, *monsieur*. Impossible, I'm afraid.'

'Everything?'

'Everything.'

Kane shrugs. Says it will have to do. Parking his life in small spaces has become a habit since Bunker Hill.

Ancille is as good as his word. A carefully typed schedule covering the days to come is delivered to Kane's room with the proviso that names and times can change. Also attached is a brisk summary of each of the attached visitors. Most of them are French and none of them appear to be a problem. Admiral Darlan, in short, has settled into the administration of Vichy affairs in precisely the way he should, with the minimum of fuss and bother.

Kane takes all this at face value. He will present himself at the outer office where Ancille has a desk at regular intervals. He will monitor the admiral's daily comings and goings, and this will include full body searches for all visitors. The latter puts a briefly pained expression on the smoothness of Ancille's face but Kane – once again – insists that there's no alternative. Not only must visitors be weapon-free, but word of the searches will quickly spread. North Africa's new High Commissioner, his Excellency, deserves a little respect. Be warned.

Of Darlan himself, there's little sign. He keeps himself behind the closed door of his office, attends to a mountain of paperwork, and encourages no social conversation. Visitors come and go, every one of them submitting to a thorough body search while raising an enquiring eyebrow at Ancille as Kane pats them down. Ancille, for his part, merely shrugs. The Americans, he seems to be saying. They've watched – and made – far too many movies. Let it ride. Because it keeps our new masters happy.

Thus Darlan settles comfortably into the torpor of Algiers life. Kane watches what little he sees very carefully and mentally tabulates his findings ahead of offering them via Murphy to DC. Our man, he concludes, is nervous, watchful and slightly surprised at finding himself installed so easily in such a role. Thanks to Gus, who has his ear to the ground, Kane knows a great deal about the various conversations that have led to Darlan's installation and senses that FDR's judgement, which is key to everything in the alliance, is strictly provisional. For the time being, the fretful little man behind the desk is earning his keep. But that may change.

Then comes the moment, late one afternoon, when Darlan opens his office door and beckons Kane inside. They talk, man to man, for the best part of an hour. His desk is mysteriously bare of paperwork. The admiral wants – needs – to know that everything is satisfactory, that everything is working the way it should, but he enquires as well about Kane's social life, about his impressions of Algiers, about people he may have met along the way.

In truth, Kane has devoted most of his waking hours to Darlan's wellbeing. This entails a great deal of inertia, of hanging around, and alas he's been devoting far too much thought to Lou Mahoney. How come something so visceral, so important, can simply vanish? How must he live with the knowledge that she's gone? That something so important is simply over?

To none of these questions does he have an answer. Neither will he share them with anyone else, even Gus, but listening to Darlan he concludes that – perhaps like Kane himself – the man is both confused and lonely. Two clues. The first is a long-ago battle in which the admiral's grandfather participated.

'It's got a name? This battle?'

'Trafalgar. My grandfather had command of a ship there. How is it that we both hate the British?'

'Both? You think we hate them, too?'

'I know you do. That's the whole point of America. You sailed there to rid yourselves of your former masters. In your case, that would have been the British.'

'But still? You think we hate them today?'

'I think the Americans have excellent judgement. You never wanted any part of this war. Very sensible. You never wanted to fight. It was someone else's quarrel. Let them settle it. And what's happened? The British are still fighting, still holding out. And now you're here with them.'

'You think we shouldn't be?'

'I think you should have stayed home, minded your

own business. I also think the British should have done the rational thing.'

'Like the French, you mean? Hoisted the white flag?'

'We bowed to the inevitable. Sometimes history teaches you lessons but the British never listen. That's one of the reasons I hate them.'

'Hate's a big word. You used it before.'

'I did. And you listened. That makes you an American, Mr Kane, and all the better for it.'

Kane nodded, remembering the Sunday morning in the White House when the phone exchange lit up.

'The Japanese bombed us all to pieces,' he pointed out. 'After Pearl Harbor we had no choice.'

'And so you went to war. I understand that. But Germany, too?'

'They declared war on us. Again, no choice.'

'You may be right,' he nodded, playing with a pencil between his fingers. 'So you think I spoke out of turn? About the British?'

'Not at all, sir. They're an acquired taste. They also have long memories.'

'About what?'

'Trafalgar, for one thing. As your grandfather would have known.'

'*Touché.*' For the first time, a smile. 'We're good haters.'

'We?'

'Us. The French and the British. Our beloved enemy. Did you ever hear that phrase?'

Kane shook his head, said no, wondering where this suddenly vocal little man might take the conversation next. The fact that he'd opened the door in the first place had come as a surprise, but admitting to something as visceral as hatred was way more than he ever expected, and seemed, somehow, to represent a compliment. The admiral appeared to like him, trust him even. Truly remarkable.

'His name's Alain.' Darlan is nodding at a small, framed photograph on his desk. Kane's view is far from perfect, but he has no doubts who he is.

'Your son,' he says evenly. 'And he's had polio.'

'Had is past tense. I'm not sure polio is a condition that ever leaves you.'

Kane tells Darlan about little Sis, about the last Christmas he'd paid a surprise visit only to find the house empty, and about what greeted him when he finally made it to the Children's Hospital.

'She's better?'

'She's in recovery.'

'And Roosevelt? That boss of yours? That boss of all of us?'

'He'll never walk again. Not properly.' Kane briefly tallies the ways he gets through. The iron callipers, the wheelchair, the helping hands.

Darlan nods, impatient now. 'I don't think it will come to that with Alain. Not as long as the medicines continue to work.'

'That makes your son lucky, sir.'

'Not at all, Mr Kane. On the contrary, it makes him exceedingly unlucky.'

'How come?'

'Getting the disease in the first place. That's when his luck ran out.'

The two men study each other for a moment. Then Darlan enquires about Christmas, barely a week away.

'You have plans? A brief return home perhaps?'

'I'm here with you, sir. It's my job.'

'You make it sound like a prison sentence. I hope I'm mistaken but that's the inference.'

'Nothing intended. I go where I'm told and I do my best. Christmas was never special, by the way.'

'You have a wife? Children, perhaps?'

'Neither. What you see is what you get. Maybe an extra beer on the great day, who knows?'

Darlan nods, says nothing. Then, unaccountably, he's back afloat.

'I love that Navy of mine. I truly do. I also love my son. Perhaps that's where one's heart truly lies.' He nods again at the photo of Alain. 'Love rather than hate. The comforts of shared blood, am I right, Mr Kane?'

Kane can only agree. The comforts of shared blood, he thinks. The French fleet tied up in Toulon has now been scuttled by the French Navy to keep it out of German hands after the occupation of the whole of France. Kane has seen photos of the sunken remains of countless ships at Toulon. In a way, he suspects it mirrors what's happened between him and Lou Mahoney.

'Unthinkable,' he murmurs. 'Just how do you ever come back from something like that?'

The next night Kane meets Gus in the hotel. Darlan is still at his desk, beset by another flood of paperwork, yesterday's conversation doubtless forgotten. Gus, in a quiet corner in the hotel bar, brings news of a training base out near Cap Matifou, not far from Algiers.

'It's run by a Brit outfit,' he says. 'SOE, Special Operations Executive. They report to a guy called Sir Stewart Menzies, who happens to be head of Brit Intel. Just now they're hosting a bunch of French paramilitaries called the Corps d'Afrique. These are wild guys who've opened the doors to pretty much anyone with a grudge – French, non-French, monarchists, anarchists, republicans, refugees, natives, Jews, leftovers, tomorrow's lunch, whatever. They all listen hard to the Brits who generally know what they're talking about. They blow stuff up. They learn how to kill people. They shaft the Heinies any which way they can. Our people are in there too.'

'OSS?' A thin smile. 'Donovan?'

'The same. Guy called Carleton Coon. He calls himself an observer but he knows where the bodies are buried.'

'And?'

'Something's up. Exactly when's a guess but it has the backing of the Brits.'

'To do what?'

'Dunno,' he flashed a grin. 'Yet.'

On the approach to Christmas, Algiers takes a good look round. The Americans are everywhere, tens of thousands of them, Darlan is at the helm, and the word on everyone's lips is Tunisia. Very soon now, the GIs will be on the march, heading east, eager to test themselves against some of Germany's most feared troops. With luck, and good generalship, North Africa should soon be free of Wehrmacht grey. After that the door to Italy will be open, exposing the soft underbelly of Hitler's Europe. But the story of war, as Kane is beginning to realise, seldom obeys any script. The real threats might come from anywhere, unannounced, unexpected, the grubby children of a world turned upside down by violence.

Word reaches Kane from Gus on the morning of 24 December. Sir Stewart Menzies, he announces, has been spotted having lunch with some pals at a *resto* barely twenty minutes' drive from the Hôtel Palais d'Été. With events moving fast, and London the centre of the Allied drive to contain Hitler, what on earth is he doing in Algiers?

Kane has no answer to this question. Darlan is planning to spend tomorrow with his son, Alain, and a handful of close friends. Work, for once, is briefly winding down. There is even a suggestion from Ancille that today, on Christmas Eve, the admiral might host a discreet late-afternoon drinks party in his office, invitation only. Ancille has made a point that Kane will not only be welcome but that his presence will be *obligatoire*. The guests will evidently include Alain, and it's the admiral's wish that the two men meet at last.

In the late morning, Kane is therefore not surprised to receive a summons from Darlan. The admiral has a special mission in mind, something by way of a personal favour, and Kane is the person to whom he intends to turn. It involves a picture Darlan commissioned several weeks ago. It comes from the hand of an English artist here in Algiers. Her name is Verity Desrosier and all Kane needs to know is where she lives and what to do with the completed canvas which the admiral now intends as a Christmas present for his son.

Kane scribbles down the address and orders a cab from reception. With luck, he'll be back in the building within the hour. Alas, North Africa has other ideas. For one thing, the driver can't immediately locate either the area or the exact address. After circling the rising ground at the back of the city, he finally settles on a discreet villa in extensive grounds shrouded by cypress trees. This, he says, has to be the Desrosiers' address. Kane can only agree, keeping him at the kerbside while he jogs up the drive and checks with a gardener tending a bed of very early daffodils.

The second hiccough concerns the canvas itself. Madame Desrosier, speaking with an impeccable English accent, has had second thoughts about a tiny detail in the bottom left-hand corner and is waiting for the paint to dry. In the meantime, she insists on apéros and a plate of canapés.

She's a striking woman in her late forties. Her flawless complexion, carefully hidden from the midday sun, is brightened by a daub of scarlet paint, and curtained by wisps of greying hair. She's wearing shorts and an old cardigan over a plaid shirt that is way too big for her. Kane judges that the shirt has to belong to the man in the house. He also says yes to a kir royale poured from a paint-scabbed cut-glass jug.

'How long will the canvas take to dry?'

'At least another hour, to be on the safe side. Are you a patient man, Mr Kane?'

'Quincy,' Kane says, looking round for the picture.

'The painting's in my atelier. Bring your drink. The canapés won't be enough for a growing man like you. Might you take an omelette?'

Without waiting for an answer, she leads the way down a corridor and into a bright, sun-splashed room at the far end. The corridor is lined with pictures and there are more to come once they get to the atelier. Kane is brought to a halt by the view, which is sensational. The entire stretch of Algiers Bay lies before them as if the house, the room, had been specially prepared for this moment. He can see the port approaches, the harbour itself, traffic on the corniche, and the deep blue bowl of the sea. With a view like this, he thinks, you'd have no option but to become a painter.

'These are yours? Same hand?' he gestures at the art on the wall, overlooking the busy chaos of a room dedicated to producing yet more work.

'Mine, I'm afraid. Your thoughts?'

Kane takes his time to answer, impressed by the woman's directness. Most of the pictures have been shaped by the view at various times of day. By far the best have the longest shadows cast by a fierce spill of light from the right of the canvas.

'That's dawn,' she says, anticipating his judgement. 'I get up in darkness, pull the blinds, get everything ready, and then wait. Waiting can be the tricky bit. Nature seldom does one's bidding.'

'You're very clever. I'm there. You've caught me. *Joyeux Noël...*' Kane lifts his glass, more in appreciation than anything else, and she offers a private smile of acknowledgement.

'That's sweet,' she says.

'I mean it. You live here alone?'

'With my husband. He's a businessman, away a great deal, but I love the way he's always in the swim. He's my Marco Polo. I rely on him to bring me word from the outside world. He has adventures and he's generous enough to share them.'

'English? American? French?'

'French. Hence our family name. Americans are rare in these parts, or used to be. You people will take over the whole world in the end. Do you mind me saying that?'

'Not at all. Trust me, it's the last thing on our minds.'

'Should I believe you?'

'You should...' he's looking round, '...because we're way too stupid to lie.'

'It's over there, flat on its back.' She smiles again.

'The picture?'

'The very same. Take your time. Have a good look. A bit of a departure, I think, so don't be shy.' With that, she's gone.

Suddenly alone in this glorious room, Kane takes his glass of kir to the drying canvas. Once again, it's a view of the bay but in contrast to everything else he's seen it's very different. Gone are the artful brushstrokes and choice of colours that have captured this view. Instead he's looking at a wild deconstruction of the bay, perspectives torn out of context, everything reduced to a feathery nothingness, plus something brought to the canvas that Kane can only describe as a mood.

Studying it first from a distance, then closer, then closer still, he can only guess that she'd wriggled free of every constraint and taken a private revenge on real life. This canvas has the merest connection to the view from the window. Instead, it speaks of something unbound, hard to figure out, yet at the same time utterly compelling. The coming together of light and shade is perfectly caught, as are the dizzying daubs of blue. Just visible is the structure of the bay, but she's filled it with a gauzy complication of colours and lines that hint at irresolution and something maybe far bolder.

'What made you so angry? Am I allowed to ask?' He's turned to find her back in the room, two plates on a tray.

'Very perceptive, Mr Kane. One day I might get round to telling you.'

They eat on their laps, her choice, amid the muddle of dust sheets and charcoal scribbles and tossed-aside tubes of oil paint that litter the wooden floor. The cheese omelette, knocked up by someone called Marianne, who evidently has a room in the villa, is delicious. It comes with thick roundels of unleavened bread still warm from the oven, and Kane demolishes every last mouthful, unaware of how hungry he's been.

Quizzing his hostess about her husband's line of work, he gets very little in return. Instead she wants to know about the small print of Kane's own life. What does he do? Who does he work for? What kind of woman can put up with months of him being away like this?

In reply, Kane sidesteps his years with FDR and concentrates instead on Los Angeles. What he made of the city. How it seemed, in a word he now treasures, flimsy. How the place itself really belonged in a development pitch that took every producer in town by storm. LA, he says, has become the golden Pacific wave you can't afford not to surf. Miss it, and you're history.

'Very clever. Have you rehearsed that little speech?'

'Only for you.'

'That's nice, but I don't believe you.'

'Suit yourself. I hated the place.' Kane frowns a moment. 'Hate, present tense, would be more accurate.'

'Maybe you chose the wrong movie. Or maybe you caught the wrong wave.'

'Yeah. Maybe.'

'Did something terrible happen there?'

'Plenty happened there. Most of it terrible. Some of it not.'

She nods for a moment, gazes out of the window, then returns to Kane.

'She's got a name? Whoever she is?'

'Everyone's got a name.'

'Not going to tell me?'

'No.'

Kane holds her gaze. When he changes the subject, asks again about her latest painting, wants to know where it came from, she shakes her head.

'We all have our secrets,' she says.

'And yours?'

She shrugs, dips her head, says nothing. Finally, she reaches for Kane's empty plate. To his astonishment, it's nearly three o'clock.

'Still hungry?'

'Always hungry.'

'You want a little more?'

'That would be greedy.'

'Then I must bid you farewell, Mr Kane.' The faintest smile. 'We lost one of the twins at Mers-el-Kébir and I don't think I'll ever recover. The next day happened to be his birthday. He never made twenty-three.' The touch of her hand is cool. She gestures down at the canvas, at last dry. 'Should I take that kind of grief out on a picture? I suspect the answer is no.'

Kane rides back in the summoned cab, the carefully wrapped canvas on his lap. He's trying to imagine a picture like this on someone's wall, anyone's wall, and he's also wondering about Darlan. Did he ask for something so provocative? So deeply personal? Or has this woman simply decided to tackle that big fat mountain called Closure?

Kane knows about Mers-el-Kébir, chiefly because Donovan once told him. Mers-el-Kébir was the moment that the British fleet opened fire on elements of the French Navy and killed more than a thousand French matelots, among them evidently this woman's son. A death like that, so sudden and so unexpected, would be infinitely worse if it took place at the hands of a seeming ally. Why did they fire? For what possible reason has this woman's flesh and blood been wasted? Questions like these, irresolvable, would haunt you forever. No wonder she took it out on the canvas on his lap.

The Palais d'Été hotel lies in the very middle of Algiers. The moment they round the corner, Kane knows that something very bad has happened. The road has been physically blocked with cars, a truck, and even a wooden cart interlinked in a makeshift barrier. A gap between the vehicles offers access to the hotel. More security in the shape of armed policemen at the foot of the steps.

Kane is out of the cab within seconds, reaching for his pass, three glasses of kir royale the faintest of memories. The guys policing the access gap examine his pass, briefly confer, wave him through.

'So what's happened?' he's been asking. 'What's up?'

No reply, just the most dismissive of nods. A donkey between the shafts of the wooden cart is trying to escape, pawing at the cobbles and whinnying. Kane ignores it. Stopped at the foot of the hotel steps, he tries again.

'Why the security?' he gestures back at the chaos in the road. 'Give me a clue here?'

'You haven't heard?' The man, French in a police uniform, looks incredulous. 'No one's told you?'

Kane holds his gaze for a long moment, doesn't bother with a reply, then mounts the steps two at a time. The hotel door

is wide open, held by staff. They look frightened, confused.
Maybe something worse than bad. Maybe something to do
with Darlan. Kane feels the rare stirrings of something he
can only describe as panic. It's been his responsibility, his job,
to keep the little man intact. Everything he's seeing, every
shouted command down the long curve of the stairwell, tells
him he's failed.

At last a face he knows well. It's Gus, appearing out of
nowhere, seizing him by the arm, saying nothing. They
mount the stairs, pushing through the crowd of bodies.
There's a gust of sweat and effort, tainted with his own
growing despair. For some reason, God knows why, all he
can think of is the image on Darlan's canvas, everything in
bits, everything dismembered, everything lost.

Gus is sidestepping through the mill, grunting in French,
in Arabic, in languages Kane can only guess at, but it seems
to work. Kane has never seen him this way, so intense,
so physical, so nailed to the job in hand. They're on the
first landing now, the one that leads to Darlan's outer
office, and the crowd has thinned. The door once again is
open, and Ancille stands behind his desk, a phone to his ear.
Seeing Kane appear, he puts his hand over the receiver and
nods towards the door that leads back to the corridor.

'He came from nowhere,' is all he can say. 'Absolutely
nowhere.'

'Who? Why?'

Ancille stares at him for a moment before resuming his
conversation on the phone. Leave me alone. Go back outside
and see for yourself. Kane does just that, and for the first
time he looks down to see splashes of blood on the carpet.
Two men have just arrived to join the throng of people in

the corridor. One of them has a camera and is snapping the bloodstains. The other is looking hard at Kane. He carries an air of authority.

'And you are…?'

'The name's Kane. Quincy Kane. I bodyguard the admiral and I want to know what's going on.'

'You're here to keep him alive?'

'Sure.'

'Then you've failed, Mr Kane,' the man grunts. 'The admiral has been shot. He was coming back from lunch. He's in the hospital dying, chest wound. By now he might even be dead.' He pauses, then frowns. 'You're telling us this is news? You're telling us you didn't *know*?'

A noise behind him makes Kane turn. Gus is standing in the open doorway, gazing down at the darkness of the blood on the carpet. Ancille has been talking to the hospital.

'*Il est mort.*' Gus draws a finger across his throat. 'Gone.'

About the Author

GRAHAM HURLEY is a documentary maker and a novelist. For the last two decades he's written full-time, penning nearly fifty books. Two made the shortlist for the Theakston's Old Peculier Crime Novel of the Year, while *Finisterre* – the first in the Spoils of War collection – was shortlisted for the Wilbur Smith Adventure Writing Award. Graham lives in East Devon with his lovely wife, Lin.

Follow Graham at grahamhurley.co.uk